FRESHMAN DRIVE

A BASKETBALL LITRPG

SHOOTER
BOOK ONE

XANDER BOYCE

RYAN DEBRUYN

Basketball Logo

This image has been designed using images from flaticon.com

This story is a very different take on the LitRPG-GameLit genre.

We hope you enjoy it!

PROLOGUE

PRESENT DAY

"There are only five."

The reporter turned around, a look of embarrassment on his face. He had indeed been counting the rings set up in the display.

"Just sort of uncommon to be around so many at once," the reporter responded, reaching out to shake the other man's hand.

"It's a respectable amount, although who knows if they'll let me keep them after this." The large hand engulfed that of the reporter, who had to look up to maintain eye contact.

"Why do it then? No one knows, you could just walk away." They were interrupted as a small girl ran into the room. She was five or six, dressed up in a blue tutu and carrying a bear that was half the size she was.

"Daddy! Gilly says they gonna throw me in!" The girl swung the bear at the taller man, who caught it even as she wrapped her arms around one of his legs.

"Baby girl, daddy is busy." The taller man pried her arms off his leg, lifted her up, and gave her a hug before holding her out at arm's length. "Besides, Uncle Max is gonna be there, and you know he wouldn't throw you in."

"Daddy lemme down!" The girl screamed, but the man just pulled her in to kiss her forehead; she fake struggled but then kissed his cheek in response.

"Okay, find Miss Rachel and tell her to take you down to the pool with Mommy and Uncle Max." The father set down his daughter and handed her back the bear. Then, she was off again, running through the house.

"My apologies, she is a bit high-energy and I let the kids come in any time they want as long as the door's open." The man closed the double doors into his den and gestured for the reporter to take a seat. "Please, sit. I believe your last question was why? Why am I telling you this?" The tall man sat down in a comfortable armchair and leaned forward. "Honestly, it's because of the girls. Because I don't want to have to lie to them. My wife has known for a long time. She figured it out back when we were going to school together.

"But the girls are getting old enough that..." The tall man shook his head as he trailed off. "It's important that they know the truth. It all comes down to that respectable thing. When I was a kid, I wasn't respectable, and I've spent a long time trying to get there. So, I'm telling you the story, because they deserve it, because it will make the world a better place.

"I have learned that sometimes you must walk to the end of the light, and a few steps into the darkness, before the light can return again. I've spent a lot of time in darkness and I'm hoping I can save some kid who's like me from having to do the same."

"You do so much to help the kids of the community already. Are you sure you want to ruin your legacy? What if you want to come out of retirement, like Jordan..." The reporter tried one more time as he motioned to the many pictures of the legendary man at charity events. It was already a shock that he was retiring so young, and at his prime, but now this? Not that the reporter knew exactly what was going on, but he was sure it was big enough to force early retirement on a man who stood atop the NBA; atop the world.

"If it's hard to accept that my love for my children and family isn't enough, then let's just say that the forces that I've been subduing alone this whole time, need more than just me to keep them in check," he responded, as his face broke into a marvellous smile. It was the same smile that had captured the hearts of so many fans and reporters of the NBA. The charisma that led people to nickname him the Smiling Assassin on the court.

Deke Mills, the man who'd won five NBA championships with only six years in the league, began his story, and the reporter rushed to get out his paper and pen. Mr. Mills had been adamant about not letting him record the interview.

ONE

SATURDAY, JULY 30TH

The office had that dark stillness all busy workplaces get after the attending drones depart for the day. The man who entered the locked room, following an electronic chime, looked nothing like the jolly Santa Claus on the stolen photo ID he used. The smell of cotton candy filled the space as he took a heavy draw off his vape. The red light of the vape pen contrasted with the muted blue glow from the dormant monitors.

Walking up to the big panoramic window, he looked down at the school's gym below, watching the returning, or early committed, college athletes put in work in a preseason tournament. After a long stare, a placard to the man's left with a no smoking/vaping notice caught his attention, and he exhaled a steady stream of smoke at it. Seeming unsatisfied with the dissipating smoke cover, the man snorted as he tore it off the wall before crumpling the metal in his hands like it was a piece of paper. The sign protested with a whine that sounded alien. Even then, he wasn't finished, and an expensive shoe ground the now unrecognizable sign under his heel, flattening the ball just a little bit more.

Finally satisfied, he returned his attention to the players, and the clock that backlit their futile sports competition. He knew just enough about basketball to know that UCSP, the home team, was winning. His tongue moved over an incisor as he saw a few bench players run to the scorer's table. The most impressive specimen exited the game, and in came what he would have deemed scrawny new recruits, in his old line of work.

Sniffing disdainfully, he kept his eyes on the large second-year, who would soon be a member of his organization. They'd been working with a great deal of local assets to reel him in, and it was almost time to fulfill the mission. One of the kids leaped off the floor right in front of number thirty-four, which obscured the man's view of the target. He took a drag of his e-cigarette and admitted that the jump was mildly impressive, physically.

The leaper was another member of the UCSP Baguettes and while he would never recall the name of the youngster, he did recollect that forty-two was a scholarship athlete. His basket had gone in, and "uno-reverse Santa Claus" breathed out another lungful of smoke as he watched the kid on defence.

Over the next two possessions, the black-garbed man grew more impressed with the clear athletic talent this first-year possessed, and even considered putting the boy in a report as "someone to watch." He clicked his tongue and took another drag. A long exhale later, forty-two was lying on the court screaming and clutching his knee.

The youngster had risen up for an impressive move, the one where the player threw the ball through the net while practically still holding it. They had some inane term for it, like a throw-down. Unfortunately, an opposing player—either unintentionally or, as the dark-garbed man suspected, intentionally—had clipped him. From his own experience in causing injuries, that kid had just torn his ACL. Too bad, was all he thought as he clicked his tongue disdainfully. That boy might have been agent material.

An electronic ding vibrated from his pocket as a text message arrived. He pulled it out and glanced at the device. A grim smile slowly spread across his lips as he read. His eyes flicked up through the window and fixed on the massive specimen of a man again. Still grinning, he responded with one hand while taking another heavy draw on the pen, before blowing out a smoke ring. It was time.

"Confirm readiness: Battle of Waterloo." -
UPLIFT Einherjar

"Looking at the subject now."- Agent
Smoke

"Proceed with operation."- UPLIFT Einherjar

The heavy security door swung shut with a well-oiled hiss as the man exited, smoke rising off his jacketed back.

Monday, October 31st

"It's still early season, we should replace
Mills with someone that can actually play." -
Ed Rooney - Athletic Director

"That's not something I'm comfortable with.
We gave him a contract, we'll honor it
unless he violates it." - Coach Skip

"We can talk about this next Tuesday." - Ed
Rooney - Athletic Director

"Not gonna happen." - Coach Skip

Something prodded Deke's shoulder and he started, raising his head from his chest. He had fallen asleep in history class again. He gave the neighbor who'd poked him out of his horrible daydream a thankful smile and then shook the sleep out of his eyes with a quick back and forth of his head.

The chairs were uncomfortable, and he couldn't believe he'd managed to fall asleep in one. They were spaced for someone significantly shorter than his six-and-a-half-foot frame. Which left him with a couple of choices—he could sit in the back of the lecture hall, at the top of the auditorium, or he could sit in the front, right next to the professor.

Unfortunately, the brace on his leg made the top of the auditorium a no-go. That many stairs would have been next to impossible to navigate. So here he was stuck in the front like some try-hard, his leg sticking out halfway through the open area at the front of the lecture hall, and his butt almost at the edge of the seat so he could be slumped over. All in an attempt to not block the view of the two rows behind him. The students behind him always complained if he sat up straight. It didn't help that the teacher was droning on about something completely uninteresting. Deke felt his attention wander again, and he turned his head to the side.

Three rows up, on the other side of the room where it was easy for him to see her, was the redhead. She had a habit of wearing shirts that accentuated every ample curve of her body, and Deke found his eyes drifting to her far too often. She glanced in his direction, and he flashed her his winning smile. She winked back and then turned to her friend with a half giggle. Deke let his eyes continue wandering through the seats. A blonde there—she wasn't sitting in her usual seat, which was with a short dude who played soccer for the university. Trouble in paradise, maybe? She was cute enough. It might be worth trying to talk to her after . . . Deke's ruminations were cut short when he heard his name.

The professor had called on him and he glanced toward the front of the room. There was nothing on the projection that would indicate what the question had been, so Deke shook his head. He had always hated when professors called on you specifically because you weren't paying attention.

"What?" Deke asked, and he had to stop himself from slumping further into his chair as the room broke out into soft laughter.

"I asked what your thoughts were on the subject of secret societies," Doctor Tawn asked again, his voice unamused but still polite, and Deke had to shrug.

"They're good in stories, but I don't think they really exist."

"And therein lies the rub, Mr. Mills. If a secret society did exist, the fact that the common man, or woman, does not believe in them is their first and most important line of defense. Ignorance! Ignorance is the shield of the peasant. What was the greatest trick the Devil ever pulled? To make people believe he didn't exist." Such an over-enthusiastic repetition of the answer made Deke roll his eyes. Deke tuned out the rest of the class, his mind wandering in aimless bored circles.

"Mr. Mills, if you could spare me a moment?" Tawn called out over the sound of the bell. Deke winced. Clearly, his inattention had drawn the ire of the professor, whose goodwill he needed to cultivate. After all, he needed the professor to like him enough to give him an undeserved A. A perk of being on an athletic scholarship was the instructors were usually inclined to let the athletes slide by with enough of a GPA to stay on the team. He really needed the A in this class to boost that GPA, especially since this was supposed to be an easy course. Deke winced as he stood, his leg protesting the movement and throbbing as blood rushed into it. He grabbed his crutches before stumbling his way over to the professor.

"What up, prof?" Deke asked, just as some kid asked about an assignment due next week. Deke mentally labeled him as a try-hard and confirmed it when the kid enthusiastically complimented the quote the professor had used earlier.

"Mr. Mills, I know history is not everyone's favorite subject, but if you could please at least pretend to pay attention during lectures, I would appreciate it."

"Of course, Doctor Tawn." Deke flashed his winning smile at the older man. Then, thinking of a different well-known quote, he added, "You know what they say about those who ignore history?"

"That they are doomed to repeat it," Tawn finished with a smile and shook his head. "All right. Make sure you get your paper done, the rough draft is due this Friday." Deke gave him a mock salute with his crutch, but he misjudged the length and he clipped a student's backpack on its way up.

"Watch it!" Deke muttered at the try-hard, as he nodded to Tawn. "I'll get it done, Professor."

"Okay, enjoy your Halloween and be safe!"

That seemed to be enough for the man, and Deke made a hasty exit. He was finished with all his classes for the day and made his way back to his dorm, intent on taking a nap before dinner. He pondered the elevator for a moment. It was an ancient thing, built sometime around Woodstock, and took nearly twice as long as even his gimpy ass took to ascend. He opted for the stairs. Of course, he had been told to take it easy, but after three months, he thought he must be ready to start rebuilding his strength. Awkwardly, he put both crutches in one hand, the other gripping the handrail as he hopped and clacked up the stairs.

The effort took more out of him than he wanted to admit, based on his heavy breathing. His huffing became an embarrassment when he discovered that Lee was in the dorm room. His assigned roommate was short, just over five feet tall, and on the pudgy side. He was also apparently *raiding* already. That's what Lee called it when he had his headset on and was shouting things like, "More dots!"

Deke wasn't sure what it all meant. Luckily, those headphones meant Lee probably wouldn't hear his labored breathing. So he took a moment to collect himself before he picked up one of the dirty shirts on his bed and threw it at his roommate.

"Quiet down, nerd, I'm going to take a nap," Deke said as he flung the crutches down on the ground and slumped onto the bed. He had to shift uncomfortably to kick a pile of clothes with his good leg. The pile had collected on the bed while he looked for something clean this morning. A kick deposited them back onto the floor where they belonged.

"Sorry guys, my Neanderthal roommate just threw a—" Lee stuttered to a stop as he sniffed the shirt. "Gross, this thing is nasty. Do your goram laundry!" He clicked a button on his keyboard again and finished his original sentence, ". . . shirt at me." He threw the shirt back toward Deke, but since it missed and landed on the pile of clothes-ramp that led up to his bed, Deke decided to let it slide. He was too tired from the walk back to the dorm to put up much of a fight as it was. Wincing as a shift caused more pain to shoot through his leg, he grabbed the pill bottles next to him and downed the one that he was supposed to take with his next meal.

Burping from the effort, he lay back down and willed the drugs to act faster so the pulsing in his leg would die down. At some point in time, he must have fallen asleep, because when he woke up it was already getting dark. Getting up with a groan, he pulled off his shirt. The dorm was uncomfortably hot, at least by his Canadian standards, and he had sweated through the shirt in his sleep.

A few quick sniffs found him a new shirt that, if not clean, was at least a little less ripe. He pulled it on. There was about an hour to kill before the party, but it was off campus on Frat Row and he was both poor and injured. He would need to hobble his way there, and if he took the time to rest along the way, he'd get there in good shape a few minutes after the party started. Dumping the contents of his backpack in the middle of the floor, he grabbed his costume, which was a simple Scream mask, and put it on before slinging the pack over his shoulder.

Deciding he wasn't in a rush, he opted to wait for the elevator this time and avoid sweating through his current shirt. While he waited, he fiddled around on his phone. This old clunker wasn't nearly as fast as some people's, but it was still enough to allow him to check some scores. Once in the elevator, he pressed the ground floor button and waited as the thing slowly made its way to the lobby. When the doors opened, he was surprised to see Lee on the other side, a bag of food in his hands.

"Hey," Deke said as he crutched out of the elevator.

"I, uh, noticed you didn't make it to dinner and thought you'd like some food," Lee said, holding up the bag. "Got enough for you if you'd like?"

"Thanks man. Yeah... Can we eat down here? I don't really want to wait for the elevator again," Deke said, pointing to some of the couches in the public area.

"Sure. Any big plans for the night?" Lee asked, as he set the bag down and pulled out a couple of tacos before handing them over to Deke. Deke's nose scrunched up slightly at the oily smell. Fast food tacos weren't something he normally ate, but beggars can't be choosers and he didn't even have money for an Uber. He grabbed a hard shell and let it settle into his empty stomach.

"Going to a house party down on Frat Row. Yourself?"

"Oh, we're gonna try and make another attempt on the Red Mage tonight. He's still kicking our asses." Deke had no idea what that was, so he just let the comment slide with a noncommittal grunt. "You're going to be back before your curfew, though, right?"

Deke groaned.

After the accident and subsequent *issue,* he had been put on a curfew, which meant he had to be back in the dorm before midnight on weekends. He also knew that his invite to this party was only an afterthought since he was on the basketball team. Yet, he had sulked in his room enough. It wasn't like he was going to drink or do anything other than hang out and talk to a few girls.

"Yeah, yeah. I'll be here on time," Deke grumbled. Lee seemed happy enough with that so he went back to eating while his roommate went on about this Red Mage fight, and how several of the casters kept standing in some sort of magical storm that the guy summoned. Deke's long experience with his mother's rants had taught him how to keep a conversation going with just grunts and the occasional, "That sucks." Now he used those skills to good effect with Lee. It was nice of Lee to bring the tacos though, and Deke ate four of them before the supply ran out.

"All right, well thanks for dinner, man," Deke said, using Lee's shoulder to help him stand up. "I gotta get going if I'm going to show up before all the pretty girls get drunk." For a moment he considered asking if Lee wanted to come with him, but then decided there was a small chance he would say yes. Having a nervous wingman when talking to girls was one powerful motivator, but the second and more important reason was he definitely didn't want Lee's judgmental eyes on him when he inevitably stayed out past curfew.

"See you later," Deke called as he crutched his way out into the night and toward his less-than-moral adventures.

CHAPTER

TWO

MONDAY, OCTOBER 31ST

"He's ahead of schedule, but he isn't going to have a full season."- Doctor Dan

"So you want to redshirt him?"- Coach Skip

"He'll be worth a full four years if he can stay clean."- Doctor Dan

"I agree. That's his best chance for a real NBA career. I'll put in the paperwork tomorrow."- Coach Skip

It had taken Deke forty minutes to walk across campus, and it usually would have only been ten. His leg had a decidedly unhealthy ache to it that throbbed past the remnants of the painkiller, but since he was the one who had stopped at his locker in the gym to ditch the brace and crutches, he ignored it. He told himself this trip was to help strengthen it. Ultimately, he knew that being on crutches would make him stand out—in a bad way—at the party. Navigating the campus under the moon and street lights used to make him smile, back when he first arrived and for the first month after his injury. Even tonight, this degree of warmth in October should've boosted his mood, but deep down something was off with Deke, and he knew it. But if he was going to make a better life for his little brother, Max, Deke needed to push forward—to find a way.

In his hometown of London, Ontario he was considered a star basketball player, sure, but he had a group of guys around him that kept him sane. Sadly, those guys were thousands of miles away. Deke was just a freshman fish at the University of San Pedro or UCSP; he had potential but was in a huge pond. It was like the game had changed and he couldn't put his finger on the why. Add in his injury and isolation from practices—and thereby the team—and it had been a *long* first semester.

Hopefully, this party would allow him to let loose for a bit. Take out some of that frustration. The house was a massive wrap-around Victorian construction and Deke could only shake his head, thinking about all the guys living there. Suddenly recalling that his last time at a party like this hadn't ended well, he almost turned around and went home, excruciating leg or not.

"No, you can't keep wallowing in your room, listening to Lee play games," he grumbled at himself before taking a deep breath and letting it out. "Fake it till you make it," he quoted from a self-help book he had recently skimmed.

Approaching the door, Deke had no idea what the prominently displayed Greek letters meant. Still, it was easy enough to tell there was a party going on. He had been hearing the music from more than a block away. Loud, manly cheers were answered by feminine shrieks of delight, as young men and women mingled in the backyard.

Deke walked into the fenced area like he owned it. Overly casual, he grabbed a red solo cup and filled it from one of the soda bottles on the collapsible table, while avoiding the side with the alcohol. He then headed over to a set of lawn chairs. In his short walk to the table, he hadn't noticed any eye-catching costumes, which was slightly disappointing, but either way he really needed to sit down and give his throbbing leg a break. His stomach was in knots, but he assured himself it was only because he wasn't in the mood to mingle just yet. Sitting down with a wince and a muffled grunt, he pulled a chair over and propped the offending limb up for a second while he surveyed the crowd.

Everyone had the telltale blush of alcohol glowing on their cheeks, and he glanced meaningfully between their booze and his cup of soda. Sure, he drank on occasion, and with his current mood he definitely could use a stiff drink, but after the *incident* he couldn't afford another strike. Plus, the doctors had been clear about his rehab. Alcohol was something that would hinder his recovery, and he needed to get back on track far worse than he needed a mild buzz. He transferred his frown to the other end of the soda table, which had a keg and plenty of mix spread out. Maybe a single drink wouldn't . . . his eyes caught some blonde hair bouncing away from the table and he used it to distract himself.

"Lots of talent here tonight," he amended his earlier thought under his breath, as he appreciated the sexy blond cat girl that flounced back to a group playing beer pong. She was basically in a black one-piece swimsuit, with a tail, ears, leather gloves and boots. He smiled at her when she looked his way, forgetting for a moment that he was wearing a mask, preventing her from seeing the gesture. He shrugged nonchalantly and took comfort that his awkwardness was covered by the mask.

No point in worrying if no one else could see it. His stomach clenched with nerves again, but he told himself it was from the Taco Bell he'd eaten.

"Ronald. You know I do not like crowds." A quiet but commanding voice cut through the din. Was that coming from behind him?

"Yeah bro, that's why we're in this little alley and not in there." Ronnie's voice carried over the fence at Deke's back. He made a slow turn, glancing through the gaps between the boards. It was difficult to see anything in the relative darkness of the alley, but there were clearly two figures facing each other.

In the semi-lit corridor, light from a faraway lamppost reflected off of the chrome dome of an older gentleman wearing sunglasses. With his shaved head and expensive suit, Deke thought he looked like some sort of B-movie hitman. In his hands, at the end of muscular arms that seemed to want to break out of the suit, he held a matte black pouch.

"That's not a bad costume, for an old dude, still I probably would have tried for a wrestler with that build," Deke whispered as he continued scanning the second figure. From the voice, it was clearly Ronnie, one of the team's physical therapy assistants, wearing scrubs and a surgeon's mask around his neck.

"Come on man, that's so lame," Deke mumbled before remembering he was in a scream mask and black hoodie. He shrugged off his self-burn, and continued to adjust his view through the fence.

"Very well. Here is the package." The suit handed the pouch to Ronnie, who took it and began to open it. "Do not open it here. In fact, it is better if you do not open it at all. You have about seventy-two hours before the material goes inert; make sure DeShawn takes it before then."

"Yeah, yeah, I get it, bro. Give the Duke the package, don't look inside it. What about my money?" Ronnie put the package in what looked like an old-school doctor's bag and closed it. Deke took another moment to mock the team trainer for his inaccurate costume. It made him feel slightly better about his own. The second man was too intimidating to be mocked and now Deke knew why. This was a drug deal, and by all appearances, the B-movie hitman look-alike was Ronnie's supplier.

"You will be wired the money upon confirmation that DeShawn has signed the contract and taken the dose," the suit said as he pulled a vape pen out of his pocket and took a long drag. The faint smell of cotton candy drifted into Deke's nose before the breeze carried it away. "If there are no further questions, I will leave you to your—"

The man paused, a look of disgust on his face. "Adolescent debauchery." He waved the vape pen in the air vaguely.

"All good bro, I've got a few more deliveries tonight. I'll get it to the Duke first thing tomorrow," Ronnie said, hoisting the bag over his shoulder and turning to head into the party. "I'll see you later."

The vaping guy took another strangely refined drag, and then the suit and the man wearing it disappeared from where Deke could see through the crack. He shifted in his seat as he tried to see where he went, but the fence and the angles blocked his sight. Was it worth it to stand up and try for a better look over the fence? Nah. Better to pretend he hadn't seen or heard anything. He frowned, though, when he realized he recognized the name of the person they were talking about.

"What the hell would the Duke be taking?" Deke mused softly. DeShawn "the Duke" Wellington was the team's center and best player. When the information clicked Deke exclaimed, "I knew that guy couldn't be as good as he pretends to be!" His knee gave a violent twinge and he jerked before using his hands to readjust its propped-up position on the chair. He took a long gulp from the cup as he wondered further what exactly the Duke was on. Was there a shortcut to his recovery? No, the doctors had told him that his new ACL would take some time to heal into place.

"Hey, can we use that chair?" A guy dressed up as a cowboy said, pointing to the one he had his foot propped up on. Deke looked at the chair, and his leg, which still throbbed, and then frowned back at the group of six that only had four chairs between them. Sure, they didn't know he was injured and using the chair for some needed relief, but it was still a bit of a dick move to ask him for it, right?

"Nah, man, saving it for someone hotter than you," Deke said, before wriggling contentedly into the lawn chair he was sitting on.

"Asshole." The cowboy walked away. The group all shot him dirty looks but Deke ignored them. Across the way, he saw a certain surgeon with an old-school doctor's bag come through the entrance to the party. Before he could decide whether to confront the "surgeon," a girl wearing an overly large basketball jersey and volleyball spandex shorts distracted Ronnie. Deke had to admit that the sports bra underneath, combined with pool floaties, goggles and face paint would distract him too. The small glimpses of covered sideboob paired with the skin-tight aerobic bottoms kept Deke's eyes oscillating between her assets, and he was across the entire party from her. In fact, it was distracting him right now, he admitted to himself.

Deke wasn't sure what the outfit was supposed to be, but he was up to talk to anyone that looked that good in a basketball jersey. Standing up, he nodded to the group of guys that had just asked for the chair earlier.

"Changed my mind, you can have them." Deke flipped the group off even as he gave them what they wanted.

It was a bit of work to navigate through the close press of bodies, but Deke managed to do it, while hiding any limp. Walking up to the girl, he was pleasantly surprised that she was close to six feet tall herself.

"So." Deke tapped her on the shoulder. "What are you supposed to be? Some sort of basketball diver?" The girl rolled her eyes and gave him a quick up and down.

"I'm supposed to be a Dunkin' Donut."

"Like the coffee?" Deke asked, looking her up and down in turn.

"Yes, like the coffee but punnier, okay?"

"Well, I might not understand the joke but damn girl, you got legs for dayz." Deke exaggerated the ending, making it extra corny. She looked down at her outfit and blushed a bit, but then returned her gaze to his with a slight smile on the corners of her lips.

"And what are you supposed to be?" she asked, her voice tinted heavily with sarcasm, as she waved a hand up and down over his rather lackluster outfit.

"I figured I should be what I elicit in bed," he responded with his best sexy voice. She chuckled lightly.

"What you cause your boyfriends to do in the privacy of your bedroom shouldn't be advertised so publicly." Her voice was so spot on in maintaining both a mocking and playful tone that he wasn't sure how to react. His mouth fell open as he half laughed and half flushed with heat. He had to admit that it was a rather good comeback.

"I've certainly never gotten to try a Dunkin—" While gesturing in a way that seemed to take all of her in, the entire party laughed at the same time, which made both him and the Dunkin' Donut girl turn around.

Deke found a crowd of his teammates standing off to the side of the pool. Always the prankster, Mac performed an impression that made Deke's teeth clench under the mask. He turned and started walking toward the gate even as he saw a shirtless Mac pretend to stumble around, before falling flat to the ground and holding the same leg Deke had injured three months before. Deke shook with rage as he snapped his head away from Mac just in time to catch sight of Ronnie a few steps ahead of him, leading two guys in full masks out of the party.

Deke took one glance back at the Dunkin' Donut girl, but she was still watching Mac pantomime to the pretend campus security that was now "escorting" a rendition of Deke from the pool area. Deke growled when he saw Mac's pants around his ankles, remembering the image that had been posted on social media. He wanted to march over there and punch Mac, and tell the whole party that it was his fault in the first place. His knee protested him just standing and watching the horrible acting, which reminded him he was in no shape to fight. The Dunkin' Donut chuckled, causing the skin under his mask to flush with an unbearable heat, and he turned away in shame.

Blood pulsed achingly against the ace bandage around his knee and down his leg as he strode away from Mac and everyone at the stupid party. It would seem that he would indeed be keeping his curfew tonight. He passed through the gate as he heard howls of laughter erupt at his expense.

As he frowned, those howls faded, replaced by the novel sounds of grunts and groans. He tilted his head, adjusting it to better hear.

Following the sound, he found the two masked men with Ronnie kicking the trainer as he lay in a fetal position on the gravel of the alleyway.

Fists fell fast and when each one landed, Ronnie grunted. The hands looked like pecking bird beaks, thanks in large part to the tattoos of bird heads that were visible on each assailant's wrist. Deke snapped himself out of his shock, this was serious!

"Hey, stop that!" Deke shouted the first thing that came to his mind. Then felt rather silly as the two men traded punches for kicks to Ronnie. He glanced around and found the old-school doctor's satchel he'd seen Ronnie store the drugs in. Surely this assault was because of them, right?

Its contents were spilling from the top of the bag, indicating it had clearly been dropped or fought over. Without thinking, he stuffed the barely visible brown bottles, greenbacks, and papers back inside before picking it up. Once he had it, he hesitated then held it up high, shouting, "I've got his bag!"

One of the two twitched in Deke's direction, and he spun and sprinted away. His only goal was to stop them from beating Ronnie. If he could get somewhere safe he could stash the bag, and tell Ronnie where it was later. Or maybe he should drop it now?

"Drop that bag right now!" One of the two shouted, as gravel shifted simultaneously, telling Deke they were now pursuing *him*. If he dropped the bag right now, they could just pick it back up and keep killing Ronnie.

He reached out with his arm and grabbed a fence post, swinging himself around a corner and out of their line of sight. His knee torqued excruciatingly as he took the corner; he knew he definitely wasn't going to win a race with his knee messed up. In fact, he shouldn't even be running at all. A black dumpster and green recycling bin inside of a garbage disposal shed caught his eye, and he painfully lurched in that direction. He just managed to get behind the dumpster when he heard the two pursuers slide around the corner behind him.

Deke tried to steady his breathing and not scream in pain as his knee throbbed angrily at him. He ducked down farther behind the dumpster as he heard one of the two assailants shout, "Shit, that kid is fast! I don't even see him!"

"Idiot, he's probably just hiding somewhere," the other responded, and Deke felt his heart nearly thump out of his chest with each breath he took. The breathing in his ears sounded like a hissing cat, and he was sure they would find his rather lackluster hiding spot in moments.

Deke ducked down even farther and felt a twinge in his quad from his injured leg. For a split second he thought it was just his leg's usual protest, but a slight movement sent a shriek of lightning up and down the limb. He would have screamed, but the threat of a brutal death by beating clamped his lips shut. As he straightened up, he felt a strange pulling sensation in his leg that seemed to resist him moving the doctor's bag off his lap.

Attempting to pull the bag straight up off his leg sent another jolt of agony through his quad and up into his nether regions. Sweat broke out over his entire body as he fought internally to prevent any sound. His breathing grew louder and even through his mouth he could smell, or maybe taste, the garbage and slowly rotting food from the enclosure. Peeking around the side of the bin showed him the lights of the street, but thankfully there wasn't anyone visible.

The scratch of gravel moving underfoot came a moment later from the other side of the street as he attempted to get his breathing under control. With the strange pain in his leg, he failed miserably and transferred his attention back to the doctor's bag. Slowly and carefully, he pulled the bag off of his quad at an angle, and watched in horror as a needle seemed to grow from his leg. His stomach threatened to disgorge his earlier tacos and soda, but he desperately beat the bodily reaction into submission. Thankfully, he managed to not only avoid vomiting, but to choke down the noise of his heavy breathing and near-scream of agony and horror.

A huge part of him wanted to tear open the bag and find the

offending item, but he couldn't spare the noise or attention that it would need. Every slight sound was already too loud in his ears as the two muggers searched the area for him. His brain did scream at him though, reminding him in vivid detail that he might have just been injected with who knows what! He fought with that urgent nagging and tried to return to breathing evenly.

It was probably just an empty, unused needle that lost its cap during the mugging, he told himself. He heard the door of the garbage shed creak and he held his breath as his entire body screamed in both pain and distress. His breath caught in his throat as boots scraped against the grit of the concrete floor. Stale sweat and the sounds of heavy breathing assaulted him as one of the men drew closer. The oppressive weight of the air covered him like a blanket as a gnarled and muscular hand came into view and gripped the side of the trash can, Deke's final bastion of safety. The muscles and tendons in the man's hands flexed powerfully as he began to pull the can away with the scraping squeal of a dying animal. Suddenly the man froze, seeming to catch sight or sound of something Deke couldn't quite grasp through the hammering blood in his ears.

"Those must be the two! Get them!" someone shouted from the direction of the party.

"Let's go, Rick!" another voice shouted, and Deke heard two pairs of boots scrape on stones again as he hoped the two assailants had fled. Then again, he had no idea. He chanced a peek behind him and found a slightly ajar door off the back of the shed. He eased himself through it and into a backyard. It was a relatively simple backyard with no grass and two tiers. He tiptoed over the concrete stone slabs and made his way to the deck stairs. He slowly climbed them, and peeked above the top stair to find two men fleeing around a corner, pursued by a group of four.

For the first time in what felt like hours, Deke breathed a huge sigh of relief, before remembering he had been stabbed by an unknown needle. He tore open the bag and carefully picked through its contents, trying to avoid any other stray needles in the process. He found pill bottles, cash, a stack of paper, but no needles, until one particular movement of the bag revealed a glint of silver protruding from the side of a black case that blended into the shadows of the "doctor's" satchel.

Carefully, he lifted the bag out, which pulled the full needle from the side of the costume satchel and allowed its entire length to be visible. He shivered at the stain of red blood, his blood, on the needle point. He unzipped the bag and took out a metal case that had an absolutely terrifying symbol of a man with six legs and arms on it. There was also a large letter R in the center of the man's chest. The entire thing reminded him of some sort of spider, and his brain of course chose to hit on how poisonous those could be. A crazy thought hit him. Could they have been trying to poison the Duke? Was that poison inside of *him* right now?

Putting down the metal case, he looked back into the satchel. There was a needle cap, which obviously should have been on the syringe that was poking through the side of the matte leather bag. He returned to holding his breath as he extricated it and turned it over in his hand. The same creepy spider guy was on it, but this one had a P on its chest. The metal syringe had a tiny glass opening inside the tube-like shape. The stopper was depressed and there wasn't anything visible in the syringe. Seeing the empty syringe, his stomach tied itself into a hard knot in his middle. Either the syringe had already been empty, or whatever substance it had contained was now in his body.

Wiping his forehead, he found it drenched with sweat. He looked down to find his shirt soaked entirely through. That was when he realized his body felt numb; his pants were drenched as well, and he didn't feel the wetness. Distantly, he also catalogued the missing pain in his leg. He looked at the limb and the small needle-sized hole in his pants with wide eyes.

Nano-Primer taken. Radanium must be consumed

within five minutes to supplement growth and prevent adverse effects.

Letters flashed across his eyes as Deke carefully inspected the P, and the R, on the creepy figure depicted on the metal case in front of him. Primer and Radanium? Adverse effects didn't sound like something he wanted to experience...

Two minutes remain until Nano-Primer begins consuming organic matter from the host. This often leads to death or serious debilitation.

"Fuck!" Deke said, and then considered whether he was actually seeing the letters and if he was, in fact, seeing them, whether they were trustworthy. His body shuddered; what little sensation he could feel was clammy and his hands were shaking. His stomach, which had felt knotted, twisted further, causing him to enter a semi-fetal position. His leg spasmed out, kicking a stone paver, but he didn't feel anything. His body was already totally numb. His other limbs started spasming and he took all of it as a sign that he wasn't crazy. The letters floating in the air must be there and telling the truth.

Struggling against the shaking, he fumbled to open the metal case. It took several attempts, but he found a metal canister with a screw lid. The canister read 'DeShawn' on the side and was sealed by two stickers. The liquid inside was a bright neon blue and seemed to glow from within. Deke didn't hesitate as he spun the lid, trying not to spill the contents. Despite his shaking, he brought it to his lips and chugged the contents. The liquid was thick and viscous but tasted similar to a handful of skittles.

Too much sugar, he thought as his muscles stopped spasming.

Analyzing host.

"That... can't be good..." he managed to groan as his eyelids sank closed, and he fell to the deck board. There was a split second where a fuzzy, distant part of himself realized that his awkward face plant should have hurt; however, he fluttered on the edge of consciousness before the substance swept even that tiny tether away. Everything went black.

THREE

TUESDAY NOVEMBER 1ST
JUST PAST MIDNIGHT

"Bossman, I got robbed, someone attacked me!"- Ronald

"Did they get the package?"- Cotton Candy Vaper

"I'm fine, btw, probably got a shiner. Someone took the package, saved my life."- Ronald

"I cannot stress enough how bad for you it would be if you do not recover the package."- Cotton Candy Vaper

Water splashed in Deke's face and he sat up with a start. For a moment he was confused. Nothing was familiar. He shivered as the cold breeze coming in off the ocean interacted with the liquid he was soaked in, both sweat and whatever had woken him up. His eyes focused on the wooden floor he half-lay and half-sat on, which confused him even more. He swept his eyes up and found a long pair of legs barely covered by tight booty shorts. A loose-fitting crop top covered the rest of the blonde's perfect body.

"Water?" Deke's throat burned and he had to croak out the words. The girl glared at him. In one hand she held an empty glass, presumably the one she had thrown on him to wake him up. In the other was a mug. With a shrug she handed him the mug and he took a gulp. It wasn't water. His throat protested and he turned his head away from the babe as he spit out the substance, coating the deck in whiskey.

"Lightweight," the girl said with an eye roll, as she reached down and grabbed the mug out of his hands before disappearing into the house. Deke stood up, wincing as his head pounded—this all had to be some sort of crazy dream. He sat back on one of the benches and breathed in the cool air. His hoodie was soaked, both from his intense sweating earlier and the water. He pulled it and his shirt off. Then he hid the canister that had caused him to black out in the central pocket of the hoodie. A glass appeared in front of his eyes and he looked up to see the girl had returned, having filled the glass with water.

"Thanks," Deke croaked as he sniffed the beverage first. The girl laughed in amusement, which made him clear his throat awkwardly, but he had to check. It didn't smell like alcohol so he tossed it back, draining the entire thing in one long gulp. The water went a long way to reducing the strain on his throat and he sighed in relief after it was gone. Looking up, he realized the girl had been giving him a very thorough once-over. So he returned the favor—her clothes didn't leave much to the imagination. The crop top rose tantalizingly as she reached out to take the now empty cup.

"You best get moving," she said with a dazzling smile, "You're trespassing, after all."

"And give up this view? Never." Deke gave her his best smile in return.

"Well, if you're going to stay and possibly get me in trouble, you'd best entertain me." She set the glass down on the bench and then lowered herself down next to him. He blinked as the familiar motion of her joining him for a chat changed. She lifted her legs up so that they were at his eye level as she draped them across his lap, her back against the arm rest. Deke's brain spun for a moment as the golden length of her legs filled his vision. She was taller than Deke originally thought and her hand was on his bare shoulder. She traced the line of his biceps with her fingers.

"Uhm, of course. Do I get to know your name first?" Deke struggled to find something entertaining to say to this Californian Goddess.

"Maybe..." She leaned in closer, her other hand on his peck. "You got a purpose for all these muscles or just a gym rat?" Deke swallowed hard; he had been working on his upper body as much as he could, since with his leg out of commission it was the only workout he was allowed.

"Yeah, I'm on the basketball team here. Name is Deke Mills." Deke let his hands glide along her smooth legs, unsure what to do with them as the girl basically sat in his lap.

"Oh? What a small world. I'm on the cheer team, I look forward to seeing you at the games." She leaned forward, pressing her legs down so she could whisper into his ear. "I'm Valerie, and it's getting cold, let's go inside." Her hand slid across his chest and up to twist his head toward hers. Their lips met. The warm heat of her whisky infused breath mingled tantalizingly with her strawberry lip gloss. He slid a hand under her legs, the other around the smooth skin of her back as he stood, lifting her in a princess carry. His brain shouted down any pain his leg chose to protest with.

"Where to?" Deke asked, when Val clutched him tight. She smiled as her finger pointed to a door. Then she leaned in, nibbling on his ear. Deke didn't have to be asked twice and his leg pain seemed to fade to the very corner of his mind. That, or his second brain wasn't listening to its helpless complaints at all.

"Shut the front door!" Valerie shrieked, startling Deke awake. "Like, I knew I remembered your name. You're like, the freshman that nose-dived during the preseason game and broke his leg. Oh my gawd, are you even still on the team?" Her valley girl accent was heavy, and Deke could blearily make out an open pink MacBook in front of her on the bed. His eyes slowly came into focus, and he saw his recruitment picture staring back at him from her screen. A glance at her tabs told him she had done a little bit of reading on him.

"Baby," he said exaggeratedly as he sat up and slapped her thonged behind. "Yeah, of course, I'm still on the team. Before you know it, I'll be healthy again and a starter, I practically was but—" She jumped up from the bed, interrupting his joking rant. He appreciated the view of her top half bouncing until she wrapped herself in a heavy cardigan and crossed her arms. Almost like she regretted him seeing her naked in the first place. Deke's eyebrows rose, and he slid to the end of the bed to sit up.

"I don't see the problem." Deke tried hard to avoid looking at the long, shapely legs that were still exposed from the thigh down, under the wool. "I didn't lie."

"You also didn't tell me the whole truth! No wonder you showed up drunk last night. I should have known. You aren't going to get tested. So what do you care?" Valerie half shrieked as she began grabbing his clothes from all over the room and gathering them up into her arms. Deke managed to snag the rolled-up sweater before she did. Unfortunately, with his stiff knee from all of the activity yesterday, that was all he managed.

Hugging the worn sweater to himself might have made him look like an insecure man-child, but it was still better than trying to explain the presence of a certain clandestine, villain-fueled needle full of... steroids? Soul-crushingly addictive narcotics? Flesh devouring poison? Shaking his head violently, he cleared his thoughts.

Think about it later. Regardless, it was best that she didn't find out anything about whatever was going on. Not with the level of crazy she was displaying. The show continued as she stormed around the bed, kicking her own clothes out of her way, and slamming open the window. Deke managed to take a step forward, but it was too late. Without hesitation, she tossed his clothes out the window onto the lawn below.

"I would have left faster with my clothes on." Deke rubbed at his neck, suddenly glad he slept in his boxers. "Christ woman, am I next?" he asked as he approached the window to look down at his slightly unraveled bundle of clothes. He thanked God or whatever power was at play that it wasn't windy this early in the morning.

His phone was down there in his pants, too. Looking at the position of the sun, it was just after dawn. He tore his eyes off the orange-tinged skyline as the sun inexorably chased the black out of the sky, and turned back to Valerie. The woman he'd had a blast with the previous night, who had inexplicably and bafflingly transformed into this... devil woman from hell. *A succubus perhaps*, he thought idly, his eyes tracking the hidden curves that he still vividly recalled. She was standing there, arms crossed, clearly expecting something from him.

"That was your invitation to get the fuck out." Valerie uncrossed one arm and made a clear open-handed motion to the window, indicating it as his point of egress. Deke blinked at her and then looked first at her, then the bedroom door they had entered through the previous night.

"Am *I* next? Well you can eff right off. Can't I just sneak through the house?" Deke questioned, rubbing the quad of his bad leg and thinking about the danger of climbing out a second-story window. She shook her head emphatically and pointed at the door but her words made it clear she meant what was behind it.

"Any girl who has a guy on any floor of this house besides the first gets in trouble. I'm not going to go through a cleansing just so your lying ass can avoid a workout." She hadn't said it in an informative manner, and Deke heard the clear threat under those words. Still, she clearly wasn't sure if he got the hint because she continued, "Plus, any guy caught above the first floor is reported for trespassing and arrested."

His options were gone right after she said arrested—not with what he was carrying. Not with his probation after his last run-in with campus police.

"Right." Deke sighed heavily and looked down at his clothes. He hadn't even meant to sleep here, but the girl had taken multiple rides on the merry-go-round to satisfy. He took a look at her face, tossed his hoody down to join his other clothes on the lawn, and then climbed out the window. Once he had a good grip and had maneuvered himself to hang from the window sill, he took his revenge.

"It isn't like I haven't had better," he called loudly through the window, and he saw a few faces peeking through the curtains as he climbed down. After that, he took his time dressing on the front lawn and could even make out Valerie's silhouette watching with crossed arms from her now-closed bedroom window. He smiled, flipped her the finger, and walked back to his side of campus.

Once away from the house, he double-checked the case to ensure that the glass capsule suspended in the metal remained intact. It was unbroken, and the few remaining drops of liquid seemed to glow even more strangely in the early dawn. What the heck was in this thing?

"Later, not now... later," he chanted to himself like a mantra.

Closing the lid, he continued his journey, waving cheerfully to the catcalls from people who loudly insinuated that this was a "walk of shame" due to the early morning hour. Many of those same people were likely on their own way home after their own exciting nights. He didn't mind at all, and he would never be ashamed of having slept with Valerie. If anything, he would be bragging about it before long. Two guys wolf-whistled at his smile and waved. They even asked "who the Goddess was."

"You tell me, have your moms made it back home yet?" Deke

yelled back through cupped hands, and received a pair of half-hearted middle fingers and eye rolls in return.

Arriving back at his dorm almost disappointed him after those interactions. He moved up the stairs and fumbled his keys out to get into the dorm. That was when an unavoidable yellow sticky note caught his eye.

Report to the Coach's Office immediately.
- Assistant Coach Boogie

Shoot, he had missed his curfew and then some. He stashed the hoodie inside his room and tried to ensure the vial and its case were tucked as deeply into his laundry pile as he could manage but still find them. Then he rushed out of the room to try to fix what he just *knew* was going to turn into a total cluster.

FOUR

TUESDAY NOVEMBER 1

"sluuuuut if I see u with that pity fuck again u are getting dish duty for a month"- Big Sis Eva

"Bitsh I was drunk on the whiskey you gave me – lol so if u do ever see me with him just shoot me"- Valerie

"will do. now report for your sorority cleansing in five"- Big Sis Eva

"FUCK"- Valerie

The athletics building wasn't far from his dorm, but Deke's leg was already bothering him from the previous night. He really needed to get a golf cart or something if he kept having to go across campus like this. The walk did give him time to think of what his approach might be. He had broken his curfew, and honestly, he should have remembered it, but with the excitement of the chase and then Valerie... he couldn't help a smile from appearing on his face as he remembered *her*. Then he recalled the blue letters, and the rodent . . . admant . . . nah that wasn't right, rhododendron? No, he was pretty sure that was a flower... the radium drug thing.

He shook off that line of thinking; hopefully that was just a fever dream or something. He hadn't drunk either, which in retrospect he probably should have called Valerie on when she kicked him out. However, he knew it was useless—after finding him apparently blackout drunk on the ground, no amount of excuses would convince her that he was telling the truth. He could barely recall how they had gotten to her room. Had he carried her?

It gradually pieced itself together. The trash cans he'd hidden behind must have been their sorority house. Wait... She'd walked outside onto her deck just to pour water in his face?

"That witch." Despite the harsh words, his tone was admiring.

Still, Valerie had been the best piece of luck he could recall in months. Everything about last night just felt... right? Just a perfect alignment of hundreds of little things that all combined into a very memorable experience. His mouth soured and turned into a frown. Yet again, it was all possibly ruined because of his leg injury, which in turn led to this stupid curfew and this meeting with the coach.

"That's right, Deke. It's the leg injury and not your own bleak downward spiral into the abyss," he muttered to himself as he mentally glanced a little too closely into that dark place inside. He flinched back instinctively and shut that door firmly, and locked it for good measure. "Well, that's enough self reflection for the year. How about you focus on figuring out what story you're going to tell to keep from washing all the basketballs with a toothbrush? Maybe this time he'll change it up and I'll get the joy of washing the team's jock straps by hand."

Shuddering, he resigned himself to whatever fate the coach had in mind. Deke slapped his access card against the scanner and walked through the heavy doors. This area of the gym was dark, especially after the early morning sun had tried so valiantly to blind him, so he paused to adjust his eyes as someone bumped into him. "Bumping" was much too mild of a term for what more closely resembled being bulldozed by a silverback. It felt like his shoulder had collided with a concrete wall.

"Look who finally decided to show up." The Duke was on his way out of the building, a gear bag slung over one shoulder. Clearly, he'd already cleaned up after his own early morning workout. "You were starting to get a little scrawny-looking," the older player teased. Deke stopped rubbing his shoulder, partially embarrassed about the mild discomfort that running into DeShawn had caused him.

Deke himself was tall, but only the regular kind of tall. Any guy he had to look up to was massive, and Duke was the team's center. The man clocked in at a whopping six foot ten, making him four inches taller than Deke, with a much thicker build to boot. His dark hair curled a few inches off his head, but he somehow managed to make it look tamed. Deke shook his head slightly when he saw Duke was wearing his jersey, proudly sporting the number thirty-four. Was he worried people wouldn't recognize him without it on? Deke was sure it was hard to miss the towering giant even without the Shaq comparison the number elicited.

"Well, can't be showing you up *all* the time," Deke quipped even as he squared his feet to hold his ground in the middle of the hallway. His stance should have forced the larger man and his bag to shift so they could get by him. To his annoyance, Duke chuckled.

"Good one, kid." Duke paused for a moment to see if Deke was going to move to allow him to move through the corridor; the two men locked eyes for a moment and then Duke shrugged and walked around Deke. "Have a good workout, Mills," he said as he pushed through the heavy doors like they weighed nothing at all.

"He thinks he is so much better than everyone," Deke muttered to himself as he limped down the hallway toward Coach's office, absent-mindedly rubbing his shoulder again. The door was open when he got there but Skip was on the phone. He tapped lightly and the coach looked up. Beckoning him in, Coach gestured silently toward a chair.

"I understand, Mr. Rooney. Look, can we put a pin in this? I've just had a player come to my office that I need to talk to." A pause as the person on the other side of the line answered. Deke took a seat across the desk from Coach Skip. "Of course, I'll call you back as soon as I'm done. Yes. Okay. Go Baguettes."

Setting the phone down, Skip stood up and closed the door. Then, he went to a filing cabinet at the side of his desk and pulled out three stuffed yellow folders. Skip's desk was a mess of paperwork already, almost an inch thick of white paper strewn about the mahogany surface. Trophies lined all of the flat surfaces in the room and Deke surveyed them, wondering what the best one was. These collectively were the record of Skip's career, both as a player and as a coach, if you took the time to look through them. Then, there was *that* ring. Deke turned back and gave the NBA champion his full attention.

"This is the recommendation letter from Dr. Dan, a report on how your leg is healing." Skip slapped the first stack of paper down on the desk in front of Deke. "This is the paperwork I was working on earlier this morning, giving you redshirt status for the season. I was gonna have you come in here and sign that, but instead—" A second stack of paper joined the first, but Skip's voice turned disappointed in a way that stopped all blood flow in Deke's body. "This is a termina- tion of your contract with the university, based on your lack of coop- eration with your disciplinary actions. That kills your scholarship, and your enrollment at the school." A much thicker stack of paper joined the three.

Deke swallowed. This was not at all what he came in here expecting. Things had quickly escalated past his expected slap on the wrist. The hand wearing the aforementioned ring sat on top of the third stack of papers—Skip's eyes never wavered from Deke's face. He couldn't breathe, his heart couldn't find a tempo and instead, oscillated between several simultaneously. His hands were cold and sweaty at the same time. This couldn't be the end...

"I need to shred one of those two stacks of paper," Skip said, putting a hand on both the redshirt folder and the termination folder, as if to ask "red pill, or blue pill?" "Give me a reason, and by God, a damn good one, for which one should I shred, Deke."

Deke froze, a paralytic fear creeping into his bones as his mouth was suddenly unable to produce even a trace of saliva. The idea that the coach could and *would* terminate his scholarship and send him back to Ontario had never truly registered with him. He had just assumed that like every adult in his past, "last chance" meant that the coach just wanted to be taken seriously. When Deke didn't respond immediately, he flipped the page and pointed to a line.

"This is your dorm log for the last twenty-four hours. You didn't come home. Coach Jeff said your roommate hadn't seen you since earlier in the evening. Were you out drinking?" Skip walked over to another cabinet and pulled out a breathalyzer. He handed it to Deke.

"No Coach, I wasn't drinking." He managed to squeak out from his tight throat. His euphoria from only having spat out a mouthful of whiskey and swapped spit with a certain voluptuous booze-mama, almost made him dizzy with relief. Deke blew into the device, slowly catching his breath and thinking furiously. He wasn't out of the woods yet. He was way past annoyed by the fact that he wasn't old enough to legally drink in the US, but that was likely only because the age differed for him as a Canadian. When the device cleared him, Coach nodded his head, put it away and sat back down in his chair.

"I noticed you walked in here without your crutches. I would ask if Doctor Dan cleared you of their use, but since I just read his report . . ." Skip tapped the first folder three times and produced a patronizing smile that he leveled at Deke. "If you aren't going to take your recovery seriously, why should I fight to keep you?"

Deke's brain, which had recently been focused on what he might say to excuse his late night and missing curfew, was forced to scramble. Inadvertently, he told the truth out of desperation. "Uh, well the crutches are in my locker. I wanted to go out last night for Halloween and just be one of the guys. You know?"

Skip's face softened slightly, and he looked down at his own leg sympathetically, for just a hint of a heartbeat. Then his hard eyes and disapproving frown were back on Deke. "All right, so what's the story?"

"Uh..." Deke paused, looking down at one of the trophies. "I met a girl and I spent the night at her place." He told the truth again. What other choice did he have? He looked up to see the coach's reaction to his words. Skip leaned back and steepled his fingers together, the massive championship ring visible on top of his large hand, before letting out a heavy sigh. His frown and disapproval receded slightly.

"I don't suppose this girl would be willing to corroborate your story? No, I guess I already know the answer to that. She kicked you out this morning or you wouldn't have been back to your dorm as early as you were." Skip closed his eyes and rubbed his nose. "But that hickey and glitter on your neck tell me you aren't lying."

Deke shifted uncomfortably in his chair; he hadn't stopped to look in a mirror yet, so he had no idea how prominent the mark or *marks* that Valerie had given him were. He self-consciously rubbed his neck, feeling for the bruised flesh.

"Look Coach, you should have seen this girl—" Skip cut him off by raising a hand.

"Deke, I know you're not going to believe this, but I was a young man once myself. I understand the lengths that people will go for a pretty face. The difference here is that you're being held to a higher standard than your average college freshman. *You* have a chance at a career in the big leagues, a chance to earn more in a season than most people make in a dozen years. I don't want to see you throw all that away because some floozy smiled at you.

"More than that, this demonstrates a lack of critical thinking. A methodical mindset is the difference between someone with talent and someone with work ethic, discipline and commitment. You jeopardized your life goals for transient pleasure." Coach's demeanor had shifted subtly into something potent, with purpose. Deke knew that Skip slid into this persona only when he was absolutely, unequivocally, not messing around. "This is something normal people do all the time, but I see in you the potential to be more than just a normal person. I *know* that you have a unique talent for basketball, but it's almost like you're afraid of being great. You are terrified of actually achieving something meaningful, and so you sabotage yourself at every turn. You keep making these *stupid*, and I'm going to emphasize that word again, just *idiotic*, absolutely stupid, horribly impulsive life choices."

Every inch of Coach's bearing conveyed a steely resolve as he leaned forward and pointed at his two eyes with two open fingers. "Look right at me, Deke. Look right in my eyes and tell me. What are you so Goddamned afraid of?"

A heavy silence blanketed the room as a thick knot of heat choked Deke's throat, preventing him from speaking. Something deep within him knew the answer to Coach's question, but he'd already used up the year's quota of self-reflection not ten minutes ago. Coach held his gaze for a tense moment before he leaned back into his chair.

"It's going to ruin you, son. Maybe not today, but soon, if you don't stop using the muscle between your legs and start using that muscle between your ears." Deke focused on that phrase, "not today."

Deke cleared his throat and composed himself. "Of course, Coach. What can I do to prove that this won't happen again?"

"Well, you can start by not doing it again. I understand that it was a holiday last night and you're still injured. I understand needing to blow off some steam. But I need to know you value this team more than your own pleasure. I didn't make these rules myself Deke, but I believe in them and I abide by them, and what's more—they work. They aren't there to keep you down. They're a guide left by the coaches and players that came before you. They'll help you make better life choices; become the sort of man I know you're capable of being. You're not there yet, and it seems like for every step forward you achieve, you take two steps back.

"Your excuse of being a kid is done, over, grown out of." He pointed to a cabinet behind his desk. "In there is the document you signed, a scholarship you received to attend this school. Yeah, your mother's name is beside yours on that piece of paper, but that was the last time you got to be a kid, Deke. Once that ink dried, you were a college athlete, and athletes are held to a higher standard."

Coach Skip tapped his ring and met Deke's eyes. The man nodded several times and held that gaze, seeming to hold his attention like gravity itself was centered there, on the other side of the desk. Deke held his breath, the atmosphere in the room somehow clamping down on his lungs like vise-grips. After a long enough time that Deke thought he might pass out, Coach Skip turned to look through his cluttered desk, searching for something. Deke exhaled as if he'd surfaced from the Californian sea.

"I want you to take the day off. Think about the choices that led to this. While we're at it, I'm going to have you talk to the school's psych counselor. Because everything you're doing is throwing up red flags in my head. You think I didn't see that look in your eye when I asked you what you were afraid of? I'm old, son. Not blind. Your actions scream lack of impulse control, which is something you can fix, but it's going to take time. Time, effort and work. I know you're capable of doing that—if I didn't, you wouldn't be on this team. I'll have Coach Jeff give you a call with the appointment details. Miss one meeting and that's it." Skip pushed a paper toward Deke, who scanned the document. It contained the office number and building of a doctor who worked at the school.

"No more chances. No more concessions, you hear me? This is well and truly your last chance. You fall off the straight and narrow path that has been laid out before you like a Sultan's promise and I will sign these papers myself, in a heartbeat." Deke knew that the coach was serious when he began to wax poetic. Skip pointed at the third monstrous stack of papers that Deke wanted nothing more than to rip to shreds. "That means if you're even a *minute* late for curfew, or I get *one* report that you're putting in less than one hundred percent in the classroom—then you're done. Off the team. Back to Canada. I hear the weather's nice up there this time of year."

It's *winter*, Deke thought with a morbid chuckle. Skip tried to meet his eyes again but Deke refused to look up and experience that uncomfortable feeling of his world on the verge of collapse... again.

"Of course Coach, I'll do whatever it takes," Deke mumbled as he stood up a little too fast. A twinge of pain shot through his leg and the coach saw it.

Skip sucked in a breath and shook his head, shedding the mantle of whatever God of War or kingship every coach seemed to be able to channel at will. "Like I said, take the day off from practice. Go to your classes and think about it. I want five paragraphs detailing the choices you made that got you here and how you intend to stop yourself from making those same decisions again by the end of the week. I'm not going to shred this paperwork just yet. Let Damocles' sword be just another reason for you to try harder."

"Right, of course, Coach." A second groan escaped Deke's lips at the additional homework, but more so at the coach's correct guess of Deke's thought. He glanced at the paperwork one more time, willing it to burst into flame. That of course didn't happen. Deke made a hasty retreat from the coach's office, his thoughts in turmoil at just how close his night with Valerie had come to costing him his scholarship—his future.

When he did get back to the room, Lee was already gone. Deke kicked off his shoes, not caring that they landed on Lee's bed as he crashed down on his own.

"Shit man, that was too close." He stared up at the ceiling above him and felt a wide range of tumbling emotions. He went from blazing hot hate for pretty much anyone he knew here at UCSP, to nearly wanting to slit his own wrists to not disappoint those same people again.

"I could really use..." Deke began, hot tears held back in his eyes by a force of will. Who could he use? What? He had been about to say his mom, but the coach was right. He wasn't a child anymore. A drink? Wracking his brain, he couldn't think of a faster way to torpedo his life. He needed a release, which was why he'd gone out last night in the first place. But look where that landed him.

What did he really need? He glared at his leg. What he really needed was for his leg to not have torn an ACL in the preseason. He needed to have laid up that basket, instead of dunking and getting clipped. It had been an impulsive thing he regretted, but couldn't change now. He had dunked his first ball at a college level and some jealous prick on the opposing team clipped him, causing him to land horribly. He had felt the pop and subsequent numbness from the limb like a gunshot wound.

Deke rubbed his leg, and then recalled rubbing his chest not even an hour ago as he quite literally ran into the Duke. That syringe and subsequent glowing blue liquid had been meant for DeShawn, but now it was in *him*. Deke felt sweat break out on his forehead as he considered that implication further.

Had he taken some sort of drug? So, if Coach Skip had pulled out a urine test instead of the breathalyzer this morning...

Fists thumped into the narrow cot-like bed beside him as he fumed. That was more like his luck, and perhaps his night with Valerie had just been a tantalizing hint of wonder before his world burned. The threat of tears returned but he forced them down as he thought furiously.

Since he was a redshirt, there wouldn't be any drug tests by the NCAA for him to take. So, that left the team administered tests, which were highly unlikely to happen unless they had reason to believe someone was doing drugs. Deke nodded to himself a few times. He was safe, for now.

Surely there was something he could do right now. Something that would help Coach see that he was serious about getting back on track. He rummaged through his pile of clothes until he found his loaner brick of a laptop. He tried firing it up but realized it wasn't plugged in, and since the battery was about as useful as sand in the desert, it wouldn't work unless firmly affixed to a wall outlet.

Plugging it in, he pushed the power button multiple times before the backlight finally told him that it was in the process of starting. That paper for history class was a good—

Physical analysis of the host is complete. Moving to mental analysis. Host will be rendered unconscious.

"You've got to be shitting me," he managed to say. Surely, it couldn't override his actual body, right? He managed one more blink, and then all his thoughts of his own terrible situation were shoved out of his head by an all-consuming nothingness.

CHAPTER

FIVE

TUESDAY, NOVEMBER 1ST

"Have you recovered the package?"-
Cotton Candy Vaper

> "nah. Look I'll cover the cost of the drugs.
> just get me another injector and I'll convince
> the Duke to take it."- Ronald

"The package was priceless, you skidmark.
This will have consequences."- Cotton
Candy Vaper

> "Look, give me some time I'll make it
> right."- Ronald

"48 hours. I expect results."- Cotton Candy
Vaper

Deke cracked an eyelid, trying and failing to recall where he had been before. Where was he now? Why did he feel like he'd been out drinking all night? His eyes slowly resolved the kaleidoscope of colors assaulting them, adding layers of resolution in an agonizingly slow process. Something or someone was standing above him with hands planted on hips. Lee. The shape focused into the image of the small Chinese man, in a "where the hell have you been" pose. God, he could *hear* the disapproval in his body language.

"You missed all of your classes today, and you never came home last night. Are you dying? I really need to know if you're dying so I can drop our shared classes and get into some harder ones. Plus, I wouldn't mind freeing up some mental load, from not having to carry your intellectually heavy ass through class anymore." Lee asked him, the sarcasm and condemnation practically dripping into Deke's ears.

Lee was never loud, but even the light volume he did put out amped up Deke's headache from pounding to excruciating. It was taking everything Deke had to try to make sense of the scene above him. Why in the hell was he on the floor? Was Lee wearing a cloak?

System Initialized.

There was only a moment between the blue letters flashing in his eyes and the gurgle of his stomach, not even enough time for him to comprehend the meaning. Despite the headache, the very visceral threat his stomach just issued took total precedence. He rolled over and shot to his feet, ignoring the pain in his leg as he double-timed it to the bathroom. Trying to hold it in, he covered his mouth, the first few coughs filling his mouth with liquid even as he tried to keep his teeth shut like they were gates to hell.

Practically diving from the door to the toilet bowl, he spewed out the contents of his stomach. His brain distantly registered that the vomit was a bright yellowish-green liquid, with no hint of food in it whatsoever. Some of his initial projectiles splashed onto the old tile around the toilet. He even created a thin trail of bright yellow bile up the bowl before he heard it splash home into the water reservoir.

Deke's knee spasmed in protest and he slipped across the floor, his arm smearing the yellow bile across the top of the toilet bowl even as he continued to heave more of the pus-like liquid out of himself.

He was supposed to be, if not a pro, at least competent at making shots. If this wasn't his worst career miss to date, he didn't know what was. His brain catalogued its disgust at his body's betrayal and its current filth with a level of contempt that can only be summoned through self-hatred. Waves of vomit, like dirty motor oil, continued to spew from his mouth as Deke continued to convulse and hug the toilet like it was a long-lost friend.

What the hell was in that vial? he wondered miserably. It was strong enough to instantly numb his entire body, force him to pass out, and cause hallucinations. The violent vomiting worried him as well, and he couldn't help but think that the neon blue liquid had turned out to be poison. By the time his stomach stopped spasming, he was thoroughly covered with the viscous, neon-yellow liquid from about the neck down. The stall didn't look much better, as splatter marks covered every flat surface.

Deke hopped into the dorm's too-small shower, not even bothering to strip out of his clothes. It took a steady stream of about two minutes of hot water to calm his quaking body. Once his body's insurrection was quelled, he scraped vomit off of his clothes before stripping out of them. Peeling off the now heavy clothing, he dropped it to the floor with a slimy, nausea-inducing splat. He needed to take care of himself and wasn't sure if the fix would require steel wool or a blow torch. As he scrubbed, he considered what he knew about alcohol poisoning. It was only dangerous if the individual couldn't purge the substance themselves, right? Now, the real question was whether that neon blue liquid was similar to alcohol or not. No amount of hangover cures could put a dent in this problem if they weren't even dealing with similar substances.

Someone else came into the bathroom, loudly complaining about the smell and then whistling as they caught sight of the nearest stall. The curtain was only up to Deke's shoulder, so it would be clear who had caused the mess. Deke ducked his head down, telling himself that it was just to get it under the showerhead and not to hide.

Thoroughly clean, Deke felt mostly human again by the time he stepped out of the cramped shower. At least, as human as you could feel after the type of convulsive vomiting he had just experienced. The cold sweats and upset stomach were gone, at least. His brief moment of humanity faded as he realized he didn't have any sort of towel or covering to use, other than perhaps his defiled clothing. He picked up the cotton T-shirt, which now looked like a one color tie-dye. His stomach rumbled threateningly and he hurriedly found the garbage for the entire soaking wet pile of rags.

Thankfully, there was a full roll of brown paper towels above the garbage receptacle. He dried himself thoroughly before wrapping his midsection with the scratchy, thin, brown paper towels. The "Imhotep" look would have to do, since he had nothing else. Even the short speed walk to his room almost ripped off his makeshift "towel." His roommate Lee was gone, which was a godsend. At least Lee didn't have to see Deke attempting to keep his package contained behind his dumpster skirt. Distantly, Deke wondered if Lee had late night classes or some sort of streaming party.

Deke moved to his pile of clothes and sniffed his way to a mostly fresh pair of underwear, pants, socks, and a T-shirt. Something chimed quietly in a way he didn't recognize, and he searched the room absently as he dressed. His phone was dark, its power drained, and his old brick of a laptop that needed to stay plugged into a wall at all times was currently unplugged again, and thus had died an ignoble death. Had he buried something electronic under his laundry? Who cared—he needed to figure out what *exactly* was pumping through his veins at this very moment that could cause him to be able to audition as a stand-in for The Exorcist.

Searching for the vial, he found it after only a cursory glance. It had rolled into the corner of his single bed and lodged itself, half-hidden under the dirty clothing that had long since overfilled that particular hiding spot.

Picking it up, he gave it the thorough examination that he should have given it this morning. It was a metal cylinder that seemed to have been fitted around a glass canister. Stamped on the bottom side of the vial, the side he hadn't drunk from, was a "CAUTION: Handle with Care" warning. On the curved metal surface, there was that strange spider/man image. He twisted the vial, trying to change the lighting to better examine the weird figure with eight limbs and a bunch of lines surrounding it. Last night he had thought of a spider. But at the center of the human-looking appendages was a torso and head.

"I'm not sure if I wouldn't have preferred a spider. At least then I would have known what this is," Deke complained as he tried to understand why this image gave him the creeps. It was a man, as evidenced by the rather stingy depiction of the guy's junk. A large circle surrounded the whole thing, and it was either trying to depict a man with four legs and four arms or a single man in multiple positions for his arms and legs. Deke wasn't an expert, but he could almost recall a name for the figure, probably attributed to one of those renaissance dudes. He delved deep into his elementary school days and came up with the term The Vibrating Man. He knew it wasn't right as soon as he thought of it, but that was the closest he was going to get in his current condition. Unfortunately, that memory didn't help him understand what was inside of this thing.

Who would use this creepy thing as a logo, anyway? The nakedness and posing of the man seemed to bring to mind human testing or cadavers. Deke shook his head and continued examining the rest of the vial. Unfortunately, the logo and the R were the only two adornments that the thing had.

"I'm gonna call them Evil Corp because that old bald drug dealer was too creepy." Recalling the man who dressed like a B-movie hitman reminded Deke about the metal case the vial had come in. "Shoot—I should have taken those papers that were in there. I bet they could have told me what that stuff is." Where had he dropped the rest of the case? Had he put it in his sweater when Valerie woke him up on the deck? He began digging through his laundry again, searching for the sweater, but he froze in place like a startled animal as more blue lettering seemed to print itself on the air in front of him.

Condition Analyzed. Displaying…

Stats:
Locked.

Skills:
Locked.

Status Ailments:

- *Atrophied Muscle in Right Knee Healing (43%)*
- *Ligamentous and Meniscal Tears Repairing (12%)*
- *Scar Tissue Dispersion Removal (42%)*
- *Unbalanced Neuroinhibitors, Amino Acids, and Hormones Reworking (31%)*
- *Poisoned: Competing Substances Purged (99.9%)*
- *Unhealthy Living Condition (0%)*
- *Sleep Deprivation and Insomnia Resolving (25%)*

Status Enhancements:
None.

"Now I know I'm going insane. What is this crap?" Deke placed a hand to his forehead and felt the cold sweat he thought he had overcome coming back. He collapsed butt-first onto his bed as he tried to shake the letters from his view. They slowly faded, only to be replaced by more damn writing. *Like some kind of hallucinogenic text message from God.* The thought only exacerbated his discomfort.

Host confusion detected. Switching from diagnostics mode to operator mode.

Genetic Deficiencies (Locked)

Genetic Enhancements (Locked)

Injuries:

- *Torn ACL: Repair 32.3% complete. *Three contributing effects.*

Debuffs:

- **Depressed**
- **Sleep-Deprived**
- **Poor Hygiene**

Buffs:

- **None**

The new list was much easier to read but left him with even more confusion. The "three contributing effects" to the ACL tear must have been the original three status ailments. Competing substances purge must have been the poisoned status effect, which is probably what all that gross green stuff had been. Sleep-deprived and hygiene were pretty self-explanatory, but he was clean and felt pretty good, so those should have disappeared, right?

Log of Status Changes

- ***November 1st: Poisoned: Competing Substances +99.9%***
- ***November 1st: Unbalanced Neuroinhibitors, Amino Acids and Hormones +31%***
- ***November 1st: Sleep Deprivation and Insomnia +25%***
- ***November 1st: Excessive Activity on Torn Meniscus - 4%***
- ***October 31st: Atrophied Muscle in Right Knee -2%***
- ***October 31st: Ligamentous and Meniscal Tear -15%***
- ***October 31st: Scar Tissue Dispersion -10%***

The physical representation of the damage from last night's adventure was painful to see.

"First of all, it's garbage that it didn't upgrade the log to the new menu style. Second, the log only displayed things related to my injury. Third, surely if a higher power was cataloguing my life, that wouldn't be their main concern, right? Fourth, fuck this thing. I mean, 'buffs: none'? There's *nothing* good about me, you ass?" he told himself, his voice hoarse. If this wasn't hallucinations during his throes of death, though, what else could the menus and the strange log be? He felt the sudden need to see Doctor Dan.

Shaking Lee's mouse, he woke the computer up and saw that it was still midafternoon.

It took him a few minutes to scrounge some cleaner-smelling clothes from the pile in the middle of the room. Thanks to the blunt and far too direct message of the injuries caused on Halloween by going crutchless, Deke intelligently took them with him this time.

Trying not to think too hard about this morning's events, he was waiting for the elevator, annoyed that he hadn't remembered to charge his phone before or after Vomit-pocalypse, AKA: that-time-he-lost-his-soul-through-puking. The black screen of his phone taunted him, reflecting his bedraggled appearance, while he waited for the relic of the 70s to make its way to his floor. He shoved the phone back into his pocket as the door opened and he shuffled in. From there, it was an agonizingly slow crutch walk back to the practice building.

Thankfully the elevators here were much faster, and it only took a few minutes before he was in front of Doctor Dan's door.

"Doc? I've been feeling weird and was hoping you had a minute to give me a once-over?" Deke asked the Santa Claus looking man who was the team's physician.

"Sure Deke. Give me a minute to finish some paperwork and I'll take a look at you."

Deke nodded and headed over to the side room where Dan did his examinations.

Deke had tried to steer the conversation away from his leg, but Dan wanted to test it first thing. Deke winced as he went through the series of tests to determine how much movement was back in the joint.

"Well, it's not any worse than it was a few days ago. Which is something, considering I saw you come in this morning without your crutches," Dan said, frowning at Deke. "Like I told you many times before, you've got another four or five months of recovery at least. This season is out, Coach told me he signed the papers to get you redshirted already. But you'll be in fine fighting shape for next season. Now, what exactly did you mean when you said you'd been feeling... I think the word you used was 'weird'?"

"Uh, yeah. Like, I dry heaved pretty bad this afternoon and I've been feeling more tired than usual." Deke only realized after the fact what it must sound like to Dan. "I haven't been drinking or anything. You can ask Coach, he breathalyzed me this morning."

"Well, your temperature is fine. So is your color. Just dry heaving and fatigue? Any other symptoms?" When Deke shook his head, Dan continued, "How long has this been going on?"

"Just today."

"Have you ingested anything unusual?"

"I mean, I had some snacks at a party last night..." Deke trailed off; he wasn't about to tell the doctor about the canister and injector.

"How is your appetite?" Deke accidentally responded with a loud stomach growl and Dan laughed. "Look, it was probably just some bad food and the stress. Take it easy for a day or two. Listen to some of those meditation CDs I gave you and make sure you're eating healthy."

It was a clear dismissal, and Deke took it as well as he could. As he hobbled out of the office toward his crutches, he saw an agitated-looking Ronnie coming in, heading toward the lockers. The signs of the beating he had endured the night before were clear; he had a cut lip and a black eye. He was focused on his phone, clearly sending a text message, and he accidentally kicked one of Deke's crutches, sending both of them spilling to the floor.

"Shit! I'm sorry Deke," Ronnie said, standing up and then holding the crutches out for Deke.

"It's all right, man. You look like you lost a fight with industrial machinery. Did someone's dad object to you flirting with his 'little girl'?" Deke joked to assuage his guilt for not stopping the fight earlier, figuring he still deserved points for leading those jokers away from Ronnie.

"What? Oh, yeah, biffed it bad longboarding last night." Ronnie touched his lip. "Look, I'm in a bit of a time crunch. You good?"

"Yeah, yeah. I'm fine, man," Deke said, and Ronnie walked back into the staff locker room area. "Take care of yourself, Ronnie!" he called after the trainer, who raised a hand to wave him off without looking back.

Deke considered squeezing Ronnie for information. He was, after all, right in the middle of whatever was going on. Watching Ronnie disappear, he reconsidered it; he needed more information—more leverage—before confronting the trainer. Taking a deep breath, he decided to take things one step at a time. Dinner first, but then he was going to get to the bottom of this. Whatever it took.

CHAPTER

SIX

TUESDAY NOVEMBER 1ST

After the doctor's appointment and the run-in with Ronnie, Deke made his way back to his dorm, eating a hurried dinner before heading back upstairs and collapsing onto his bed. What was he going to do about this drug?

Not just this drug, but about Coach's threat of possibly being kicked off the team?

Deke shot back to his feet and looked out the window as a realization struck him. What had happened to Ronnie's bag? He had the canister and syringe, but what about the papers in the case? Wait, what about all those other pill bottles and drugs he had seen inside the bag? If someone had them and could tie them to him, he was as good as gone, but more importantly—what if he needed them to keep away side effects? He still recalled the notification about "adverse effects." Adverse effects sounded like something he didn't want any part of.

He wasn't going to get any answers sitting on his own bed. The logical next action was to make a trip back to the frat house where everything started. He needed to find Ronnie's stupid costume bag. His body was covered in a cold sweat and he was about to rush out the door when he recalled his crutches. They'd fallen on top of his clothes-ramp when he got back. Even though he felt the need to rush he dutifully placed one under each arm, and grudgingly used them to transport himself through the dorms and back down to the street.

After getting outside, he cursed. One issue with the dorms was that they were so packed together that his window faced another dorm's brick wall. From Deke's room, he hadn't been able to tell that it was flat-out pouring outside. He stood just outside of the doors under the canopy that gave a measly ten feet of protection from the elements. The enthusiastic splashes that echoed up from the ground didn't indicate small raindrops either. Deke resolved himself to getting drenched and crutched his way into the deepening gloom of the approaching sunset.

Even in the rain and with it being late in the year, California was still warm compared to London, Ontario. He'd bet that his mother and little brother were dealing with snow already. He hoped they were doing okay and that his mom wasn't too strung out from working multiple jobs to make ends meet like she usually was. Most of all, he hoped his brother Max was happy. His close brush with suspension from the team, and his possible poisoning, had been an uncomfortable reminder that what was going on back home might soon become his normal life again if he didn't get things sorted out, and fast.

Unfortunately, the trip across town took twice as long on crutches, but felt three times as long in the rain. Deke's panic grew ever higher the closer he crutched to the dumpsters. Each garbage can he'd passed so far was upside down and left on the curb. Had it been garbage day?

When he reached the enclosure he thought he had used to hide, he found the massive containers empty. He walked around the back and confirmed that these were, in fact, the dumpsters he had hidden behind. He exited the enclosure the same way he had last night and began combing over the deck.

"Maybe the garbage men found it and threw it all out?" he whispered to himself after ten minutes of fruitless search. While that wouldn't help him with the papers he needed to find, it definitely was better than someone being able to link the drugs to him in some way, and getting kicked off the team.

"What are you doing back here?" a cold and clearly annoyed voice whispered just as Deke heard the sliding door hiss open. Deke looked over to the door to find Valerie glaring at him as she stepped through the doorway. She motioned at his crutches. "Nice of you to come out of costume and as your gimp-ass self."

Blinking at the rather unnecessary insults and tone, he considered the best way to answer her initial question. "I got the message loud and clear when you forced me out the window, but I was holding something for a friend and dropped it somewhere. I'm just retracing my steps... no need to be a bitch about it."

"A bitch about it? Do you even know what I had to go through today because of your lame ass?! No of course you don't, so whatever. Just get out of here before my sorority head gets back, or she'll call the cops and I'll be going through this whack cleansing again."

"Wanna help me look then, maybe?" Deke responded dryly as he lifted the lawn chair cushions for the twentieth time. Suddenly, his stomach rumbled a threat. A minor threat when compared to the Vomit-pocalypse but still a warning that he knew the meaning of. He hurriedly rushed to the side of the deck and vomited over the edge onto the unkempt gravel below.

A sound pinged within his mind, as more of the blue text wrote across his vision.

Poisoned effect has been successfully removed.

"What the fuck?" Valerie squealed. "Like, you're a fucking total slob. This hangover, vomit shit is going to get me in trouble! Look, you've been out here for fifteen minutes already, if you haven't found it yet, maybe you dropped the stupid thing somewhere else? Get the fuck out of here."

Deke pulled himself back from the edge of the balcony. At least this episode was short, plus the color was more of a yellowish brown, and far less obvious in the dark night. Relief flooded him at the message, even as he read it. He'd be lying if he hadn't been concerned over the poisoned status from before. Closing his eyes, he collected himself before opening them to stare at Valerie. "Come on, lady, it's important. I won't ever come back if you just give me a hand! Can you at least go check with some of your sisters to see if they saw anything?"

"This is such bullshit. You didn't even seem that drunk last night. Now you're vomiting off my deck, and blackmailing me?" She seemed to resign herself to the situation with an exasperated sigh. "What the fuck does it even look like?"

"It was a stupid medical bag from a bad doctor costume." Deke saw something cross her face and he blinked. "Have you seen it?"

"Well not really..."

"Valerie, please what do you know?"

"Can you even prove that it was yours?"

"It wasn't mine!" Deke responded. She jumped a bit at the increased volume and intensity of his response, so he held up a hand. "Sorry, it wasn't mine. It was some guy's that was getting the shit kicked out of him..."

Valerie raised an eyebrow and spun her finger thoughtfully through her hair, before crossing her arms over her chest. Tonight she was wearing an orange sweater, and salt-and-pepper sweats. The way she was currently standing told Deke she was going to be stubborn and not give him anything unless he elaborated. So, he told her the mostly truthful story about him leaving the party last night and finding Ronald being jumped. He then modified the truth to explain that he saw the guy at the clinic today—not looking particularly good —and the guy had asked him to come and check for the doctor's bag that he lost, since he wasn't in any shape to come check himself. Deke felt like it was a good mix of truth and convenient excuse to be here searching for the thing himself.

After his story Valerie just stared at him for a long moment, and the measuring look in her eyes told him she was calculating some- thing. Finally she uncrossed her arms. "Look, gimp, I found the bag today because I was forced to clean the entire house as part of my punishment. Once I saw what was in there, I threw it out."

Deke looked back at the dumpster enclosure below them and felt both relief and frustration. On the one hand, it saved him from being connected to the drugs in any way. On the other hand—he turned back to Valerie. "You didn't keep *anything* that was inside?"

"Dude, are you stupid? This whole sorority would get disbanded if any of that stuff was found on the premises! I'm not an idiot! I tossed it immediately and then washed my hands several times!" Valerie exclaimed.

Rolling his eyes at her tone, Deke didn't press the issue. He was pretty sure there had been a wad a cash in there, and he highly doubted that the girl would just toss—

"Shit that's big sister's car! Get the fuck out of here! Now!" Valerie went as far as to close the distance and start shoving him lightly. He sighed and turned to go. Unfortunately on crutches it wasn't fast, and he was forced to hide inside the dumpster enclosure again to avoid the woman who parked her car and walked down the alleyway to the front of the house.

"Big sister" had a look on her face that Deke couldn't quite make out before slipping into hiding. Had she seen him? One thing he did catch sight of was that she seemed intent on heading right for where he was hiding.

This is going to be bad, he thought with a resigned sigh.

CHAPTER

SEVEN

TUESDAY NOVEMBER 1ST

"A major donor just called me and told me
to help you. What did you do this time?"-
Director Rooney

"Got jumped on the way to get the package
to the Duke. Couldn't find the guys
afterwards, can you get me traffic cams
from Frat Row last night?"- Ronald

Deke braced for the inevitable conflict as he was found out. To his relief, however, she simply threw away some trash from her car into the dumpster he was hiding behind. Valerie anxiously cleared her throat and made small talk with her "big sis," gradually drawing her away from Deke and giving him the opportunity to slip away.

The walk back without the rain was just as bad as the walk there had been, but at least Deke now didn't have to worry about the discovery of drugs. It was just his luck that he got caught in the rare California rainstorm and then needed to return while drenched. The standing water kept causing his crutches to slide along the wet

61

concrete, only catching after they slipped a few inches. Cursing to himself every time it happened, he was just glad that everyone else was taking the rain as a sign that they should stay inside, and he met no one else on the way back to the dorm.

There was a whiteboard on Lee's side that had the kid's schedule for the week on it. Today's schedule had the letters denoting Lee's dangerous dragons night, or whatever that nerd called it. Deke figured that meant that tonight he would be out late playing games with his friends, which explained the cloak he'd been wearing earlier.

Deke stripped off his wet clothes and tossed them on the pile of his other dirty laundry, which, as indicated from his search-and-sniff method for finding clothing this morning, was *all* of his laundry. Pulling Lee's towel off the hook, he dried himself off as best he could before hanging it back up where he had gotten it. His own towel was in the pile somewhere, but it was too much of a hassle to find it when he needed it. For a while now, he had been using his roommates', and the kid never seemed to notice. In fact, Lee's Turtle Ninja towel was still wet from Deke's earlier shower.

It was too late for a snack at the cafeteria, and while he had enough money for a small meal, he had no desire to go back out on the wet sidewalks to get anything. So, back to the pile he went. He shifted it around, looking for a dry pair of underwear and some gym shorts. He considered hiding the canister and syringe somewhere outside of the dorm room for a moment, but that posed the same problem of going outside in the rain. He couldn't think of anywhere in the dorm that would be safe, so he tucked them into the pocket of a different hoodie and then shoved the hoodie deep into the clothes pile under his bed.

Falling back on his bed with a sigh, he tried to get into a position where his feet weren't hanging off the end of the too-small cot-like contraption as he pulled his covers around his body. Hunger fought with his tiredness to keep him awake, but his exhausted mind eventually pummeled both biological needs into a restless sleep.

ding woke him up and he fumbled for his phone, only to discover that it was five minutes before his alarm was due to go off. Glancing over at Lee, he saw it didn't seem to have been *his* alarm either, as he was still asleep, wrapped in his cloak from the previous day. Before Deke could question the ding further, more of the glowing blue words appeared in front of him.

New task assigned. One old task pending.

Daily review of progress:

Insufficient nutrient count for activity.

Sufficient non-REM sleep reached for typical daily activity.

Poisoned effect has been successfully removed.

Torn ACL debuff still active, 32.4% progress toward recovery.

Active tasks: Acquire Nutrients, Remedial Hygiene.

The remedial hygiene task sort of pissed him off. He had showered and even taken a walk in a downpour yesterday! Focusing on that task brought up a more detailed window.

Remedial Hygiene: Created by environmental factors which are having a detrimental effect on the operator's health. Remedy by removing environmental factors contributing to detrimental effects.

Deke lifted his arm and smelled his pits but couldn't smell anything. There must be some sort of issue with the sensors or whatever allowed the blue text to create tasks.

Well, the insufficient nutrients were easy to explain, he *had* gone to bed hungry, and he was positively ravenous now. Focusing on the task, he saw a more complex line, telling him to acquire a certain number of grams for proteins, carbohydrates, and fats. Before he could really read much of what it said, it shifted to simply read, *Eat Breakfast.*

That was easy enough. Unfortunately, the hygiene task had no such simplification when he flipped back to it. The damn boxes were worse than his mother, for crying out loud. He decided to shower due to the nagging thing, but since Lee was home, it would be dangerous to use the kid's towel again. He dug through his pile of clothing and discovered his only towel wasn't in it. He eventually found it when he saw a corner of the gray rough-spun cloth under his bed, where he must have kicked it. Since it was early, he didn't have to wait in line for one of the floor's showers.

Scrubbing himself down, Deke took extra time to make it a thorough cleaning. He was usually a pits, butt, and crotch believer, but the Remedial Hygiene task made him feel just slightly insecure. It wasn't until he went to dry off that his nose detected the first clue as to what the problem might be. His towel radiated odor, and it wasn't the pleasant fresh smell of a winter-spring or whatever laundry detergent is supposed to smell like. The stench of mildew wafted off the towel in putrid waves that seemed both offended and ready to put up a fight. Putting the towel down, Deke used his old friend, the paper towels, again to mostly dry himself off and then returned to his room with the offending towel loosely wrapped around himself to get dressed.

Looking at the pile of dirty clothes that surrounded his bed, it became obvious to him what he would need to do. But he had a class in an hour and a half, so he would have to do laundry later. Fishing out some clothes that smelled cleanish, he put them on. Lee had woken up, removed his Dangerous Dragon cloak, and was mechanically putting clothes on at the same time as Deke. They finished getting dressed and both exited the room. Lee clearly wasn't fully awake yet; half the time, his eyes weren't even open as they waited for the elevator to go down.

On the ground floor, Deke started crutching toward the cafeteria and realized that Lee had kept pace with him.

"Morning," he said finally, and Lee just grunted something in return. After flashing their IDs to get into the mess hall, Deke crutched over to the line's start while Lee walked straight over to the coffee pot at the end of the large mezzanine. Deke used his hip to slide his tray down the line while grabbing food out of the middle. His mouth watered from the smells of the buffet line, and his stomach rumbled loudly to chastise him vehemently for going to sleep hungry. Motioning for a serving of bacon and then some hash browns, Deke managed to convince the server to give him an extra helping of each. Finally, near the end of the line, he snagged a heaven-sent pastried ambrosia of an apple tart.

Sitting down with a smile, he tucked into his peanut butter toast with the eagerness of a squirrel recalling his buried horde of acorns. He smashed together the hash browns and bacon with a generous helping of Texas Pete's hot sauce on top. He was about a third of the way through when another ding sounded in his mind.

You have reached your daily allotment of polyunsaturated fats. Additional consumption will have negative effects. Excess consumption will require purging. Enhanced visual display activated.

Additional notification: You have already consumed 31% of your daily allotted nutritional intake of fats. Consuming fat in high quantities will cause sluggishness and lethargy.

Deke growled; looking at his plate, he realized that the entire thing now glowed slightly red. The one exception was the glass of milk which had a *healthy* green aura. Remembering his last "purge" and the gross green substances that had poured out of his mouth made him instantly both horrified and nauseous in turns. How was he supposed to eat breakfast with something like that hanging over his head?

Deke stood up mid-breakfast and stared at his plate as if it had just slapped him. Putting his tray in the washing receptacle, he eyed the glowing red apple tart with regret before heading back through the line for more food. To his further annoyance, most of the things he wanted, almost craved, seemed to be highlighted in that soft red glow. Seeing fruit salad with a green glow around it, he took a bowl even though he didn't particularly like cantaloupe.

He reluctantly followed the glow's unsubtle-as-a-hammer-to-the-skull prompting to the omelet station and ordered an egg white omelet with just the vegetable mix. The bacon was highlighted red, as was pretty much anything else that actually tasted good. By the time he sat down, his plate only had half the food he usually ate, and none of those were things he actually wanted to consume. The unlimited food at the buffet was one of the few perks of his scholarship that he had intended to *thoroughly* abuse. To add insult to injury, Lee moved from where he had initially sat to a seat across from Deke. His roommate's entire tray was filled with red-tinted food, which he ate unapologetically.

"So, what was that all about?" Lee asked, gesturing to the plate and then vaguely toward the tray return.

"Oh, I just remembered that I'm supposed to be eating healthier," Deke muttered forcefully, looking away from Lee's mountain of deliciousness and chewing on a piece of tasteless orange fruit.

"Only just now?" Lee asked with a laugh. "Haven't you been on a diet since you got back from surgery?" Deke growled and reached automatically for the Texas Pete. After picking it up on reflex he stared at it, turning it in a few directions waiting for a glow, but it remained clear. He put a few drops on his omelet and waited, still nothing. Then he liberally applied more, hoping to drown the cheese-less tastelessness in spice. At least his favorite local hot sauce hadn't been taken from him.

"Yeah, but Coach came down on me hard for missing curfew. Figured eating right might get him off my back," Deke lied; really, he just didn't want to have another blue text initiated purge. It had been, by far, the worst vomiting experience of his life. He felt the hair on his arms stand on end at the memory.

"Oh," Lee said, and he finally seemed to get the hint that Deke wasn't happy with the choice so he chewed on his cereal with a loud crunch and a satisfied smirk. "Hey, what did you do for the American History paper?"

Deke only responded with a grunt as he ate his food mechanically. He hoped that Lee would stop talking, but to his dismay, the effort was unsuccessful. Lee instead began to regale him with his DnD group's exploits last night. He discovered to his utter lack of concern that apparently, that acronym didn't stand for dangerous dragons.

In large, gesticulating, excited detail, Lee continued to describe a fight between them and a giant Basher, which sounded cool till Deke found out that it was a rabbit. Then he thought the game must be stupid to make a rabbit a hard battle. The guy managed to talk with half his mouth full and still not spit everywhere, which Deke found to be the only heroic part of the story.

Finally, the breakfast from hell ended, and he got another ding from the blue letters.

Task: Acquire Nutrients, completed.

You have been awarded 2 evo points for successfully completing this task. All progress has been diverted to

fixing your active injury (Torn ACL, current progress 41.3%)

Deke froze solid in the cafeteria's entryway, his mind spinning with the implications of what he had just read. He was blocking two students behind him, but he didn't care. 41.3%. That was a full five percent higher than the recovery had been previously. That meant that every time he got an evo point, he would get two and a half percent recovery.

"Lee, how much is sixty percent divided by two point five?" Deke asked his roommate.

"Twenty-four. Why?"

"No reason..." Deke said, and he finally crutched forward. Twenty-four points—if he got two points for eating every meal, he would be completely healed in what, four days? It had taken him *four months* to get to 35%. That one breakfast was worth like... *two weeks of recovery?* Deke's cheeks started to hurt from how big his smile got. *Four days* and he'd be back to one hundred percent, four days and he could be on the team again. He could play basketball again!

A second ding, and Deke hurriedly called up the info on the next task.

Task Issued: Acquire Knowledge. Fully engage yourself in the learning activities assigned to you.

Deke's smile grew even larger. If he got credit for going to class, the recovery would take less than four days. That was no time at all! With renewed vigor, he began hobbling toward the building where his American History class was held.

What followed was an hour and a half of trying to follow along, as the instructor explained the history of industrialization, and its lead-up to the American Civil War. Deke could tell that the other students were following along, because many, including Lee, nodded their heads and took minimal notes. Unfortunately, he hadn't been paying attention since he returned to school after the surgery, and he couldn't remember half of the stuff that he needed in order to comprehend the discourse.

Eventually, he asked enough questions that the teacher told him to just hold off and see him after class. Each question asked changed the look Lee gave him, until his roommate's stare was so complicated that Deke couldn't begin to interpret it. He might have called it confusion mixed with sympathy, but he tried to avoid looking at his friend as his incredulous glances grew more and more pronounced.

"Mr. Mills." The tweed-clad professor looked up from the pile of papers he was accepting from the other students. "I'm glad that you took my words from Monday to heart, and that you're choosing to be a more active component to our class time, but perhaps it would be best if you reviewed some of the basics in the textbook? I don't want to hold the rest of the students back to answer questions from last month's assignments."

Deke swallowed and shifted awkwardly. This was a big part of why he didn't pay attention in the first place. No one wanted to feel stupid, right? But if this was going to get him back on the court sooner, well, then he was willing to bite that bullet—in fact he'd eat the whole damn gun if it came down to it.

"Right. I'll go do that..." He nodded his head and turned to crutch away. After two clacking steps, he turned back, "Uh, which one is the course textbook again?"

The professor didn't even look up from the papers. He just pointed to a corner of the whiteboard where the textbook information had been written down. Deke added an embarrassed throat-clearing to his awkward shifting, because he vaguely recalled the professor writing it up there that first day at the start of the semester. Sheepishly, he cracked his pristine white planner's spine, which was unused and also from the first week of classes, and wrote down the information.

Task complete: Acquire Knowledge. 2 evo points gained. Injury (Torn ACL, now at 46.3% recovery).

"Just twenty-two more to go." Deke's lips curled up into an antici-patory grin as he crutched off to the gym for practice.

EIGHT

WEDNESDAY, NOVEMBER 2

SPIDERSLAYER LEE: "I THINK MY ROOMMATE
FINALLY LOST IT. HE'S GOING CRAZY."
TOXXXIC: "JOCKS ARE ALWAYS CRAZY, MAN."
SPIDERSLAYER LEE: "I SWEAR, HE VOMITED
AN ENTIRE KEG OF BEER THE OTHER DAY, AND
HIS GARBAGE DUMP OF A BED WAS PILED SO
HIGH HE PASSED OUT ON THE FLOOR. ALL
DAY!"

Deke eagerly laced up his Jordans. He couldn't recall ever feeling this high on life. Whatever that Evil Corp, Radanec stuff was, it was making him better. This made the possibility of the NBA after three years of college possible again. If he was brutally honest, he would have gone right out of high school if he had the talent some of the best in the world possessed. Still, he patted the Air Jordan emblem on his sneaker—after all, the king had done three years of college.

He wished that his pursuit of a higher level of play was just for his love of the game, but he—

"Heard the coach handed the golden rook his own season ticket." Mac mocked Deke from near the starting fives' lockers, and Deke felt himself tense. That jerk just wouldn't stop, and maybe it was past time to confront him, thinking back to three months prior and the events surrounding the timing of his injury. While the injury was a freak accident, it was definitely that asshole's fault that he was on probation in the first place! Deke spun to find Duke standing nearly right on top of him. He jumped a bit but tried to pretend that he hadn't.

"Rook, I know the coach is going to redshirt you." Duke's deep bass voice vibrated the insides of Deke's chest. Ignoring his clear surprise, Duke went a step further and wrapped a large, thick-fingered hand around his shoulder, which effectively brought him up short. "Don't listen to that idiot. The redshirt is a good thing. This gives you an extra year to learn the ropes and come in stronger next year. Coach would have just taken away your scholarship if he didn't believe you were worth it."

Jerking away from the man's mitt of a hand, Deke narrowed his eyes at the giant center. Was this guy serious? He should be happy to accept a redshirt and sit out the year? Huh? So, what, he was supposed to just let Mac get away with his comments? That didn't sit right. It didn't matter that Deke was allowed to keep his scholarship; his family didn't need money they couldn't use. His mom and brother needed something real. They needed NBA money!

Knowing that Duke was close friends with Mac didn't help either. Deke felt his clenched fist shake. The night of his injury, Deke had been forced to attend a party with "the guys." The team had been tasked with looking after the injured Deke, and collectively decided that they could do that at a party. Since the team was "away" none of the players wanted to be left back at the hotel to babysit. So every player went to the party, and Deke was everyone's responsibility. Since the injury was fresh, Deke began the night exhausted—both mentally and physically. Mac had been the one to "generously" offer to get him his prescribed pain medication. "Saving" Deke from having to stand up. Deke, being the stupid and overly trustworthy lamb that he apparently was, had taken the medication, no questions asked. He still wasn't sure if the overdose was intentional, or not... but one thing stuck out to Deke. According to the bottle, a side effect was drowsiness.

Thinking of his prescribed pain killers, an image of the creepy spider-man thing and the glowing liquid popped into his head. Deke started to sweat as he looked at Duke. Wasn't that glowing vial meant for this guy? Wait—was this friendly facade nothing but that? The real question was whether Duke knew about the vial and was complicit in trying to take it, or if it somehow was supposed to be forced on him. On the one hand, it would enhance Duke's performance and really put him center stage. On the other hand, it would mean that this thing could have a different function to it, designed to control the person who took it. One that someone could possibly use on Deke, now. A cold knot formed in his stomach as he considered the second possibility. While he usually would have dismissed mind control as something science Fiction-y, or whatever, in the last few days he had seen a few things that fit with the whole Star Trekker vibes.

Deke forced his anger down and unclenched his fists.

"Don't worry, your emanents," Deke scoffed, trying to defuse any awkwardness by mocking DeShawn's nickname of the Duke. Unfortunately, as soon as he attempted to pronounce the word it jumbled in his mouth. Deke shook off any awkwardness and straightened his back before continuing. "I'm going to get better *before* the end of the season. Once I get back, I will get us to Mercenary March and carry the team to the finals. Then, I will have teams sending feelers for a first-round pick! I guarantee I'll be out of your hair before next season." The large center leaned back from the barrage, before tilting his head as a smile crossed his lips.

"Rook, I like the fire!" Duke rubbed at his fade and looked sheepishly back to his cubby and the other starter's lockers behind him. The group of bootlickers guffawed as Mac said something else that Deke couldn't hear. He was relatively sure that the jibe was centered on him. Every other joke Mac told revolved around him, after all.

The anger he'd fought off earlier surged with a vengeance and he glared at the back of Duke's head. Was his anger with the Duke justified? Probably not, but Deke knew it was that entire group of guys who had refused to miss the party after the preseason tournament, and he couldn't help but hold Duke somewhat responsible for their decision as well. Even though Duke wasn't present for the actual decision, he was the team captain and was responsible too, right?

Duke turned around and shrugged. "We're a team. We all look good together, just like we all look bad together. Just take your time, do the work. We're going to need you." Duke gestured over his shoulder at Mac. "That *clown* is graduating."

Deke watched Duke rejoin the others, and the ones that were already dressed for practice followed the big man out of the locker room toward the gym. Deke wasn't sure what to make of the interaction. Still, after some consideration, he couldn't get over his anger at the center. He likely just wanted to look good for the other guys—like a captain. Yeah, right. They needed Deke because another player would be gone? If the oaf really cared about him, then he would be pushing the coaching staff to have him back sooner.

Entering the sideline of the basketball court with crutches soured Deke's mood further. Still, he needed to let this new drug or system, or whatever it was, work its magic. Scanning the massive gym, he found the coach on the first of three courts. Each time he bounded forward toward Skip on the crutches, they whined and squeaked. It was going to be amazing when he could break them in half, or burn them... Now there's an idea, kill them with fire. It's the only way to be sure that he'd never see them again.

"Mills," Coach Skip said without looking at him. "Get your hundred foul shots in, and then go see the therapists."

Deke inhaled through his nose, opened his mouth, and then thought better of it. It had only been a day since he almost got kicked off the team. He couldn't think of anything to say to turn that around just yet. So, he crutched over to the free-throw line and was joined by one of the team trainers. Dropping the crutches, he began taking his well-practiced foul shots. He had always been a good foul shooter, averaging about seventy percent, even in high school.

Today, he counted up and was on pace when he reached fifty shots, having sunk thirty-five. He raised his elbows to shoot the next ball, and the glare of the gym lights created a faded red rainbow between him and the hoop. He dropped the ball back to his hip, expecting a wave of dizziness or disorientation. However, the strange, almost invisible light faded along with his head motion. He tried three more times, but each time he raised the ball to shoot, the glare from the lights bothered him with a red arc.

"I think I am good for today," he said, and tossed the ball to the trainer. "My head is a little off." He explained further when the smaller man gave him a tilted head "you aren't done yet" look. Once the assistant seemed satisfied, Deke picked up his crutches and headed to the elevator to go downstairs and into the physio clinic. That had been strange, and Deke hoped that it was just a side effect of his lack of sleep. A thought struck him that maybe it was a product of his new diet.

"That apple tart would have never betrayed me like this," he whispered to himself bitterly as he worked the elevator buttons.

Downstairs in the clinic, he found himself staring at the rather shapely behind of a new therapist he hadn't met before. She was kneeling over a track athlete's ankle and was finishing up an ultrasound. He only knew what the strange gun-like wand and blue gel did because he was subjected to it daily. According to Ronnie, it helped break down scar tissue. Of course, Deke had no way of confirming that story.

"Hey man, have you seen Ronnie?" Another therapist walked by, and Deke stopped him. The student helper—Deke read his position from his nametag but ignored the student's actual name—looked around startled, as if he had just remembered he was in a clinic.

"Nah, man. Like, haven't seen big Ron all day." The slightly hanging jaw and red eyes told Deke the story, and he just shook his head with a chuckle. As if that wasn't enough the sour, dank smell of cannabis practically radiated from the guy's clothing. He wouldn't be learning anything from this guy. Whatever, he would just sit on a bed and wait for someone to come by. Hopefully, they would know where Ronnie was. Or not—his new miraculous road to rehabilitation was already laid out for him, and he wasn't in any hurry to go through painful therapy if he didn't have to.

He lay back on the clinic bed and was just settling in to enjoy his view when the new therapist turned around, and their eyes met. She squinted and tilted her head before making her way nearer. Deke was more attracted to her the closer she came. From across the clinic, it wasn't tough to tell that she was near six feet tall and beautiful. The only part of her appearance that soured his mood was the brace she wore on her leg. Not because it made her less attractive—no, because it was a reminder of what he too would have to wear.

"Who're you waiting on?" She arrived at the table and found Deke frowning, staring at her brace. He looked up to meet her green eyes, framed by long dirty-blonde hair. He realized with a start that this was his Dunkin' Donut!

"Oh." He stuttered for a moment before remembering his therapy appointment. "Ronnie's got me," Deke said, pointing at his own knee. At her look of confusion, he added, "ACL tear."

"You must be Deke Mabes?" The woman placed a finger up in the air in the universal "one moment" gesture. She jogged across the clinic, accompanied by the squeaking knee brace, and grabbed a clipboard before returning. Deke frowned at the brace a bit harder due to the noise. "I'm Abbie McDugal. *Ronald*," Abbie said, emphasizing the name Ronnie preferred to be called, "is sick today. So I am handling his patients. Let's just check what he usually does."

"It's Mills." Deke coughed to get her attention as she read.

"Oh—my bad, Ronald's handwriting is a complete mess, just look here." She moved close to Deke, pressing her abdomen into his shoulder to point at a word on the top of the clipboard that resembled Dele Mabez more than Deke Mills. "Don't worry, I have been on the receiving end of all the treatments listed here." She pointed under his name at the paper and then at her own knee brace. "Let's get your muscles warmed up with some ultrasound."

"Your form isn't correct, and you shouldn't be adding weight yet. This exercise is only to maintain the balance between your muscles. Right now it's about combating muscle atrophy in your bad leg. We'll work on rebuilding after it's healed," Abbie scolded. Her voice was getting more stern as the rehab workout continued and Deke performed one exercise after another improperly.

Deke admittedly was showing off a little for Abbie. He'd added more weight when she wasn't looking, and he hoped it was making his calves and quads look great. Abbie might not be as cute as Valerie, but it wasn't often he met girls that tall. He looked over at her and was forced to readjust that statement. She was rocking a crazy hot body.

"Look, I got this. I have done a hundred million half-Bosu-ball squats. Ronnie usually bounced after the warm-up and demonstrations," Deke retorted, trying to convey in his tone that he was strong and cool simultaneously. Plus, he didn't need a babysitter.

"Fine." Abbie threw her hands in the air in an "I give up" gesture and turned to leave. Before she made it out of the rehab zone, she turned back. "Look, I'm just here for my clinical hours. I need two hundred before I can apply to the physical therapy undergrad program. But my final destination is physiotherapy. I don't like you or your attitude, but I know what I am talking about, and it's kinda my job to help you. So, when you're ready to actually heal, come find me." She finished storming off and Deke shook his head with an exaggerated eye roll.

"What a drama queen." He dipped into another rep of the squat and felt his legs begin pistoning on separate timing from each other. He bore down on his focus and forced them to fire in sync, completing the rep with a self-satisfied smile. Why take things slow when you can *crush it* now?

Moving through the rest of the workout, he enjoyed the feeling of the sweat dripping off his brow. He was already halfway done with today's workout and would likely be finished before practice ended. His initial motivation for this workout had been the task created by Evil Corp's strange system, but now he was hoping for a nap before lunch.

Once the list of exercises was completed, he started into his stretches, and the strange system chimed again. Deke smiled and eagerly willed up the update, causing the scrolling text to appear.

Task failed. One old task pending.

New task issued: Injury Rehabilitation. Created by seeking assistance from an expert in rehabilitation. Complete the workout assigned.

Injury Rehabilitation Failed

You have lost 5 evo points for failing to complete this task and further injuring yourself from working counterproductively. All progress has been diverted to fixing your active injury. (Torn ACL, current progress 28.8%)

A wide range of sensations assaulted his body. It flushed with heat and then chilled drastically at the final line. He had lost twelve and a half percent and was even farther away from healing his injured knee. Earlier today, Deke had thought that he might be better with eleven more tasks, but hadn't considered that those tasks could take away progress as well.

Sweating from his internal rage at the system, himself, and Abbie, he stood up. It took a moment for him to admit how stupid he'd acted, but he was also unwilling to go find the girl to try to apologize—his blood was still too hot. Instead, he crutched to a back stairwell and struggled up it. Avoiding Abbie, the gym and all the people in practice entirely. He just couldn't face the coach or the guys right now.

Making his way back to his dorm, his angry flush diminished, and the shame finally washed over him. Why had he insisted on lifting heavier just because a pretty girl was around? Sure she was gorgeous, and he wanted her to be impressed, but he was pretty sure all he had accomplished was the opposite. His knuckles whitened around the crossbar of his crutch.

The door to his shared room with Lee banged open, and he stood in the doorway staring at his side of the room. A part of him wanted to lie down, bury his head in his blanket and pillows and sleep—then maybe he could wake up and hope he forgot the embarrassing choices of the day. Instead, he focused on the laundry and state of his room.

Deke was relatively sure that the state of the room and his clothes were all contributing to the Remedial Hygiene task. If he wanted to minimize the damage caused earlier, it was time to do something about this mess. He borrowed Lee's laundry hamper and stuffed it full before realizing he would need more space than it provided.

Finding his travel bag, the one his mom had saved up for when he told her he got accepted, he stuffed it full. He then awkwardly wheeled the whole thing down the hallway to the dorm elevator and pressed the basement button. He was relatively sure that was where the laundry machines were, but honestly, he hadn't ever been down there. When you traveled with the basketball team, you could throw your laundry into a bag, and it came back cleaned and folded...

He grimly girded his mental loins as he prepared himself to face his greatest enemy yet. Laundry.

CHAPTER

NINE

WEDNESDAY, NOVEMBER 2

The laundry room was easy enough to find. A dozen large machines lined both walls, with a sizeable table in the middle and numerous desks spread throughout. Clearly, the space was designed for students to study as they waited. One other resident was there, but he was lost in a romance novel. Deke smiled to himself at the kid's choice as he picked the largest machine and dumped both Lee's basket and his own suitcase into it.

"Hey man, where do I get soap?" Deke called out to the romance kid when he realized he was missing something. Of course, the kid was listening to music and couldn't hear him. Frowning, Deke looked around. Had there been a vending machine outside? Using the table as support, he hobbled over to the door. A newer machine stood just outside, and he slid his card. He didn't use the card often but was relatively lucky he had free use of it, thanks to the team. Throwing the newly purchased package of gels into the washer, he turned it on.

After eyeing the chairs and desks nearby dubiously, he realized that he wouldn't do much work down here. It was loud and poorly lit on top of everything else. Not to mention the *tiny* problem in that he hadn't brought any books...

Was it worth going back to his room and working on that stupid paper? He decided it was, and set the alarm on his phone to remind him to come back down. It made for a much easier way back upstairs without the laundry or baskets. It was time to rewrite his American History paper. He actually made good time, thanks to Lee's advice about the rubric. The rubric-thing basically spelled out exactly what Professor Tawn wanted.

Three quarters of his paper was written before his alarm went off, and he smiled at his laptop. Maybe he was smarter than he recalled, because with this rubric the paper was practically writing itself. Standing up, he grabbed his crutches and spun to head to the door. One of the crutches snagged the power cord and pulled the thing out of the wall.

"No!" he screamed, far too loudly. The white screen of the word processor turned black with a strange electronic click, as his brick of a laptop died a very untimely death. For a split second he considered throwing the loaner out of the dorm window, but settled on clenching his fist harder on the crutch's cross guard. Surely, he could rewrite what he'd had.

"It was only forty-five minutes of work." He kept repeating the mantra over and over in his head as he first waited for the elevator and then rode the hunk of junk to the basement. He exited the elevator, placing the rubber stops on his crutches onto the floor, and instantly felt them slide. Thankfully the crutches hit the wall on the other side of the hallway, which prevented Deke from taking a fall. Who had left a puddle of water here?

Using the wall as support, he abandoned his crutches and turned toward the laundry room. The clues to who was responsible for the water weren't hard to follow. The same student Deke had seen with the romance novel was pushing a mop and bucket down the hallway back toward the laundry room. About halfway down the hallway stood the open laundry room door. The door almost seemed alive as it regurgitated bubbles slowly into the hall.

The kid looked up and took in Deke leaning against the wall with two crutches under his arm. His facial expression changed a few times, leaving Deke unsure if the hopeless romantic was upset with him or if he felt sorry for him. Eventually the guy said, "Happened to me the first time I used the machines too. I'll start cleaning up, out here. You should go transfer your load to a new machine and start it up. Just an FYI, you used too much soap."

Deke blinked, having expected a completely different response from the guy. After a moment of stunned silence, Deke realized he should probably say something. He managed a weak chuckle. "That obvious that it was my first time using the machines?"

"Nah, but if this wasn't your first time, and you caused this... well, then I wouldn't be as forgiving. You know?"

"I feel you." Deke's earlier anger at losing his history paper seemed to fizzle in his chest. Something about the fellow student's response made Deke feel a bit more human. While this was still a horrible, terrible day for him, at least one person seemed to get it. Deke whispered, "I really appreciate the help, man."

The next forty-five minutes were spent attempting to help the other kid clean up. Deke wasn't very helpful with his leg, but something inside him wouldn't just let the romance dude do it by himself. This time Deke was there when the buzzer for the laundry machine sounded, and he limped over to transfer it to the dryer.

When he opened the lid, he didn't recognize the contents. He pulled out the shirt on top and spread it out. What he saw caused him to slowly inhale through his nose. It was one of his white Baguettes warm up tees. It was now blue, with hints of red. He closed his eyes for a brief moment before opening the front of the dryer and whipping the shirt to the back of it. Thankfully, he only owned a few white shirts, and the other darker clothes inside the load didn't look worse for wear.

"Before I eff this up, is there anything I need to know about the dryer?" Deke asked the other student.

Romance guy chuckled as he pointed to a shelf with an orange box on it. "Nothing you can really do wrong with that one. I suggest throwing one of those sheets in there. It adds some nice smells and is supposed to soften the fabric."

Deke nodded, and crutched across the mostly dry floor to procure one of the white, slightly scruffy-looking sheets. "For next time, how much soap am I supposed to use?"

"One gel. You'll also want to wash the white clothes and the color clothes separately, or you get the funky tie-dye clothes like that." He pointed at Deke's once-white warmup tee. "Trust me, you'll never make that mistake again. At least your clothes are going to smell super fresh!" Romance guy laughed, including himself in the joke with his earlier admission of having also caused a similar problem.

After Deke started the dryer, he thanked the guy and excused himself to go work on his history paper, *again*.

An hour and a half later, he reread the paper while he folded his laundry on his bed.

Lee opened the door to the room, causing him to look up from the laptop.

Deke watched as Lee walked in, his eyes on his phone as he cautiously inched forward to navigate through Deke's dirty laundry without looking up. He didn't stop until he ran into the base of Deke's bed.

"Huh?" Lee said, looking up for the first time since he entered the room. "What the..." He glanced from Deke's pile of folded laundry to the now clean floor next to his bed and then back. "What's going on? Is there some inspection I've never heard about or something?"

"Don't act shook," Deke growled, but continued to fold his laundry. He was getting hungry and wanted to have it all folded before he went to the cafeteria. He had to admit it was somewhat amusing to watch Lee look back at the number on the open door, to ensure he'd walked into the right dorm. "Got sick of the mess." He preemptively explained, which was even partially true. Still, he was looking forward to getting the evo points from completing the task even more than any other motivation.

"Do you have a fever? Oh God Deke, are you dying?" Lee reached over and laid the back of his hand on Deke's forehead to add to the joke. "You missed that hoodie under your bed, by the way." Deke slapped the hand away and then lightly shoved the Asian kid toward his own bed, trying to make sure he didn't reach for the hoodie currently housing the Evil Corp drug packaging.

"Shut up." Deke chuckled despite himself, then returned to folding his laundry even as his stomach marched in the streets and held up metaphorical signs in protest. "I'm grabbing food as soon as I'm done, if you're hungry."

"I could eat," Lee said, still giving Deke the side-eye as he folded laundry. "You sure you're all right?"

"I'm fine," Deke muttered. He stood up to move clothes around so that he could continue folding, and he grunted as he put weight on his knee again. The removal of progress in the system was reflected in the increased pain, compared to before his regretful mistake at the rehab clinic. Deke considered the new uncomfortable sensations as a good reminder. He *would* get better and stop messing up.

"I can help..." Lee said, moving to pick up some of the folded underwear.

"Don't you dare." Deke pointed a finger at his roommate. Honestly, he was afraid that someone else working on a task might invalidate his effort in completing it. Or, if he was honest, he was more concerned that the kid might grab the hoodie in a misguided attempt to be helpful. Deke pushed Lee's hand away as he put his laundry away and folded the last quarter of the basket.

"Is that my laundry basket?" Lee sat back on his bed and continued to watch Deke fold the laundry.

"Yeah," Deke said as he upended the dregs of the thing and tossed it at his dorm mate. Deke decided that he probably didn't need to match up his socks and stuffed them into the drawer. Finishing allowed him to breathe out a sigh of relief as the last of the clean clothes disappeared from his sight. "Right. Dinner?"

"Yeah." Lee finished putting his own dirty clothes back into his basket. He followed along as Deke crutched his way over to the cafeteria. "Are you sure you're all right? You seem... different."

"I'm fine. Hey, random question. You know that logo I was asking you about? The bivuvian man?"

"Vitruvian Man," Lee corrected automatically, but then snickered a bit at the way Deke said it.

"Yeah, the Vitruvian Man. Do you know if that's like... a symbol of something? Does it mean anything?" Deke corrected hurriedly, not liking that Lee laughed at him.

"I don't think so. I wanna say da Vinci took it from some architect who said it was supposed to be the ideal measurements of a person."

"Why would an architect be concerned with the ideal measurements of a person?" Deke asked as they passed through the entryway. It looked like the doors had just opened up for dinner, but there were a few students ahead of them in line already.

"Well, there is some speculation about that, if you're actually interested. You see, there are at least two schools of thought in the implementation and usage of measurement; which, as you might imagine, is incredibly important to nail down for all kinds of fields, including, yes, architecture. The first orthodoxy, for lack of a better term, structures their use of measurement around the measurement of the planet. A kilometer for example, is nothing more than one forty-thousandth of the circumference of the earth, approximately anyway. From that foundation everything else is simply breaking that single measurement down into lesser and greater orders of magnitude; the meter, centimeter, millimeter, etcetera."

"Lee. Bro. What's this got to do with the Vesuvius Man?" Deke interrupted.

"Vitruvian Man," Lee corrected absently. "And I'm getting there. The second school of thought organizes the structure and implementation of measurement around... can you guess?"

"Feet?" Deke brought up the simplest form of measurement he could think of, feeling like an idiot.

"Hey, that's really close, man. Good job," Lee said encouragingly, giving Deke a proud slap on the shoulder. "The answer is, in fact: the human body. You were on the right track. Feet were, and are, a measurement of the very present and available unit of measurement of a person's foot. The inch, however... Twelve inches in a foot? How does that make any sense? It's because the inch was derived as the distance between the tip of your thumb and the first crease of your thumb, again, an easily accessible unit of measurement regardless of vocation. Thus, we come full circle. The *Vitruvian Man*. The perfect man. Perfect in measurement, form, and function. You know the term renaissance man?" Lee asked, and Deke grunted noncommittally. "It is supposed to mean someone can do a lot of things really well, you know? Da Vinci was a famous painter, for example. But he was also an inventor and a philosopher. The sum of human knowledge was a lot smaller back then, so it was possible for a single person to become an expert in everything. People like da Vinci were like, the smartest engineers, doctors, scientists, and artists all rolled up in one. So naturally it wouldn't be surprising if architecture was just one of the guy's many hobbies."

"Damn, Lee. Where do you even learn all of this stuff?" Deke muttered as he went through the line. Lee was ahead of him and already had a serving of greasy meatloaf, fries, pudding, a slice of pizza, and a fruit cocktail. Everything on Lee's plate but the fruit glowed slightly red to Deke's eyes. Sighing the sigh of the downtrodden, he had a large salad, several dried-out chicken breasts, and rice piled on his tray. The portions were about the same, but Deke had a feeling that his meal wasn't going to taste anywhere near as good as Lee's.

Deke topped off his tray with two glasses of milk and a bowl of fruit as a dessert. Lee, true to form, had opted for two glasses mixed between blueberry blast Mountain Dew and Gatorade and a slice of chocolate pie. Deke ate his food in moody silence as Lee nattered on about the Renaissance. Once he'd finished his entire tray, Deke eyed Lee's; he hadn't touched the fruit cocktail, so Deke took it off of his plate and began eating it. Lee didn't even seem to notice. They finished their plates and were headed back to the dorm when Lee stopped for a moment.

"I just remembered something. I saw a video game that used the Vitruvian Man. It was this weird open-source game where you had to fight these robots or something. The UI was pretty clunky, so I didn't actually get very far into it. But I remember all the menus used it as... like a backdrop."

"What sort of game was it?" Deke asked, getting a little excited. The blue letters and tasks could easily be considered a video game interface. Perhaps he could learn more about what all this meant by looking at the game.

"Oh, just a normal cyberpunk, stealth assassin game."

"Stealth assassin? Aren't all assassins stealthy, like ninjas, right?"

"Yeah, I guess stealth games are their own genre, though. There is usually an assassination or two in them, but also stealing or infiltrating to plant evidence or something." Lee shrugged. "This one seemed to focus almost exclusively on killing targets, but like I said, I didn't get very far."

"How did you unlock your skills and stuff in the game?" Deke asked, thinking about the locked sections of the menu. Lee gave him that same wide-eyed look from earlier.

"I mean, they were all unlocked at character creation; you just had to finish tasks and assign points to abilities." Lee continued to look at him as if he was cracked. "Are you sure you're all right? You've never been this interested in a game before—well, a video game at least."

"Oh, my brother really likes those cyberpunk games, the ones where you can replace body parts with mechanical replacements and stuff. Figured this might be up his alley. Not sure if I want him playing as an assassin, though." Deke was luckily saved from answering any more questions by the simple expedience of the crutches not allowing them both to walk through the narrow entrance side by side.

They made it back up to their room, both young men silent in their separate contemplations. For Deke, he was lost in thought. Despite his considerations, a distant part of himself understood that he still hadn't finished his remedial hygiene task, so he began cleaning off his desk mechanically. Most of it was pamphlets and stuff that he wasn't going to need, so he just threw them all away. The layer of junk on the top slowly thinned out, and an old pizza box was revealed. He didn't even remember when he'd eaten a pizza last.

Desktop clear, he found his math textbook, which he actually needed. Grabbing his math homework, he looked at the assignment but couldn't really figure out what the first problem was even asking. He glanced over at Lee, who had his headset on and was fighting a giant converted building-looking monster with a sword, the blue letters above the creature's head reading "Empire."

Lee was already getting too suspicious of Deke. So, instead of bothering the guy, he would just go to the math lab after American History tomorrow. Closing the newly uncovered math book, Deke slid it into his backpack then pulled his laptop over, careful not to unplug it. He knew that this time the paper was saved but the damn brick would take a full fifteen minutes to reboot if it shut down.

Carefully, he went over the paper a final time, deciding it was good enough. After saving it one final time, just to be sure, he submitted it online. Sighing, he moved on to the next overdue assignment, then thought better of it and started on his essay for Coach Skip, which took him almost an hour.

Finally done with his homework, Deke yawned as he glanced around the room. His clothes were folded and put away; his sheets still hadn't been put back on the bed, though. The rest of the room looked much cleaner, although the trash was stacked pretty high in a corner. Trash was hard for him to do on his crutches, so hoping that Lee would do it, he decided it was time to go to bed. As he finished making his bed, the notification he'd been waiting for showed up.

Task complete: Remedial Hygiene.

Remedial Hygiene: Your person is suitably clean and the surroundings are now suitable for habitation.

You have gained 2 evo points. All progress has been diverted to fixing your active injury. (Torn ACL, current progress 33.9%)

Deke lay down on the bed with a sigh of relief and pulled his blanket over his head to block out the light from Lee's monitor. Unfortunately, there was no blocking out the obnoxious clicking, but Deke had gotten used to it a while ago. Thirty-three point nine was a third of the way to the finish line. Yet he felt annoyed; he was almost exactly back where he'd started this morning. Completing three tasks today gave him six evo points and he'd failed a fourth one, which lost him five. He would be almost halfway healed if he hadn't pushed too hard with his rehab.

Twisting in bed to try to get into a more comfortable position, Deke determined that the most annoying part of his self-recrimination is that he kept hearing it in Duke's voice. "Take it easy," he'd told him. "Do the work but don't strain yourself." He was just so smug about the whole thing. It was no wonder Deke pushed himself too hard. That guy was probably using inverse psychology or something.

Wait, it was inverse, right? No, that's a math term for when you... put something upside down. Deke popped his earbuds in, switching his phone to play one of those meditation YouTube videos the doc assigned him, and then tried to relax. If he wasn't going to fail any of the tasks tomorrow, he needed to be on top of his game.

"No time to take it slow, gotta crush it," Deke muttered to himself. Finishing the tasks was his ticket to playing this year, and he had no intention of letting the Duke, Abbie, or anyone keep him from his destiny. He was going to be playin' the NBA before long. He was going to be rich. That's right, he was gonna buy a big house, and his mom could quit all her jobs, and Max... Max would get to live any cyborg dream he wanted.

Deke drifted off to sleep, images of his little brother shooting bad guys with lasers playing center stage in his dreams.

TEN

THURSDAY, NOVEMBER 3

"Progress report."- Cotton Candy Vaper

"I spent all night looking through the video, but the guy who saved me disappeared into a shed."- Ronald

"You have 18 hours." - Cotton Candy Vaper

Waking up was usually a struggle for Deke, but this morning it wasn't. He opened his eyes and was just wide awake in a way that he couldn't remember being since holiday mornings as a child. He reached for his phone to check the time, hoping he wasn't this awake in the middle of the night. His hand hadn't touched the phone when his alarm started blaring. He turned it off and heard Lee groan before the kid's mattress creaked from him turning away.

Today, he was going to complete all the—

Daily review of progress:

Nutrient levels: Sufficient. Adjusting requirements based on previous activity.

Non-REM Sleep: Sufficient. No additional adjustments required.

Torn ACL debuff still active, 33.9% progress toward recovery.

Active tasks: None

New task assigned.

Healthy Living: This task includes the four following sub-tasks—each with its own subgoals.

Acquire Nutrients: Eat a total of 2810 calories for the day—macronutrient goals: 220 grams of protein, 280 grams of carbohydrates, and 90 grams of fat.

Hygiene Maintenance: Maintain a healthy living standard. Goals: brush teeth twice (0/2), keep odor output within acceptable limits, and maintain environmental status.

Scholastic Betterment: Attend, listen and comprehend the scholastic endeavors of the day.

Injury Rehabilitation: Perform the prescribed activity assigned to you by a recovery professional. Goals: Get treatment, do not deviate, and follow instructions.

Sub-tasks complete: 0/4

What had just happened? The letters scrolled by, and he couldn't recall the sheet again. Still, it had just informed him that instead of three separate tasks, all of his activities from the previous day were now combined into a single task.

"What sort of bullshit—" Deke blurted and cut himself off when Lee groaned from his bed. He almost dismissed his dorm mate's issue and went back to shouting. Lee had chosen to stay up all night gaming, after all. Yet, Deke realized it wasn't the kid's fault that he now had some sort of big brother device-thing in his head.

A part of him understood that he was upset because he'd been hoping for three underhand lob tasks again. He'd been planning on knocking the covers off the tasks and hitting them out of the park. Now he wondered—would he have to complete each one perfectly to get any evo points?

Getting out of bed, Deke tried to figure out if he needed to shower in the morning or if the task would consider him hygienic enough as he was. He decided he was clean enough from the previous night still. Instead, he got dressed from a stack of folded clothes, being careful not to disturb the other piles accidentally.

At breakfast, there was a new addition. On top of food glowing green, yellow, orange, or any other Fruit Rings cereal coloration, each item, when focused on, would display three small numbers. Each number was followed by a P, C or F, and he made the great logical deduction that they were calculating his macros. He picked some items that glowed green like he had yesterday and deliberated. Deke wasn't good at math, never had been, and never would be. Sure, his first class today was calculus, but the Student Advisor claimed he needed it for his degree. Now the system wanted him to do mental arithmetic? Okay, it was actually a simple deduction, but he didn't like the tedium of it.

Sighing heavily, Deke pulled out his planner, wrote down the numbers he remembered, and then copied his breakfast values underneath. He needed to get better, and if this was what was needed, he would crush it.

The numbers in the book and his ineptitude at math made him sigh. His next class was calculus, and he knew it would be even worse than American History had been. The only good news was that Lee was in a more advanced block of classes and so wouldn't be giving him strange looks as he tried to piece the teacher's words together.

Deke wouldn't ever have said something like this in the past, but he wished he was in American History right now. The calculus teacher, Professor Wing, droned on about tangent lines and rates of change at the front of the class. Deke looked around at the other students madly scribbling in their binders. He exhaled and glanced at his own brand new book. He'd managed to write each of the topic's headings, at least: Chain rule, implicit differentiation, inverse trigonometric differential... Yeah, he needed help—he needed to talk to Professor Wing after class.

Speaking of talking with professors, Deke realized that Professor Tawn might know something about the Vivuvyant Man thing. He opened up his planner and wrote that down. If he could learn something more about that blue liquid he drank, it might give him answers on how to speed up recovery. Or at least tell him what he took...

New task assigned. One task pending.

Math Help: Seek assistance in completing your math-related assignments. Assigned based on detected stress from the operator concerning the subject.

"Saweeet!" Deke crowed from his seat and heard the unanimous stop of scribbling pens and chalk. The teacher and all the students looked up at his seat near the front of the class. Thinking fast, Deke pointed to the board. "Sorry, got the same answer—first time... today. Big ups, Teach," he explained and scratched the back of his neck.

The class ended shortly after that, and Deke sheepishly approached Professor Wing. There was a small line of other students asking questions about—log-at-tisms? Listening, Deke became surer that it was about converting something in a game. Honestly, if they wanted to talk about their base tens or whatever, they should go elsewhere. He had important questions to ask.

"Professor Wing," Deke called when it was finally his turn. "I am wondering if you have time to give me some extra help. I just feel like I am not understanding the Derivy's like I am supposed to."

Wing just stared back at Deke, then pointed to the corner of the chalkboard. Deke groaned at the repetition of Professor Tawn's actions from a few days ago before following his gesture. There in the corner of the board that was otherwise filled with numbers, sat some scribbled words. "Math Lab Hours 8:00 a.m.–5:00 pm. room CMB A510, Office Hours M,T,W 1–3p.m. CMB 130J." Deke nodded and wrote down the information dutifully. He was about to turn and go but was brought up short.

"Mr. Mills, while I don't mind letting you skate by—Go Baguettes!—I do not like interruptions. Please refrain from them in the future." Professor Wing began collecting his notes off the lectern. Deke gave him an awkwardly wide full-toothed smile, and after he was sure nothing more was coming, he fist-pumped.

"Go Baguettes?" He returned the teacher's cheer unenthusiastically and hurried out of the classroom.

"**Y**ou following me, gimp?" Valerie greeted Deke at the entrance to room A510. He gave the beautiful girl an appreciative look and smiled at her.

"Good thing I have a third leg, right?" He joked back in her direction, indicating the crutches and winking at her simultaneously.

"And a fourth one," she said, pointing at the other crutch. "You should really get that looked at, could be serious. They may need to amputate." A tiny smirk crept onto her face, but she hid it a moment later. He could tell she wasn't in the mood, so he gave her a serious answer.

"Nah, I'm here for math help. Not that following you wouldn't be as rewarding an endeavor. Have you seen dem legs? They go on for dayz." It never hurts to compliment a woman.

Feeling his hair stand on end, Deke looked at Valerie, thinking he'd crossed a line, somehow. Valerie was ignoring him, from what he could tell. He scanned the room and saw another familiar face sitting at a table. Abbie sat at a table and glared sharp enough daggers that he wondered if she was picturing murdering him. He gave her a smile and a shrug before turning to the attendant as he returned from the back of the room.

"You two here for extra help?" At their nod, the Poindexterous man continued, "What class?"

"Calculus," Deke and Valerie chimed in unison, and then looked at each other. Valerie didn't match Deke's smile, and his face fell a bit. Guess he wasn't going to be seeing her naked again. Bummer, she definitely wasn't hard on the eyes in her birthday suit.

"32B or A?" the nerd asked. Deke had no memory of what either of those meant, so he just shrugged. Valerie did the same. "Whatever, doesn't really matter."

Abbie glared at him again, but started when she realized she was supposed to be tutoring a student. The student looked between Abbie and Deke as he tried to get the therapist's attention back.

"Sorry, bro, can't help the animal magnetism," Deke muttered to himself and chuckled.

"What?" Valerie asked in her high valley girl accent. Deke ignored the question, and the attendant finished looking through his notes.

"We only have a single tutor available at the moment. Luckily it's the same class. So, you two can share, right?" Valerie sniffed as Deke shrugged. "Good, since neither of you objects," the man placated hurriedly before Valerie could speak about whatever her haughty expression meant.

An hour and a half later, Deke was actually rather impressed with himself, the tutor, or some combination of the two. He could partially understand how the man turned an equation with an X into something that he solved for the letter. They might have done even better, but Valerie flirted with the man whenever she needed his attention. Deke would've been upset, but she unclenched enough to flirt with him too, so he let it slide.

Valerie got up to leave, and Deke checked his watch. He needed to get to practice in about a half-hour himself. But getting up to pack his stuff now would seem too clingy. Instead, he let Valerie pack her things and appreciated the double-sided show whenever she leaned over to collect something. Far too soon, she was walking away.

"Damn, I would let that girl do anything she wanted to me," the tutor said once she left the room. Deke smiled and remembered the night they'd shared, silently agreeing with the man.

"Already did that once, but I'm looking forward to the rematch," Deke responded and held up his fist for some proper respect on the situation. The tutor pounded his fist happily, with a broad grin.

"No way. How'd you do it?" The tutor asked for the details in a conspiratorial tone. Maybe he was hoping for some sort of tip to come out of the exchange. Deke was about to tell him all about it when he felt those same goosebumps return. Abbie's glare felt like the stabbing he'd assumed earlier was morphing to castration.

"Some other time, my man. I gotta run to practice. But hey, I'll hit you up, next time bro." Deke packed up his things. As he did, a piece of paper fell out of his notebook. He leaned down to pick it up and found a number written in sparkly gel pen, signed, "-V" in the corner. "I might have a better story then." He winked at the tutor as he slipped the paper into his pocket.

CHAPTER

ELEVEN

THURSDAY, NOVEMBER 3

Deke put Valerie's number into his phone and waited for the elevator, leaning on the wall to remove pressure on his armpits. The subtask for math scrolled by and changed to completed, but he didn't get any evo points. His jaw muscles tensed; he'd been right this morning, but he would have been even more upset with the system if the blond bombshell hadn't slipped him her number. He was surprised at how good he felt, even a bit optimistic, as he crutched over to the gym and practice.

His crutches clicked into the relatively empty locker room, and Deke scanned the area. Only three other guys were already suiting up, a far cry from the usual activity level. He must have mistimed the trip from the tutoring lab to here. Deke changed in peace, slightly hopeful that his early appearance would be noticed by the coach. He really needed to rebuild that relationship.

Instead of reporting to Skip, he grabbed one of the assistants. Deke assumed the coach would have him do free throws and figured this might be something the coach might label as "good work ethic" for starting early. He noticed that the hoop started changing colors again, flickering slightly between red and blue midway through his hundred shots. Deke narrowed his eyes. Was that the same blue as the menu? He tried going slower and faster, but if it was from the vial he'd acquired from Duke, it wasn't consistent enough to mean anything. It did distract him enough that he began bricking multiple shots in a row.

"You all right there, Deke?" Coach Skip said after one awful shot that fell through the open air beside the hoop.

"Just one of those days." Deke hid a wince. At least he had been early?

"We all have those. Head down to the doc's, no point in building bad habits."

"Sure thing, Coach," Deke said, and he turned away to pick up his crutches and head down.

"How are things going, anyway? Everything good with your mom? Little brother?" The coach was giving him the same look Lee had been throwing his way the last two days.

"Yeah, Coach. They're all good." Deke tried to head off that line of questioning before it got too involved.

"You know I have an open-door policy if you ever want to discuss something. Have you had an appointment with the therapist yet?"

"Uh, no Coach, I scheduled a meeting, but it's not until next week... I think." Deke winced. He had totally forgotten to call the therapist. Hopefully, the coach didn't have a way of knowing he hadn't actually scheduled an appointment yet.

"All right. No rush. We've got a year to get you back in shape."

"Yeah. I'll be fine before that, though, Coach," Deke said.

"We'll see. Go check in with the doc."

"A'ite." Deke pushed to a little faster than his normal speed. He got down to the physio room and winced, as Abbie was the only assistant present.

He put his crutches down by the friction massage and sheepishly waited in a chair for Abbie to finish what she was doing.

"You're early." Abbie's voice was skeptically surprised as she finished up with her previous patient and came over to check on him. She flipped through a chart for a moment. "All right. Let's get started, up on this table." She patted the nearest blue upholstered bed, but Deke saw a slight clench to her jaw. Guess her earlier pronouncement of not liking him still held up. Keeping her head down as she worked, she rubbed his knee as Deke sat there.

"So, you're a math tutor too?" Deke tried to break the ice, but Abbie's only response was a slight nod of her head. Deke frowned. He should have known better than to ask yes or no questions. "How long have you been doing that?" Abbie just shrugged her shoulders slightly. And Deke lapsed into an awkward silence. The woman clearly had no intention of responding to his conversation attempts.

The cold shoulder continued for each exercise she assigned. Abbie just told him what she wanted him to do, and that was it. She didn't even attempt to correct movements. No other words left her mouth, and Deke sighed deeply. Therapy was going to feel twice as long if this was the new normal.

Deke started scanning the room instead, bored without some conversation. He saw Ronnie rush into the clinic, through a side door and into an office. There were plenty of windows, so Deke could still see the assistant's haggard appearance. The kid looked like he hadn't slept in days. Heavy bags hung under his eyes, and his hair was clumped up into greasy chunks that he half hid under a tuque. He was distracted for a minute trying to remember what the American word for that was... something to do with beans?

"Beaner!" Deke muttered to himself, and Abbie looked up at him, confused.

"What?" she asked, and Deke jumped on the chance to have an actual conversation.

"I was trying to remember what Americans call a tuque. It's a beaner, right?" Deke pointed at the room Ronnie disappeared into, and Abbie turned to look at him.

"That's extremely offensive," Abbie said with a frown.

"What do you call that style of hat then?" Deke said, scratching his knee. Luckily, the top of Ronnie's head appeared in a window just as she turned to look.

"Oh. That's a beanie." Abbie shook her head, "Beanie, not bean... what you said. That's a slur."

"A hat is a slur?"

"No, it's because Ronald is from Guatemala. That's a racial slur for him," Abbie said Guatemala with an accent, probably using the Spanish pronunciation, but Deke wasn't sure.

As they were talking, Ronnie had turned around and was talking to someone out of sight around a corner. Ronnie was looking somewhat agitated by the conversation, and Deke's curiosity about who he was chatting with was piqued.

"Actually, I need to talk to Ron—" Abbie's cell began to ring, cutting her off. She gave Deke a look that was impossible to read—it seemed almost accusatory. Then she pulled out her cell to look at the screen.

"I gotta get this. I'll be back in just a minute," Abbie announced as she strode away from Deke, her brace squeaking with each step.

Deke decided he could alleviate some suspicion if he had a reason to go chat with Ronnie. He figured he could ask Ronnie why he hadn't been able to find him at the party. He made his way over to the office door. However, as he got closer, he caught the scent of cotton candy. Deke broke out in a cold sweat as he immediately remembered the vaping man who had given Ronnie the package for Duke. Not wanting to get on that guy's radar, he changed course, angling toward the free weights near the office entrance so that he could overhear their conversation.

"...but I haven't been able to find the guy anywhere. It's like he never came out of that shed thing."

"I am not interested in your excuses, Ronald. Where is the canister?"

"Dude, I can pay you back. How much do you want, five grand?" Ronnie's voice sounded strained, scared. Deke put his earbuds in but didn't have anything playing. He began doing some bicep curls while he listened.

"Ronald. Do you know how much eight hundred milligrams of Radanium costs?" The vaping man snorted. "There is no way you'll be able to pay us back for its loss. The sample should be inert by now, and we've been monitoring the hospitals and haven't seen any Radanium poisoning. So whoever stole it must not have drunk it. You caught a lucky break there."

"Look, I'm sure I'll be able to find whoever it was. Just give me some more time."

"Ronald, that is something you are fast running out of." The vaping man's arm came into view through the open door and grabbed Ronnie's shoulder. Ronnie's head fell, and Deke actually watched his Adam's apple bob up and down.

"I've got a few more leads I need to check," Ronnie pleaded. Deke could hear the warble in his voice, and when his head came up, Deke could see the fear in his eyes.

"Don't make a scene, Ronald. We need to discuss your failure and how you are going to make it up to us." The arm pulled, and Ronnie's feet slightly dragged across the floor before he took a step to follow.

Deke had been watching the whole thing unfold from the corner of his eye, and he turned away slightly. Whatever mess Ronnie was in, Deke had no intention of getting caught in the same net. Maybe if he was back up to full strength, he could help Ronnie. But with a gimped leg? No chance. Besides, it wasn't his problem—he had already gotten more involved than he should have. Ronnie should have known what he was getting into with this guy. Everything about him screamed danger; even the weird cotton candy vaping pen somehow turned ominous in that guy's hands.

Ronnie was led out of the clinic using the old fire escape doors.

Deke put down the dumbbell and considered the information he had learned. The vial had contained something called Radanium. He was pretty sure that name wasn't on any periodic table, though, so it must be some kind of drug. But they were also expecting anyone to have drunk the vial to get poisoning from it. Why would they have given it to Duke if they expected that? Was *Deke* poisoned? He didn't feel poisoned. The vaping man's words gave him more questions than answers, but at least it was a place to start.

As for Ronnie? Deke wanted to do more but couldn't think of a single option available to him. The kid was into drugs, and he lost the product. Surely that wasn't as bad as Hollywood made it out to be, right?

"Why are you lifting weights?" Abbie asked from behind him, and he turned to look at her. She stood with her arms crossed, which enjoyably emphasized her breasts. Deke forced himself not to look at them, though, since she was clearly not in the mood, based on her tone.

"Chillax, I figured I could get some upper body stuff in while you were off talking to your boyfriend or whatever. Ain't nothing wrong with my arms." Deke did an exaggerated bicep curl to help his case, before he stood up to his full height and looked down his nose at Abbie.

"I don't even have... You know what, that's none of your business. Come on, let's get back to work." Abbie turned around, marched back to where they had been before, and Deke followed. Years in the gym were the only reason he kept his eyes up above her waist, but he sorely wanted the distraction after the Ronnie thing. He let his mind wander instead. They continued with the rehab, and by the end of it, he was confident she'd added plenty of exercises to the menu. All the small muscles that surrounded his knee ached in a way he'd never felt before.

"All right, we're done for the day. You made some good progress." Abbie's words sounded strained, like it physically hurt her to compliment him. "I'll see you back here tomorrow for some more of the same." She turned around and walked a few steps before turning back to Deke.

"No, you know what? You're a pig. I'm going to speak for every woman in the world here and say that the way you treated that girl at the math lab was absolute horse poop. Props for sleeping with her? Just 'cause she was flirting with you both doesn't make her a piece of meat. She isn't some conquest or trophy to brag about. Ugh, you make me sick. You deserve everything that happened to you. The fact that your leg is going to heal and you'll be fine is just proof that the universe isn't fair."

Deke tilted his head at her first accusation, actually curious why he was a pig. But by Abbie's final words, he could feel his blood boiling just below the skin. Abbie stormed away before he could say anything, which left him nowhere to release his anger at her unfair accusations. What made it worse? Two of the other guys in the gym were obviously trying to hide a laugh at his expense.

"That girl is batshit. She's clearly just jealous and needs something between her legs not powered by batteries," Deke muttered, louder than he probably should've. Face red with both anger and, surprisingly, embarrassment, he made his way to the locker room to shower and change. Thinking back, he remembered how angry Abbie had looked in the math lab, how she had glared daggers at him for doing whatever Valerie asked of him. Then he remembered how hard it had been for him not to stare at her tits and ass during the workout. His mom would have smacked him upside the head if she'd seen that.

The menu dinged, telling him he had successfully completed the subtask for the rehab. But even that wasn't enough to shake the slow drop of his stomach. Maybe Abbie was right? And his first thought was that she needed sex? The fear that he might have poisoned himself with the serum swarmed back into his mind then. What about Ronnie? He could have at least stopped the guy from taking him out of a very public clinic, right? Where would the Evil Corp guy have taken the dealer?

His throat tightened, and he decided that he didn't want to go back to the dorm and work on his homework. Deke needed some fresh air, so he crutched his way out toward the ocean. One of his favorite parts about being in California was the gorgeous golden beaches that were so different from Ontario's.

Finding a bench on a cliff overlooking the water, Deke looked out at the setting sun. The blue waves crested in white caps that rolled forward, before crashing into the rocks at the bottom to send a thin spray up into the air that fell like mist. Feeling the wind pick up, he closed his eyes for a moment, drinking in the moment of peace.

That moment was ruined by his phone ringing. Deke had to struggle for a second to pull the old cell out of his pocket. It was his mom. For a fleeting moment, he thought she somehow knew about his confrontation with Abbie and was calling to yell at him for his behavior. A more rational part of his mind dismissed that as impossible, but he clicked the button to answer the phone.

"Hey, Mom. What's up?"

CHAPTER

TWELVE

THURSDAY, NOVEMBER 3

"**B**ig bro!" Max's voice crowed from the handheld speaker, and Deke had to pull the phone away from his ear because of the sheer excitement those two words held. Despite his disgust with himself, Max's voice brought a smile to his face.

"Maxie!" Deke began, matching his brothers' excitement as best he could and using one of many nicknames he bestowed the kid with. "What's happening on the home front? You crushing it?"

"I caught my first baseball today!" Max shouted, and Deke heard a man's voice acknowledge the accomplishment from somewhere in the background. His chest tightened slightly, but Max continued, "You gonna crush your season opener?" Deke's heart tried to soar and fall simultaneously. His brother used his own saying, and Deke wanted nothing more than to pump a fist and answer it in the affirmative. But his question dug at Deke's soul. Now, he needed to disappoint his biggest fan.

"I'm not playing the home opener, bud. Coach has other plans for me," Deke said around a lump in his throat. "Leg hasn't gotten better just yet. Trust me, I'm working hard at it."

"Dude! Johnny got us the extended sports pack on the TV. You said you wouldn't be out for more than a few months." Deke's brother's disappointment turned his stomach, but what made it worse was the name mentioned. That piece of shit was still in the picture? Johnny never spent money without expecting something in return. What had Rhonda done?

"I know, Maxie, I'm closer than you think. Just not one hundred percent yet," Deke responded, and was about to continue when he heard Johnny's voice in the background.

"What'd I tell you? I knew he weren't gonna be playing this season. Damn spaz kid don't know to land on bent knees, takes more'n a couple months to fix stupid." he said, and Deke's heart finished falling as he felt his earlier anger with Abbie come storming back. Only amplified and somehow more focused.

"Max, can you put Mom on the phone please," he forced out from clenched teeth. Max responded and called out for their mom. Deke waited, and as soon as she greeted him, he yelled, "What the fuck, Rhonda? That piece of trailer trash is back in the house?"

Rhonda sucked in a heavy breath, and she didn't respond right away. Rustling and a closing door reached Deke's ear, and he figured she was taking the call into the bedroom. The squeak of bedsprings confirmed it as she simultaneously took a deep breath.

"D, he helps out around here. With you gone, I can't do everything on my own." Rhonda huffed into the phone, returning Deke's anger. "He's been straight sober for nine days already. Quit cold turkey, and he promised me he wouldn't bring another drop into the house again." Her words only caused the pit in his chest to drop further. When he'd gone back to London, Ontario to visit after the surgery, he had arrived to find his mom with a fading bruise on her shoulder. She said she fell, but Deke eventually got her to tell him the truth.

"Mom, he hit you! That's why I got rid of him when I was home. Now you're letting him back into the house? What if he knocks Max around and he has another incident?" Deke shouted into the microphone and heard his voice echo off the sand and water below him. He didn't even care.

"Shut up, D. You go to some party and take too many pain meds as soon as you get back and want to criticize me? I sacrificed everything to get you into that school and you're doing your best to ruin it. Then you have the balls to criticize Johnny for *accidentally* knocking me down." He heard the tone of his mom's voice and tried to cut her off, but she overrode him. "I can't just leave Max with the crazy cat lady next door. He needs round-the-clock care. Having Johnny around lets me work only two jobs, you ungrateful little shit!"

"Mom, Cathay isn't so bad, and he hit you!" Deke repeated with more emphasis. "You didn't get knocked down. What if he hits Max?"

"That didn't actually happen. You forced it out of me, and it wasn't true. I just fell down, okay? Look, you worry about yourself, or you'll be back here next week without a scholarship!" His mom finished and clicked off the call. Deke blinked stupidly into the setting sun. He still held the phone to his ear. His hand clenched down on the device, and he heard his knuckles pop from the force.

Closing his eyes, Deke imagined the world falling away. His heart had just been run over by a dump truck. Air came out of his mouth in shallow bursts, and he recognized he was crying only because a breeze highlighted the cold trails of salty tears down his cheeks. A quick flex and he swung his legs over the railing, sitting up on the square cement post overlooking the cliff. After a glance down he pulled his legs up to his chest. He hated this. He knew his mom worked hard, and she deserved happiness, but Johnny wasn't it. Why did she keep falling into that trap?

Not only wouldn't she listen when he was out here, but she'd called him out and was so accurate. He'd almost lost his scholarship two days ago and she hadn't even known about that. That was by far the worst part—he was on his last chance here. Maybe even past that. That didn't mean he was wrong, though. Now that fucking pile of shit was poisoning Max with his nonsense?

Deke realized what the worst part actually was. He couldn't *do* anything. He was on the other side of the continent. Three hours behind them, which meant they'd all just finished dinner and were probably getting ready to watch a movie or something. He dropped his phone to the ground and wove his fingers into his hair before flexing them and pulling on it frustratedly. The pain felt good somehow, like he deserved it.

Blue letters scrolled by, but he didn't even read them. This stupid thing was probably poisoning him slowly. Especially if what he'd heard Ronnie and the vaping man talking about was correct. Should he head to the hospital? No, from what the man said, they were monitoring the hospitals. He opened his eyes, his chin resting on his knees, and his gaze turned downward.

A litany of his wrongs ran through his mind, Valerie, Abbie, Max, and even Ronnie. Had his theft killed Ronnie? No, you couldn't get money from a dead man. The vaping man was probably just gonna beat him up or something. Still, Ronnie wasn't going to just be okay, and that all started when Deke took that damn satchel.

Even realizing that Ronnie would be in the same exact situation if it were the thugs putting the boots to him who'd taken the satchel didn't help. It was clear that was what they were after. They'd stopped assaulting Ronnie and immediately taken off after him when he'd grabbed it. Despite all of that, however, it *hadn't* been the thugs who had taken it. It had been him. He had intended to give it back— he thought?

Ocean spray hit his face; the breakers under him were sixty, maybe seventy meters below, and the slick rock glistened with the last rays of the sun. He slowly stood up, balancing on the post with his good leg. He looked down and considered jumping, crashing into the rocks like the waves below. Would anyone even care? He was a loose knife, hurting everyone close to him lately. Wouldn't it just be worse tomorrow? Having to live knowing Johnny might be hitting his mom, or somehow worse, his brother Max.

He leaned forward, his eyes fixed on the jagged lines of golden serpentine coast below.

"Deke? Is that you?" Lee asked incredulously from behind him. Deke ran his forearm across his face and shook his head. The moment of disorientation unbalanced him, and he jolted backward. His fear of falling in the moment of dizziness fired every muscle in his body, shooting him back. He turned and tried to catch himself with his left leg, but the pace of the action twisted his right leg because it was still dragging on the rock. He fell to the ground and held in a shout of pain, turning it into a long groan.

Re-balancing surge of neuroinhibitors, amino acids, and hormones complete.

Damage to existing ACL tear detected. 3% loss of progress assessed.

"Lee! Shit! Man, you startled me!" Deke called from the ground, trying to hide his hyperventilation as fright instead of a coping mechanism for the pain.

"Dude, it looked like you were gonna jump?" Lee retorted, his voice concerned.

"Nah way, man. You want to get a new roommate that badly?" Deke injected as much humor as he could into his voice. "You surprised me, Tiny. Mind helping me up and grabbing my crutches and phone?" Deke continued, but rubbed at his knee as soon as Lee wasn't looking at him. It hurt like hell, and he just hoped he would get enough evo points to make up for his current stupidity. He couldn't help Rhonda or Max if he died.

Once Lee helped him to his feet, Deke tried to send Tiny ahead of him. He didn't feel like being grilled the rest of the way back. But the kid refused to leave without him and led the way to the cafeteria and dinner, talking about goblins and dragons and how he was DMing the next game. How Lee was sliding into some girls' DMs talking about goblins or dragons was beyond Deke, but he nodded along like he understood as he considered what had happened on that cliff.

The letters that scrolled by on that cliff must have been about the neuro-whatevers. The system had mentioned depression in the past. Was that what had just happened to him? Did he hit bottom? If Lee hadn't interrupted him, he might have stepped off that cliff. Part of him said that was not possible, but a dark corner of his mind he'd never paid much attention to, knew he would have done it. He shook that thought off and used a phrase he'd heard in a few movies.

There's nowhere to go but up, he thought to himself as they entered the cafeteria.

Deke sat down before getting a tray and then to distract himself, he ran the final calculations for his nutrition sub-task. The numbers left him with ninety grams of protein to consume, with only ten grams of fat and about fifty carbs. He tapped his pen against his lips, leaving his crutches behind for the first time that day. He couldn't carry a tray, notebook, and crutch around. Instead, he used nearby furniture and, in a few cases, other students' shoulders to move about. At their questioning looks, he apologized, and they seemed to forgive him.

Once in the line, he discovered that each chicken breast contained around forty grams of protein with decimal points of fat and no carbs. Well, that was the answer to his first problem. He crossed it off after taking three breasts that totaled over a hundred grams. He figured he would just throw out the extra. Everything else he passed, glowed green but were over his totals in fat, except for plain white rice. He inhaled through his nose and asked for two helpings. After those filled up his plate, he took a single piece of cheese as dessert.

As he shoveled the tasteless food into his mouth, he realized he could probably come up with a meal plan in the future. Something that spread everything out and didn't make his last meal bland chicken and rice. Then he dismissed the thought. He knew he wouldn't actually do it. That was like those resolutions you make with yourself while going to bed about waking up early and putting in extra work to compromise for going to bed early. Never worked.

Lee sat down and began eating as he flipped through a colorful hardback book. It had some sort of title about finding a path, and he thought it had a dragon and a ship on the front. Whatever path the kid was trying to find, he was scribbling notes with one hand and shoveling food into his mouth with the other. Deke left him to it and kept forcing his food into his mouth. Every so often, he nibbled on some cheese and gulped water to help lubricate the dryness in his throat.

The system scrolled an update notification when each macro hit, and Deke stared down at a plate with half a chicken breast, a quarter of the piece of cheese, and scattered rice. Normally he wasn't one to leave food on his plate, but other than the small bit of cheese, he was happy to put this food in the trash.

Deke got back to the room first, leaving Lee with his book and mad-doctor scribing. He grabbed his folded towel and made his way to the shower to complete yet another quest. Wasn't that what Lee and Max's game called their missions? Vaguely surprised, he kind of liked the sound of that, it had a nice ring to it. He smiled after brushing his teeth and seeing the hygiene subtask completed. Lee was back after Deke's shower, and he'd already stuck to the chair in front of his computer, headset on.

Checking the notebook, Deke was disappointed. He'd completed every task he wrote down. But the evo points hadn't come yet? He tried to remember this morning or call up the tasks through a force of will. Nothing happened, and he was forced to shrug. It would scroll

letters at him again tomorrow, of that he was certain. That, or...
maybe the poisoning was getting worse?

He shook that thought from his head and got dressed. Climbing
into bed, Deke tried putting in earbuds to help distract him from the
intense key-clicking going on. It worked to mute the keys, but every so
often, Lee would yell something through his headset. Deke cracked
an eye and shook his head at the kid. If only he was so commanding
in the real world, or at an earlier hour. Right now, Deke was considering going over and ripping the power cord out of the wall.

He turned up his music instead and fell into a restless sleep.

CHAPTER

THIRTEEN

FRIDAY, NOVEMBER 4

"Local asset on Battle of Waterloo failed delivery. Package total loss."- Agent Smoke

"Message confirmed. Tie up loose ends."- UPLIFT Einherjar

"Affirmative. Delivery agent handled, will escalate through local assets. Reattempt?"- Agent Smoke

"Aesir will be consulted, stand by for decision."- UPLIFT Einherjar

Deke realized he was awake, but he also understood that his alarm clock hadn't gone off yet. So he stayed in that state of semi-consciousness, which allowed him to continue his dream. He was back in Valerie's room. She was turned away, but her bare back was visible. He watched the smooth lines of her muscles contract as she heard him approach. She twisted to see who was behind her, the movement slow, graceful. The shift revealed her side boob, but she kept turning, a smile on her beautiful face. She turned more, and—

Subtask complete: Rest and Recovery (broken)

Partial task completion. Healthy Living, 4 evo points awarded. Two out of four subtasks completed.

The scrolled words interrupted his rather pleasant waking dream but instantly got his attention. He'd failed two tasks yesterday. It continued to scroll. He noted both of the failures, his mouth twisting, right up until it gave him a summary of his injury recovery.

Torn ACL debuff still active, 43.5% progress toward recovery.

Tutorial period is complete, aggregating subtasks

New task assigned:

Healthy Living

Checking that progress made him more disappointed with himself for failing the rehab subtask again, and the even easier hygiene task. Both were marked as partial failures, but he could have had a higher recovery if those failures had held back evo points.

Deke lay back on the bed and considered the implications of everything the blue letters showed him. His knee could be healed before the season opener, despite his mistakes. That seemed insane, since it had been bouncing back and forth around the thirty percent mark for a few days. He'd gotten four points for two completed tasks. Did that mean each subtask rewarded a full point? Something about that math seemed off but he had just woken up so he shrugged. It was close, he figured. If so, completing two more would make a huge difference. He promised himself to complete everything today.

The alarm on his phone finally went off, and he sat up; glancing over, he snorted. Lee had his arms up on the desk, his head cradled between them and a small puddle of drool forming under his mouth. Deke grabbed a sock and went to throw it at Lee but blinked as a spot on his face lit up slightly right before he threw it. The sock landed exactly on the area. Deke shook it off as some weird reflection.

"Wha'?" Lee wiped the drool from his chin as he looked around.

"You fell asleep on your chair, and we've got class in an hour," Deke said, pulling his shower stuff out. To date, he had generally avoided showering in the dorm since he had to literally duck to get anything below his shoulders wet. Yet he definitely needed to satisfy this damn big brother Raderium thing. The reason for his failure of the hygiene task seemed to be from his haste to leave the gym yesterday, without showering. That neglect had cost him evo points, or fractions of one. As Deke walked back into the room after showering, Lee had only managed to shift from his chair to his bed. Deke threw his wet towel on the kid's face.

"It's time to wake up," he said, and Lee groaned, then sat up like a bolt and threw the towel back at him.

"Gross man, my mouth was open. Wait, did you throw a dirty sock at me earlier?"

"Good, I scrubbed *everywhere* with that towel," Deke taunted, pulling on a pair of clean shorts. Lee's face suddenly drained of color, and Deke laughed. "Let's go, sleeping beauty, we gotta grab food and get to class."

Lee stared at him for a few minutes, scraping his tongue across his teeth before sliding off the bed and getting ready. Deke didn't have the heart to tell him a massive rooster tail stuck up from the back of his head from the awkward sleeping position. Or maybe it was also for the comedic effect when he learned about it later. Deke wasn't really sure.

Breakfast was a much more complex affair as Deke tried to balance his consumption so he wouldn't be stuck with chicken and rice for dinner. This made breakfast even more depressing, and Deke wondered if there was an actual solution or just varying levels of hell to this food allowance bullshit.

Class was moderately interesting, since Deke had done the assigned reading. Professor Tawn was a good lecturer. The subject matter was mostly new to him, having never really gone in-depth into American history rather than Canadian. They talked about the oppression of the Irish following the mass immigration caused by the Potato Famine and how that applied to current-day politics. Lee still had a flag of hair that stuck straight up, and every time he ducked his head to take notes, Deke chuffed lightly. He couldn't wait to see the kid react later. The bell rang, which seemed to surprise Tawn because he glanced suspiciously at the clock.

"All right. Have a good weekend, everyone. Mr. Mills, please come see me." The man made eye contact with Deke to make sure he'd heard him over the sound of students getting up to leave the room. Deke moved slowly, not wanting to fight the stream of students leaving, not on his metal death sticks, anyway. Still, it was a longer wait than he anticipated while a few other students asked the teacher questions about homework.

"Mr. Mills, I just wanted to say how much I appreciated the re-write of your paper. It was unconventional, but that led to some unusual insights."

"Thanks, Prof," Deke said with a smile. He was totally okay with being called up to be praised.

"I also noticed that you haven't turned in any of your other late homework. You're going to need to do those if you intend to get a passing grade in the class."

"Right. I'll work on that this weekend. I was just busy in my other classes." Deke's words drew an arched eyebrow of inquisition from the professor, and he changed the subject. "Hey, teach. I came across a weird reference to some secret organization that used the Byruvian man as a logo. You ever heard of something like that?" Tawn cocked his head to the side for a moment, thinking.

"I assume you mean the Vitruvian Man, one of da Vinci's more famous pieces of art. If I recall, there have been several organizations that used that symbol throughout history. It's compelling imagery that lends itself easily to a particular ideology. Although there are some studies I've seen that place its creation to long before Leonardo. These sources claimed it was attached to things like the pharaohs, Greek demigods, or even the Viking berserkers and Valkyries.

"They even claimed that some of Hitler's super-soldier programs were based around those same concepts." Tawn frowned, "It's an interesting topic, and I applaud the expansion of your interests. Do you have any particular source that incited this line of inquiry?"

"Oh, uh, Lee, my roommate. He showed me this video game. The baddies used it as a logo, and Tiny said it was based on real life. I was sort of just hoping to prove him wrong."

"Ahh, yes. Tiny being Mr. Wett, in this circumstance?" Tawn responded with a slight smile on his lips. "I can't say that there are any specific secret organizations that use that symbol... But they wouldn't be very good secret organizations if everyone knew the symbols they used, if you know what I mean. Tell you what, you've piqued my curiosity, so I'll look into it a bit as well. But I'm almost positive that your roommate is correct on this one, I'm sad to say." Another professor politely coughed, and Tawn nodded his head.

"Well, we should clear out and make room for the next class. Good luck with that homework, Mr. Mills. Go Baguettes."

An echo of "Go Baguettes!" rang out around the room as the incoming students took up the call. Deke shook his head. The school's mascot was a bit of an open joke. Everyone knew it sounded ridiculous, and they sort of carried that as far as it could go. It was one of those things where it had become so terrible that it threatened to get back into the good zone. According to most of the students, anyway. Deke was still firmly in the terrible camp.

Crutching out of the class, Deke realized that he had a few hours before practice. His current classroom was pretty close to the student union. So, he decided to stop over there and sign up to see a shrink.

The coach had given him a room number. Still, it was in a section of the building that he hadn't bothered to spend much time in yet, so he wandered through a few mostly abandoned hallways until he found it. The waiting area was huge, with an open area balcony that looked out on the ocean. Deke made his way over to the reception office.

"Hi, how can I help you?" The guy at the desk looked like he was a student.

"Yeah, uhm." Deke reached into his backpack and pulled out the paper Coach Skip had given him. "I'm supposed to talk to this dude?" He handed the paper over to the receptionist. He looked it over for a moment, even as he was pulling out a clipboard and attaching a couple of documents to it.

"All right, this is our patient intake form. Go ahead and fill that out. We'll get you sorted out with an appointment with Doctor Pinsonneault after that."

The first page was just a bunch of questions about his student status and other personal information. Still, after that, there was a sheet of questions to get a baseline for his mental health. Does seeing blue lettering and following its directions count as mentally cracked?

Deke sat down and answered a bunch of questions about his mental state. He hesitated on the question asking if he'd had any suicidal thoughts lately. He tried to decide if he should be honest, then he shook his head. No, the rhyno drug was handling that for him. He was just here for what the coach wanted him to work on—no need to add anything that might give them a reason not to let him play. At the rate his leg was healing, he should be completely recovered for the home opener next weekend.

The rest of the questions he answered more or less honestly, with a slight shifting of everything in the direction that seemed least dangerous. It took him almost ten minutes to fill the thing out because the annoying pen they used was attached to some sort of fake flower that kept getting in his mouth.

"All right, I'm done."

"Okay, let me just check this." The receptionist took the page and perused his personal information. "Good, let me see when we can get you in." He began putting stuff into his computer and checking a few things. "All right, I actually have a cancellation in about thirty minutes. If you can wait, I'll get you in to see her today."

"Uh." Deke grunted in surprise, not quite mentally prepared to dive right into his issues right *now*, even as he pulled out his phone to look at the time.

> "You dick"– Tiny Lee, ten minutes ago
>
> "You could have told me my drool got in my hair"– Tiny Lee, just now

Deke chuckled; he'd really wanted to be there for that one. Based on the time, he'd be rushed for lunch, but he could eat somewhere other than the cafeteria and save some time crutch-hobbling across campus. "Sure. I guess I can stay. I'll just be out on the balcony," he said, and the receptionist nodded.

Deke stepped out onto the balcony. There were a couple of benches and a couple of hammocks. Deke felt that "broken" sleep the words had described, so he decided to lie down on a hammock in some shade and enjoy a quick fifteen-minute nap. He was surprised they had these out here and that there weren't more students using them. It wasn't uncommon to see people curled up under tables or on couches taking a nap.

"Deke?" A woman in her early thirties stood over him carrying a clipboard. She had wavy brown hair and a big smile.

"Yeah?" Deke said, struggling to sit up in the hammock and rubbing his eyes.

"I'm Dr. Pinsonneault. If you'll follow me?" Deke made a quick adjustment of his earlier assertion that he was seeing a "dude." Deke tried to stand up, but his crutch got caught on the netting, and the doctor had to help him untangle it. Which was pretty embarrassing.

"Sorry about that. I tore my ACL a bit ago, still recovering." Deke followed the doctor into a room in the back of the little clinic. She had a couple of comfortable couches and chairs. He picked one that looked like it would be the easiest to get into and out of before sitting down in it.

"All right, how about we get to know each other a little bit first. I'm Dr. Pinsonneault, but you're welcome to call me Danielle or whatever you're most comfortable with. Full disclosure, your coach called me a few days ago to talk about your situation, so I know his side of everything that happened. But this is about us figuring out a way forward for you. I will be reporting progress to the university as part of your scholarship, but only in a general sense. Any details you share will be kept confidential." Deke pondered for a moment, looking around the room. He saw that she had graduated from a college in North Dakota.

"You're from the Northern States?" he asked, pointing to the diploma on the wall. "So, you actually know what snow looks like?"

"Ha." Danielle chuckled while nodding her head and looking at her own diploma. "I moved out here a few years ago. Decided I couldn't take the winter depression anymore. You're from that area too, right?"

"Yeah, Ontario." They talked for a few more minutes about where they grew up.

"Is it hard being so far away from your family?"

"Uhm, a little. Mostly I just miss my little brother. My mom's never had good taste in men, and Max is..." Deke frowned, glancing down at his hands. "Max can't take care of himself the same way I can."

Deke was almost surprised when the hour was over. Talking to Dr. Pinsonneault had felt natural; she had been interested in his life without seeming to be overly preachy about what he should do.

"All right, Deke. That's all the time I have today, but one further question. How do you feel about next weekend's home opener?" Danielle asked, her face telling Deke it wasn't meant as a hurtful question, just as a probing one. He examined that thought and realized that he was excited after this morning's progress and his promise to complete all the subtasks today. When he explained those feelings to Dr. Pinsonneault, she tilted her head. She wrote something down, which admittedly made Deke curious, but she spoke before he could ask.

"Let's meet again next week and discuss this some more. In the meantime, I'm going to give you a quick homework assignment. I want you to write down ten things you like about yourself. You can do more if you like, but bring in that list the next time we talk."

"Uh, sure I can do that." Deke shook his head. Ten things would be easy. He pulled out his planner and wrote it in, trying to keep himself on task.

The rest of the day was pretty normal—he got lunch, and he peppered Abbie with questions during rehab. She, in turn, was giving him the cold shoulder again but did provide direction for his exercises. He thought he made some headway by the end of the session and tried his best pickup line again.

"Girl, even in that brace, you got legs—" he began but cut off instantly from the icy glare he received. He pulled on his collar awkwardly while making a noise between a growl and a whine, and left the clinic.

Dinner was bleak—another tasteless collection of chicken and rice. Deke hadn't been able to restrain himself at lunch after having a subpar breakfast in the taste department. When he collapsed onto his bed, he noted the absence of his roommate. Dismissing it with a shrug, he pulled out his planner. Inside, each subtask had a check beside it, and all that was left was sleep. Maybe Lee wasn't there because it was 10:00 p.m., and Deke was never in bed this early?

Still, if going to bed at ten was the answer to getting more evo points, which in turn would put him back on the court sooner, then Deke would buy a pair of grandpa pajamas and get on the sleep train. As he put in his earphones and turned on the meditation track, he spared one thought to wish for a deluge of evo points tomorrow.

FOURTEEN

MONDAY, NOVEMBER 7

"I just realized who it was in that scream mask you asked me about it's that lazy freshman Deke Miller or whatever."- Abbie 4 days ago, message unread

"You didn't show up to work all last week. Everything okay, Ronald?"- Abbie, just now, message unread

"You can't have my leg, Margot!" Deke shouted as he awoke from a strange dream where Margot Robbie was taking his limb off at the knee with a neon-blue laser beam. The heat somehow transferred over. He could feel the residual memory of it. "Ah shit, I'm on fire." He shouted again when he saw a strange blue glow coming from under his covers.

"Off with her head," Lee slurred sleepily from his bed but didn't bother turning over. Deke was about to shout for additional help from the lazy little shit when scrolling letters notified him that the burning pain in his knee didn't mean an agonizing death by fire. Or worse, an STD.

Subtask complete: Rest and Recovery, full night's rest.

Task complete. Healthy Living, 10 evo points awarded. 5 subtasks completed.

Torn ACL debuff resolved, 100% progress toward recovery. Beginning final healing.

The same task assignment followed, but he was too preoccupied with the searing agony of his glowing blue knee. This was *healing?* Deke could feel sweat dripping down his neck as waves of pain crashed through his leg in time with his racing pulse. He fumbled behind his bed at his tiny fridge and pulled out an ice-pack from when the injury first happened. It was covered in freezer snow, but he didn't care; he slapped the gel-filled ice pack onto his knee and sighed as the soothing cold struck the area. The pain was still there, but the ice helped immensely. Thanks to all the scrambling and noise Deke was making, Lee finally turned over and cracked an eyelid.

"What the frak, Deke?" Lee sat straight up, his eyes wide. "Why is your knee glowing?" Deke looked down at his knee and then lay back down with a sigh.

"Sorry, Tiny," Deke said. "Just a bad dream, and my cell startled me awake. Ain't no superhero shit happening today..." Lee gave him a look that told him he wasn't buying any of the bullshit.

"Whatever, I've got to pee." Lee got up to go use the dorm bathrooms. Deke swallowed hard. His knee better stop glowing by the time Lee returned, or that explanation wasn't going to fly.

Torn ACL healed. Foreign metal objects detected. Evaluating rejection protocols. Objects deemed useful structural material. Absorbed and merged with bone. Scar tissue 100% removed.

The blue light faded away like a blown incandescent, and Deke pulled off the ice pack and threw it on top of his mini-fridge. Without waiting, he swung his leg over the side of the bed. Carefully he bent and then straightened the limb and felt no pain. He put his weight on it and performed a few air squats. Nothing—he really was healed. After all that work, all that pain, it was over? Just like that? In a few minutes, it was healed.

He could play in the season opener this weekend. He needed to tell the doc. Lee walked back in to find Deke, performing air squats.

"Dude, it's zero dark thirty in the morning. What's wrong with you!" Lee groused as he pushed past Deke to get to his bed to go back to sleep. Admittedly, Deke hadn't looked at the time and had gone to bed even earlier than usual last night. Still, it had all been worth it! He could *play*.

He grabbed his toothbrush and headed to the dorm facilities himself. He was brushing his teeth in the empty room when the blue lettering returned—this time with something new.

Operator state analysis complete.

Status

Control - 5.925
Power - 6.305
Finesse - 5.525
Endurance - 5.410
Overall rank assigned. Trainee.

Had those *stat* thingies Lee always talked about, just unlocked? That would imply that this really was like the video game. Was it called a [Status]?

The blue letters popped back out, and Deke abandoned his toothpaste to rush back to his room and write them down in his planner while he had the chance. He wasn't sure what they all meant but could guess that Power was the most important one. They faded away again halfway back, but he thought he got them all. He might not know what they meant, but he knew who to ask. Lee was still sleeping, and he figured he should try to get him in a good mood since he needed something from him. Grabbing his towel, he trudged out of the dorm.

Lee was awake when he got back, and Deke didn't miss the stink eye he got when he walked back in, either. He got dressed and put away the ice pack before turning to his roommate, giving him a winning smile.

"You're not about to try to sell me something, right?" Lee retorted before Deke could even get a word out. His smile faltered, and he snatched the ice pack from the freezer and threw it at his roommate. It slapped him wetly in the face, and Deke put both of his hands up in the field goal gesture. "Frak you, dude," Lee said and threw it back weakly.

"Sorry, man." Deke caught it out of the air with ease. "I didn't mean to wake you this morning. I had a bit of a nightmare..."

"Margot Robbie was in your nightmares?" Lee asked.

"You heard that, huh? Long story," Deke countered with a wink. "Anyway, I've got a stumper for you. I know you're into these role-playing games. Ever run across one with status stuff in Control, Power, Finesse, and Endurance?" Lee tilted his head and blinked. "Also, how do you max Power in those games?" Deke added offhandedly. He figured he did a good job appealing to the kid's nerdiness.

"Dude, if you want to bang a hot cosplayer, you're on your own, man." Lee threw his hands up in the air, then pointed to a poster. "Just dress like that dude and hit up a con. You'll do fine."

"God of Death has that status stuff?" Deke asked curiously as he read the headline. Deke studied the red and black poster with a scarred man holding two axes on the front. "What's a hot cosplayer?"

"You're fracking joking, right?" Lee exclaimed and rushed over to his computer. For the next ten minutes, Deke appreciated A Slideshow of Epic, which was the actual name Lee gave the thing.

Deke was impressed, though. He didn't know there was that quality of tail at these events. He'd have to get Lee to take him to the next one.

"So, if you're not trying to bang a cosplayer, why do you want to know about those *stats*," Lee corrected, emphasizing the final word. Deke figured he had been pretty close with "status." Now he felt like an idiot for not taking the excuse Lee had provided. What was a believable reason?

"You gonna tell me what's best or what?" Deke retorted and crossed his fingers. Lee was smart, outrageously so, and if there was one thing smart guys liked, it was to explain their passions. That or he would just pester him daily until he cracked.

"Fine, fine. You said Control, Power, Finesse, and Endurance? Only four?" Lee cocked his head as he typed those into a google search. If he'd wanted to google it, he'd have just done it himself, but Lee didn't hit send. "Well, almost all games have the holy six attributes, strength, constitution, dexterity, wisdom, intellect, and charisma. So let's look at it from that perspective... Do you know much about what the stats do?" Deke shook his head.

"Okay then, well, the easiest one is probably Strength and Power. If I was to guess, they would be the same. I think Marion's Trench did that with their stat sheet"—Lee tapped the screen on Finesse—"which would make Finesse something like Dexterity—"

"Stop, bro, you comparing them to other games isn't really helping," Deke interrupted. "How about telling me what you think they might do in that game you were talking about the other day?"

"Oh, okay, that's relatively simple, I guess. Control would likely be something to do with spells and skills or how you can control the fighting space. Power would be pure strength, like how much you can lift. Finesse would be fine motor control for melee fighters and some kind of spell modifier. I guess? Maybe even like an energy consumption modifier which would fit best with Endurance. Endurance would be your character's stamina or how long he can fight. You know, like how long you could stay on the turf in basketball."

"It's called a court, but I catch your meaning," Deke responded and scratched his head. "Any chance that *antivyman* game used these?"

"Vitruvian Man, but nah, that game had eight stats, if I remember it right," Lee said dismissively. "I didn't play it long. It was kind of all assassination with no real endgame. Like some overlord was planning the whole thing but no hints to the reasoning."

"Breakfast," Deke stated firmly and shrugged, pointing over his shoulder with a thumb. Then with a smile he joked, "Or do you need a moment with your cosplayer chicks?"

Lee punched him in the arm, and they got up to head to breakfast. Now that Deke was done healing, he treated himself to whatever he felt like. It was quite enjoyable to eat a mound of bacon, hash browns, toast slathered in butter, and an omelet with fucking cheese in it.

They headed to American History again shortly after, and Deke got stopped on his way in by Professor Tawn.

"I see you left the crutches at home today, Mr. Mills," Professor Tawn pointed out. "Any shot of you being cleared to play this Friday?"

"No doubt. I've gotta talk to Doctor Dan this week and get cleared," Deke said with a cocky grin.

"Go Baguettes," Professor Tawn called loud enough that a few students who were walking by jumped. "Sorry, students." He scrunched up his face while holding up both hands. After they continued on, he picked up a stack of papers from his desk. Deke had already gotten his assignment back, so what was this? "Here, Deke, this is what I could find on the Vitruvian Man symbol and the organization connected to it. I actually recalled that I had an old hand-written journal about it. It was called Project Ultra and was all the rage for a while, right up until someone came forward and claimed they wrote it as a fictional piece. So, it's a fun read, but everything inside is a conspiracy theory, I'm afraid. I'll keep looking, though..."

Deke grabbed the papers and flipped through them, not noticing anything about stats or blue liquids. Still, a few headings did stand out, like Super Soldiers and Assassinations.

"Thanks, Prof. Really appreciate this. I'll tell you what I think about it later," Deke said awkwardly when he looked up to find the teacher regarding him with a raised eyebrow.

"I'd like that, Mr. Mills. Thanks for completing the online assignments too. Good luck with the knee," he said with a point, then did a mini fist pump and whispered, "Go Baguettes!" The name was so ridiculous, but combined with the gesture, Deke couldn't hold back a smile at Tawn's exuberance. Were all the teachers in on a huge gag or something?

As he walked out of the classroom he gave the teacher a raised fist over his shoulder, basically agreeing with the sentiment of cheering for the basketball team but not saying the name. Deke was all better now, though, which meant he could actually start contributing to the Baguettes' success.

FIFTEEN

MONDAY, NOVEMBER 7TH

"Hey girl, this is the laziest robber."-
Dekester

"I think you have the wrong number. I don't
know any robbers, just broken basketball
players."- Blonde Valerie

"Well, we can always discuss that next time
we do a sleepover."- Dekester

"I'm listening, gonna need to sweeten the
pot though."- Blonde Valerie

After American History, Deke ate another indulgent lunch. A Philly cheesesteak that dripped so much grease he was going to have to spend five minutes washing his hands when he finished. He paired it with some deep-fried, over-salted french fries and a cheesecake with plenty of blueberry marmalade on top. He felt like he was probably overdoing the grease as his stomach gave a discontented grumble, but he didn't care. It also took long enough that he would have been late to practice if he was still on crutches. But that wasn't a limitation he had anymore. Excited to be able to get up to full speed on his knee for the first time in months, he ran to the gym.

Getting suited up as fast as he could, Deke got to court just a few minutes before regular practice was supposed to start. He gave a fist pump and prepared to step over the sideline and onto the floor—

"Mills, where are your crutches?" Coach Skip yelled at him, interrupting the moment of glory.

"Don't need 'em anymore, Coach! I'm all healed up!" To demonstrate his fitness, he jumped as high as possible, miming that he was shooting a fadeaway. Coach grunted and even cocked his head slightly as Deke came back down. "And I'm ready to crush our season opener."

Coach Skip's eyes narrowed as he considered Deke, "You owe me one hundred free throws, and then you're going down to the trainers."

"But Coach, honestly, I'm..."

"Don't want to hear it. Until Dan clears you, you're not playing." Coach Skip turned away from Deke, shouting at Mac, who was attempting to perform some type of trick shot.

Turning away from Skip, Deke resignedly jogged over to a ball rack and then wheeled it toward the free throw line alone, deciding he didn't want to wait for someone to rebound for him. By this point, he'd gotten used to the weird glare off the hoop that he saw every time he took a shot, but it seemed like it was particularly bad today. There almost seemed to be a dotted line between his hands and where he was aiming the ball. Shooting the first dozen balls, he jogged out to pull them back to the top of the key.

Deke continued to shoot and collect the balls until he was about halfway through the shots. Then the blue letters appeared before his eyes.

Five hundred projectiles thrown. [Aim Assist] skill has been unlocked.

Deke blinked the letters away, realizing that he had just phased out in the middle of his shots. Shaking his head, he noticed that the glare and coloring wasn't from the neon fluorescents or their reflection off the shiny varnish. A glowing blue line extended from the ball, showing an arc that moved as he adjusted his elbow angle. Dropping the ball back to his waist, he turned it over in his hands for a moment. There was nothing extraordinary about the ball.

"All right, let's see how this works," Deke muttered to himself, as he adjusted his throw to make sure the ball would swish through the net rather than hitting the rim or backboard. At the last second, he jumped, and it threw his aim off, the line showing it would bounce off the rim and down through the hoop. Which was exactly the path the ball followed. "What are the odds..." Deke trailed off, picking up another ball and trying again. This time he didn't jump, and the ball went exactly where the line had predicted. Again!

With a devilish grin, Deke quickly finished his daily shots, not missing a single one after he had unlocked the [Aim Assist].

"That's impressive." Deke turned around to see The Duke standing behind him. "I didn't see a single miss." The towering center gave him a cant-headed smile, and Deke nodded his head in confirmation.

"Just crushing it. And don't worry, you'll get to see plenty more this weekend," Deke said as he re-racked the balls and wheeled them over to the side of the court.

"I thought you were red-shirted? Wait—where are your crutches?" Duke asked, and Deke almost growled. Why was everyone asking him that stupid question? Couldn't they see that his leg was fine?

"Don't need 'em," Deke shouted over his shoulder as he angrily pushed the rack the last few feet into position. He took the stairs two at a time, just to prove to himself he was all better. They'd all see when Doctor Dan gave him the green light! When he got to the bottom of the stairs, he looked around and frowned. Abbie was wiping down some of the mats, but there wasn't anyone else waiting for her services.

"I'll be right—" Abbie started before she looked up. Her neutral expression morphed into a frown as she saw Deke. ". . . with you. Where are your crutches?"

"Honestly, is everyone gonna ask me that? Where's Danno? I need him to clear me for the game this weekend. I just took the stairs at a run to get here," Deke countered. Abbie's face frowned further, and he grinned before looking around. The physio's office was dark.

"*Doctor* Dan," Abbie emphasized the title, "is busy, and he's not gonna rearrange his schedule because you decided you're all better." Abbie frowned. Her voice went up a couple octaves, "Did you just say you ran down the stairs? Going downstairs is quite literally the worst pressure you can put on an ACL injury!"

"Calm down. I think you're missing the point, Abbie. My knee is fine. All I need is for 'Doctor Dan'"—Deke put finger quotes up to show he was annoyed by the need to use the title—"to clear me. Then I'm good to go." Deke repeated his earlier jump, and Abbie frowned.

"Bullshirt, don't act like that didn't hurt." Abbie pulled up his chart. "Your surgery was only a few months ago, and we've only just started you on the second phase of recovery; torn ACLs don't heal over the weekend."

"Well, call it one of those miracles Coach is always talking about, then, because I'm healed," Deke said the last in his best preacher voice and then lowered his head to show he meant the prayers before games.

"You're going to pretend that jump didn't hurt?" Abbie asked, her voice slightly amused, and when Deke shook his head, she shook her head and grinned rather evilly, "I'll do some range of motion tests. And you know how much they can hurt, right? You won't be able to hide your pain, champ." She used finger quotes around "champ" like Deke had earlier to show her annoyance with him. She gestured to the table. Deke hopped up eagerly and looked at her expectantly. She blinked, and her face twisted in confusion. She really must have thought Deke was making it up. After a moment, she placed her hands around his ankle. "All right, raise your foot toward the ceiling. I'm going to test the structural strength first."

Deke easily pushed past the light pressure she was putting on his ankle to fully extend his leg. Her eyes widened as her body shifted back with the motion. She'd clearly been increasing the weight to try to match his output strength and failed. "See, I told you, I'm fine."

Abbie was staring at his face with a look of confusion on her own, "Huh? That didn't hurt?"

"Nope. Like I said, I'm healed."

"I'm going to try and push your leg down. Try to keep it straight." Abbie said, putting one hand under his knee and the other on his shoe, pushing it down while watching his face.

"Come on, my brother can push harder than that." Deke's leg didn't waver from its position straight out.

"You're not having any pain?" Abbie continued to stare at his face, her eyes narrowed. He shook his head again. "All right, lie back fully on the table." Deke slid back. The table wasn't quite long enough for him, so his feet dangled over the end. Abbie lifted his leg up, bending it, and braced his foot in position with her thigh. "I'm going to pull on your shin forward, and it might be uncomfortable. Let me know if there is any pain." Deke remembered this test, as it was the one that confirmed his ACL tear in the first place. It was called Lockman's or something.

She pulled forward on his shin while ensuring his quad stayed still. Deke just looked at her with a bemused expression as she continued to run a multitude of tests on his leg. When she was done, she checked the charts for a minute and then tested his other leg with the same battery.

"I don't get it," Abbie said when she was done, "You don't have any pain, your range of motion is higher on both legs, and while the injured leg is a little weaker than the other, there doesn't seem to be anything wrong with it."

"Girl, I told you. I'm healed. Will you go get Doctor Dan now?"

"Don't call me girl, and I told you, he's busy. Tell you what, do all your exercises for the day, and I'll tell him he needs to look at you." Abbie was still looking at him like he'd grown a second head.

"Fine," Deke said, and to his surprise, a task popped up. He pretended his phone had rung so that he could read it without looking off into space.

New task: Rebuilding.

Imbalance detected in the muscles surrounding the joint (right knee). Increase joint stability by increasing strength and combating atrophy in your formerly injured leg.

Deke grinned and went through the exercises that Abbie gave him, adding weight every time she wasn't looking. It felt good to be able to work out at full strength again, and he actually really enjoyed the routine. Abbie kept looking from his knee to his face like she was trying to figure out what the catch was. Eventually, she set him on an elliptical machine.

"We were going to start you on jogging this week, but I think this is still a good precaution 'til Dan—I mean, Doctor Dan—takes a look." Her cheeks flushed a bit at her mistake, and she hurried off to help other athletes who had shown up while she was testing his knee.

An hour later, he was done with the exercises she had set him, and he headed up to the locker room to use their heightened shower. He stood in the warm water, enjoying the fact that he could stand up straight and still have water on his head, as the blue text appeared in front of his eyes.

Task complete: Rebuilding.

You've listened to your trainer and diligently done your rehabilitation. Your muscles are returning to their former state.

Bonus stats granted: Power .04

Deke blinked and fumbled the soap. Hurriedly, he grabbed a towel and streaked through the locker room, drying his hands on the towel as he ran. He got to his locker and scrambled it open, looking for his planner. He ripped it out of his backpack and turned to the back where he had recorded his values earlier, putting a +.04 next to Power. What was the number from before? He tried to remember what his [Status] had said. And to his surprise, the blue letters reappeared.

Control: 5.925

Power: 6.325
Finesse: 5.525
Endurance: 5.410

"What the hell?" Deke growled. The number that he had recorded for power was 6.305. Meaning that the system was only registering .02 growth rather than the .04 it had told him he had gotten. Someone walked by and whistled at his still dripping naked body. Deke flipped them off even as he wrapped the towel around his waist and sat down, trying to figure out why the system would be lying to him. Had he written the number down wrong?

"Stupid math shit." Deke tossed his planner back into his backpack with a frustrated growl. What was the point of having this weird thing in his head if it was just going to lie to him? He began toweling himself off and instantly felt annoyed that he would have to put his socks on a wet floor. He pulled his boxers and shorts on and then threw the towel on the floor, mopping up the liquid he had dripped before putting the rest of his clothing on. Picking everything up, he tossed it all into the dirty hamper on his way out. It was nice to have the team doing some of his laundry again.

"I'm gonna have to ask Tiny again about the reason why the stats lied. And he is already getting suspicious." Deke slowly walked back to the dorm, trying to think of a good way to ask his roommate. As he went, his phone dinged with his text message alert, and he looked at it.

> Tell you what, if we win this weekend you
> can see me again. - Blonde Valerie

Deke grinned. That was something else to look forward to, especially since this time he wasn't going to have to baby his leg. The spring returned to his step, and he speed-walked back to the dorm.

CHAPTER

SIXTEEN

MONDAY, NOVEMBER 7

"One of my student helpers claims that Mr. Mills has made a miraculous recovery. Drugs??"- Doctor Dan

"What do you think? I saw him jumping today. Are there even drugs that would do that?"- Coach Skip

"I can't see another explanation from the charts. I will run him through the tests again."- Doctor Dan

"I'll make some calls."- Coach Skip

"Nerd king!" Deke exclaimed as he walked into the dorm room and found Lee predictably at his computer. Lee reached up with a hand and bit his thumb, his other hand still mashing keys. The mouse moved at speeds Deke didn't know the kid had in him, and the rate of clicking from both hands was relatively impressive. Deke went to sit on his bed. On his way, he picked up a few pieces of discarded clothing from the morning to put into a laundry hamper. After a few minutes, Lee fist-pumped and took off his headset.

"Complete victory," Lee crowed. "That dude didn't know what he was getting into, trying to zerg rush the spiderslayer." After a moment of awkward silence, Deke nodded.

"Okay, Tiny. Your definition of dude and mine are vastly different. Mind if I ask a question of the great Spiderslaver?" Deke said with a grin that promised to never let the kid live this down.

"Slay-er, and whatever, man, that win advanced me to the gold league! Gaming is a legitimate sport," Lee countered, and Deke just let his eyebrow raise to contradict that statement. "What? It is!"

"So, do you know any games that lie to the players about the stat things?" Deke asked, changing the subject rather pointedly. He didn't want to bother correcting the kid. After watching Lee click the keys, he was impressed, but he wasn't willing to grant gaming sport status.

"Lie to the player about stat points?" Lee began and then took off his headset and fully turned his computer chair to face Deke. "Celestial Feces, Deke, just tell me what this is about?"

"Like, let's say one of your games told you it was increasing a stat by four, and it only gave you two. What would it mean in that game?" Deke asked, ignoring both Lee's probe and his strange choice of swear words.

"I don't know. It could be a bug, I guess, or you're looking at the wrong stat. Or you're looking at the modified value, not the base value. Or... the point could be splitting between two different values. Those are all guesses. If you want more accurate responses—you can tell me why the sudden interest! And no more dodging it!" Lee grumbled, before he turned back toward his monitor. He glanced back once and then put his headset on again, clicking off the "victory" screen and back to a different page.

Stunned, Deke sat on his bed, blinking. Could one of those be it? It didn't make a great deal of sense, but they were better explanations than the neon blue drink stuff lying to him. He wanted to ask follow-up questions, but Lee was clearly getting suspicious, plus the whole ultimatum thing. Maybe it was better to go and experiment a bit. Try to get some more increased stats and see how that played out.

Deke stood up and looked over to Lee before choosing to go to dinner without his friend. Just like his dorm mate, he didn't want more questions. Not until he knew more, himself. He made it to the cafeteria and filled his plate with pizza and deep-fried chicken. Even treating himself to a second plate of a Canadian delicacy using fries, gravy, and loads of cheese. It was called poutine and if done right, it was amazing! The curds and gravy available in the cafeteria were disappointedly lacking, though.

His stomach gurgled in displeasure at him as Deke stood to leave, but he refused to listen to it. That week of tasteless food was enough to last him the school year! Even though practice for the day was over, he headed to the gym again. He had unlocked a skill today from shooting free throws. Could he unlock more? Maybe he'd get another task and figure out this stat stuff.

The gym still had a few guys practicing, and Deke wondered if any of them would be the type to run to the coach about him. He shrugged after giving it some thought. He had already told the coach he was better. This would just further prove it. He took a ball out of the rack and started with the simplest skill, dribbling.

Bouncing the ball, Deke went through some slow starting movements, warming himself up. After five minutes and a light sheen of sweat, he continued into some more advanced stuff: cross-overs, jukes, hezzies, between the legs, behind the back, and even some playground stuff. He didn't start noticing strange lights or lines in any of his actions and stopped after about a half hour. He had worked up a sweat and couldn't help a smile. It had been a long time since he'd done that. Just like with running earlier, he had enjoyed the activity for its own sake even if he didn't get a new task or skill.

He did remember it was only after a week of practices at around a hundred shots a day that the other skill had activated full-time. Maybe he just needed more? Nah, those strange lights and glows began hitting him almost the day after he drank the neon blue vivue man shit. Okay, what else could he try? Jumping seemed like an excellent skill to improve on. He could even do it while perfecting his [Aim Assist]. Deke pulled up at the three-point line and leaped, entering an easy jump shot. The line flashed into existence as he tried to line the shot up and release. His focus on the line caused him to land back on the ground with the ball in his hands. The landing jolted his entire body, and he tried to release the shot, but the aiming line jumped as well. He watched in horror as the ball sailed through the air and hit the ground about midway to the net. He scratched his head and was just glad no one saw that.

Duke picked up the ball, and Deke swore under his breath. Just his luck to have preachy McGee show up.

"I like the extra effort, man. But you don't think this is overdoing it?" Duke said as he stood back up with the ball. Deke held his hands out in front of him in the classic "pass me the ball" gesture. Duke's mouth twisted up, and he shook his head.

"*Duke*, I already told you, man. I'm all better. Now toss the rock, or I'm going to start thinking you're scared of losing the spotlight." Deke egged on the large center, trying to persuade him to give the ball back.

"Rook, it ain't happening today." Duke walked over to wrap a very large and heavy arm around Deke. He was then escorted off the court and back to the locker room. Once there, Duke sat him down in front of the starter lockers. The locker room was empty, save for both of them.

"Big guy, if you're about to give me some preachy lecture shit, I'm out!" Deke exclaimed and stood back up.

"Deke, sit back down. I'm gonna spit some truth at you. And you're gonna listen," Duke said, his deep voice making Deke feel like he had no choice. "Listen, Rook, I get it. You want what I have." Duke began and gestured at his open starter locker, which contained a picture of a gorgeous babe Deke kind of recognized. "You can try to get here by taking shortcuts, but I can guarantee you, they'll leave you hollow." Duke continued with a far-off look in his eyes, and Deke rolled his eyes. The dude was going to preach at him after the blue stuff he took was meant for him?

"Duke, I'm not in the mood. I get it. You think I need to take my time. But I'm better, and I'm gonna be playing. By the end of this year, I'll be having NBA agents and scouts knocking down my door," Deke groused and stood up. "I'm out." He walked away and heard Duke chuckle to himself for a bit.

"Kid, I hope you're right," Deke heard Duke mumble as he walked out of the locker room. He pulled out his phone. If there was one thing Duke had the right idea about, it was his cheerleader. He pulled up Valerie's message chain.

> Someone just reminded me that the right girl makes the hard work worth it. You game for a late-night workout?- Dekester

He was about to put the phone away and keep walking when three dots popped up. He stared at them till they disappeared. Deke growled. She was going to ghost him then? The phone dinged.

> I could be convinced but we'll have to meet in Winchester's Mansion, it's on loan from a graduate of Kappa Kappa and our seniors are doing meet and greets. Still, I'm sure I can find an area without people.- Valerie

> Don't worry. I'll play the plumber and lay down some pipe...- Dekester

Deke smiled. His night had just gotten a whole lot better. He made a pit stop in his room and changed into some fresh clothes. Lee was still clicking away at his computer but now had a half-eaten pizza in a box beside his chair. Deke got a wave as he entered and another as he left, but that was all the interest the kid showed.

It was hard to forget the way to Winchester Mansion, since it was quite literally the largest building on Frat Row. When Deke had first seen it, he assumed it was a fancy lecture hall, that's just how massive the place was. Now, thanks to Valerie, he knew it was just owned by some rich girl who used to be a Kappa Nu.

Thanks to its size, even while it was dark out, he found the place without effort. He walked up to the front door and knocked. When no one answered, he creaked open the door and peeked his head in. There was a bit of a gathering happening on the first floor. Nothing as obnoxious as the party he had expected. What the heck was a "meet and greet" then? Some college-aged girls and older men and women were intermingling. The dudes were all wearing suits and the girls gowns, and Deke instantly knew he wouldn't fit in.

Still, Valerie was somewhere inside, so he circled the outer edge of the gathering until he found a discarded jacket. He threw on the too-tight black material and found a logo on the breast as he did. It read Mondo's Catering and he smiled to himself. There couldn't be a better disguise, right?

He began moving among the crowd, totally ignored. As he walked he studied the ongoing activities. Deke tried to understand the tables' setup and failed. There were a bunch of inconsistencies that he wasn't able to solve. The ages of occupants varied so drastically, he might have called it a wealthy get-together with prostitutes if he didn't know better.

There was a table set up every twenty feet, with someone sitting at it. A young woman sat at each table and they almost fell over themselves as they gushed about their accomplishments. He considered the term Valerie had used in her text—meet and greets? For what? Were these people donors to the sorority? Marriage? Speed dating? That thought seemed off, since some of the tables held two women, and others had three people, and the wide age gaps made things even stranger. Not that there was anything wrong with that kind of action, but it definitely didn't seem to fit the dating consideration.

Deke shook his head after a time. What the hell did he care... he moved to the stairs and began climbing the stairs. Call him a pirate, because he was looking for that *booty*. He wasn't a hundred percent sure which room he'd find Valerie in, but he didn't mind some hide and seek as foreplay. Last time they'd missed out because they had been too busy pulling at each other's clothing.

At the top of the stairs, to Deke's surprise, the girl in Duke's photo stood with her hands on her hips.

"What are you doing coming upstairs? Wait, you're not even one of the caterers! So, what are you doing in the house and coming to the second floor?" The girl planted herself at the top of the stairs, physically blocking Deke's progress. Her words practically shrieked at him.

"Relax, I'm just looking for a bathroom," Deke responded and tried to move past her.

"We don't allow professionals or caterers onto the second floor or above since they could pester the sisters! It's time for you to leave," she snapped back as she moved to block his path again. He chuckled and made a spin move to pass by her with ease.

"Come on, lady. You gotta do better than that to stop a shooter!" Deke said and looked over his shoulder to wink at her playfully. She was holding a cell phone, and Deke stopped short.

"Security, I need you at the Winchester Mansion, now!" she spoke into the phone. He blinked at her stupidly. She clearly wasn't playing around. He held up his hands and moved back to the stairs.

"Look, I'm just looking for the toilet, I'll go somewhere else," he said as he backed away from the girl and hurried down the stairs. He pulled out his phone, intending to text Valerie, and found a message waiting.

> I'll be in the pool house around back. Don't get caught.- Valerie

"Shit." Deke cursed to himself. He might have normally attempted to make his way to the pool house now, but the girl shouting from the top of the stairs made him change that thought immediately. Instead, he took off the jacket and sprinted for the door as the well-dressed people downstairs turned and watched.

SEVENTEEN

MONDAY NOVEMBER 7

SPIDERSLAYER LEE: "ANYONE KNOW WHAT
THIS VITRUVIAN MAN SYMBOL IS? I WAS
TRYING TO FIND VIDEO GAMES BUT I FOUND
THIS CRAZY ARTICLE ABOUT SOME SUPER
SOLDIER MOVEMENT."
NOMOONLANDING: "YEAH MAN, CRAZY SHIT.
I'LL SEND YOU A LINK ON TOR."
SPIDERSLAYER LEE: "ANYONE ELSE HAVING
ISSUES UPLOADING IMAGES? MINE KEEPS
GETTING DELETED."
MESSAGE NOT SENT, PLEASE CHECK YOUR
CONNECTION AND TRY AGAIN LATER.

"Look, officer, I understand what this looks like. Truthfully, though, I was invited." Deke had been stopped by one of the university's rent-a-cops before he got halfway back to his dorm. "That girl was just actin' crazy!"

"Kid, we get a call every week for this. You're gonna say the same stuff a thousand other freshmen have said before you," the officer said as he cuffed Deke's wrists. And guided him into the cruiser. "We treat all trespassers the same." He closed the door behind him and walked over to where Valerie and Duke's girlfriend were waiting. Surely, Valerie would help his case here. He could just hear them through the cracked front windows if he tried. However, from Val's body language, he already didn't like what was going on.

"He says that he was invited," the officer said on approach.

"None of the sisters would invite him into a house we don't own." The older girl, who matched the picture in Duke's locker, responded with a pointed look at Valerie.

"He claims she texted him and told him to come." The cop turned to Valerie as well. She looked to be in tears as she shook her head, clearly denying everything.

"No, sir, I would never invite someone like him to one of my sorority events. He's just some washed-up basketball star who has been stalking me," Valerie responded.

That bitch!

The officer looked from Valerie to the other girl and then back at his cruiser. He said some more, but Deke was too upset and didn't have the energy to listen anymore. It was clear "his girl" had thrown him under the bus to save her own image or avoid some stupid sorority punishment. Of course, the cop had taken his phone before cuffing him but surely the texts would clear him, right? If Deke could just show him the texts, that would be enough?

No way was it just their word against his? He hadn't done anything wrong! Why did this keep happening to him?

Mac's face appeared in his mind. "Here take your stupid medication, I ain't babysitting a dweeb all night!"

Deke banged his head back against the cruiser seat in agitation. The day of games, injury and subsequent extra painkiller had sent him into a drowsy state. The seniors had then taken him to the party, where he was left in the coat room. Next thing he remembered he felt like he was on fire, all over. Then he was lying on the wonderfully chilled concrete of the sidewalk in front of the house in his boxers. Just like this time, the cops had been called...

A few minutes later, the rent-a-cop got in the car, radioing that he was coming in before they took a two-minute drive to the campus security station. It was unsurprisingly located near the Alumni Hall since the building was so central. Deke didn't even try to talk to him as he seethed at himself for somehow putting himself into these messes. This was his last chance, too.

Pulling Deke out of the cruiser, the officer guided him to a small interrogation room and cuffed him to the table. "Captain Dutchman will be in to talk to you in a minute."

Since he was cuffed to the chair, Deke couldn't rest his head in his hands, but he really wanted to. So he just laid his forehead down on the edge of the table. While he waited, he tried to think his situation through. If he tried to get the coach involved, he was almost guaranteed to be kicked off the team. He was pretty sure a trespassing charge would break whatever thin ice he was on. The look in Skip's eyes as he had shown Deke the completed expulsion paperwork kept scrolling past his closed eyelids as he pressed them harder into the metal tabletop.

The door opened, and Deke looked up. The man who entered was wearing a white shirt and a sweater, like those cops in Hot Fuzz. There was a folder under one arm and a mug in the other hand. Setting the folder down, he took a long sip. It smelled like strong coffee, black enough to curl Deke's nose hairs even across the table. The captain flipped through the folder for a minute before finally breaking the silence.

"Deke Mills, freshman. Managed to get a starting position on the basketball team, but landed wrong in preseason and tore his ACL." Captain cop slid a picture of his knee over to Deke. "Pretty nasty injury. Then recently, we didn't charge you for underage drinking or drug use at the behest of the dean. It says here you're doing some therapy with Dr. Pinsonneault. Yet by all accounts, you should still be on crutches, and somehow you managed to run halfway back to student dorms after you trespassed in the Alumni Hall, tonight.

"Let's start with that. You care to explain how you're walking, Mr. Mills?" Captain Douchebag looked up, forcing eye contact with him for the first time since he entered. Was the man implying he had taken drugs or something?

"My knee's all better. I was celebrating that with a girl," Deke blurted, wanting to cut off that line of conversation immediately. Like last time, if they thought he was taking illicit substances they would run it up the chain of command. He pleaded with the man using his eyes as he continued, "She told me to come to Alumni Hall and meet her on the third floor. If you'll let me get my phone, I have texts that prove it."

Some of the information he had recited was in Deke's file, but something told him that some of the more minor stuff wasn't. Maybe this guy was a basketball fan. Did that mean he still had a chance? "Look, it was just a misunderstanding. Let me show you the texts, and I'll never go near a sorority ever again. Fu—fudge, I'll never go near Alumni Hall ever again!"

"Technically, I'm supposed to notify the standards office any time a student-athlete gets brought in." The cop had a nametag on it that read Dutchman, which Deke noticed as he looked away from the man's eyes. That at least reminded him what his actual name was. It would probably be counterproductive to call him by the wrong name while pleading for leniency.

"Please don't do that, Captain Dutchman. It was just a misunderstanding. I just barely got rid of the crutches, and I'm on thin ice as it is. I'll never be able to play here if you do." Deke banked on the fact that no one was happy with Mac, the senior shooting guard. Mac's poor showing on the court was one of the reasons why Deke had been able to make a starting position in the first place. Dutchman gave a loud sigh and slouched down in his chair ever so slightly.

"Well, that would be a shame. I caught your preseason game on the local NCAA coverage. I was really looking forward to seeing you play this season." Dutchman scratched his cheek.

"On the TV? They don't give you guys free tickets?" Deke could sense there was some negotiation room here, and he had to take advantage of it. Clearly, he couldn't straight-up bribe the guy... but maybe he could indirectly sweeten the pot.

"Only if you work it, but then you don't get to watch the game."

Captain Dutchman's eyes narrowed slightly like he understood what Deke was getting at.

"Well, I think we'd all feel much safer if there was a stronger police presence in the stadium. Especially closer to the floor," Deke said. He had a half dozen tickets each game he could give out to friends and family. But he could easily put the cop's name on the list. "As it happens, my family are all on the other side of the continent and are unable to come to the games. I'd be happy to donate my friends and family seats to the hard-working men and women here at the security office. Of course, that would require me to still be on the team."

"Well, that's very generous of you, Mr. Mills. Especially given the news I've just heard that you volunteer at the community center ten hours a week or until you reach fifty hours." Dutchman pulled a card out of his front pocket and slid it over to Deke. It was a business card of a Mr. Shane Rogers, the founder of Growing Men, a charitable organization of some sort.

"Do you always carry around one of these?" Deke asked. Dutchman just smiled at him.

Damn, this card wasn't usually in the man's pocket! Which meant...

"I had a feeling it would be relevant. Although it was going to be fifteen hours. We'll send you an email with the names to put on those tickets, though. Just make sure Shane knows to send your hours to me."

Deke realized he'd been played by Douchebag over there. Chuckling in a helpless mixture of admiration and anger, he was more relieved that the cop wasn't charging him with bribery. Or anything else for that matter.

"Well, I'll be sure to let"—Deke had to recheck the name—"Mr. Rogers know that we're friends." To his embarrassment, Deke's stomach gurgled loudly. Douchebag was already unlocking his handcuffs.

"I'll have one of the guys take you back to your dorm. I wouldn't recommend being seen on Sorority Row for a bit, since any girl who thinks you looked at her funny could complicate this..." Dutchman stuck out a hand for Deke to shake, "I look forward to seeing you play, Mr. Mills, and winning a few more games than last year. Go Baguettes!"

"The pleasure is all mine," Deke said through clenched teeth. He really hated the team name and large bread mascot.

"Oh, I doubt that." Dutchman patted his shoulder as he opened the door. "Gerry, take Mr. Mills back to his dorm for me, will you?"

"Sure thing, boss." The cop that brought Deke in was leaning against a wall, looking at his phone. Apparently waiting for the two of them to come out. As they got into the car, Deke's stomach rumbled again. The roiling was gaining in volume so much that he could tell Gerry was looking at him in the rearview mirror.

"You all right, kid?"

"Something I ate isn't sitting right," Deke said, fighting down a bit of nausea. Was this the system punishing him for eating all that greasy food? Was it going to purge him again?

Purge imminent.

"Oh God, no!" Deke mumbled as his stomach gave another monstrous grumble. This one didn't feel like it was going to come out through vomit either.

Sweating profusely, Deke could see the houses passing faster as Gerry stepped on it, clearly worried about a mess in his cruiser. Deke's stomach gave one last grumble and then started to do back-flips. He was clenching his entire body and drenched with sweat as he tried to hold the purge inside. The car pulled to a stop, and Deke stumbled out of it, tripping on the curb as he did. His stomach lurched, and his colon leaked some of whatever his insides had turned into out into his pants.

"Oh God, please no!" Deke prayed as he turned toward the dorm, moving as fast as he could with awkwardly narrow steps. He could feel something dripping out of his boxers and down his leg. He desperately needed to get out of the public eye to avoid the humiliation of shitting in his pants. Taking the stairs three at a time while clenching his butt-cheeks, he cursed the dorm for making cards that only worked on the occupant's floor. He needed a bathroom, now! Not three floors up! His door took three swipes before it registered his card, and he pushed the door to his floor open. He duck-walked past his door, only realizing then that one of the assistant coaches was outside his room writing something on a clipboard.

"Mills, are you okay?" he asked, and Deke shook his head. "What the hell is that smell?"

"Can't talk," Deke shouted as he waddled the last twenty feet to the dorm bathroom. He pushed it open and stumbled to the stall, dropping his pants and relaxing his control over his bowels.

This was definitely the system purging him. He had never heard or smelled anything quite like it. Even after multiple courtesy flushes, he had to cover his mouth and nose with his shirt to stop from gagging. He heard the door open behind him, only for an immediate cursing to bounce around the room. Deke had to breathe in shallow spurts through his mouth to stop the smell from triggering his gag response. Vomiting wouldn't be pretty right now! He ripped off his shirt and wadded it in front of his mouth and nose. His eyes teared up from the teargas-like expulsion painting the toilet bowl. He kept depressing the flusher in an attempt to wash away the foulness, but it couldn't keep up.

Then it was over. He felt his stomach give one last gurgling lurch and settle down. That signaled the beginning of the humiliating process of cleaning up, and he started with his pants, which were a lost cause. He just shoved them in the trash. Only to realize he had left his phone and wallet in them as well as the card. For a brief moment, he considered just leaving them, but realized he couldn't afford a new phone, so he had to dig through the garbage to get them. Grabbing the scented spray from the counter, he gave the whole room a thorough coating of orange vanilla bean mist, which somehow made the smell worse than before. He wondered if the janitorial staff would start telling haunted house stories about the third floor bathroom after the exorcist vomit-pocalypse and now the shit-ageddon.

Remedial task assigned.

Healthy Living: This task includes the four following sub-tasks. Each with its own subgoals.

Acquire Nutrients: Eat a total of 2810 calories for the day. Macronutrient goals: 220 grams of protein, 280 Grams of carbs, and 90 Grams of fat.

Hygiene Maintenance: Maintain a healthy living standard. Goals: brush teeth twice, keep odor output within acceptable limits, and maintain environmental status.

Scholastic Betterment: Attend, listen and comprehend the scholastic endeavors of the day.

Increase Capacity: Perform at least two hours of physical activity to improve your physical performance.

Sub-tasks complete: 0/4

- ***Operative's failure to maintain discipline has led to a remedial task. Do better!***

Walking out of the bathroom naked wasn't an option, so he grabbed his old friend, the brown paper towels, and wrapped them around his midsection *again*, and then marched out of the bathroom and toward his room. He stopped in front of the door, glaring at a yellow paper stuffed into the crack.

"Mills, you clearly were dealing with something, so I'm not going to write you up for being late. But you cut it close."

The note was written on the back of a progress violation report. The information on the front was half-filled in with Deke's name and showing that he was five minutes late for curfew. Someone whistled at his mostly naked form and Deke pushed the door open hurriedly.

Sitting on his bed, holding the canister with the Vitruvian Man on it, was Lee. He looked up as Deke came in.

"What in the abyss is this fracking thing? And why in the nine hells are you naked?"

Deke stared at the canister, then up to Lee's face in shock. It seemed like Deke's night was just getting better!

CHAPTER

EIGHTEEN

MONDAY, NOVEMBER 7

"You're covering your man meat with paper towels and all you can say is 'long story'?!" Lee began, but then inhaled deeply to keep going. Midway through the inhale he almost choked. He gagged visibly and then continued in a hoarse groan, "God, that's awful. Go shower or something!" Deke was glad the lack of good oxygen forced Lee to tone down the volume. The coach might still be around outside.

"Okay, but keep it down. I will tell you everything when I get

154

back, okay?" Deke pleaded with his dorm mate. He was pretty sure Lee wasn't the type to snitch, but you never know. At Lee's insistent gesticulation toward the door, he snagged his towel off his floor among his pile of dirty clothes, albeit only a day's worth. Along with the lack of nutrition, he'd also thought he could stop folding all of his laundry. He hurried to the shared showers as he internally growled at the system. Did this mean he could never just veg out for an entire day again? Glancing down at himself with a shudder, he gave himself a thorough cleaning in record time.

Deke found Lee sitting on his bed when he returned. The kid was examining the vial, turning it this way and that; Deke realized that after cleaning his pile of dirty clothes, hiding it under the bed in a rolled-up hoodie was stupidly obvious. Dammit! Too late now. So, did he have any options left?

"Okay, Tiny," Deke began as he threw on some shorts and an old-school Jordan jersey that always made him feel a bit better. "I'll tell you everything, but you can't share it with a soul. You feel me?"

Lee perked up but squinted his eyes. "Frack no, man. I can't make that promise. Like, these photocopies of Project Ultra basically imply you're some sort of super-soldier assassin! If you're killing people, you gotta turn yourself in!"

Deke blinked. He hadn't expected *that* direction to the conversation. He also hadn't fully read the Project Ultra documents that Professor Tawn had given him. He squinted back at his roommate. If he really was a killer, wouldn't confronting him and telling him he couldn't keep a secret be the dumbest thing to do? Lee stared back at him as he seemed to come to the same conclusion. Deke could see a hand quaking, and Tiny was trying to hide it. It was taking all of Lee's courage to confront Deke like this.

The ridiculousness of the situation forced a laugh from Deke. Not some chuckle either, but a tear to the eye, full snort of uncontrollable laughter.

"Dude, you think—" Deke was forced to laugh harder when Lee

began to blush furiously. "You think... Oh my God! This is fucking hilarious." Deke broke into laughter again. Admittedly, the situation was still dire, but the over-exaggeration and the starting point of the accusation were just too much. "Dude, I haven't killed anyone!" he finally managed to force out.

Lee slouched onto the bed and even smiled slightly when Deke finally forced out the response. Sheepishly, Lee raised both the Project Ultra documents and the vial. "Well, can you explain what this all is about then?"

"Shit," Deke swore and sobered. That vial was still some sort of super-drug, and he didn't know how Lee would respond to *that*. Still, if anyone could help him with this whole blue letter thing, it was Lee! He began explaining the story, trying to make sure Lee understood the stakes of the situation. Not just the stakes of turning Deke in now, but the situation that had forced Deke to take the second half of the drug.

"So, like I said, I didn't have a choice, the stupid thing said I would die or *could die*, I guess? I've got no clue what this thing is, or how it works, and need your help," Deke recapped.

"Let me get this straight, you poured some random glowing neon liquid down your throat, instead of calling an ambulance, and now have some sort of game interface in your head?!" Lee asked, his voice filled with an emotion Deke couldn't place. Did the kid think that Deke could have killed himself? Because that was certainly true, but he hadn't meant . . . "That's so boss! Like can—how do you increase your stats? Is there any farming you can do? Can you loot stuff? What skills do you have? Can you level them through use or do you have points to spend? Whoa! Is this the kind of system that is best to min-max or use an equal stat allocation?"

"Nerd king! Hold up," Deke interposed a question as he stopped his pacing. "Are you saying you're going to help me?"

"Are you zarking me right now? You're like a real-life video game character! Of course I'm going to help." Lee shot up from his bed to grab a notepad. "What are your current stats?" Deke handed over his planner, and Lee copied down what was there before gesturing with his pen at the line that read "[Aim Assist] after 500 shots." "Is this a skill? How does it work?"

"Yeah, man! Watch this," Deke exclaimed and picked up a nearby mini-basketball. He then lined up his shot with the mini hoop hanging across the room and swished it through.

"And?" Lee asked. Deke motioned at the basketball hoop meaningfully. "Sa'hut, you're a basketball player. Sinking a shot doesn't mean anything about a skill! Please tell me that isn't all it can do?" Deke scratched his head. Well, he'd never tried it for anything else...

"I'm not sure, to be honest," he said, then picked up a Swiss army knife from his bedside table and extended the pinky-sized blade. Remembering the sock throw, he considered the very unbalanced blade, maybe? He lifted the blade like he was going to throw it and noticed a much thinner and dashed blue neon line lining up a relatively straight path between the knife and the wall near the foot of Deke's bed. He scanned over and found a poster at the foot of Lee's bedside. He lined up the head of the strange blue creature with arm blades, and when the head glowed green, he loosed the blade. "Crushing it!" Deke exclaimed as the knife plunged into the wall.

"You zarking Belgium! That's my zealot poster! I had it signed by Won-Lee Sak," Lee jumped up from the bed and pulled out the knife from the wall. "Just 'cause you can throw a knife doesn't—"

"Lee! I've never thrown a knife before in my life!" Deke explained, but Lee just gave him a death stare as he caressed the hole in the poster and the wall behind it. "No, seriously, man, and that was a Swiss army knife. I doubt anyone throws those!"

"But then why would you throw one inside, and at my side of the room!" Lee hissed back. "Like, that doesn't prove it any more than your basketball shot. I'm wondering if the lack of an intelligence stat isn't explaining this whole thing." Lee gesticulated with the notepad in his hand as he continued to split his attention between Deke and the mutilated poster.

"Whatever, man." Deke sighed. If Lee was just going to disbelieve the whole thing, then he was better off going to sleep. "I've had a long night with the system purge, the campus cops, and now you not believing me. I'm going to bed!"

"Man," Lee said, his voice a little less excitable. "It isn't that I don't trust you. I was thinking I will make some sort of testing system, and we can work on it together."

"In the morning," Deke grumbled, not really caring anymore. As long as Lee didn't turn him in, then he was going to be okay. He would love the kid's help, but honestly, he'd settle for him answering questions here and there again. He performed a quick clean-up of his clothes from the floor and lay down to sleep, turning his back to his dorm mate.

"Don't worry, man, I'll have something figured out by morning," Lee whispered, and Deke just shrugged before burying his head moodily into his pillow. He didn't like not being believed when he was telling the truth—mostly.

The act of actually confessing everything that had been going on in this absolutely insane week, and then having it thrown back at him with suspicion and skepticism, weighed on him like a dark sea. He closed his eyes and let the inky waters take him.

Tuesday, November 8

"Look man, this is better than getting caught in the school gym," Lee insisted for the third time, motioning at the beach fitness center. It consisted of colorful metal tubes dug into the sand, with such a varying degree of people using them that Deke thought he saw four generations of a single family all here together. His biggest problem with the set-up was that there wasn't a single weight in sight. "Stop being a Reaver! Do you want to get kicked off the team for overdoing it? Look, you can do pull-ups there, and most everything else, you can do bodyweight exercises or use those jugs and fill them with sand. These places are a really great program the city set up to keep people in shape."

"Tiny, this place is to keep people in shape, not to create all-star athletes. Like, I'm not going to get anything from bodyweight work. I've been lifting heavy since I was thirteen," Deke explained the situation so a non-athlete could understand.

"Giant, I've been up most of the night researching a lot of ways to utilize bodyweight exercises for elite athletes. What I have in my hands is a certified Mamba workout! I had to pay five dollars for the trial." Lee waved his notepad like he had the previous night.

"Wait, you have a workout that Kobe himself performed?" Deke asked, feeling his motivation skyrocket.

"Kobe? I didn't say anything about him. No, I said Mamba," Lee explained, and Deke felt his eyes widen in horror. There was no way this kid was that sheltered, right? "Anyway, it literally said Mamba was one of the greatest NBA legends of all time. You ready to get to work?"

"I can definitely get on board with a Black Mamba workout!" Deke said, choosing to ignore Lee's blasphemy.

"Sweet, you've heard of him. I knew that five dollars wasn't going to be for nothing!"

New task: Elite Exercise.

Perform bodyweight exercise to increase your synapse memory and muscle firing rates. Follow the proper forms, rest times, and set instructions to gain optimal results.

Deke told Lee exactly what the task said, and he wrote it down verbatim.

"Seems pretty basic," Lee remarked after reading it over. Lee pulled out the timer app on his phone so he could ensure Deke followed the workout precisely. Having done plenty of workouts before, Deke wasn't convinced it would ding him for a few seconds here and there, but there also wasn't any harm in it.

By the end of the bodyweight workout, Deke was still only slightly sweating. Still, it was also clear that the workout Lee had purchased was an entry-level one for younger athletes. Most of his sweat came from sand sprints, shuffles, and rocket jumps, which scaled to the strength he put in.

Task complete: Elite Exercise.

You've listened to your trainer and diligently completed the regimen. Your body is beginning to improve. 1/10 perfect routines completed. Complete 9 more for a bonus reward!
Task on cooldown for 24 hours.

Bonus stats granted: Power .02, Endurance .02

Again he dictated the task as quickly as possible before it vanished, and Lee wrote it down. "Cooldowns and a bonus—this is exactly like a video game daily! Okay, but I remember you saying that the stats won't increase by the numbers you just told me?"

"Well, it didn't last time. I have no way of controlling when it shows me the page with all the stats on it. Sometimes it will do it two times in a row really fast, and sometimes like this morning, I haven't seen it at all," Deke responded as they began walking back to the dorms. Lee had woken him up pretty early, and it was now past the time the cafeteria doors opened for breakfast. Deke was definitely not looking forward to bland eating again, but admitted that he might be willing to do it if he got stat gains or skills from it.

"Your status page?" Lee asked, but as he said it, Deke saw it pop into his vision.

"Hold on, here it is. Yeah, those stats only increased by half of what the numbers were again. Otherwise, no other changes!" Deke cursed the thing. "See what I mean, it's full of shit!"

"I don't think so. If what you're saying is true—" Lee shook his head as Deke growled. "Sorry, just meant it as a saying. If what the system did is accurate, then my guess is that it's splitting stats somewhere. Not sure why it would be doing it for you and not showing you the subcategories, maybe it's something to do with your level."

"My level? I don't have a level."

"Levels are like... milestones to measure how strong you are."

"Did you just say I wasn't strong enough?" Deke asked as they climbed the stairs up the rise and off the beach.

"Dude, quit being so sensitive. I'm just saying that it will probably open up more of the system if you gain more strength. Like what happened when your injury got healed. Frackin' crybaby!"

Deke punched Lee in the arm, and the rest of the trip was somewhat silent as Lee wisely chose not to complain about the charley horse, while Deke hoped he would. Lee knew Deke too well, it seemed, because he had been planning to slap him with a retaliatory "Frackin' cry baby" moniker if he did complain.

When they made it to breakfast, Deke began explaining in more detail than the previous night how this part of the system worked. Lee nodded along, writing down some of the numbers and checking them against something in his phone.

"They are all pretty accurate to what My Fitness Guru says, so I think we can optimize what you're eating to balance what you want to eat with your limits," Lee explained, as he put back some of Deke's fruit and added a Danish and some bacon in its place. At Deke's shocked look, he said, "It's all about moderation and math. We can definitely do this."

Deke had never wanted to hug a man so much in his life. As they were about to sit down, Deke caught a glimpse of the clock. "Shit! I'm going to be late for calculus," he explained to Lee as he stuffed his yogurt in his pocket and shoveled some of the hot eggs and bacon into his mouth in a hurry. "Gotta go, man. Tonight we will work on the [Aim Assist] stuff."

Deke stood and polished his plate off as he carried it and his tray to the cafeteria cleaning racks.

CHAPTER

NINETEEN

FRIDAY, NOVEMBER 11

The crowd jeered from all directions as the Bulldogs increased their lead. Deke glanced around, still in awe of the number of fans in the stadium. This was the main floor, and while they often practiced here, it was never like this. People sat in the thousands of seats that lined the court on all sides; all but the very top levels of the bleachers were full. The playing surface had been recently buffed and waxed, so it reflected the light in a near glare. That polish also made the squeak of the players' shoes audible, even over the roar of the crowd as the Baguettes inbounded the ball after the opponents' basket. UCSP began fighting their way to half-court despite the efforts of some energetic players on the opposing team trying to force a turnover.

163

Deke shook off his awe of the crowd and leaned back on his chair. He wanted to be out there, but instead was in a second-hand sports jacket and slacks, sitting on the bench. Technically it was a cushioned chair that had the team logo on it, but he was sidelined all the same. So he ground his ass into the smiling Baguette logo under him. It was the first game of the year, and it was not going well for UCSP, not at all.

They were ten minutes into the first half and already down three points, which wasn't terrible, but the writing on the wall was obvious. Their opponents, the Brockton Bulldogs, were playing hard. They were pushing a full-court defense that was rapidly wearing out the home team's starters. The depth of the Bulldogs' bench was allowing them to cycle through players and keep fresh legs out there. Duke, the UCSP star center, had managed to regain a momentary lead in the first few minutes of the game, but he was now getting double-teamed, and the rest of the squad wasn't handling that well.

Deke turned to scrutinize the current play. Arthur, the Baguettes' starting point guard, managed to pass back and forth with Mac to get the ball past the half-court line and held a hand in the air with two fingers upraised. Deke leaned forward as the team got into a triangle offense, placing Duke at the top of the key, with Mac outside the arch near the baseline.

Arthur dribbled to a position high and outside the arch, shifting the defense to the right side of the court. His defender played off of him, giving him space and daring him to shoot the three-ball. Deke clenched his fist, wishing he was out there. He could have tried out his new [Aim Assist]. However, Arthur didn't shoot despite the defender's disrespect.

Since Duke was double-teamed, that meant someone was open, so it might not be a bad decision to find an easier shot. Arthur screened off Duke and found Mac, the open man. Arthur passed the ball to Mac, then cut to the hoop and was replaced in his spot by another teammate as the offense cycled.

Mac, the team's starting shooting guard, began to dribble before faking a shot, his quick hezzy catching his defender off guard. Deke grudgingly admitted Mac performed the fake shot... adequately, and the Bulldogs' center rose up onto his toes trying to block a shot that wasn't there.

Mac took off, driving baseline, and the opposing center gracelessly spun in an attempt to catch the much quicker shooting guard. The center's rapid turn ended with an elbow colliding with Mac's face, knocking him to the floor.

A sharp whistle stopped the action as the ref called a foul. Deke leaned farther forward when Mac didn't jump back to his feet.

"Damn!" Deke grumbled, as he discovered the reason. It was quite apparent when Mac did finally stand. A thick stream of blood poured out of his nose, dripping off his chin onto the court. The soft appendage had clearly taken the offending elbow at full force.

"Jones, get in there," Skip shouted from Deke's side. The coach was sending in the third-string shooting guard to replace Mac until he stopped bleeding.

Jones wasn't a true shooting guard, and should be considered more of an all-round player. The team's lack of depth was genuinely depressing. Deke almost groaned out loud but managed to stop himself. Mac wasn't a great player, but he was still a senior and created opportunities. Jones was, well... he was the best "bad" option, but if Deke was allowed to play this game, Jones would have only seen some play late in the second half, and even then only if the Baguettes were up by twenty.

Mac glared daggers at Jones even as Abbie and Dr. Dan held an ice pack on his face and the back of his neck, attempting to slow the blood flow. They moved Mac into a sitting position at the end of the bench, relatively close to Deke.

"This is such bullshit," Mac shouted, and Deke wasn't sure if he was yelling at his nose or Jones, who had just bricked the free-throw Mac's injury and the opposing team's foul had earned for UCSP.

"Lean your head back, Mac," Dan said, pushing Mac back so that he was lying on the bench. Deke turned his attention away from Mac to watch the game.

"Argh!" Mac growled as Abbie pushed the tissues and ice pack onto his nose. "Deke, you should have just stayed in Canada. Maybe then we can at least get a scholarship replacement that knows how to shoot."

"Shut up, Mac. I'm sure Abbie has a tampon you can borrow, so you can stop leaking like a sieve," Deke retorted hotly from the side, pulling at his jacket angrily. Not only was Mac an asshole, but Deke hated wearing this stupid suit to the game. A reminder that he wasn't allowed to play. In fact, he couldn't even stand up to cheer unless someone called a timeout. Utter bullshit was right...

"Both of you, zip it. Mac, lie back. The more you move, the longer this is going to take," Abbie snapped as she pushed Mac back down. Deke could see her turn to glare at him from the corner of his eye. But he didn't really care; Mac had finally shut up. Deke winced as Jones let another free throw fall far short of the hoop, only for the opposing rebounder to turn it around for a long pass and a fast-break layup. Mac's nose continued to bleed, and the point difference continued to climb in the Bulldogs' favor.

To take his mind off the ongoing tragedy that was Jones's playing, Deke thought about the progress he had made this week. Since telling Lee his secret on Monday, he'd had to go back to doing remedial tasks for the week. Which was sort of nice in the fact that it gave him points, even if he didn't care for the names. He and Lee had continued to sneak down to the beach to do some new workout Lee had always found on the internet the night before.

Deke had tried to sneak the kid into practices, but the coaches had refused to allow him to stay. They had cited some bull about the practices only being available to family members. Still, his stats had continued to go up steadily, if only by half the amount the messages said they were improving. They had been working on getting a passing skill, and Lee was almost able to chest-pass a decent ball back to Deke at this point, but it had been a sad display for a while. Still, no new skill had spontaneously arrived yet, and Deke thought the problem was that he needed to use it in a game, so to speak. When someone was trying to stop him, not just playing catch on an empty court.

The halftime buzzer sounded, and Deke looked up to the scoreboard before groaning. They were down eighteen points. As much as he hated wishing well for Mac, hopefully, he would be back on the court for the second half. Jones was just the absolute worst. He probably shouldn't be thinking that, but right now some of his anger at being sidelined was manifesting onto the guy.

He turned to follow the rest of the team into the locker room, walking past the cheerleaders. They were heading onto the floor to get ready for their halftime show. Valerie paused when she saw him in the suit and gave him a leering once over. He was still angry at her for the whole trespassing thing, but that didn't stop him from doing the same to her. The skirt and top accented her curves perfectly; her long legs were exposed to beautiful effect.

If only she wasn't a total bitch.

With a wink, Valerie reached out and brushed a hand across his shoulder as he passed her in the tunnel. He turned to follow her with his eyes, and her hand that had touched his shoulder slapped her own ass. Causing the slightly exposed bottom cheek to jiggle in a decidedly pleasing manner.

Okay, maybe she wasn't a total bitch... she *had* told him to come to the pool house, after all. He had just been so excited to see her that he didn't check his phone once he got there. So it was at least partly his own fault...

Deke shook his head, Valerie's ass bouncing still replaying in his mind even as he had to mentally remind himself that he hated her. Even then, he knew he'd jump at a chance to hit that again. Then the cheerleaders were gone, and he was back in the locker room. Deke took a seat next to his locker, behind and away from where the starters were. Coach Skip waited until they had all sat down before he looked around.

"Men, I know this game isn't going how we wanted it to." Skip started his speech stoically. Deke mostly tuned him out. There was nothing the coach could say that would be relevant to him. Even with tuning him out, Deke heard Coach talk about their bench stepping up, and he felt a surge of annoyance because he knew he could take these Bulldog slouches. He was at least as good as Mac and would likely be better than him if he hadn't been injured. Mac was a ton better than Jones for sure, and Deke would have been in the game even if it wasn't as a starter. If the coach would just stop blocking him and let him play, they could turn this game around.

"Remember! An athlete is not crowned unless he competes with perseverance and integrity!" Skip ended his halftime pep talk the same way he opened up their practices. Deke shouted "Go Baguettes!" with the rest of them, even though he didn't really feel motivated.

Mac did manage to get back into the game, but they had already lost so much momentum that it didn't really help. The Baguettes were obviously flagging, as their players were forced to stay in longer than the Bulldogs.

Deke's team was running haggard by the time the final buzzer sounded to the announcer declaring a 53–84 score. The coach sat them down and gave another speech ending it with another scripture reference. Deke idly wondered if the coach would have been this religious if they were winning.

Deke hadn't brought a second change of clothing, so he was still in his suit as he walked home. The dorms were somewhat near the stadium, but Deke was trying to avoid the crowds, so he took the long way around campus. He passed two fire trucks on the route home. Their sirens were blaring as they responded to an unseen fire deeper into the campus. Deke wondered if it was just a faulty smoke alarm or some kid hotboxing his dorm room. Aside from preventing him from crossing a road when he wanted to, the trucks weren't much of an inconvenience.

About halfway back, he got a text from Lee asking if he wanted a late dinner. Deke agreed but suggested a little diner near the beach that they had used a few times in the last week. Lee responded that he was already there.

"Hey," Deke said morosely, as he sat down and pulled out the menu. He wasn't even in the mood to tease the kid. Although he hadn't been doing much of that lately anyway. The two of them were spending a lot more time together than they had before as Lee ran his system through its paces.

"I saw the game was over. Is a thirty-one point difference a lot?" Lee asked, pulling out his earbuds to talk to Deke.

"Yeah. It was a bad game. Mac took an elbow to the face and had to sit out most of the first half while the bleeding stopped. And Jones is just awful. He barely made the squad before I was injured. He might have even been taken off of redshirt status when I was given mine.

"If the coach let me play, it would have been better, but the other team took advantage of our weaker bench." Deke ordered an egg white omelet with a ton of veggies that he had grown to love, with enough salt and pepper. It was one of the reasons they ate at this café; it had a full nutritional list. The two chatted for a bit about Lee's raid and the rest of the basketball game as they ate.

After the meal, they began walking back to the dorm together, and Lee rubbed his chest.

"Man, I don't know how you do this soreness thing," Lee said with a wince as he rubbed his sternum. They had been trying to get a passing skill, and Lee's ability to catch a ball was distinctly lacking. Also, Lee was afraid of hurting his hands, which made sense to an avid gamer. So, unfortunately, Deke had hit him in the chest often enough that it was bruising by the time the two had called it quits.

"You get used to it, then you get to the point that you feel weird when you aren't sore," Deke said, then paused to think. "Although I think the burn is worse since I started the 'sports drink.'" They had agreed to call the Vilubia Man-vial a *sports drink* in public to not arouse suspicion.

"I think you're healing faster," Lee said as they got back to the dorm and began climbing the stairs. "Compressing the soreness into a shorter period of time, which makes it worse while it's there."

"Huh, I guess that makes sense," Deke said, opening the door to their hallway and holding it open for Lee. His phone buzzed, and he paused to pull it out.

"Arsebasket," Lee cursed, and Deke looked up from his phone to see what had caused such a response.

"What's wrong?"

"Someone broke into the room!" Lee shouted, and Deke hurried over to look inside.

The room had been tossed. Clothes and books were lying all over the floor, the mattresses were on their sides, and the bedding was stripped off. The door's handle was clearly broken as well, having been forced open.

"My computer is still here!" Lee said, gently caressing the large glowing box.

Deke had a bad feeling about the whole thing. Someone broke into their room and tossed everything but didn't take any of the expensive items? Immediately, he remembered the canister. Had they been looking for it? Lee had insisted on storing it down by the beach, and they had hidden it under the pier in a hole they dug. An *unnecessary* precaution Deke had only agreed to so that Lee would shut up about it. But, suddenly, that precaution didn't seem so excessive anymore. A cold sweat broke out on his skin as he considered what they were going to do next.

CHAPTER

TWENTY

SATURDAY, NOVEMBER 12

"Deke Mills should be showing up tomorrow
to help with the kids."- Officer Dutchman

"Saw the game, that was a pretty rough
showing."- Mr. Rogers

"Don't remind me, I was there. Just let me
know if he doesn't show up."- Officer
Dutchman

Deke walked through the gray fog of early dawn, making his way toward the community center that was just off campus. He knew many older students left their kids there for the weekends when they attended classes, and he wondered what that meant for his upcoming day.

He actually liked kids; he had taken care of his brother after Rhonda had started working two jobs. At least when they were on the same campus, it had often gotten him looks of pity from others. But those people didn't understand the joy of being a big brother. That drive gave him the courage to come out to California and he hoped it would get him to the NBA. He would do anything for Max...

171

The fog hung low to the ground, a product of the Californian sun cresting the horizon and removing the previous night's chill. The campus felt like a ghost town this early on a Saturday. The majority of students were sleeping off hangovers or late-night study sessions, or in a few rare cases, all-night raids on video games, like Lee, who had only finished as Deke was waking up. Conquering the Red Mage of Rock Land was a huge accomplishment for the nerd king. At least, according to the caffeine crazed ramblings of his friend this morning. Deke chuckled and continued down the sidewalk.

Out of the gray, Deke thought he saw what he was looking for. The large gymnasium-like building, the play structure, splash pad, and gazebo picnic areas likely meant he had found the community center. His excitement crept up a bit when he caught sight of the outdoor basketball court. He hadn't been to this side of campus before, but to find a place he could practice with Lee was a boon he hadn't expected. He jogged the last hundred meters and felt that small glimmer of hope start to fade.

This wasn't a basketball court so much as a tetanus hazard. A rusty fence surrounded cracked asphalt and two somewhat vertical poles. Not only the posts but both hoops were bent at horrible angles and missing nets, clearly the work of some drunken escapades. The court had copious weeds growing up through the cracks that criss-crossed the entire area. To be fair, the court did remind him of the one near his house in London, Ontario, and all that it needed was some elbow grease and sweat to be usable.

Setting his bag just inside the gate, Deke spent the next quarter of an hour pulling weeds while waiting for Officer Douchebag's contact to show up. He managed to clear the key of the slightly less bent basket and was just about to start in on the three-point area when a shoe scuffed the gravel that surrounded the court.

"You must be Deke Mills?" a middle-aged man called from near the gate, and Deke turned to examine him. He was dressed in cargo shorts, T-shirt and sported a red fanny pack around his waist. His hair was brown, but his temples had a gray streak that was combed backward to almost make it appear like a silver stripe.

Deke nodded at the silver-hawk and stood up straight to go greet the head counselor. The man held up a hand and began walking toward Deke instead. "Nice to meet you. I'm Shane Rogers. People call me Mr. Rogers because of the job and the kid's show... Anyway, we still have fifteen minutes 'til the kids arrive. Why don't we continue working? I keep meaning to fix this court up, but I just haven't been able to find the time..."

Deke gave a smirk and bent back to continue pulling weeds. "To do it properly, you would need a winch to straighten the posts and rims. Plus, probably some weed killer to prevent them from growing back."

"I've actually got both. Mind continuing while I go grab them from storage?" Mr. Rogers responded with an eyebrow raised. Deke nodded again. He was enjoying the work and if they truly could fix this place up. . . Well then, he could come here to shoot hoops. Maybe even get a few new skills from this "system" of his.

"I t's starting to look like a court!" Mr. Rogers exclaimed as the basketball post slowly unbent, with the help of the winch that was tied off to the nearby fence post in two places.

At first, Deke thought they would only succeed in bending the metal of the cage, but since Mr. Rogers had tied it off low first, it seemed to distribute the weight better. Kids had begun arriving and forming small little groups under the watchful eye of some other counselors who'd shown up while Deke and Shane worked.

Some of the kids were watching from around the cage as Deke gestured for Shane to give the winch one last crank. Deke motioned to a counselor simultaneously to ensure kids didn't get too close to the tetanus hazard of the rusty areas of the chain link. They complied with a look that told him his worry was unfounded and they were already aware.

The thick basketball pole groaned and straightened a hair more. It wasn't perfect, but it was near to vertical again and the net was definitely at the ten-foot mark. Deke nodded and surveyed the court. This single half was now passable as a basketball surface again. Deke managed to spray all the cracks with Weed be Gone, Maximum Strength. Since he had used the entire jug, he was pretty sure that anything left would be dead soon. Mr. Rogers plucked the basketball out of Deke's bag and chest passed it over to him with startling competence.

A smile broke across his face, and Deke lined up his shot using [Aim Assist] and fired. The ball passed through the hoop without touching a single side, but thanks to the missing mesh it didn't make the satisfying swish sound. Mr. Rogers threw the ball back. After Deke's fifth in a row, Mr. Rogers held the ball. "Why weren't you playing yesterday? You're clearly better than some of the guys on the court."

Some of the braver kids came into the cage and sat down on the edges of the court. Mr. Rogers smiled at them, and that seemed to encourage more to venture inside. The ball came back to Deke, and he caught it as he considered his answer. With the kids here, he didn't want to whine about the unfairness of the coach not playing him. It just didn't seem right.

"I'm just getting back from injury, and the coach isn't sure if my leg will hold up to the stresses of the season. So, right now, I'm a redshirt..." Deke stated and shot the ball again.

"Well, I can honestly say that's unfortunate. I like Mac, but whoever that kid off the bench was, he definitely isn't ready for the show yet," Mr. Rogers said as he passed the ball back again. After a few more minutes, there was a crowd of almost twenty kids watching the small game, and Deke could hear them whispering.

"He hasn't missed yet. I think that's number eighteen!" Deke distinctly heard one of the older kids fill in to a newcomer.

Mr. Rogers caught the shot and turned to the group. "Some of you might not recognize our new counselor. Let me introduce Deke Mills, rookie shooting guard for the Baguettes!"

The announcement drew every gaze to Deke. The kids had the same look in their eyes his brother did whenever they were hanging out. It was a look that told Deke they wanted to be just like him. That they were all picturing themselves standing where he was. He smiled at them all and caught the ball in one hand as he turned and dribbled toward the group of them on the sideline. "Who here wants to learn how to shoot?" Deke asked, and was answered with a unanimous raising of hands. He turned to Mr. Rogers. "Do you have any extra basketballs around here?"

Mr. Rogers nodded and turned to someone outside of the cage. "Abbie, can you go grab them? With our special guest counselor, I think today should be a basketball day..."

Deke started and turned to find Abbie leaning against the fence pole near the baseline. How long had she been there? She was looking at him and not Mr. Rogers as she nodded and turned to go. The look was one of the first non-hostile ones, other than at the party, that he could recall from her. Shielding his eyes with one hand, he had to admit that with the early morning sun, her eyes seemed to shine.

"Okay, since we don't have the basketballs yet, you's all don't have an excuse to not listen to my instructions, right?" Deke shouted to get their attention back and then turned to give them a side profile. "Who here likes to eat 'BEEF'?"

The looks of confusion he got made him laugh and reminded him of his first time hearing the term. One of the smaller kids put up a hand, and Deke pointed to him. The kid shyly asked, "What does beef have to do with basketball?"

That was the exact same question his brother asked him when he was first teaching him. Deke couldn't help but tilt his head and smile at the kid.

"I'm glad you asked. Why don't you come up here and help me

demonstrate." Deke began, and when the kid got up to him, he raised the basketball above his own head into a shooting position. "The B in BEEF stands for balance. What's your name, kid?"

"Jeremy," the kid squeaked, and Deke tracked the kids' eyes up to the basketball in his hand.

"Well, Jeremy, you and everyone else are looking at the wrong place. Balance comes from the feet. Check out mine. See how they are around shoulder-width apart. Notice I am balanced and can move in all directions from this position."

A few of the kids muttered in acknowledgment, and Deke smiled wider. "I'm sorry, I can't hear you. Why don't we try again; can you all see how I can move in every direction?" There was a chorus of assent. "Good!" Deke continued. "Why don't you all get up and try to mimic this position?"

"Excellent!" Deke stated as the kids jumped up to mime his positioning. "Now, what do you think the E is for, Jeremy?"

"Umm... execute?" Jeremy tried.

"Ahh, that comes at the end. First, you need to have your eyes on the target. Right?" Deke responded, correcting the answer, and watched as all the kids turned to face the newly straightened hoop. "Exactly. Does anyone want to guess the second E?"

"Execute!" Jeremy shouted exuberantly beside him, and Deke chuckled and ruffled his hair.

"Not quite. Elbow is the second E. Notice how my shooting arm's elbow is pointing at the rim. And my supporting arm has its elbow up and cocked to protect the shot? Yeah, like that, Jeremy," Deke exclaimed. "Now Jeremy, what's another word for Execute?"

"Finish!" Jeremy crowed his answer, and Deke could hear the excitement in the kids' voice.

"Perfect. The F stands for two things, Finish and Follow-through. Complete the shot and follow through with your hands, so they point to the basket." Deke followed through with the action and, with the help of [Aim Assist], drained a near half-court shot.

"That was number nineteen," one of the kids exclaimed.

Abbie had returned with a bag of balls, and Deke pointed to them before he said, "Why don't you all pair up and work on BEEF with your partner. I will walk around and help!"

The kids all rushed forward, and the ones who got a ball were able to pick a kid to work with. Jeremy, the smallest kid, was left without a partner, and they'd run out of balls. So, Deke tossed his to Abbie, "Do you mind working with Jeremy while I correct forms?"

"You all are going to have to practice if you want to take on the king!" he crowed jokingly. Deke shot a three and watched as it sank home to knock out the final kid in the game of bump. He raised his arms in a victory pose. He'd considered allowing the kids to beat him, but he wanted them to aspire to be better and practice basketball seriously. He figured letting them win now would be counterproductive, plus his competitive side wouldn't just let him miss on purpose.

"All right, everyone, we can do some more after snack time. Go find Mr. Rogers and wash up," Abbie called from the sideline. "Slow down, take your time through the gate!" she shouted as the kids bolted for the door. Some of the older ones realized the problem and tapered back to make sure they didn't attempt to push through the small opening at once. It was a close thing, and Deke felt his eyes widen as one of the kids tripped and sprawled out before jumping back up and continuing his sprint.

"Don't worry, they're like rubber," Abbie chuckled as she took in his open-mouthed stare. "We always called that game Lightning, growing up. Kind of weird to hear it called 'bump.' How'd you get so good with kids?" she asked as she walked over. Deke turned away so she couldn't see his face fall, and began gathering up the basketballs the kids had abandoned during their mad dash for snack time.

"Well, I always wanted to be able to teach some kids back home,"

Deke hedged, unwilling to tell Abbie about his brother. "Plus, I've been around good coaches my whole life."

"Why didn't you just teach the kids you wanted to back home?" Abbie asked, her voice neutral. Deke glanced at her and saw that she was walking over with two basketballs. He held the bag open as she dumped them in.

"So, what do the kids do after snack time?" Deke deflected.

"We move inside, we wind them down and do some board games, crafts, or dodgeball usually. But maybe they will want to play some more basketball today..." Abbie said with a wink and even nudged him with an elbow. He blinked at her and returned her smile. "I mean, it's not every day that the kids meet *the king!*" she teased, and he laughed.

"Well, I couldn't just *let* them win!" Deke responded with a chuckle.

"You made that abundantly clear when you sank that dagger in my back," Abbie mock whined, referencing the low arcing shot he had drained on her at the beginning of the bump game. "When do you get in to see Doctor Dan?"

"First thing Monday," Deke responded excitedly as they walked into the community center. This was the first time they had talked without an underlying tension behind every word. Grinning as he followed her inside, he decided he liked it.

CHAPTER

TWENTY-ONE

SATURDAY, NOVEMBER 12

"I've got the tests scheduled for Monday."-
Dr. Dan

> "Is there any way this could be legit? Kid
> seems to be getting his act in gear."-
> Coach Skip

"I mean, with God, anything is possible.
Isn't that the quote you're always telling
me?"- Dr. Dan

> "So, short of divine intervention, the answer
> is no?"- Coach Skip

"I don't need to answer that, do I?"- Dr. Dan

The sun was hanging an hour above the horizon. A strong breeze from the ocean allowed Deke to smell the rust off the community center equipment. Deke eyed the plates he was using and saw the places where the plastic had chipped off, exposing the metal underneath to the elements. Putting the last of the circular weights back on the rack, Deke leaned back and smiled. It had been a good day. The chime from the system told him that he had gained point zero six in power, which only added to his post-workout high.

Being able to use actual weights instead of the sand buckets from the beach meant he could push himself harder. However, the lack of a spotter meant he had to be careful which exercises he did. The workout and "six" points had given him an increase of three to power, which was one more than the beach workouts. Deke was still annoyed that it was halving his rewards for some reason, but he just tried to ignore it since there was nothing he could do.

Thinking back on the day, the slight downward turn of his lips from the system's strange inaccuracy vanished. The biggest reason for his change in mood was the kids; they had held him in a kind of reverence that reminded him of Max and home, and it felt good. On top of that, he hadn't missed a single shot all day—even with the sub-par basketball hoop. Not that anyone had been able to properly guard him, but it had been good to be able to play again. Most of the kids were better basketball players than Lee, who was the only person he'd been able to "play" with since he was healed. They hadn't cared about his leg, and he was able to remember the pure joy of playing basketball again. It wasn't the same as pushing himself against a really talented opponent, but it was still more than he had experienced in what felt like a really long time.

The memory of the home opener played through his mind, and he picked up a ball before heading back out to the court. Idly dribbling it on the uneven court, his mind repeated some of the moves that their opponents had used. He went through the motions that he would need to counter those moves. Dribbling, fade-away shots, and footwork played through his mind as he replayed the game. He practiced movements he had used his whole life in an attempt to burn them back into his muscle memory.

The sun was close to setting when he finally finished. He stood at the free-throw line and tossed a few more balls into the hoop as he cooled down. He was actually surprised to realize that the breeze was cooling off a thin sheen of sweat—he had gotten so caught up in the moment of reliving the game that he hadn't realized how much he was pushing the envelope until he finally came back to himself. Wiping an arm across his forehead, he walked over to his bag and collapsed onto the ground, resting the ball under his head.

He pulled out his phone to check if he had any messages. Lee was on his way to meet him, having tracked his phone's location.

Task Completed: Conditioning

Train your body and mind to respond to external situations. Finesse gains .04 points.

"Well, that's new," Deke muttered to himself. That was the first time he'd gained Finesse. Was it because he had never been able to consciously work on his footwork and handling before? Something to ask Lee when he got here. He glanced around the vacant community center, which had slowly emptied out of kids over the day. The adults that were left had cleared out just before dinner time, and were replaced by some part-time students, which left him time to get in a workout alone. Looking over, he saw Lee coming into the parking lot with a couple of takeout bags from a nearby restaurant in his hands. Deke blinked, confused by the generosity of his roommate but unwilling to comment on it. He had already explained to Lee that they needed to cut down on the off campus café trips because he couldn't afford anymore restaurant prices for himself, so this would be a treat.

Deke didn't bother standing up. He just took another gulp from his water bottle and scooted over to make sure Lee had room on the ground beside him, where the tetanus hazard fence wouldn't cut him.

"Hey, Tiny." Deke's voice was more tired than he was expecting.

"Hey yourself, you ogre." Lee threw one of the bags at Deke and sat next to him. "Got you some dinner, figured you hadn't eaten yet."

The two settled into a comfortable silence as they ate. Deke had gotten a chicken wrap of some sort, it was a bit light on seasoning, but that was pretty normal for Deke's meals these days. Lee had taken charge of Deke's food plans even in the school cafeteria. Admittedly, it was far better than eating one good meal and multiple bland ones each day, so he tucked in to enjoy it. Deke informed Lee about the new stat increases as they ate, and he could see the brainiac's wheels churning away at something, so he let the other kid think.

"I am pretty confident now that there must be two substats for each major stat," Lee said finally, "and the reason you can't see them is you're not high enough level. But either way, knowing that you're getting better numbers from heavier weights means we should probably avoid the lighter stuff. I'll make a new workout plan that includes all this." Lee motioned to the community center as a whole. "I think I understand it enough at this point that I can at least do that. And we probably need to get you... "street" games, or whatever, so you can discover new skills. Or level your existing ones..."

"Street games? Do you mean pickup games?" Deke half laughed at the terminology his roommate used.

"Yeah, sure, pickup games. It's clear that you don't get much playing against me. Still, if we can find better people, then maybe you'll develop skills faster while actually using them in a competitive environment."

"I got [Aim Assist] in practice. I almost never miss with it," Deke said after a moment of thought.

"Yeah, but aiming is an internal thing. I bet it'll level faster if someone is trying to stop you from aiming. Wait, does it even have a level?" Lee said after a moment's thought.

"I don't know man; it's just [Aim Assist]," Deke answered, mentally calling up his [Status] screen. Lee had figured out the trick of calling the screen during the week leading up to the game. Just mentally commanding [Status] was enough to bring the blue letters to his mind. "Yeah, on my status thingie there ain't nothing there about a level."

"I bet it's hidden too," Lee said. "I went back and played some more of that game that looks... suspiciously like what you described, and they had skill level-ups."

"All right... I won't pretend to understand hidden levels but as long as you do, I'm good. So back to the workout. I need cardio, burpees, and supersets." Deke grew slightly uncomfortable every time Lee brought up anything to do with Evil Corp and knew that the game would inevitably lead to a conversation about the Project Ultra Vivuman thing. The fact that they couldn't find the photocopied papers from Professor Tawn anywhere in the dorm, despite its newly cleaned state, was sending goosebumps over Deke's shoulders. Plus they'd reported the break-in but since nothing was thought to be missing at the time, there was nothing to be done other than to chalk it up to 'student shenanigans.' So, to find the papers missing made that assessment hair raising.

"What's a superset? Is that like a normal set, but it can fly and shoot lasers from its eyes?"

"No, smartass. A superset is where you switch between two exercises immediately without a rest cycle between them. So like, bicep curls and tricep dips. You alternate between them until you've completed the full set."

"I'm guessing a burpee isn't just belching?"

"Nah, they're a full-body workout. You jump up in the air from a standing position, then drop, do a push-up, get back to your feet. Stand straight and then jump, at the top of the jump, you clap your hands above your head and begin again. It's a way of turning an anaerobic workout into an aerobic one while still getting strength training."

"So I can just write, 'do a thousand burpees' and you'll know what I'm talking about?" Lee asked.

"Yeah, but don't make me do a thousand, that would kill me," Deke said with a laugh. They had finished their meals, and Lee helped Deke put everything away, ensuring the community center's gym was also tidied up before they headed out.

"Did you get this email from Tawn? He says his office caught on fire, and tomorrow's class is canceled. He's still trying to reorganize everything. We even all got full credit on the homework because it got burned to ash," Lee said as they opened the door to their dorm room. "Wait, didn't you say you saw firetrucks on the way home from the game? The same night someone broke into our dorm?"

Deke wasn't paying a lot of attention, though, because his phone had just buzzed.

"u up?"- Blonde Valerie

Deke shot off a quick response before stepping through the door and putting his stuff down next to the bed.

"Don't feel like getting arrested again."- Dekester

Lee continued to talk, but Deke just watched the three little dots in the bottom corner that said she was responding. He collapsed onto his bed before she finished a short message.

"Don't h8 I can cum over there"- Blonde Valerie

"double entendre intended"- Blonde Valerie

Deke shot off a quick yes, before looking around the small room he shared with Lee. It was relatively clean. Lee had clearly spent most of the morning putting everything back together after the break-in, even going as far to tidy up what Deke hadn't had time to this morning. He had only been able to refold and put away his laundry this morning, despite the early hour, and now with Valerie coming over, he was immensely thankful for his and Lee's hard work.

He hurriedly kicked his dirty workout kit under his bed and then thought better of it. He pulled it back out before grabbing the pair of socks, shorts, and a T-shirt out of the bag to toss into the dirty laundry basket.

"Look Tiny, I hate to do this but you need to leave," Deke said, turning to Lee. "I got a girl coming over!"

"What? No." Lee said, looking up from his computer desk with a frown, "I have a raid tonight! And we need to talk about if Tawn's fire is related to whoever broke into the room."

"You can..." Deke's eyes frantically searched the room before landing on Lee's expensive gaming laptop. He picked it up and then shoved it into Lee's hands. "Play somewhere else. Dude, this is bro code. You gotta clear out for a few hours."

"No, you're not going to sexile me!" Lee whined. "And you haven't said a word about Tawn's office, wasn't he looking into Vitruvian Man stuff for you? What if they found out about that?" Deke winced as the goosebumps from earlier came back. Why did Lee keep bringing up Evil Corp? Luckily, Lee hadn't taken his shoes off yet, so Deke strong-armed him through the door.

"Nope, you gotta go!" Deke stated as Lee's shoes slid along the carpet. "We can talk about this later. Can I take the weird alien poster off the wall? Sweet thanks." Deke asked and then ignored the answer as he slammed the door shut behind Lee. He locked it from the inside to prevent the kid from coming back in right away. Looking around, he saw that Lee had laid his wallet and key card out on the desk. Lee timidly knocked on the door, and Deke slid the wallet without the card under the slot.

"Dude, no, you can't take Zeratul off the wall." Lee increased his knocking to pounding on the door and then paused. Clearly stooping down to pick up the wallet. "Be careful with it! You already cut it! And give me my gaming mouse and headset!" Lee shouted.

Deke owed the brainiac that much, and so he passed the aforementioned items to him. Lee seemed to understand and didn't try to barge back in. He did, however, give another warning about damaging Zergul-whatever. Deke waved him away before closing the door and beginning to pull the pins out of the poster and rolling it up —carefully. He hid it behind Lee's monitor. He understood how much the kid liked the poster and still felt bad about throwing the pocket knife at it, so he was even extra careful as he laid it down.

A quick glance around the room showed him a few other things that needed to be taken care of before Valerie could see the room, but he looked at his phone.

"brt 10 min"- Blonde Valerie

"Okay, that gives me... some time," Deke said as he shoved his old laptop into his backpack and then tossed the thing under the bed. He didn't want Valerie, who had displayed a new model laptop, to see his turn of the century brick. He then lifted his arm to check his pits and shuddered slightly. He didn't have time for a shower with the time-line Valerie had thrown at him. Still, a full day outside in the sun and then a workout had left him in a state well below "fresh." So, he pulled off his shirt, rubbing it into his pits to get rid of the sweat. Then he put on an extra thick layer of deodorant to be sure. He followed that with clean clothes and an extra helping of cologne that was hopefully enough to mask any stale sweat smell that remained.

"Shit! How am I gonna get her up here..." Deke muttered to himself as he changed into a pair of board shorts that looked like he was trying too hard, but better too hard than not at all. A few more quick glances around the room, and it was as tidy as he was gonna make it. He pulled out his phone—she would arrive any minute, and he still had to figure out how to get her up without the RA noticing.

Flying down the stairs four at a time, he got to the bottom only slightly winded and glanced around. No sign of Valerie yet. He saw a bunch of people coming in and out of the public spaces still. Enough that a girl heading upstairs clearly wouldn't be that big of a deal, and he sighed in relief.

"Hey there, lazy robber." Valerie's words from behind him caused him to turn. The blonde was wearing a thin white sundress that hinted at her beautiful body underneath rather than displaying it openly. Deke let his eyes drink her in for a minute while he grinned. Valerie laughed and shook her head.

"Stop staring and take me upstairs. It's impolite to make a lady wait."

CHAPTER

TWENTY-TWO

SUNDAY, NOVEMBER 13

Deke's arm falling to the bed woke him up, and he blinked as a perfectly formed butt bounced away from him. His broad smile didn't even slip when he saw clothes flying from his shelves onto the floor in messy piles. He could clean that up later. He tracked Valerie to the closet and watched her pull on a pair of his boxers and a button-up. She didn't bother to fasten any of the buttons, leaving a tantalizing strip of flesh visible down the middle. Her tight body getting the thinnest of covering was somehow arousing even though he'd seen all of it again last night.

Someone else's breathing in the room caught his attention, and Deke looked over to find a wide-eyed Lee staring openly at Valerie as well. Deke turned a stretch into a quick grab and threw his pillow at the kid. Deke wasn't upset or jealous, but he wasn't sure how Valerie would respond to the kid ogling her. When the pillow thumped home, and Valerie turned to follow the sound, she spotted Lee and Deke watched as a smile crossed her lips. Guess she didn't care.

"Morning!" she chirped at Lee and bounced over to his bed as he attempted to throw the pillow back at Deke. The pillow landed halfway between the beds, and Deke wasn't sure if it was the kid's lack of athleticism or the loosely shirted and braless Valerie's approach that caused the pathetic attempt. She sat down on his bed, and Deke almost guffawed as Lee's face went so red that he looked like he was going to pop. "I'm Valerie. What's your name?"

"Uhh... Lee. I'm sorry, I didn't mean to..." Lee stuttered out as he tried to both introduce himself and apologize for taking in a show that Valerie may have even intended. Her mischievous smile reminded Deke of a few moments from the night before, and each time it creased her cherry mouth, he knew he was in for something...

"Are you the whiz kid that Deke kicked out of here?" Valerie asked, ignoring the kid's attempts to apologize.

"Umm, well, I'm Lee..."

"Probably not the intelligent one, then," Valerie retorted, clearly poking fun at Lee not being able to find the words. She then practically lay down in Lee's bed with him to give the kid a hug. "Just kidding!" she chimed and slid back out of the kid's bed to make her way over to Deke's again. Deke actually laughed at the looks that crossed the kid's face. He was clearly torn between something close to euphoria and likely some sort of loyalty, judging by his quick glances at Deke.

"You shouldn't tease the nerd king," Deke chided as Valerie slid back into his bed and pulled his arm back over her. "Normally, when he can talk, he is really cool."

Lee blinked at Deke, and a subdued smile came onto the kid's face. Then Lee sat up and grabbed a stack of papers Deke recognized. That was his calculus homework. "This is way better, Deke. You made a few mistakes when you transferred values across the equations, but you seem to be understanding it now."

"Wait, you have someone doing your calculus homework for you? That's, like, totally unfair!" Valerie said as she pulled herself out of Deke's arm and spun in the bed to look him in the eyes. "Like, you know I struggle in calculus too!"

"He is only helping me check my answers, Val," Deke said, caught by surprise. He couldn't tell if Valerie was actually upset or joking with him.

"Yeah, sure," she said, stretching out the words and increasing her pitch to clearly convey her disbelief in the situation. She turned to Lee. "Perhaps you can 'help' me with my homework as well. Especially after the show you just got!"

Lee squinted at the girl and then looked at Deke. The morning amusement was turning a bit sour, thanks to the situation. Deke still wasn't sure how to defuse it but tried his best. In a light, playful tone, he said, "Stop teasing him, Val. You know he didn't try to peek at you. Plus, you chose to stay here, remember?"

"Yeah, whatever. Oh right, my clothes!" she exclaimed and slid back out of bed to rifle through her sundress's pockets. Deke wasn't sure how the thing had pockets, but when she pulled out a rolled spliff, he hesitated. The lighter that followed told him she clearly intended to spark up in here.

"I'm not sure that's a great idea. Hotboxing the room is just asking for trouble!" Deke said, stuck between his desire to keep Valerie happy in the hopes of a repeat performance and not get caught in his dorm with drugs.

"Come on. It's just a pinner," she responded as she lit up. Deke rushed to the window and opened it before snatching the lighter and "pinner" from her hand. He hurriedly chucked the drugs out the window and then tossed the lighter to Lee.

"Can you light some candles, bro?" he asked, and when Deke turned back, he found Valerie sulking. "You know I can't, I'm hoping—"

"Don't be a buzzkill, I can't believe you wasted good weed!" Valerie whined. Deke took a deep breath and accidentally inhaled some remnants of the smoke that hung loosely in the air. He felt his throat burn and his lungs spasm.

Recreational Drug detected. A decrease in body funtions is imminent. Purge initiated.

"Oh no!" Deke sputtered and felt his stomach begin churning. Valerie attempted to grab him for a hug, but he held up a hurried hand while lunging toward the corner of the room and the garbage can there. He was just in time as he violently vomited on top of the condoms and wrappers inside.

"What the? Ewww... gross," Valerie cried out in shock. "I wouldn't have pegged you as such a lightweight. Not with that bag you left at my place! Ugh, that's so disgusting. I can't be here. I'm so out!" she finished, and Deke heard her move around the room as he continued to dry heave into the bin. He could hear Valerie throwing stuff around as she put on her dress.

"Stop leering," she commanded Lee, pulling the dress down over her head. She pulled off the boxers from under the dress and then threw them at Deke's back. She grabbed her own undies off the floor and pocketed them. The door opened and then slammed closed before Deke could feel Lee move to stand next to him. Deke continued to be violently sick as Lee hovered over him. After a few moments, the spasming in his chest subsided, and he set the garbage can down and leaned back. Lee cleared his throat.

"Well, while you're down there and a captive audience, I learned some more about the fire at Professor Tawn's classroom," Lee explained, seemingly eager to return to the topic of the previous night. "The fire started in Tawn's office and was intentionally set among his books. The school thinks a student did it to get out of the homework assignments, but what if you didn't lose those papers on Project Ultra? What if our papers on Project Ultra went missing the same night? I think the fire and the break-in are connected.

"We really need to find that contract that you told me about. If someone is out there destroying evidence of this Vitruvian Man organization, we can't continue to stay in the dark. There are just so many questions . . ." Lee continued. Deke attempted to glare at him but a final dry heave made him double back over.

Purge complete.

"I'm fine, thanks for asking, Tiny," Deke said with as much scorn as his wrung-out diaphragm could manage. "Here's what the system just said..." Deke began explaining the purge, and Lee reluctantly pulled out a notepad to copy it down.

Almost as soon as Deke finished, Lee looked back up and asked, "So, how are we going to get ahold of Evil Corp's contract?"

Deke felt the goosebumps return but shrugged and let his silence be his answer. Admittedly, he was slightly upset that Valerie had lit up in his dorm room. Not only were random drug tests a thing in sports, but if he hadn't acted faster, someone outside might have smelled it. That would have definitely been the end of his time here at UCSP.

Sighing deeply, he finally responded. "Yeah, I checked the bin Valerie dumped it all in, but it was empty." Deke looked around, thinking. "Our only other option is paying Ronnie a visit, I guess, but what if that hitman dude is lurking about his place?"

"First, are you sure she tossed the bag? And secondly, I've never seen the guy, but you think he would be just hanging around at Ronnie's place?" Lee asked, his voice a bit squeaky, and he hadn't even seen the creepy vaper dude.

Deke looked at the door Valerie had just exited through, and shrugged by way of responding to the first question of Lee's.

"She told me she did, and I doubt she would admit to having it, if I asked again. As for B-movie hitman dude, I don't know what this virusman crazy company is capable of. Neither do you, and he basically escorted Ronnie out of the physio clinic with one hand," Deke said and dropped his head, still worried he let something terrible happen. Still, Ronnie got himself into drug dealing, right? What was Deke supposed to have done?

"Well, he is one of your trainers. You'd have a plausible reason to go check in on him," Lee countered, and Deke tilted his head in consideration before nodding. Perhaps, that would be enough to go unnoticed by the vaper.

"Should we go check the garbage dump first?" Deke asked instead of agreeing. He wanted to avoid discovery at all costs.

"You know how hard it will be to find a specific bag of trash in a garbage dump?" Lee asked, his voice dripping with incredulity.

"So... Is that a no?"

CHAPTER
TWENTY-THREE
SUNDAY, NOVEMBER 13

There weren't really any run-down areas near UCSP, not like the trailer-parks Deke was accustomed to from back home, anyway. There might have been some farther away from the beach, and still near the university, but almost all the students stayed within a few miles of campus and the area reflected that choice. Still, Ronnie's apartment was in the slums of San Pandero. It was a rundown two-story building built in a square shape with a small internal courtyard with only dead grass inside.

There was a gate blocking access to the "desirable" courtyard, and a set of doors into the apartments that cut off Deke and Lee's access. Deke buzzed Ronnie's apartment and they waited to see if anyone would open the gate for them. Deke and Lee had both made the trek out here, having to use two different buses. Deke had just wanted to walk but Lee had insisted.

"How do you know where he lives again?" Lee asked as he looked through the iron bars.

"We dropped him off with the travel bus in preseason, and I helped carry the medical bag and table into his apartment. I think he used the table to earn some cash on the side." Deke glanced at Lee before he shrugged "That was in the first tournament when I got here in the summer, a bit before the knee blew up." Deke rubbed at the offending limb out of habit.

"Yeah. I remember moving in with you, while you waited on surgery. Angry would be an *understatement*. I think you snapped at me a few times for breathing too loud," Lee said with a laugh.

"Yeah, it was a low point in my life for sure. Thinking back, I think Ronnie insinuated a few times he had drugs that could help me." Deke thought back on those interactions and considered some of the wording and hinting the trainer had used. Then he wondered if the trainer was implying regular drugs or the Radanium... In the end, he could only shrug it off and change the subject to stop thinking about it.

"I'm sorry if I treated you poorly, man." Deke let his head fall, embarrassed about needing to apologize but also knowing Lee deserved it.

"Yeah, I get it man. I remember you were stressing over your scholarship," Lee said, reaching up to pat him on the shoulder. "I know stress... My parents have been pressuring me to become a doctor for as long as I can remember. They are the epitome of the stereotype." His face screwed up into a wrinkled facsimile, and the thickest Chinese accent Deke had ever heard came out of Lee's mouth. "Why you no' doctor yet? You wan' be a failure? You musta' geta' good grades." Lee's face relaxed with a self-deprecating chuckle. "They just don't get that I don't wanna do that stuff."

Deke burst into uncontrolled laughter after Lee's impromptu impression, wiping a tear away, as he asked. "They don't know you're studying game development?"

"Nah, they think I'm pre-med. They expect me to go to Stanford and become a doctor. They mean well... but they're both from a different world, right? They both immigrated here from—" Lee's explanation about his family was cut short as one of the residents, a kid their own age carrying a dozen bags' worth of groceries, walked up behind the two.

"Hey could you get me in?" he asked, lifting the groceries slightly to indicate that his hands were full.

"Sorry, we don't know the code," Lee said, but the guy snorted.

"It's five-four-three-two, just put it in," the guy responded, clearly not caring about the security much, as Lee jumped to help. "Star after that," he corrected when the door didn't buzz open immediately. Lee pressed the button and then pulled the door open, holding it for the guy. "Thanks."

They followed him in, and Deke led the way to the back corner where Ronnie's apartment was. The door was slightly ajar and there was a paint bucket and some brushes sitting outside. Deke glanced over at Lee, who just shrugged. Deke knocked lightly, then called out.

"Hello? Ronnie?" Deke's knock had opened the door a little and it was clear that the front room had been cleared out, as only a pile of tools and some old carpet were left. A man came out of the back room; he had a tool belt on over a stained jumpsuit.

"Sorry, it's not up for rent yet," the man said, wiping his hands down his pant legs.

"Huh? What happened to Ronnie?" Deke asked, and the man's earlier friendliness vanished in an instant.

"Never heard of a 'Ronnie'. This apartment has been empty for a few months now. We're just now getting around to renovations." The hurried man turned back to the tools in the front room, shifting stuff around and clearly trying to dismiss them.

"What? That's bullshit, my friend Ronnie wouldn't have moved out months ago," Deke insisted, and the man turned around, a long colt revolver in his hands. The weapon was pointed at the two of them. Deke was shocked by the gun's appearance but simultaneously surprised by the fact that the system had filled his vision with tags, warning him against the guy's sudden movement but also identifying the gun with a small tag.

Threat detected: Combat tactics and assessment activated.

Prepping release of norepinephrine, increasing metabolism, activating reactionary regions of the cortex.

Colt Python double-action revolver detected, ammunition size: .357 Magnum.

Time slowed, the moment being drawn out thin as piano wire as the system highlighted the weapon in green; the cylinder in particular drew his attention and he could see that it didn't have any bullets loaded. The system confirmed that assessment by listing the gun as unloaded. The man clicked the hammer halfway back and it made an intimidating sound. The system added a tag saying the gun was now completely non-functional and still unloaded, which left Deke with a strange sense of confusion.

Weapon status: Unloaded and inoperable.

No threat detected: Deactivating combat tactics and assessment.

Restoring homeostasis.

"Are you two with him, that god damned cotton candy smelling bastard?" the man asked, his voice raising a few octaves, and Deke could see that his hands were shaking, clearly in fear.

"Whoa man, we're just looking for Ronnie," Deke responded,

feeling strangely relaxed, and holding his hands up to show that he meant no harm. Deke wasn't sure why, it just felt like the right thing to do, especially since Lee's hands were already above his head. Yet, the system clearly indicated that there was no threat from this man's gun.

"I already told him and I'll tell you guys too. Kid paid off his contract and disappeared one night. No idea how he got all his stuff out, it was all just... gone one night. Now you two can go for a hike for all I care, but if I see you around here again I'm going to call the cops. I know what sort of guests Ronnie liked to have." Deke nodded his head in response to the man's words and grabbed Lee's shoulder.

"All right, we're heading out." Deke pulled Lee out of the room; his roommate seemed to be locked up in fear, so the action of leaving took some coaxing. Deke made a quick escape out of the complex and down the street before he slowed down, guiding Lee down onto the curb so he could recover. "You all right?" he asked his roommate, unsure what was wrong with the kid.

"No!" Lee said as he pushed his head into his hands, trying to block out the world for a moment while he recovered his breath. "That was the scariest thing I've ever done!" Lee exclaimed in a hoarse whisper.

"The gun wasn't even loaded. The guy was shaking and was clearly just as scared as you are." Deke flopped down next to Lee.

"What?" Lee's confusion was enough to shock him out of his fear, and he looked at Deke in surprise. "There is no way you could know that."

"The... sports drink—" Deke had almost been about to call it the system. A habit he had gotten into with Lee, but he'd remembered at the last minute they were in public. "—told me." He described the popups and green outline to Lee, who stared at him for a few moments and then shook his head.

As he described them, the system created another prompt.

Trainee's response to verbose mode reporting in combat

was detrimental to outcome. Engaging color coding of responses. Active threats assigned red, potential threats assigned orange, inactive threats assigned green.

"That's crazy. Also sort of telling us that the 'sports drink' is totally training you to be a secret assassin or something."

"Yeah, let's hope not," Deke muttered. He wondered if the system was also making him calmer. He didn't feel out of sorts at all, and judging by Lee's response, that wasn't normal.

"Well, I don't think we're gonna get anything from Ronnie," Lee said, his breathing seeming to now be under his control. Deke was glad to hear him thinking rationally again. "I don't know where else we would be able to look at the contract though. Duke maybe?"

"They were *giving* him the contract, he wouldn't have one just sitting around." Deke shook his head. "I think we're probably up shit's creek on the contract."

"Yeah... you're probably right. I mean, unless we find the vaping man's house," Lee said after a moment of thought. Deke laughed at that *horrible* idea.

"Something tells me his gun wouldn't be empty if we did that." Deke stood up. "Come on, I need to get a workout in this afternoon." Deke offered his hand to help Lee stand. "We'll walk over to the community center, that'll help calm your nerves."

Monday, November 14

D r. Dan loomed over Deke's leg, twisting it for the third time. Dan's eyes were on Deke's face but aside from feeling a stretch, he was even less bothered by the motion than he had been when Abbie did them. They were in the back of the physio clinic and Dan was running him through the same series of tests that Abbie had already done. With the same results, only extraordinary, from the expression on Dan's face. Deke and Lee knew the reason—the sports drink. Deke had also put on some additional muscle since then, and due to the motion elongating those muscles, he could tell that he was getting a little stiff, and mentally added additional stretching to his routine.

Deke figured the system added to his strength faster than normal workouts and he would need to stretch more to accommodate for the faster muscle growth.

"This doesn't make any sense," Dan repeated himself. "You're building muscles fast and you're a little stiff, but you don't seem to be in any pain."

"I told you Doc, I'm all better," Deke answered with a grin. The older man's befuddlement was actually pretty amusing to watch, as he tried to reconcile what he knew of Deke's injuries with the healed leg that he was examining.

"Honestly Deke, that's impossible. So either you're the best actor in the world, and you're just hiding the pain or..." Dan didn't finish the sentence but Deke was suddenly nervous. Dan was clearly implying that he was taking some sort of drugs. The experience with Valerie's weed told him that he absolutely didn't have any of the normal illicit drugs in his system. That didn't mean they didn't have a way to detect whatever serum he had accidentally taken which had actually healed his leg.

"Can't we just put this to bed with an MRI scan?" Deke asked, trying to get ahead of a possible drug test.

"All right, follow me, we've got one more test to do," Dan said, ignoring his suggestion, as he stepped away and started putting on some latex gloves. Deke followed him into his office, where Dan started pulling down the blinds. "There is a drug kit on the table. Check it to ensure that the seal is intact..."

Deke looked at the Styrofoam box with tape sealing the top. Inside there was a urine sample test. He'd taken enough of them in his career at this point that it was clear what the doctor wanted him to do. Deke reluctantly moved to the box and pulled the tape to release the seal, pulling out each item individually. Two glass bottles with twist seal lids, with an A and B label on top, sat at the top of the Styrofoam box. As he removed them, a plastic cup that also had a lid with something that looked like a sippy cup spout resided under them. Dan opened a drawer and took out some pH strips and a refractometer.

Deke sighed and dropped his shorts, ensuring Dan could see him fully. He picked up the plastic cup and began. Dan watched the whole thing. Deke felt a bit weird but it was a familiar sense of discomfort. A lot of people had watched him pee into cups at this point, and he willed himself to fill the container. Once he ran dry, he placed the cup on the metal table in the center of the room.

Dan moved to the sample and with an iodine dropper, transferred some of the urine to another cup. He then placed a drop on the open screen of the refractometer before closing it and holding it up to his eye and the light in the room. His face was serious and Deke felt his unease grow. He knew this was just Dan ensuring that his urine was concentrated enough for the lab to test, but the disapproval from the man brought home how much was riding on those results.

The pH strip was placed in the second cup and urine was dripped over it from the iodine dropper. Deke used the hand sanitizer on Dan's desk, lathering it on twice as he waited for Dan to finish the procedure. Dan then split the rest of the urine from the plastic "sippy cup" between the A and B bottles and sealed them before motioning Deke closer.

"Go ahead and tighten them to ensure a good seal," Doctor Dan stated, and Deke complied. Once the lids clicked home and were back on the table, Doctor Dan motioned to the door. "Thank you Mr. Mills. I'll send this off to USADA immediately. You're welcome to leave now."

"So, if—no *when*, that comes back clean. Am I going to be able to play? My knee is healed, you said so yourself."

"*If* the test comes back clean, that'll be up to Coach Skip to decide," Dan answered, not even looking up from packing the bottles back into the Styrofoam case. He clearly was not buying the idea that the test wouldn't show some sort of drug use.

Deke grunted and left the office. What would happen if they found the blue stuff? What if they *didn't* find the blue stuff, but still didn't clear him to play? Was there someone that could protect him from that kind of thing?

Deke saw Abbie out of the corner of his eye. She had just walked out of the elevator and was looking over a few charts. He had genuinely enjoyed his time with her at the community center, and thought she was warming up to him by the end. Walking over to her, he put on his most winning smile.

"Hey Abbie."

"Oh, hey Deke. I didn't see you come in," Abbie said, looking up from the charts.

"Yeah, Doctor Dan had me come in early to run a bunch of tests. I was just in his office..." Deke paused, trying to think of a polite way to say he pissed in a jar.

"Filling up some bottles?" Abbie came to his rescue and he just nodded his head. "Anything you're worried about specifically?" Deke blinked, was he that obvious?

"Not... really." Deke paused and then shrugged slightly, "I walked by some idiots smoking weed on the street and got a lungful. Could that mess with it?" He thought back to his purge and hoped that meant what little got into his body was quickly removed. He shook himself, and vowed to talk to Valerie about boundaries.

"Ooookay," Abbie said, clearly confused by his reaction. "I mean, that shouldn't even be a problem. It would be a miniscule amount. You sure you aren't worried about anything else?" Deke allowed the genuine relief he felt to show. He actually *was* worried about the joint Valerie had tried to smoke in his room.

"No, seriously, I haven't taken anything else," Deke half lied. He truly couldn't admit to the neon blue raderium. He changed the subject instead, saying, "Hey look, I was wondering if you had a rehab workout I could use for my leg? I'm getting stiffer than I'd like to be, and losing some flexibility."

"Oh. Uh, yeah I guess I could put something together." Abbie paused, then glanced at Dr. Dan's office. "But if you're using any drugs, I'm never going to speak to you again. Got it?" She gave him a steely gaze.

"Crystal clear, don't worry. My pee is gonna crush that test, you'll see." He sat in the long and awkward moment created from his choice of words, and wondered if he was only flustered because of the sports drink, or if her threat was bothering him that much. Coughing, he continued, "I just need to get back in the game."

Deke felt a surge of surprise when he found his final statement to be the total truth. More than anything else, he wanted to go back to playing against real opponents. Not the kids at the center or Lee, but someone that could actually give him a run for his money.

Everything was riding on this test and in a few days, he would find out if everything would come crashing down around him.

TWENTY-FOUR

THURSDAY, NOVEMBER 17

"Sample sent for rush testing is complete. Results are negative for drugs."- Larry-USADA Contact

"Thanks, Larry. Can't believe I am saying this, but that leaves me stumped."- Doctor Daniel Graham

"Glad I could help. Good luck with the season."- Larry-USADA Contact

Deke walked stiffly down the school hallway toward the gym and practice. Abbie's workouts were a far cry above what Lee had been finding online and Deke was feeling them. The strange blue stuff seemed to shorten recovery for his muscles, which would have been amazing if it didn't compress his delayed onset muscle soreness, or DOMS, into a shorter time frame. There was no free lunch in this world, he supposed. Now, instead of seventy-two hours, it was usually the next morning that his muscle pain was at its peak. At least that's what Lee had theorized to Deke the morning after he started his new workouts, but knowing the cause did *not* make it better.

Abbie had also continued talking to him, so he was relatively sure the testing hadn't been able to detect the sports drink. The last two days had almost been pleasant while in physio and he was starting to look forward to each treatment. Well, he would trade the friendly banter with Abbie to be back on the court, certainly. But since he had to be there, Abbie definitely made the treatments better.

Once Deke arrived at the team room, he moved to his locker and got changed quickly before jogging out onto the court. Any day now the coach was going to get told the results and Deke would be allowed to join the practice.

"Mills," Skip called from the center of the gym and Deke jogged over, his excitement already bringing beads of sweat onto his skin. "Take your hundred shots and go see the trainers for your rehab," Skip finished in a more manageable volume once Deke drew close enough.

"Come on, Coach! Dan has to have told you I'm all healed. Why can't I practice today?" Deke exclaimed, his excitement giving way to frustration. It had been *three days* since the assessment and the coach still refused to let him play.

"Doctor Dan *still* says something is off. Until he clears you fully you can't play," Skip said, his emphasis on the word still catching Deke's ears.

"So, the drug test came back negative but he still isn't going to let me play?" Deke said while blinking stupidly at the coach. "That's bullshit, I put in a ton of work to get back. You gotta let me try!"

"Were you expecting a different result?" Skip asked, raising an eyebrow. Whatever the coach saw on Deke's face appeased him and he continued in a more consoling tone. "Yeah it came back negative, but he's worried you just have a really high pain tolerance. No one should heal as fast as you and he doesn't want to see you reinjure yourself."

"What can I do to convince you? Like, you've got to be able to overrule him, right?" Deke pleaded with the coach. Skip's more caring tone had emboldened him.

"You're barking up the wrong tree, Mills," Skip stated flatly. "There isn't a single person at this school who would overrule the doc. You'd have to be crazy. The man's been here for twenty years, he's an institution and pretty much came with the building." Skip scanned the area for one of the assistant coaches. "Boogie, go work with Deke. He can put in a hundred foul shots and twenty jump shots today. Keep track."

Deke sighed but let it go. It was clear that Skip respected Dan too much to go against him. Boogie grabbed a ball rack and rolled it to one of the side hoops. He chest passed the first ball to Deke, and for a half-second, he could almost swear he saw double. The ball almost jammed his finger because he tried to catch it before it arrived. Boogie shrugged in apology and Deke waved it off.

Then he began shooting jumpers. The feeling of being in the air and releasing the ball from his peak felt so right. He'd been doing far more than twenty a day out at the community center. So, he figured he would push it and force Boogie to rein him in. Thanks to the system, he knew he was fully healed, and maybe he could get the coaches talking about it too. He began dribbling and crossing over before jumping into the air and lining up his [Aim Assist].

Boogie's eyes widened after every shot he hit. Deke only missed a single one in the twenty shots. He knew he'd reached twenty when Boogie didn't pass the ball back to him. "That's twenty already, kid. Move on to foul shooting..."

"Boogs just throw it back... please man? I've been shooting foul shots for months. I can hit them with my eyes closed," Deke said somewhat boastfully, but he'd worked with Boogie a few times and he knew that the assistant coach had also made note of his increasing foul shot percentage.

"Deke, I can't," Boogie said with true disappointment in his voice. "I ain't losing face with Skip so you can take a few extra jump shots.

Get cleared and I will push to get you on the floor. Honestly, we need you, Jones can throw a brick better than a mason..."

"The coach won't overrule Dan, so I'm basically screwed, Boogs," Deke whined.

"Just go talk to the Athletic Director then. He's the only one who could overrule the doc anyway. I mean, they have an agreement and don't usually interfere in each other's spheres, but it's the only higher authority. Worth a shot, right?" Boogie stated and Deke blinked.

A trembling flame of hope rekindled in his chest and he moved to shoot his foul shots without further complaint.

"I shouldn't have sat down after warming up," Deke complained, as he gingerly walked into the physio clinic. Abbie watched him approach a smile building on her face. She gave him a once-over and began to laugh at his slow approach. "Oh come on! Don't add to my embarrassment!"

"You look . . . like a . . . giant penguin," Abbie said between gasps for air. Deke slowly moved right in front of her and tried his best to loom as he frowned. She continued to laugh but eventually got a hold of herself. "Okay, up onto the bed, happy Mumble," she teased.

Deke chuckled. Mumble was the penguin in Happy Feet, which was a movie his brother and he watched together. The memory was a good one, so he maintained a smile as he remembered his brother's tear-filled eyes as he watched the little guy finally get to dance free. He eased himself onto the bed face down and let out a long breath as the new position eased some of his muscle soreness.

"I'm going to do some effleurage to flush the muscles of any built-up lactic acid. You've clearly been pushing yourself way too hard. You know you're not Superman, right?" Abbie said. She began cupping her hands around his calf and applying pressure as she ran them toward his heart in long, pain-inducing strokes. Each wince and groan he gave seemed to make Abbie chuckle, if the shaking of her hands was any indication.

"Come on, Abbie," Deke said. "I just want to get better. Your workouts are really good, that's why I'm so sore."

"Yeah, sure. You suck-up!" Abbie said with an exhale of breath. "I purposely did make them a bit harder than I probably should've, but the pain you're experiencing is far and above what you should be. You know I put rest days in between, right?"

Deke did know that, but the system eliminated the need for off-days. Lee had run some experiments that first day when Deke woke up in absolute pain. He'd concluded that the pain was actually a good thing. The entire healing process for his muscles was happening at almost three times normal speed. Which meant he was near the peak of delayed onset muscle soreness in twelve to eighteen hours, and then ready to push himself hard again. There was just no way to tell Abbie that...

"Yeah, I saw that. But if I feel I can lift, why wouldn't I?" Deke said, trying to act merely stubborn and not... genetically modified, or whatever he was, now.

"You're the idiot who is probably just extending his recovery time." Abbie continued the treatment. When he flipped over and she began working on his quads, he could tell by her eyes that she was seriously worried for him. What a change... a few weeks ago he thought she probably would have stabbed him in the chest rather than talk to him. He tried to hide the white-knuckled grip he had on the table throughout her ministrations, even as he considered her. Maybe the concern he saw was just professional courtesy. Or possibly worse, sympathy from one gimp to another...

When she moved on to the electro-stimulus machine, she looked him right in the eye and said, "Look Deke, I get it. No one can say what will happen and that you're actually gonna reinjure yourself, but you've worked hard and climbed back. If you keep pushing yourself too hard, you definitely have a higher chance of ending up back on this table for something else. Can you just take your time? I promise you that you will come back stronger than ever."

Deke looked at her and when he didn't nod right away, she chuckled and shook her head. "I really shouldn't have given you those workouts. Don't blame me for saying I told you so later, dummy…"

"Have you ever met Director Rooney?" Deke asked, effectively changing the subject and trying to find out more about his final hope.

"Strange question," Abbie said, a small frown coming onto her face. She looked at him again before sighing. "Yeah, I met him once. He's the one who took away my scholarship after I tore my ACL." Deke felt a lump build in his throat as Abbie turned away, dabbing at her eyes. He hadn't known she was a scholarship athlete here.

"I didn't know—" Deke began and was cut off.

"Skip is a great coach; he must have gone to bat for you. My coach didn't. They handed my scholarship off to a new recruit as soon as they found out I'd been hurt," Abbie continued in a low voice. Deke held his breath to make sure he didn't miss anything. "Now, I can only rehabilitate myself and try out next year."

Deke felt his mouth go dry. She was living his worst nightmare. He glanced down at her brace, which took on a whole new meaning for him in that moment. Abbie followed his gaze. "Actually, we should get you sized for one, Deke."

"I'm all better, though," Deke stated. "Do I actually need it?"

"Well." Abbie shrugged. "If you have one, you are way more likely to be allowed to play and practice. It protects you from reinjuring yourself. Normally we would have started getting you fitted around now anyway, if you were on a normal recovery path…"

"You're serious?" Deke asked, feeling that sense of hope return and burn more fiercely. If he had a brace it might just show the coach how serious he was. Show Doctor Dan, too for that matter. "Let's do it! Anything to get back on the floor."

Abbie smiled and moved to a desk to pull out some equipment and a form. She returned and began taking measurements of his quad, knee, and calf before filling out the form.

"Do you think I will look as good as you in my brace?" Deke asked after she was done.

"Oh stop it! You're like a used car salesman." Abbie slapped his shoulder lightly. "Let's finish your treatment and I will show you some good partner stretches that should help keep your muscles a bit more supple."

Abbie moved around the clinic cleaning up, as Deke sat with the electrical stimulus machine attached to his legs. After the timer beeped, Abbie motioned him toward the weights and rehab section. She instructed him to begin a seated hamstring stretch and Deke reached for his toes.

"Okay, meet my resistance," Abbie said, as she leaned into Deke's back. He slowly ramped up his strength and her breathing grew a bit heavier as she fought back. After about ten seconds she forced out, "That's good, now lean more into the stretch and try to drop deeper into it."

"Okay, let's switch to a groin stretch," Abbie continued after they finished the other leg. "So, what are the chances of the team winning the game tomorrow?" she asked as he met her resistance again.

"Honestly, I'm not sure." Deke sighed, not really wanting to talk about the team when he couldn't play. He hedged by focusing in the direction of the mental side of it all. "Skip and the coaching staff are pretty on edge. I can tell how much they *need* a win before the Booster event this weekend."

"You think it's affecting the rest of the team?" Abbie asked as she motioned for him to return to the stretch.

"Well, if I can feel it and I'm not even playing... yeah, I think the other guys are feeling it too," Deke explained. The recollection of the Booster event reminded Deke of his surprise for Lee. He wanted to get the kid something for all of his help and the event had some special guests that Deke thought the kid might enjoy meeting. "You excited for the Booster club thing?"

"They don't send us *lowly* student assistants to do the Booster stuff. And this year especially, I probably wouldn't want to attend...

with everything so fresh. This year they really managed to take the sky from me," Abbie responded, her last phrase hanging in the air oddly to Deke. What in the heck did she mean?

"Well this event has the cast of some old TV show attending and I plan to surprise my roommate with tickets. Do you know anything about Firebug? Do you think a self-professed nerd would like meeting them?"

"You've got extra tickets?" Abbie said, her voice was overly excited, and again Deke wasn't sure why.

"Yeah, all the athletes get some tickets for their families. I've got two extra, but my mom and brother are nearly an entire continent away. I just don't want to invite Lee if he won't enjoy being there. You know how stuffy these events can be."

"Gao Guhn," Abbie exclaimed, and this time Deke had enough.

"What is going on with you?" he asked, relaxing the stretch and turning to look at her. Her face was flushed a bit and she was smiling.

"I think it meant amazing on the Firebug show. Honestly, they mixed in Mandarin and I only heard it in the context of the show, but Lee isn't the *only* one who would enjoy meeting the cast of Firebug!" Abbie answered.

"Okay?" Deke began before the realization hit him. "Oh! If you came too that would be awesome. I always just stand around awkwardly at these events. But you're saying Lee would enjoy the surprise?"

"He may wet himself! Pick me up at five?" Abbie said while doing a cute little dance that made Deke's eyes widen. The ball of nerves he had been feeling for the past few days eased, and he couldn't help but think that at least he might make Abbie and Lee happy...

CHAPTER

TWENTY-FIVE

FRIDAY, NOVEMBER 18

Deke couldn't really lie down on Dr. Pinsonneault's couch, he was too tall for that, and that was separate from the fact that the brown leather was too nice to put his shoes on anyway. Coming in the morning made the office completely different, as the wide wall of windows now streamed in California sunshine in a way that highlighted the doctor's love for plants.

Despite the open feel of the room, Deke felt awkward. He felt like some of that awkwardness was from that lack of ability to lie down on the couch. Instead, he sort of sprawled across the surface of it down to his knees and then let his calves hang off the side uncomfortably to the floor. On top of that, he was staring at a poster of Arches National Monument on the wall, trying to think how to respond to the question the shrink had posed to him, which was the cause of the other unpleasant feeling he was experiencing. How should he talk about his clenched-gut anxiety and rising sense of helplessness?

"I think the worst part is that I *know* I'm better. I know I'm fully recovered but I'm still sitting on the sidelines. I *hate* not being able to play, I hate that everyone tells me to listen to my body and then ignores me when I tell them it's fully recovered," Deke finally answered. The therapist had asked him what was driving some of his more negative thoughts lately. "I hate that I'm watching others play because no one will actually let me try."

"I understand how frustrating it is when people won't listen to you. I want to focus on that last thought though, about not being able to play." The doctor was sitting in a comfortable-looking armchair. She had a notepad in front of her, although she wasn't using it much. From their previous meetings, it seemed she mostly used it to assign him homework. If she ever took notes she did it after the session. "Surely you can think of ways to challenge yourself off the court? You're doing well in your classes—do you not think that was a challenge?"

"I mean, sure. I guess. It's just..." Deke struggled to find the words he wanted to use. "It's not the right kind of progress. That stuff doesn't... fulfill me? Or some other technical term. More importantly, it doesn't get me closer to the NBA."

"Well, surely there are non-basketball skills you can work on that would improve your NBA career. For example, you mentioned you're going to a Booster meeting with your roommate tonight." Dr. Pinsonneault tapped her pen on the pad and Deke grimaced at the reminder. "I imagine learning how to schmooze Boosters and fans will be a valuable skill in the future."

"Yeah, I think that might terrify me more than never being back on the court again," Deke grumbled, and Dr. Pinsonneault laughed.

"Oh come on, didn't you just ask to be challenged? What scares you about meeting them?"

"Well, my family never really had much money. So my suit looks like something from the eighties," Deke grumbled. It barely fit him, his mom had to let all the fabric out of the legs so that it would land properly against his shoes and with his height, it meant that it was a few sizes baggier than it should have been. "I'm also not used to being all... fancy-like."

"I know you won't believe this right now, but the Boosters are just people too. They paid a lot of money to be able to talk to *you*. They aren't going to think less of you because you're not comfortable in the penguin suit. You have more leverage in the power dynamic here than you realize. Plus, everyone likes a good underdog story, right?"

Deke wrinkled his nose; was there something about him that made people think of penguins? Abbie had called him one just the day before. "Doc, what if they ask me why I'm not playing?"

"Now we're getting somewhere. Now you're actively planning and considering your available options. I can work with this. Tell me, what would you say if I asked you that same question right now?" For the first time, Deke heard the slow tapping of the doctor's pen come to a stop. Her armchair leather squeaked slightly as she leaned forward, clearly intent on his answer.

"I'd tell them I was all better and should be playing!" Deke exclaimed, his voice full of confidence.

"Good! That's called Positive Modeling. The more you can picture yourself on the court, the faster you'll be back." The conversation continued on from there. Still, they only had a half-hour time slot. "However, that's just considering your inward mental state. As far as a response to a Booster, it's total dog shit."

Deke was so caught off guard by her surprising shift in language that he almost fell off the ottoman-with-delusions-of-grandeur he was resting on. Air exploded from his chest as he laughed in response. "What did you just say?"

"Dog. Shit." She enunciated carefully and primly. "There are some unspoken rules in professional settings. One of those rules is that you never countermand your superior openly. If you have to question the decisions of your coach then do it behind closed doors. You keep problems like these in-house, like family. *Especially* to a potential investor."

Deke considered her words carefully. Her mention of family really made him stop to think. He played his family situation tight to his chest, right? He even knew that bringing it up only brought uncomfortable questions. *Shit*, how often had he been airing the team's dirty laundry to everyone who would listen of late? "I'll... take that into consideration."

"Good. That's all I ask. Well, it looks like that's all the time we have today, Deke, and I think we made some really good progress. I want you to read chapters fourteen and fifteen of the book I gave you. They are about interpersonal behavior and I want to talk about how you can use the things it's talking about to improve yourself off the court, for our next meeting." Dr. Pinsonneault ripped off a piece of paper and handed it to him. "It will have to be after the break, I'm afraid." Deke glanced at the slip of paper long enough to see the homework assignment and a reminder of their next meeting. They had started to meet every Friday but with American Thanksgiving next week, the school was mostly closing down.

Deke opened the door to the dorm room. He'd returned home instead of going to the gym as usual. Practice had been cut short, since they had a game tomorrow. But that didn't change Deke's routine much. He had gotten a light dinner and done his calculus homework before heading back to get changed. Lee was standing in front of the closet with a knee-length brown coat worn over what he assumed was his suit. Deke stopped in the doorway.

"Why are you wearing a trench coat?" Deke asked, finally continuing into the room and sliding his bag onto the floor at the foot of his bed. He had begun emptying it while he waited for what he assumed would be a strange answer.

"It's not a trench coat, it's a brown coat." Lee's response caused Deke to look over at the other kid with a quirked eyebrow.

"Okay? I mean, I guess it's a *brown* trench coat." Deke blinked at the kid, trying to compromise but not understanding the distinction.

"No, you big idiot. It's a brown coat... it's what they wear on Firebug!"

"Oh, right. I guess it looks... good, then? Are you going to wear it all night? That'd get pretty hot right? And not in the good way." Even this late in the year, the weather in Southern California was still slightly above Deke's Canadian-born comfort level.

"I was trying to decide. I guess not." Lee said, pulling the coat off, his voice sounding disappointed. He began setting it on the bed carefully and as he looked at it longingly, Deke realized how much it meant to the kid.

"Just wear it," Deke said, trying to encourage Lee in what was obviously his preference. "You don't need to impress the Boosters, and maybe you can get someone to sign it or something." Lee looked at him, flabbergasted. Deke had begun putting on his oversized suit like a man dressing for the gallows and motioned down at what he was going to wear, as if to say "see, it could be worse."

"Oh man! I totally forgot to get something for them to sign! I can't have them sign the jacket, it wouldn't take... I need..." Lee looked around the room frantically before going to his desk and feverishly shifting stuff around inside it.

"I think they'll have stuff there. Wouldn't be much of an athlete meet and greet if they didn't," Deke offered and Lee turned to him, eyes wide.

"I need to bring money! I should run to the ATM and get cash!" Lee's higher-than-usual voice made Deke shake his head.

"Nah, they'll have a full register. Just bring your wallet."

They made their way over to the Alumni House, a large estate on a cliff overlooking the ocean. It was one of the nicer places on campus, and Deke had to stop a nervous Lee from going back to take off his brown trench coat. Not only did they not have time, but if he really wanted to get rid of it, he could just coat check it. They were going to meet Abbie at the beginning of the path up to the mansion and were probably already late. Turning around the bend, Deke paused.

The girl waiting for them didn't look anything like the Abbie he had come to know. Her dress was a flowing A-line in a deep ocean blue, cut just below the knee. As she moved the fabric twisted, giving slight glimpses of her calves and the hint of a knee brace. Her hair, usually up in a ponytail, was a wave-tossed ocean against the blue of her dress. The figure she cut was so different from what he had been expecting that he just stopped in his tracks. He felt Lee bounce into him from behind but couldn't find it in him to be upset.

"What the hay, man?" Lee said, rubbing his face. The kid's PG swearing pulled Abbie's gaze over to them and she waved. That was enough to get Deke moving again and he looked at Lee.

"Sorry, got distracted," Deke muttered.

"I can see why," Lee whispered back as he too blinked at Abbie.

With Lee's comment, Deke looked down at his feet, suddenly feeling very underdressed in his too-large gray suit. Abbie started toward them and they met in the middle. "You clean up really well," Deke blurted out in greeting. Abbie gave him a once-over and then tsked.

"I want to say the same, but..." Abbie moved her arms out and for a second he thought she was going to give him a hug. "Can I fix this?" she asked, dashing his momentary hopes. Deke looked down at what she was indicating before nodding. She reached around his waist and pulled the fabric of his shirt tight, then folded it back and gave it a military tuck into the back of his pants.

Deke looked at Lee awkwardly even as the scent of Abbie's lavender perfume filled the air. Then she brushed his jacket shoulders back and stepped away. She pulled a hairpin out of her clutch—Deke studied her fancy style and noticed it matched those in her hair. She had it in some sort of central braiding. Abbie fixed his jacket cuff with the pin before stepping back to take in the completed picture again.

"Well, that's a lot better. You *almost* look like an eighties basketball star! I still watch replays of the players from that era." She gave him another once-over with her eyes, and Deke felt goosebumps prickle his skin at the appraisal. "I don't mind it!" She exclaimed with a slight smile while still looking at the suit. "I could let down the hem on these and my mom can probably take in the jacket a bit for next time—show off those muscles I know you have." Abbie hmmed to herself as she looked him over once more and then turned to Lee. "That's a great brown coat. You must be the smart one. Lee, right? I'm Abbie."

"I like your dress—let me guess, you saw the ruffles and couldn't say no?" Lee responded, and for some reason they both laughed. The sound startled Deke out of the confusion that Abbie's adjustment and subsequent statement had caused. Were those compliments, or just her assessment?

"I don't get it," Deke said, looking between the two of them, but that only made them laugh more. Deke smiled a bit seeing them having a good time. "Well, this already sounds like it's going to be a bust. Maybe I'll just go home and take these tickets with me..." Deke threatened, pulling the tickets out of his pocket and fanning them out to wave in the air as he pretended to turn away.

"Deke Mills, don't you dare. Do you have any idea how long it took me to get ready for this?" Abbie glared at him, one hand on her hip. "If you walk away without letting me show off all this work I will make those workouts I gave you feel like a sweet dream compared to the pain I'll put you through." While Abbie spoke, Lee reached out to grab the tickets out of Deke's hand. But the system jittered for a moment, and he instinctively followed along, straightening his arm, keeping the tickets out of reach of the much shorter kid.

"Fine, fine." Deke chuckled and turned back before handing Abbie her ticket. Moving to put the other ticket back in his pocket while he glared at Lee. Abbie took the ticket and then handed it to Lee before holding her hand out expectantly. Deke coughed and pulled the second one out and handed it over. "That's not fair. Two against one."

"I think they call it a double-team in your sport. You should be used to it, champ." Abbie winked as she smiled back. The moment dragged for a second as Deke couldn't help but stare at her smile.

"All right, let's go do this," Lee said, and he held out an arm to Abbie. "Miss Abbie, if you would join me?"

Abbie slipped her arm through Lee's with a grin. The two turned and walked up the path, leaving Deke behind. "It would be my greatest pleasure, Sir Lee."

"Wait for me!" Deke cursed, his longer legs easily catching up with the two. Abbie turned and grinned at him, holding her other arm out for Deke to join them. Deke slipped his arm in and the trio made their way up the path. Abbie didn't let him go as they handed their tickets to the attendant and the three made their way around the building to the open grassy area behind the alumni house. Still arm in arm, they turned around the corner where a few dozen people were mingling around a set of white tables.

The backyard was ringed by paper lanterns hanging from thin white metal frames above their heads. The metal was in a boxy pattern but high enough that Deke didn't think he could have touched it even with a jump. Each lantern hung from some sort of wire that was wrapped around the metal. The tables had long white cloths that hung off them almost to the floor, and each one was about four and a half feet above the ground with no chairs, clearly meant for a standing gathering.

Deke was surprised to see Valerie standing with several old men and women. She was wearing a skin-tight, scarlet, knee-length dress with a slit on the front that exposed twice as much leg as Abbie's. Deke would have to be a complete idiot to not see her, since she was glaring at him from across the space. Immediately Deke pulled his arm away from Abbie like he had been burned, but Valerie just continued to glare.

"I uh, need to go make the rounds," Deke said when Abbie and Lee both looked at his jerky motion. "You guys probably wanna go talk to the actors anyway. I'm supposed to talk to the Boosters." He forced a smile as he gestured over to the table where the cast members were all sitting and signing posters or copies of the movie. Their smiles returned twice as big and they headed that way, wishing him luck as an afterthought. He watched them go, shaking his head and smiling.

The smile fell as he scanned back to Valerie, who was still stabbing him with her eyes. Something told him that she wouldn't appreciate him trying to explain the situation right now. Deke hoped she would understand when he explained that it was just a friend thing. Looking around the crowd, he saw Director Rooney, his bright red hair like a beacon in the setting sun. Next to him stood a large man, large even by Deke's standards; he was wearing black sunglasses and Deke froze. The muscular man stuffed into a tuxedo reminded him of the vaping man. After a moment Deke shook his head, trying to build up his confidence. He was probably just some sort of security guard. He really wanted to get over there to feel out the director. That was the only man who could overrule Doctor Dan, after all.

Making his way through the crowd, he was interrupted as Duke and a tall brunette with olive skin, wearing an orange cocktail dress, stepped up next to him.

"Mills! It's good to see you, kid." Duke held out a hand to Deke and the two large players gave a one-armed hug in the middle of the crowd. "I don't think you and Eva have met yet." Duke turned and introduced him to his girlfriend.

"Oh, we have," Deke muttered. Eva was the woman that he'd met at the top of the stairs to the second floor of Winchester Hall, and she'd called the cops on him.

"Hey, I'm really sorry about last time," Eva said, holding out a hand for Deke to shake. "I got the full story from Valerie afterward, but we had to keep up appearances for the older sisters. Otherwise I'd have Panhellenic down on me. I did manage to convince them to just take you off the Row. Hopefully they didn't scare you too badly?" Deke glanced over, but Rooney and the guard were already gone. He sighed, not seeing a quick way out of this conversation and with the director already missing, he realized he'd rather spend time with Duke than any of the Boosters.

"It was fine, they just conned me into doing some community service. But I've actually really enjoyed going to the center so I guess I can't really be mad at *you*." After being reminded of that day, Deke took the opportunity to visit his own glare toward Valerie, who was now pointedly looking away from him.

"Ouch, you piss her off again?" Eva asked, following his line of sight.

"I think it's mutual. I brought one of the trainers and my roommate to this thing. They were goofing off and we were interlocking arms when we came in," Deke muttered and Eva ooh'd in dismay.

"Did you manage to get that fox Abbie to come?" Duke asked with mock excitement, and Eva punched him in the arm. Duke chuckled good naturedly, and tilted his head in Eva's direction, giving Deke a "see what I have to deal with" expression. Deke smiled and Eva shook her head at them both.

"Thick as thieves!" She mock-exclaimed, but then softened her tone to look back at Deke. "Valerie is a little territorial, doubly so right now. Given that she's here with her dad," Eva explained. "I'll try and lay some groundwork, which should at least give you a chance to explain yourself."

"Thanks, I'd really appreciate that." Deke finally set aside his anger about the girl in question not sticking up for him that day on

Frat Row. Valerie was still not looking in his direction. "Looks like I'll need all the help I can get."

"Hey no problem, it's the least I can do after that whole... almost getting you arrested thing," Eva said with a smile.

"How's the leg?" Duke asked. "I know you've been walking around without your crutches but you don't seem to be favoring it at all since you got here."

"Leg's great," Deke said and to his surprise, a rotund man whose hair was graying at the temples pushed between him and Duke.

"Your leg does indeed look better. No crutches or anything. When are we going to see you playing again? I'd like to get some more dubs in before we get too much further into the season." The man stood uncomfortably close to Deke, looking him up and down. Deke couldn't help but feel a bit like a piece of livestock being evaluated for auction.

"Uh, I don't know, Mr..." Deke trailed off, hoping the man would introduce himself. He shot a look over to Duke and saw the large center backing away slowly. Like prey trying to go unnoticed. Deke felt sweat break out under his armpits.

"Fisher. Grant Fisher, class of '87." The rotund man flashed a class ring he still clearly wore proudly as he stuck his stubby hand into Deke's dwindling personal bubble for him to shake.

Deke took the hand, realizing only afterward that Duke was giving him the "Good luck, I'm out of here" sign. A part of him wanted to shout Duke's name to pull attention away from himself, but the session with Dr. Pinsonneault was fresh in his mind, so he only gritted his teeth. The man's hand was slick with sweat, and Deke felt like he'd just dunked his hand in a glass of water. Grant Fisher clamped on, his sausage fingers not letting go of Deke's as he pumped up and down repeatedly. Despite the sweat, Deke was unable to recover his hand from the man.

"Like I said, I'm all better, but we're still waiting on Dr. Dan to clear me for play." Deke took a half step back, trying to get his hand away, but the man followed him. He realized that he likely shouldn't be sharing his dirty laundry with the man, but simultaneously it was the truth and not something that would cause trouble.

"Wonderful! That's wonderful news, Deke. You don't mind if I call you Deke, do you? Excellent, come with me Deke, we're going to talk to Director Rooney about getting you cleared." Fisher swiveled, far too light on his feet for his mass, and pulled Deke after him through the crowd, calling out Director Rooney's name loudly. Heads turned in their direction as Deke tried to shoot a call for help to Duke but the big center himself was cornered by another Booster. Their eyes met and Deke saluted in solidarity. Misery loves company.

Fisher dragged him back and forth across the lawn three times before Deke finally managed to extricate himself, saying that he needed to use the restroom. The director was nowhere to be found, and from the sound of it, Grant Fisher was going to rather strongly inform him how unacceptable that was, which Deke wanted no part of. He needed Director Rooney's help, not his animosity. Deke did, however, wonder just how much money Fisher had to donate to the school to justify that kind of entitlement. A million? Ten?

He slipped into the house and climbed the stairs, since he found the first floor bathrooms occupied. He moved up another floor and found the bathroom there available. He washed the clammy sweat off his hands as he took in his appearance in the mirror. Abbie really had made him look much more presentable... he wouldn't quite go as far as to say *good* but... acceptable. He looked at the counter and wondered why there were three shells sitting between the two sinks.

"Rich people are weird," Deke muttered to himself before heading out. He heard Lee's distinctive laughter and followed the sound to a second-story balcony. Abbie and Lee had both retreated there and were loudly quoting what Deke assumed was Firebug.

They had commandeered a bench and Abbie must have stolen a tray of the finger foods, which they were eating from between quotes. Deke sat down on the reclining deck chair across from them and grabbed the tray.

"Hey! That's mine, I stole it fair and square!" Abbie cried out in alarm when she saw him. "Give it back!"

"You can't steal what's already stolen," Deke said as he grabbed a weird puffball-looking thing and shoved it in his mouth.

Lee playfully snatched up a puffball and gave Deke a mock stern look. "You turn on any of my crew, you turn on me!" The comment and confidence seemed out of place until Abbie laughed heartily.

"That's a good one!" she said, and Deke understood it was a quote from Firebug as he joined in on the laughing. Maybe he could hide up here for the rest of the night. Nothing crazy ever happens at these parties, anyway.

TWENTY-SIX

TUESDAY, NOVEMBER 22

> "What the shit?! Do you SEE this asshole making eyes at another girl"- Valerie

"I thought he was just a bit of fun on the side? You catching feelings?"- Big Sis Eva

> "Whatever you know I like him, stop it... What's with the bitch in the brace?"- Valerie

"Relax gurl. He told me she's one of the team trainers!- Big Sis Eva

Deke got around to finally trying to approach Director Rooney five days later. As much as Grant Fisher wasn't the most hygienic man to be snatched by at the Booster event, he did make a good point and hopefully, a case to Director Rooney on Deke's behalf. Or at least, that was what he told himself as he and Lee walked into the Athletic Department and steered toward the man's office. His roommate was here to push him forward if he thought about backing out.

The athletic department was inside the Athletic Building, and was behind a glass wall covered in decals of the Baguette logo and some older players who had long since graduated. It was probably due for a change but the team needed to have a few accolades and standout players before that happened. Behind the wall and a desk with an attendant were multiple cubicles and stations for staff. There was a walkway between the greeting desk and the glass that led to a true hallway lined with offices. The setup reminded Deke of a high school office in Canada, but with far nicer equipment and decor.

The entire room was in alternating school colors and Lee marveled at it as Deke approached Sara. "Deke Mills!" she chirped brightly. "What brings you into the Athletic Department? And who is your friend?"

"Hey Sara, this is Lee, my roommate. I was hoping I could talk to Director Rooney about something..." Deke began looking over at Lee, who was nodding along as Deke ripped the proverbial band-aid off. Still, Deke never finished the thought and eventually faded off because as he looked back at Sara, he could hear Director Rooney shouting.

"The money's already been spent, you can't ask for a donation back—" Deke followed the noise and could see a shadow pacing behind a large window with the blinds pulled. "—that's why they call it a donation!" There was a short pause, in which everyone in the office stared at the window and seemed to hold their breath. "I don't care how big the donation was, you don't get a say in what players can or can't do, much less the team for that matter!"

Lee coughed into his hand and Deke remembered to breathe. "You know what Sara, this seems like a bad time. It can wait."

Together Lee and Deke fled the Athletic Department, not even waiting for a response from the assistant. As soon as they rounded the nearest corner Lee asked, "Was that the director? He seemed pissed! Do you think he was talking to that Fisher guy?"

"I sure hope not!" Deke continued to jog at a slow pace to ensure Lee could keep up with him. "I mean all I was going to ask him was why I couldn't play. Then hope he asked if I was cleared and drug-free..."

"Pigu! That was definitely not the right time," Lee said, using the same swear he and Abbie had repeated numerous times during the night of the Booster Event. Deke shook his head at their newfound friendship. He swore the kid texted Abbie more than he personally did Valerie. Not that Valerie had forgiven him for bringing Abbie to the event yet. "We can try again next week. I'm actually kind of surprised he was in his office at all."

"Right, Thanksgiving!" Deke began to slow as they neared the dorms. "I always forget that Americans celebrate Thanksgiving now, and not in October."

"Do you have plans?" Lee asked quietly, and Deke shook his head. "Do you want to come to my place maybe? It isn't a traditional meal but it's better than spending it alone in the dorms with a pizza..."

"Dude, that would be awesome! Plus you know I don't have money for pizza!"

Thursday, November 24

"Lei says you are quite intelligent, you should go into med school, like him. It's the most well-respected career one can hold," Mrs. Wett said proudly to Deke, and he swallowed the delicious Peking Duck that was in his mouth in preparation for an answer. Thankfully he was saved because Mrs. Wett turned to her son. "That reminds me. What pre-med courses did you sign up for next semester, Lei?"

The way his mother pronounced the name clearly indicated that his friend had anglicized it at some point for those around him. It was Lee's turn to swallow his food and blush slightly as he took a sip of water. "Mom, we have company. I can tell you about this after he leaves. Also, I told you, Deke is going to go to the NBA! I'm pretty sure athletes make more than doctors."

"Until they need a doctor to heal from a career-ending injury! Everyone needs doctors, Lei," Mrs. Wett scolded her son but didn't bring up the courses again. From Lee's relieved face, he had won a small victory with that. "Deke, your mother probably tells you all this, but make sure to come out of school with a degree in case that sport you play hurts you."

Lee eyed Deke nervously, clearly embarrassed by his mother's forwardness. Deke smiled back at Mr. and Mrs. Wett, including Lee in the gesture as well. He didn't mind in the least. How could he be angry with her clear concern for a friend of her son? Not to mention, with the strange sports drink, he didn't think an injury was as much of a threat to him as to other athletes. "I will Mrs. Wett." Turning to Mr. Wett, he changed the subject. "What do you do, Mr. Wett?"

"I work for IBN and am head of server integration," he responded proudly. Deke listened intently as the man described some of the problems they were facing with downsizing and the like. IBN clearly wasn't the large market entity it had once been, but according to Mr. Wett, the company was on its way to specializing in offshore server hosting.

Lee and Deke were clearing the plates from the table when Deke suddenly punched Lee in the arm. "I thought you said your dad barely spoke English! You made it sound like he was fresh off the boat with all that 'why you no doctor' bullshit."

Lee laughed good naturedly. "You believed that? Damn Deke, in that case I've got a bridge to sell you."

Deke stepped forward to escalate the matter when his phone began buzzing. He placed his load of dishes on the beautiful black granite counter as he pulled it out to check the caller. It was his mom, and he showed it to Lee before excusing himself. He walked out of the sliding door of the luxurious kitchen and onto a back deck that overlooked a well maintained backyard with an infinity pool before accepting the call.

"Happy American Thanksgiving, Mom!" Deke said overly cheerfully, hoping to start the conversation on a good foot. Sometimes his mom's attitude highly depended on those around her. Turns out he didn't need to worry.

"It's Max!" his brother crowed into the phone, reciprocating Deke's own energy.

"Maxie!" Deke perked up and began to pace, as speaking to his little brother seemed to feed him energy through the phone. "I'm so glad you called, kid, how's everything on the home front?"

"It's awesome, Deke! I've been watching a ton of games, Mom allowed me to stay up late and watch some west coast games on the new TV channels. There's some good players in your league—none as good as you of course, but it's exciting. I keep telling Mom that I'll be able to dunk a basketball one day, since you promised."

"Of course you will bud. When you grow up you're going to be better than me. Just wait..." Deke encouraged that dream with as much earnestness as he could squeeze into those words. He noticed his eyes starting to water and changed the subject to a safer one. "I'm all better now. The doctor's tests have cleared me, so I should be able to start practicing soon!"

"Can I come to watch one of your games like we planned, then?" Max exclaimed through the microphone.

"It's a long way, kiddo, those flights would be too expensive for Mom. Remember the plan was for me to make Mercenary March, 'cause this year it's in Syracuse. That's drivable for Mom..."

"I guess I can watch it on the Super Sports package till then. Once you're back on the team, you're sure to be in some games! Right bro?" Max said, his excitement not waning at all. Deke smiled while simultaneously feeling his gut wrench sideways. He still hadn't figured out a way to have Doctor Dan overturn his stubborn decision. Deke's jaw firmed as his resolve steeled once more.

"You bet bud, you just wait and see."

Deke was running on the beach. After the Lee family's Thanksgiving dinner and his brief chat with Max, he had excused himself to allow them to have the rest of the evening together. With nothing better to do, he was taking a late-night run on the slowly cooling sands near the dorms. It was strange how much the beach seemed to change under the soft, luminous light of the moon instead of the intense white of the sun. He could see groups of teenagers ringing fire pits far off in the distance and had even run past a few other such gatherings already. The way the kids had eyed him made him think the fires weren't allowed and they were worried he was some sort of law enforcement. He considered running up to one of the groups and pretending to be a cop to bust their balls, but his chat with his little brother and worry over his current circumstances robbed him of any playful mood.

At first, the night air had felt slightly chilly, but now with his body sweating it just felt refreshing. His headphones were playing the newest Drake but suddenly cut off, and he jumped as his ringtone blared into his ears.

"Hello?" he asked after wincing and tapping the answer button that hung around his neck. He kept running as he went.

"That doesn't sound like a very enthusiastic greeting for the best girlfriend ever!" Valerie's voice mock-scolded from the other side of the line.

"I'm out for a run, so my phone is in my shorts, I didn't know it was you. Plus I thought you weren't talking to me," he accused back, adding the same level of accusation she had a moment before.

"Oh so you're already all sweaty, I guess you don't need my help..." she faded off suggestively and he smiled as he continued to jog. "Wait, even that offer didn't stop your jog?" she whined playfully.

"I thought you liked my heavy breathing?" He answered with something equally playful when he heard distant shouting conveyed through the microphone. This time he did stop running. "What's that? Are you okay over there?"

"I'm fine. My parents are celebrating Thanksgiving!" She groaned in exasperation, her voice going from playful to slightly depressed in Deke's ears. "That's why I called, do you have plans tonight? I need to get out of here."

"No plans."

"Awesome, you want to swing by and pick me up?"

"In what car?" Deke asked, returning to laughing a little bit at her assumption.

"You're kidding, right? Never mind, don't answer that; I don't want to know. I'll pick you up at your dorms. You're such a loser... It's a good thing you got a cute butt."

He had just enough time to shower, change and get back downstairs. When he got there he found a tiny Barbie car waiting for him. He stared at the two-seater Miata that Valerie sat in, looking impatient. Of course, it was a bright candy-apple red with leather interior and a convertible top. He hesitated for a split second, trying to determine if he could even fit into the vehicle, but chose not to complain. At least she'd dropped the top, and it wasn't like he was in a position to grouse about the fit.

Instead, he walked up and bent nearly double to reach the door handle from the raised sidewalk, and attempted to sit. He pulled the handle to slide the seat back as far as it would go and managed to get his shoes into the space under the glove box and his butt almost to the seat cushion before he paused and just blinked over at Val.

"Baby, this car may be the only thing smaller than you!" he teased as he settled as deep into the seat as he could and put on his seatbelt. His entire head was still fully above the windshield.

"Which one are you complaining about?" Valerie asked while

biting her lip, making her meaning clear. Deke scratched at his head and swallowed the drool that flooded his mouth.

"You know parking is just around the corner, right?"

"I'm in the mood to loosen up a bit first..."

She slammed her foot down on the gas and Deke felt his head, well above the headrest, jerk back before he had time to react. He tried to respond and might have even screamed a few times as Valerie wove in and out of traffic as if her Barbie toy was some sort of sports car, but luckily, if he did, the wind carried it away. When they pulled up to a very seedy-looking bar, Deke didn't have any drool left, or moisture in his eyeballs for that matter.

"You brought a fake, right?" Valerie asked and at Deke's head shake, she scoffed. "You really are a huge loser. Don't worry, I know the staff. Let's go!" Valerie hopped out of the car and Deke began disentangling himself from the car's interior.

"Why doesn't it surprise me that you 'know the staff' here?" Deke griped as he took in her outfit for the first time.

He'd noticed her red tank top before, but couldn't have seen the open back that literally seemed to expose the entire lines and curves of her graceful figure from waist to neck. There was just a tiny piece of the fabric showing just above her jeans, which seemed to be tight enough that Deke actually wondered how she was walking. Especially in her stiletto high heels that he estimated were nearing three inches.

"Damn girl! You look scrumptious!" Deke called out to Valerie.

"Hold that thought for dessert," Valerie said with a sly grin and half turn.

Deke hurried to catch up as she sashayed toward the bouncers and line at the front door. The bar looked more like a diner, or maybe a strip club, with its tinted black windows and two metallic swinging doors. It definitely wasn't a traditional club though, because the music inside couldn't be heard as they continued their approach.

Instead of heading to the line, Valerie walked straight up to a beefy man who was probably half a foot shorter than Deke. "Hey

Spence, can me and my friend head in for a drink?" she asked with the same playfulness she'd just directed at Deke in her best good-girl-gone-bad voice.

"You know it!" Spence said excitedly, but his glare at Deke gave away the actual status of his friendship with Valerie. Deke managed a half-grin at the man as Valerie practically towed him inside. As they moved to a table, he watched the heads of guys and girls turn to follow Val's bouncing assets. He sure was lucky...

"I'll have a whiskey—straight," Valerie ordered a server as they passed her. Deke blinked at Valerie and then the server, who looked at him.

"Umm, just some Sprite if you have it," Deke mumbled as he tried to catch up to his girl. How she was walking so fast with such tiny legs and heels he didn't know, but he kept his eyes firmly on her behind, sure that the answer would present itself sooner or later.

TWENTY-SEVEN

TUESDAY, DECEMBER 13TH

"The board is very unhappy with the team. We need to put in a good showing against the Diablos."- President Marsh

"What am I supposed to do Doug? Go over Skip's head?"- Ed Rooney-UCSP Athletic Director

"The board wants a win, I don't care how we get it."- President Marsh

December in California wasn't anything like December at home. Max had sent pictures of the snow months ago. The weather in Ontario was reaching just below freezing at its peak, and that was on a warm day. In California it was still shorts weather, although you did need to bring a jacket if you were going to be out after dark.

Yet that humid heat made the sports jacket and slacks Deke currently wore all the more uncomfortable, especially in the stifling gym. Today they were playing the Diablos, the team from the other side of the valley, and the Baguettes' rivals. The pressure while the clock was ticking was at an all-time high for his team, thanks in large part to the entire staff stressing the whole week how badly they needed this win.

Despondent, Deke watched the opponent's Devil Chicken mascot fight with the Baguette. There was an absurdity to the fight and the losing score that made him shake his head and sigh. Deke tore his eyes off the mock combat and followed the rest of the team into the locker room. Valerie winked at him as they passed each other and Deke felt a momentary pang. He would much prefer to watch her bounce around at halftime than hear the coach's tirade he was sure was a locker room door away.

Deke sat down next to his locker while all the players who were uniformed sat on the main bench around Skip. He eyed his own uniform in his locker, denied to him but still tantalizingly hung up in case he might need it. Some part of him was listening to Skip denounce the starting players, asking if they were even paying attention to the strategy meeting yesterday. But Deke's eyes wouldn't leave the jersey in his locker; he let them drift to the picture of him and Valerie at the theme park she had taken him to last weekend. He had balked at the price at first but she had insisted on paying for him, claiming Daddy owed her. It was a particularly bright memory that kept him going even through moments like this, that made him feel so hopeless. What could he do?

"Duke, you're not boxing out their center. And after a stop you need to get up the floor faster while keeping your head up on those fast breaks. We need to stop missing the easy buckets, boys," Skip continued talking as Deke forced his attention from his locker to the rest of the team. Duke and the rest of the starters looked tired—they had been playing nearly the entire twenty-minute half and it showed. Most had their heads down as they listened to the coach's words. Mac looked worse than the rest, as his hair was soaked and he leaned against his locker with his eyes shut.

"Manny, we need you to play both ends, you're lagging behind on defense and they're getting—" Skip was addressing the forward when a door slammed on the far side of the locker room. Shocked silence struck Deke out of his haze as everyone turned to look at who would dare interrupt Coach Skip like that. Director Rooney was marching through the locker room, his face red and his cheeks puffed out.

"Down by ten at the half!" Rooney shouted at Skip even as several of the assistant coaches moved between the two.

"Director Rooney, you cannot be in here right now." Skip's voice rose to match the director's even as the assistant coaches held out their hands to block Rooney.

"If you want a job next year, you're going to sit down. It's my turn to talk." Rooney glared daggers at the two assistant coaches. "And if you two so much as touch me, you'll be packing it in tonight!" The two men stepped aside hurriedly as Rooney stormed into the rubber-tiled area, and stopped by the press of the crowd right next to Deke. Skip crossed his arms and looked down his nose at the shorter man.

"Directory Rooney, you're distracting my players. If we're going to turn this around I need to discuss our second half strategy with my team."

"*Your* team? HAH!" Spit flew from Rooney's mouth as he shouted, splattering over Deke's face. Deke grimaced and wiped his cheek. Rooney's eyes were drawn to the movement and he looked down at Deke who was still sitting. "Look at *your team*! This kid? We gave him a full ride scholarship and he's just sitting there in a blazer not even playing after one good preseason performance!" Deke held back a growl as he stood up, he was almost a full head taller than the director and he used his height to his advantage, looming over the other man.

"I'm perfectly healthy and could play anytime you clear me," Deke growled, meeting the director's eyes. Rooney blinked, then his eyes roved over the room until they landed on Doctor Dan.

"Is that true? Can he play?" the director asked. Dan looked uncomfortable for a moment.

"He's passed all the tests we've given him," Dan said after a few moments of tense silence.

"Then he's playing, right damned now," Rooney said, glaring at Dan and then shifting to look past Deke at Coach Skip, daring the man to challenge his decision.

"He's not even on the roster tonight, Directory Rooney, I think we should—" Skip was making his way through the mass of players to Rooney, clearly trying to defuse the situation.

"You. Get dressed, or uniformed up. Whatever you meatheads call it. You better turn this around," Rooney said, poking Deke in the chest and then turning and storming into Skip's office. By the time Skip got to Deke he sighed, looking at the freshman. There was a moment where their eyes met and Deke wasn't sure if he should be ecstatic or apologetic. His earlier response had been out of anger at the director's accusation...

"Mills, get dressed, I'll try and sort this out. I don't know if there's precedent for adding someone to a roster mid-game, but I'm sure we'll find out in about five minutes." Skip walked away and Dan followed Rooney as well. Deke immediately began shrugging out of his blazer and unbuttoning his shirt like they were on fire, wanting to be in uniform before anyone changed their minds. His belt and pants followed shortly after as he rushed to get changed. Muffled shouting could be heard even after they shut the door but Deke just focused on pulling on his kit as fast as he could. The other players remained silent as they tried to overhear what the director and coach were saying. A few people glanced at Deke but the majority of the team seemed relieved.

Deke was just putting on his shoes when Abbie appeared next to him and held out a black piece of contoured plastic.

"Wear the brace, it'll help smooth things over with Dan and Skip," she whispered, kneeling down to help him pull the support up his leg. "Are you sure you're up for this?" Abbie's voice was quiet, but in the silence of the locker room Deke was sure everyone could hear it.

"I'm fine, you know that. My knee has never been better," Deke reassured her as he helped pull the brace into place around his knee and then put on his shoes. He kicked out a few times with his knee to get used to the restriction on his movement the brace made, and then finally turned to the rest of the team.

"It's fine guys. I'm really all healed up. You've seen me doing my workouts in the corner of the gym during practices. I'll be fine," Deke explained. Duke was standing next to him and looked him up and down.

"Well, it's a bit unconventional. But I guess you're finally back on the team full time. I think I speak for us all when I say: Welcome back, man." Duke held out his hand to shake Deke's. "We could really use the help. Those guys have our number." Duke pulled him over to the rest of the starters and nodded toward Mac. "Mac, you've been playing the most minutes. My guess is they'll start Deke..." Duke settled into an easy and natural rhythm as he took over for Coach and went on to explain a few strategic changes he wanted to make now that Deke was in the game.

A few minutes later, Skip and Rooney stepped out of the office. The director shot Deke a glance to make sure he was in uniform but otherwise didn't say anything as he stormed out of the room. Rooney's face was a pale white now, which was a stark contrast to the puffy red from earlier. Deke could tell by the set of his jaw and his lowered brow that he was still angry, but what had the coach and doctor said to the man to hollow him out like that?

"Against my better judgement, the director has made it clear that Mills should be allowed to play if he wants to. Somehow he's 'already on the roster'," Skip said, having waited for Rooney to leave before he addressed the team again. The way he enunciated the final sentence made Deke acutely aware that he disagreed with something that Rooney was going to do. "Deke, if you're hurt at all, this is your last chance to step down. Don't ruin your body for this, you've got plenty of playing time left. A whole career ahead of you."

"It's fine, Coach. My leg is healed, it's been healed for a while now. I'm ready to play," Deke responded, and Skip let out a heavy sigh.

"Well, I can't say that isn't the response I was expecting. Still be careful, and let me know if it hurts at all. This is still my team, I don't care what the director says." When Deke nodded his head enthusiastically to the coach he sighed again, "All right you lot. We still have a game to finish. And it'd go a long way for all of us if we could squeeze a win out of this one. Everyone bow your heads." Deke and the rest of the players followed his command and the coach said a quick prayer, ending it with one of his typical scriptures. "Let us run with endurance, the challenge that is set before us.

"And kick some devil ass." As Skip said those words, the team all cheered. "All right, let's get out there!"

The whole group began filing out of the locker room. Just before Deke left, he turned back to glance at Abbie and she gave him a smile and an encouraging thumbs up. He returned both gestures and then followed his team out to the court for the first time in months. Deke's eyes lidded, half-closed as he took it all in. The low mutterings of the crowd as it echoed off of the halls leading to the court; the chirp of his well-worn sneakers as he walked the once familiar surface of the polished floor; the jarring smell of popcorn mixed with that of bodies pressed close out of necessity, and the rising tide of the storm wall of emotion that threatened to drown his sense of self as he took it all in with a deep, steady breath. He was going to be playing the game again, and he couldn't help but smile. Just before the door closed behind him, his revelry was shattered in an ice-cold realization as he turned around hurriedly. Shit! He needed to tell his brother he was going to be playing.

He rushed to his locker, past Dan and Abbie who were clearly talking about him, and sent a quick message before hurrying back out to catch up to the tail end of the team.

Clearing the tunnel, he passed Valerie who gave him a shocked look and mouthed, "WTF?" Deke just gave her a winning smile, put one arm around her waist and twisted her into a kiss before letting her down again.

"I'll explain after, gotta go win a game!" Deke called out as he hustled to catch back up with the team, listening to the crowd and the announcer.

"Well, in a surprising turn, it seems that the Baguettes have been saving rookie Deke Mills as their secret weapon. This may be the first time we've seen number forty-two dressed since the preseason. Deke has been on the bench recovering from a torn ACL. But it looks like the Baguettes had him on the roster and are pulling out all the stops for this one! Is this the turning point for the Baguettes, or is it a case of too little, too late? Stay tuned folks, because I feel like things are about to heat up in the second half!"

CHAPTER

TWENTY-EIGHT

TUESDAY, DECEMBER 13TH

"I'm going to play tonight."- Dekester

"Tonight? I thought the game already
started."- Rhonda Mills

"I'll let Max know."- Rhonda Mills

"OMG I'm so excited -max"- Rhonda Mills

"Just a minute here folks! Not only is number forty-two dressing, it appears that Deke Mills is going to be starting the second half!" The announcer shouted into the stadium. Deke was walking away from the bench and could feel Mac's eyes boring into his back, but he was too engrossed taking in the scene.

The lights seemed brighter and the floor far shinier than during the practice times they were allotted in here. They were also using the central court, which was only ever used at the end of the practices for scrimmages between the starters and the bench. Deke had only ever been allowed to watch from the sidelines for the last three months during those, if he was even in the gym and not downstairs getting physio. He moved smoothly over the large black sideline and

241

onto the floor, the crowd humming with energy around him. He kissed the back of his thumb and touched it to his thumping heart.

Tim took the ball and got ready to inbound it from the sideline. Since the possession arrow was facing the Baguettes, they would start this half with the inbound. Deke got into position leaning into the opposing team's shooting guard.

"So, the bread boys are so desperate they're playing a gimp?" the opposing player chirped in his ear, and Deke couldn't help the smile that came to his lips. He had missed this!

Tim managed to inbound the pass to an open Duke on the Baguettes' side of half. Duke didn't even bother dribbling and quickly shuffle-passed it backward to Arthur, who caught it and began dribbling up the floor. Just as he was crossing the half, he held up two fingers above his head.

This indicated a set play where Deke needed to screen down and then cut to the basket along the baseline. Arthur passed the ball to Duke on the other side of the formation as he sprang free to the edge of the key, and Duke looked to both of the crossers on the baseline, but the zone defense of the Devils did a good job picking up both Deke and Little Tim as they crossed through.

Duke was about to look for the reset, as the big man was outside his optimal shooting range, when Deke's defender moved to double-team Duke instead of following Deke. Taking the opportunity, Deke shifted over to the corner as Duke passed him the ball. His court awareness had him take a half step back over the three point line. Deke took half a second to line up [Aim Assist] before releasing a wide-open three. It drained through the center of the hoop, barely touching the net as the crowd roared with approval.

"We've got a game here, folks! Mills cuts the lead to eight, with a wide-open three. It seems this kid has not let his edge dull at all during his recovery," the announcer voiced to the crowd as Deke sprinted back to the other side of the court. Duke, who was the leader on defense, held up a five. This meant man coverage, and so Deke marked number twenty-three on the other side. The same kid who had beaked at him. Deke wasn't sure how his brace would affect his lateral movement on defense and so gave the kid a cushion, which would also dare him to shoot a three. This was somewhat in the game plan from the previous night. While number twenty-three was a good field goal shooter, his percentage steeply dropped off behind the arc. The tactics of the game demanded you both know and play the odds.

The Diablos began running an offense and Deke shadowed twenty-three, trying to keep one eye on the ball and one on his man. A poor pass resulted in the opposing team's center fumbling the rock and it bouncing out of bounds for a turnover. Deke smiled as he rushed back up the court, leaving the inbound pass for Manny. "Mills, help him out! They're pressing!"

The coach's shout shook Deke as he recalled he was the relief on a full-court press. He spun and moved back to receive the inbound pass. He dribbled up the floor, turning his defender back and forth until the double-team arrived, trying to force a ten second violation. Deke then passed it off to Arthur. The point guard managed to cross the half on his dribble, which released the pressure of the opposing team and Arthur quickly flashed a one, this time. This was a play to isolate Mac—wait... isolate *Deke* for a three from the wing to the left of the line.

Deke moved through the midfield, pivoting to plant himself, screening so that Little Tim could play off him and back away from the top of the key. The ball was passed to Manny on the wing of that side and Deke sprinted to the baseline and circled around the defense on the other side of the ball. Arthur cut toward the basket, which collapsed the Diablos in toward him as the point guard looked for a return pass from Manny: the power forward.

As soon as the defenders moved on Arthur, Manny reversed the ball to Deke as he popped out behind the three-line, wide open—again! With [Aim Assist] Deke lined up his shot and let fly. This one drilled in off the inside of the rim for another three-point play.

"Like a surgeon, the rookie, Deke Mills cuts the lead to five! Get loud folks, we can't hear you from down here!" The commenter was standing, egging on the throng, as the students in the crowd waved flags and cupped their hands to their mouths, screaming and cheering with enthusiasm.

Deke sprinted back as he felt his heart soar. He was doing it. This was going to be a career-high kind of night, he could feel it. He stuck to the game plan on the man coverage and let number twenty-three shoot a retaliatory three from a meter behind the arc. He could tell that the guy was agitated by Deke's two made threes and wanted to take it back. Unfortunately—for him—it wasn't to be. The rim reverberated as the high-arced shot slammed into the back of the rim and back up into the air. Duke, Little Tim, and two of the opposing team fought for the rebound and a swatting hand sent the ball toward Arthur, who won the foot race with the opposing point guard and began dribbling up the court.

The opposing team was full-court pressing again, and so Deke was passed the ball once the defenders double-teamed Arthur. Deke crossed the half, which meant he was supposed to call the play. He held up a four, which was calling for a drive and dish to Duke. He watched his team begin moving into position as number twenty-three came out to guard him. The other team was no longer in a zone, and was now playing man to man. He should probably make a change to the play—

"Shoot it, you piece of shit. Luck don't last forever!" Number twenty-three raged out in front of him, giving him a four-foot cushion. It was the same separation Deke had given the opposing player, and he could tell that the kid wasn't happy about missing his own shot.

Number twenty-three wanted some revenge—instead of changing the play, Deke pulled up three meters behind the arc and jumped, fading out his third three-pointer attempt. His brace squeaked in protest but Deke ignored it, feeling far too good about the green line that hung between him and the basket. As soon as he released he looked the kid in the face and winked, the wrist of his releasing hand still hanging limp as he continued to hold the pose of his shot, in a mocking salute. The ball traveled right on the [Aim Assist] path and sank home with a satisfying swish.

His stupid brace squeaked on landing too, ruining the moment, but so far it hadn't seemed to limit him too much. So, he ran back up the court clenching his teeth with each hyena-like squeal the stupid thing made.

"That's nine points in three possessions! Where have they been hiding this kid?" The announcer celebrated with Deke as the refs blew their whistle. "The Diablos seem to want to regroup after their lead is cut to two. Thirty-second timeout!"

Deke walked to the bench, his skin was tingling with sensation, the heat of victory flushing it like a warm kiss. This feeling...this feeling was something he needed in his life. Number twenty-three wanted the smoke, and he was going to give it to him for the rest of the game. Coach Skip waited till the starting five were sitting on the bench, which took a bit longer than usual, as each person wanted to pat Deke on the back and exclaim something celebratory.

"They moved to man! This is what we were waiting for. As long as Mills is a threat from behind the arc they will be forced to spread out and stick close. This should open up our big men down low. This is what we've been waiting for!" Skip crowed at his team and Deke looked around. Their energy was completely renewed and each member looked to be ready for a war. Except for Mac, whose eyes never left Deke. The glare wasn't comfortable but Deke tried to let it slide off his shoulders. It wasn't his problem that he was in Mac's starting spot right now—that had been the coach's decision. Or maybe Rooney's, he supposed.

They took back to the floor and Deke found he had a new player to guard. Number twenty-three was on the bench and in his place was a smaller Latino guy wearing number eighty-two. The call was still man coverage and Deke stuck on number eighty-two, who wove through picks to receive the ball near the baseline. Deke felt like he was a step behind the kid due to the sluggish brace that squeaked intermittently. He wanted nothing more than to tear it off but knew that would mean the bench for him.

Eighty-two dribbled and began crossing over and turning Deke from side to side. From the game plan, Deke knew his goal was to force his man to the baseline, which would bring them right toward Duke or Little Tim, and so he attempted to stay on the high side of the extremely quick player. He failed, thanks to the brace choosing that moment to lock down his lateral movement and cause him to stumble. Eighty-two circled high by him and pulled up for a four-footer to widen the point gap to four.

Deke helped Arthur with the full-court press and managed to pass it back to the point guard before crossing the half. They ran another isolation for him to shoot the three but when he got the ball at the wing, Eighty-two was right with him. Deke smiled down at the smaller kid. Eighty-two couldn't stop him. Not when Deke had [Aim Assist.] He jumped up but the line that normally helped Deke became an oscillating red blur as Eighty-two took off as well and put a hand in the line of the shot. Deke tried to change the trajectory to a higher arc but his hasty release, and the line, told him that the shot was going to rattle out.

The opposing team managed the defensive board and they dribbled up the court. The Baguettes weren't playing a full-court press, because they didn't have the depth of bench the Diablos had, and they were forced to pace themselves. They needed to conserve their energy so they could play more minutes. His team tried a zone this time on the defensive end, which put Deke on the right wing. He picked up each person who crossed through his zone. On this possession the opposing team's point guard got the ball in Deke's zone and he went to engage. Again, trying to force him baseline if he drove. The opposing point guard was possibly faster than Eighty-two and, with his maneuverability limited thanks to Squeaky, the opposing player easily zipped by Deke before dishing away the ball to a cutting center for an easy hoop. Their lead was back to six.

"Dammit!" Deke huffed under his breath. This stupid brace was going to make it impossible to hold the fast player's baseline. On the offensive end, they ran a play for Duke and Deke even got the assist as the Duke powered home a dunk on the other team's center. The game went back and forth for several minutes and they managed to pull back to within three thanks to an and-one basket by Arthur, the ref having called a shot-foul on his defender.

Ten minutes had already gone by in the second half, and Deke hadn't managed any more points. He had missed two more shots, thanks to the very sticky defense of number eighty-two. Deke hadn't known his [Aim Assist] could even act this way. He realized now in hindsight, he had only ever been taking shots with no defender. What a useless skill, if all it took was a defender in his face to mess it up. He might as well go back to not having it, as it felt more like a distraction at the moment.

Mac subbed in at the fifteen-minute mark, which allowed Deke to come to the bench. Abbie was the first one to rush to his side, followed closely by Doctor Dan.

"I know the brace is uncomfortable, but don't take it off," she scolded as she stopped him from unlacing it. "Other than the brace, how does the knee feel?"

"I'm telling you—" Deke said as he reached to pull the brace off his leg.

"Mills, this isn't an argument. The brace stays on or you stay off!" Doctor Dan overrode him and Deke nodded quickly and pulled fitfully at the rubber. He leaned back into his chair and straightened the leg out. The stupid brace squealed in delight at him, mocking his acceptance of the doctor's words. Whatever, anything to stay in the game!

"The knee feels fine. No pain. I just haven't played with a defender in my face in a long time..." Deke couldn't help but offer an excuse. He felt like his three missed shots had hurt the team.

"You've taken six shots and drained nine points! Not only that, but you broke their zone defense. With Mac out there they've gone back to it. See!" Skip exclaimed as he came over to stand above the doctor and Abbie as they poked and prodded at his knee.

Abbie held up an aerosol of liquid cold, cryogenic CO_2, giving him a warning of what was coming before spraying the visible area with it. The knee instantly began to chill, not that he needed it, but appearances and all that. He smiled at the coach. "I can still play, Coach!"

"You better be able to," Skip responded as he looked up at the clock. "We'll put you back in at the eight-minute mark. Be ready!"

The other starters cycled out over the next four minutes, leaving both teams with their benches playing each other. This time though, thanks to Mac's leadership, the Baguettes fared much better against the Diablos. In fact, they pulled within one before the Diablos widened the gap again to five. Still, that was a far better result than the same situation in the first half.

The eight-minute mark arrived, and Deke was subbed in for the second-string small forward, NJ. That left Mac out there with him and to his surprise as soon as Deke checked in, Mac approached him for a fist bump. "You take the shooting guard position. I'll cycle down to small forward, let's close the gap."

"Gotcha!" Deke moved to cover Twenty-three again as that was his mark according to the game plan.

"Can't move laterally, huh; I'm gonna cross you up, shitstain!" Number twenty-three sneered at him. Deke just smiled back and continued to stick to the angry player. Clearly, he wasn't over being subbed and sent to the tank, otherwise known as a combination of the bench and your own mind prison.

The Diablos ran a play that sprung Twenty-three to the top of the arch, and Deke, currently in man coverage, got ready. The last time he was on the floor, the other team was taking advantage of his bad mobility on defense, and he was determined to overcome that problem right now! He watched closely and was shocked when Twenty-three blurred. He didn't remember the kid being that fast. He stuck his hand out where he saw the ball in the blur, trying to at least put in a token effort to stop the kid. To his surprise, he felt the ball slap into his palm and he pulled it in before throwing it down the floor to a fast-breaking Big Tim.

Timmy slammed the ball through the hoop, and even hung on the rim for a split second, taunting the opposition. Clearly the Baguettes were feeling it. The announcer said something but Deke was tuning out everything but the game.

Number twenty-three brushed by him hard as he ran back up the court to help with an inbound pass and reset the offense. Big Tim returned to defense and high-fived Deke on the way by. "Call the police, 'cause you're picking pockets out here!"

They isolated number twenty-three again, and Deke watched this time as the kid seemed to blur again. This time though, he wasn't trying to drive by Deke. Instead, he watched the opposing player seem to dribble left, then a more substantial version of him followed the strange semi-transparent outline. Deke was pretty sure that the strange sports drink was predicting what the other player was going to do. It wasn't perfect, as shown by the two images exiting number twenty-three currently, but still!

Deke moved forward to reduce the four-foot cushion, which was clearly what Twenty-three had been waiting for. He attempted to drive by him again, but the strange prediction showed only one path now, toward Deke's bad leg. Deke stole the ball again and this time passed to Mac, who took off on a fast break with Chino and Larry. They scored an easy three on two, to bring the score within one point. Number twenty-three was subbed off again, during the stoppage after the basket, and Deke smiled at the glares he received.

Maybe he couldn't make a basket but he could definitely still play! Didn't they criticize MJ as a ball hog, and the next year he came back and won defensive player of the year? Yeah, those weren't bad footsteps to follow in at all, he decided.

"Dude, eleven points in a half! That was huge," Geoff, the third-string shooting guard, crowed. "I don't know if we could have won without that jolt of energy right after the half!"

That was probably the tenth person from his team to come by and compliment him as he unlaced the brace. Once Squeaky came free, he buried it in the back of his locker, hoping that next game they might let him play without it. Maybe if he said he couldn't find the thing?

Still, even the brace couldn't dampen his mood. Deke tossed his jersey into the bin at the center of the room using [Aim Assist] and a basketball shot, for the first time since preseason. The jersey joined the others as he tilted his head up toward the ceiling and tried not to blink to stop any of the dampness he felt in his eyes from escaping. It was so damn good to be back that he didn't even know where to begin processing his emotions.

"Kid, that was unreal!" Duke ruffled his hair as he walked by in his towel toward the shower. "You better be ready for a rager tonight! But hey, I see anything other than soda in your hands and we're tying you up. Got it?"

The way the Duke said the final call made it clear that he was joking and Deke couldn't help but smile. "All right, as long as you buy the soda!"

The seniors on the team guffawed, as they clearly planned on having real drinks and must have been reminded of their earlier years. From the conversations, he could tell the older players intended to drink heavily since dead week started tomorrow. Deke couldn't help but swallow thickly, drying his sweaty palms off on his towel as he considered the last what... two parties he'd been to? Surely nothing bad would happen *this time* though right?

TWENTY-NINE

TUESDAY, DECEMBER 13TH

"the girls have convened and agree you can
be seen in public with pity fuck"- Big
Sis Eva

"i'm not that desperate"- Valerie

"girl i know you been sneaking around,
:eggplant emoji: :ok-hand emoji: with him"-
Big Sis Eva

"he needs to do more than play a few
minutes if he wants this :peach emoji: in
public"- Valerie

"shall I remind you of the kiss he gave you
as he came on court?"- Big Sis Eva

D eke had managed to sneak away from his teammates long enough to call Max. Yet Ronda cut the conversation short, saying Max needed to get to bed, which seemed unfair since Max was already awake. Still, he did have an earlier bedtime than other kids his age, and likely should have been asleep hours ago, so he didn't protest too strongly.

Walking back into the locker room, he cleaned up and got ready for the night's next excursion. Pulling on his suit jacket, he looked at himself in the mirror. Abbie's mom had fixed the suit and it now actually looked like it was made for someone roughly his size, rather than someone twice as big as he was, and his pants no longer looked like he was preparing to weather Noah's biblical flood.

"One good game ain't going to make you a starter over me," Mac said from somewhere nearby. Thanks to the content and the derisive tone, Deke knew he was being addressed. He turned slowly and found Mac not wearing a suit. Mac indicated Deke's clothing for emphasis before saying, "Don't get used to that. It's just eleven points, and the fact that it's your first game back..."

Mac stormed away, not giving Deke a chance to respond. Not that he had one. Mac had been a major reason that the Baguettes pulled out a win tonight. Without him leading the bench in the final change, UCSP would have probably returned to the court with an insurmountable lead to overcome. Deke shrugged after a moment of consideration. No one could ruin his good mood right now. He had gotten to play.

Deke turned back to his image in the mirror and nodded with appreciation. Out of the corner of his eye, he saw Mac glaring at him from his seated position near the starter's lockers. It was just a Booster's post game party, and Deke had heard every starter complain about them in the past. Still, Deke guessed not being invited was a different story for a senior starter. Especially when Duke and the rest of the starters were all getting dressed in their suits. Deke almost felt bad for Mac, but recalled the last party and Mac's incessant teasing.

Deke met Mac's eyes in the mirror and winked, and the dark scowl on Mac's face grew even more stormy. Unnecessary? Probably, but looking good and being envied for his talent felt right, and Deke wasn't worried about Mac's displeasure. Deke already believed he was better than Mac, and if not now, he would be soon. That's all there was to it.

Straightening his tie he turned, only to have Duke's massive paw land on his shoulder.

"Looking good, Rook. You ready for this dog and pony show?" Duke's smile was infectious; either the center hadn't noticed Mac's mood or didn't care.

"Yeah, as long as that Jabba-the-Fisher doesn't corner me again. Man, that guy gives me the willies." Deke shifted his suit back into position after Duke's giant mitt was removed.

"Fisher's harmless, just try not to shake his hand too much. Guy's hand is always super slimy." Duke ruined Deke's attempt to fix his suit by pulling him away from the mirror and out of the locker room. They moved to the side of the hallway for a bit of privacy.

"Look, you did great out there tonight. We probably wouldn't have won without you and that's great, but I don't want to see you injured again or worse—expelled. So seriously, no drinks tonight, eh?" Duke adopted the Canadian "eh" and Deke wasn't sure if that was supposed to be a joke or not. "You don't have any kind of pain meds? Narcotics? Prescription or otherwise. Let's just remove every possibility of something going wrong tonight, okay?"

"No, I mean, yeah, trust me, I don't plan on anything but soda. Getting back on the team is what I've been working on for...well, this entire season. I'm not going to mess it up again." Deke's words caused the big man to nod his head seriously.

"All right, I'ma hold you to that, no alcohol! No nothin'! Even if someone insists you celebrate with them at the Booster club or the real party. If it comes down to it, you come get me and I'll hand them their ass, I don't care who they are." Duke's words reminded Deke of the small accidental puff of weed, and he shuddered. What Duke didn't realize was that Deke's system wouldn't tolerate drinking anyway, so there was nothing to worry about on that front at all. Purges were a hundred times worse than normal vomiting, which already wasn't his favorite thing in the world. Especially when they... egghh... came from both ends... He had no intention of triggering another one if he could manage it.

"Of course, I wouldn't dream of doing anything offside." Deke realized that he actually meant the words and they both smiled at each other. "Only things I'm gonna crush are opposing teams..." Deke tried to steer the conversation back to the game. "Well, actually Valerie isn't off the table either, now that I think about it. Hmmm—wait, I wouldn't mind having her *on* the table, if you know what I'm saying." Duke laughed and they continued out of the locker room. As they left, he saw Abbie off to the side, going through some paperwork.

"Hey Abbs," Deke said, giving the "one minute" signal to Duke as he walked over to the trainer. "You coming to the after-party?"

"Hey Deke. I really shouldn't. I have to study." Abbie gave him a once-over and smiled. "Man, that suit looks a ton better."

"Right! Your mom did some amazing work. Thank her for me again, will you?" Deke said, smoothing the suit. He was amazed at how much better a suit that actually fit him felt. "You sure you can't sneak away for a little while at least?"

"Nah." Abbie shook her head. "Besides, you-know-who is going to be there, and you know how much she hates it when we spend time together." Valerie was distinctly not a fan of Abbie, and most of the major fights she had with Deke were over his female friend. Then again, sometimes it felt like they didn't really talk much... Almost, like they avoided conversations.

"All right, fair enough. I'm sure Lee will regale you with plenty of stories tomorrow," Deke said with a smile. "Anyway, I should get to the Boosters."

"Oh, that sounds like a ton of fun... not."

"Not? I didn't realize you were in your forties. All right, catch ya' later, grandma." Deke laughed and Abbie shooed him away while pretending to push up a pair of non-existent glasses.

The Grilled Baguette, UCSP's sports grill, turned into an invite-only meet and greet after each home game. Deke and the other starters were announced to rounds of applause before Skip told them to mingle. Deke gravitated toward the buffet. He was just starting to look through the options for something that wasn't highlighted in red when, as if talking about him earlier had summoned him from some sort of sweaty, sticky portal—Grant Fisher found him.

"Deke Mills!" The large man shouted in his ears and Deke had to hide a wince at the volume. "I knew all my calls to Director Rooney would pay off!" The man stuck out his ham hock of a hand for Deke to shake. Deke grudgingly accepted, hiding another wince as his hand was engulfed by the clammy grip. Grant pumped his hand up and down energetically. "Fantastic game, son! Simply fantastic game! Come, come! I have some friends I want you to meet."

Grant waddled through the crowd, his bulk clearing a path with practiced ease. Deke was towed behind him, like he was the man's personal trophy, since Grant had yet to release his hand. The man had a surprisingly strong grip for his rotund shape. Deke was introduced to a dozen of Fisher's closest friends before he managed to escape. Ducking back the way they had come; he decided it was time to reward himself with something that wasn't entirely healthy. As he was pushing his way back through the crowd toward the buffet, another hand landed on his shoulder.

Turning, he saw the splotchy face of Director Rooney, and the red-haired man beckoned him to follow, pulling Duke in as they went. They ended up at the edge of a platform where the band was playing. Rooney planted Deke on the middle stairs before climbing the rest of the way up and grabbing the mic from the stand. He tapped on it a few times. The squeal of feedback was enough to silence the room and everyone turned to look at Rooney, and by circumstance, Deke. Only as Deke turned back toward the room did he realize Duke was on the steps below him as well. The setup made the director the tallest person on the stand.

"Is this thing on?" Some muffled laughter followed. "Oh good, I just wanted to give a quick shout out to the players that made this win against the Devil Chickens possible! DaShawn 'The Duke' Wellington is our starting center and you all know how well he's done by us. But today I managed to convince Coach Skip to allow freshman Deke Mills back onto the roster, even though we weren't sure if he would step on the court in today's outing. Deke's eleven points, eight assists and *four steals*, are just a start to what this team is going to be able to put up the rest of the season! We're all going to be riding this train all the way to Mercenary March!" Rooney's pale face flushed in his excitement and he raised his hands over his head.

When the cheering died down Deke realized, with a frown, that he had been smelling cotton candy since the director grabbed him. It was faint, but was clearly emanating from the director's suit. His excitement was crushed in a second; what was the connection between the director and the Vaping Man? Was he involved with Evil Corp? He looked over at Skip, trying to gauge his reaction to that rather horrible speech. The coach was exchanging a look of dismay with Dr. Dan. Both of them looked like they had eaten something sour as their lips pursed in disapproval.

"Go Baguettes!" Rooney shouted, Deke having missed whatever else the director had said in his musings and worries about the connections with Evil Corp. He and Duke were released to go back into the crowd. Duke tapped his shoulder, and then gave the "let's get out of here" nod that Deke had been waiting for. He followed the center out of the grill, his appetite suddenly lost thanks to the revelations that smell brought on. It wasn't until Duke pulled him aside that Deke realized that the two of them were alone, and he suddenly realized just how big Duke was. Deke wasn't really used to feeling small, but next to the massive center, he felt snack-sized.

"Hey, I... just wanted to let you know that I've seen what you're doing. You've really turned things around in the last month or two and the level of effort you're putting forward is damn impressive. I really admire that level of dedication and I wanted to apologize for some of the things I said about you earlier in the season. I made a snap judgement and that was wrong of me. I've been wanting to clear the air between us for a while now. Tonight seems like a great time to do it," Duke said, holding his hand out for Deke to shake.

Thoughts raced through Deke's head. Why was Duke making this effort now? The sports drink was made for Duke, which meant he knew what it could do. Did he suspect it was behind Deke's miraculous recovery? Duke was the only person on the team that got any interest from scouts, too. Deke wanted that interest himself. So, was this some play that he just didn't understand? No. He refused to live a life of paranoia. Duke had always shot straight, and just because they wanted him to take the drug and sign a contract didn't mean he actually would have.

Deke took the offered hand. He couldn't help but compare it to Grant Fisher. Both were large, powerful grips, but where Fisher's had been slimy and oppressive, trying to show dominance, Duke's was warm, dry and firm but also controlled. Exactly like Duke himself, it seemed to scream "dependable." Which was exactly the adjective he would have attributed to Duke if he had been forced to.

"Thanks Duke. I don't blame you for those judgments. I'm discovering, with the help of Dr. Pinsonneault, that I wasn't really myself right after the injury. So, I made some stupid choices at the beginning of the season and I'm still paying for them. They've taught me a lot, however, and I'm strangely grateful for them at the same time, if that makes any sense."

"We all make mistakes. What's important is that we never quit. You quit once, and that becomes a habit. Never quit," Duke said with a serious face. "That's what MJ says. That's what Kobe said, and with that kind of backing, it can't be wrong." Duke tugged on his shirt. "Come on, we gotta get to the *real* party."

Deke felt himself nodding along with Duke's words; there was wisdom there. You don't have to be the best. You just have to keep moving forward. He liked that mentality. He felt himself liking the big center just a little bit more. Sure, the guy was still an arrogant jerk, but he at least had the skill—and work ethic—to back that up. Duke led him to a house just off campus; like most parties in the area, it took advantage of the warm Cali weather and was in the house's backyard. They were headed toward a side gate where Mac and another player were acting as bouncers.

"You're bringing the kid in?" Mac asked Duke, talking over Deke like he couldn't hear him.

"You know the rules, you play, you're invited to the party. What, you don't think he's earned it?" Duke answered, gesturing for Deke to go around him.

"Sounds like another drug or alcohol disaster just waiting to happen." Mac glared at Deke, who returned the glare. This jackass was the one who'd given him too much medication at the first party! Duke put an arm around Mac and moved him off to the side. He was saying something too quiet for Deke to hear, but turned around as Deke decided to head inside.

"Remember, no drinking, man!"

Deke just rolled his eyes and headed into the party. It took him a moment to take it all in. There was a pool taking up a substantial part of the property. Palm trees lined the fence and there were drinks and snacks off in one corner. A couple of his teammates were playing pool chicken with some of the cheerleaders and a girl screamed as she was pulled into the water, toppling three other people down with her.

A quick glance didn't show him anyone that he knew so he headed over to the bar, where he grabbed a sports drink—an actual one—that had been tossed into a cooler on the side. Deke laughed slightly as he snapped open the lid, and looked around for Lee so he could share the joke. He caught sight of his roommate off to one side near the beer pong table and made his way over, wondering who would be listening to his undoubtedly nerdy debate. To his surprise it was Duke's girlfriend Eva, and Abbie.

"Anyway, so that's when I told him he was pretty short for a stormtrooper!" Deke caught the tail end of Lee's story. This particular one Deke had heard before. It was about him missing a few shots while he was trying to test [Aim Assist]. The whole point had been to see if it would help him hit any target, not just a basket.

"Heya," Deke said, interrupting Lee and draping an arm around the shorter kid. "I assure you everything he says is libel and my team of high-priced lawyers"—Deke indicated his much better fitting suit—"is already aware of the problem."

"I think you mean slander. It's only libel if it's written," Abbie said with a grin. Deke gave her a hurt expression in response, holding his suit near his heart, like she'd shot him.

"Congrats on the win today Deke, you really saved our bacon," Eva said with a smile. "You being here means Duke is on his way in, right?"

"Yeah, he stopped at the side gate to talk to Mac," Deke answered Eva and she winced.

"He didn't take being subbed out well, I assume?"

"That's... umm... one way to describe it," Deke said, and Eva shook her head sadly.

"Well, I better go see if I can't help with damage control. Oh, Val is here..." Eva looked around and then shrugged. "Somewhere."

"Thanks, good luck with Mac."

"I'll need it." Eva patted Abbie on her shoulder in farewell.

"I thought you weren't going to come?" Deke asked Abbie, now that it was just the three of them.

"I used my social magic to force her to reconsider," Lee said, waggling his fingers in a mystical way with a grin.

"He means, he begged me until I gave in," Abbie informed Deke while poking Lee in the shoulder.

"Beg, convince, what's the difference," Lee mumbled while blushing.

"Well, I'm glad you did," Deke answered Abbie while putting a supporting hand on Lee's shoulder.

"Hey, I'm thirsty. You guys want anything?" Abbie asked, and Deke just gestured to his bottle.

"I'll take a beer, or something," Lee said, and Deke raised an eyebrow. Lee wasn't much of a drinker on his best days, especially since he, like Deke, was underage.

"Living dangerously, are we Mr. Lee?" Abbie said with a bad

British accent, even as she turned toward the coolers. "One beer, coming up."

"Dude, I cannot believe you got to play!" Lee said, giving Deke an awkward hug, which he returned after a moment of hesitation.

"You haven't been drinking already have you?" Deke asked, wondering at the strange behavior.

"Nope, just super happy! You were killing it out there." Deke and Lee claimed three lawn chairs while they waited for Abbie to come back with the drinks. Lee began running through every one of Deke's points, which was a little embarrassing, but he enjoyed the kid talking up everything in a way that reminded him of Max. Wondering where Abbie was, Deke stood up to get a better vantage, and to his surprise he saw Valerie making her way toward them. When she got close she threw herself on Deke, and he caught the light blonde.

"I heard you played!" Valerie's words were already a little slurred.

"What do you mean, you heard? You were at the game, didn't you see me play?" Deke said with a frown. He could smell the alcohol on her already. It had only been a couple of hours since the game.

"Oh, I never pay attention to the sports thing. I'm too busy dancing!" She tried to kiss Deke, but missed and kissed his cheek instead. "Hah! You've got lipstick on your face!" She reached up to wipe his cheek and even licked her finger first. It reminded Deke of his auntie and he pulled away, embarrassed. "You're such a prude!" Valerie laughed at him again, poking him in the chest. Deke set her down on one of the lawn chairs, not sure if she would be able to stand on her own if he didn't.

"One beer, here you are!" Abbie said and as Deke turned around, she held the beer out across Deke's chest toward Lee. Deke was happy to see the beer was of the non-alcoholic variety.

"You little whore! Trying to get *my* man drunk!" Valerie had shot to her feet as soon as Abbie spoke and slapped the innocent beer meant for Lee out of her hands.

"I was..." Abbie started, but Valerie didn't let her finish. A violent slap cracked over the sound of the music and Deke had to physically pull Valerie off Abbie as the two went down. Valerie slapped at him ineffectively as she tried to get through him and back to Abbie.

"I'm sorry... I'll just go," Abbie whispered, standing up and turning away. There was a slight catch in her voice that made Deke angry. She ran off as Valerie's shouted invectives followed her. Deke pushed Valerie down onto the chair again and glared at her.

"I'm sick of this, Val! Abbie was getting *Lee* a drink. Not me." Deke pointed to his roommate, whom the blonde had completely ignored. "I don't want to deal with you like this. Call me when you're sober," Deke growled and turned to walk away. He could hear someone following along behind him but didn't turn to see who it was until he was almost a block away.

"Can we slow down now? Abbie didn't even park in this direction," Lee said, panting a little as he tried to keep up with Deke's near run. Deke sighed and stopped so that Lee could catch up.

"Where did she park?"

"This way, I think," Lee muttered the last bit under his breath. They turned and headed back to the party. They wandered around for almost twenty minutes before Lee confessed he wasn't sure, and she wasn't answering her cell.

"It's all right, we'll talk to her tomorrow. I guess," Deke said, feeling frustrated. This was supposed to be his big night and Valerie had ruined it. "Come on, let's head back to the party, I didn't mean to ruin it for you too."

"Let's just go back to the dorm. They wouldn't even let me in until Abbie came with me. I don't have anything in common with those guys."

Deke sighed and nodded his head. They had to pass the house again anyway, since that was on their way home.

"All right..." Deke frowned, as he heard shouting ahead of them. Two women were struggling over a purse on the sidewalk.

"Give me your keys!" Eva shouted and Deke realized that the other woman was Val, standing near her car and trying to open the door. Valerie had clearly gotten even more drunk in the last fifteen minutes and could now barely stand. Still, Eva was having a hard time dealing with the taller girl. Deke walked up behind them and put his arms around Valerie, holding her still.

"I've got her," Deke said, and he could see the relief on Eva's face as she let Deke handle her sorority sister.

"Oh Deke!" Eva said as Valerie face-planted drunkenly into his shoulder and then started to try to kiss the fabric there. "Can you please get her home? She won't listen to me like this."

"Yeah, I got it. No worries," Deke said, and pulled Val over to the passenger side of her car.

"Thanks, you're a lifesaver." Eva helped Deke and Lee put Val in the passenger side of her two-seater Miata. Deke realized he had a problem when they finally got her in and he glanced over at Lee who gave him the "go ahead" sign.

"Thanks Lee, I'll see you soon," Deke said as he tried to squeeze into the driver's seat while keeping Valerie upright.

"Lee, can you come help me?" Eva asked. "We need to grab some bags of ice and I could really use another set of hands."

Deke waved again as he finally managed to push the seat back and get his knees into the car, accompanied by some light snoring. Well, tonight turned out to be a bit of a roller coaster—and Deke only hoped that Abbie was okay...

CHAPTER

THIRTY

WEDNESDAY, DECEMBER 21ST

"Hey, double date with Deke and Val after the break."- Best Girlfriend Eva

"I'm busy that night."- The Duke

"Haha, I'm serious. We're doing this."- Best Girlfriend Eva

"Oh man, do we have to? You know how I feel about her."- The Duke

"Come on, Deke's been real good for her. She's getting better." Best Girlfriend Eva

"Okay, but you're going to owe me."- The Duke

Deke handed in his final American History exam. He was relatively confident in the answers he had given, which admittedly was a first for him. Granted, it wasn't saying all that much, since he was the last student to finish and he had wracked his brain to try to get a great deal of them. Maybe it was better to say he was confident in part marks for a great deal of it.

The instant his paper touched the pile, Professor Tawn coughed politely. "Would you like me to mark it right now?"

Deke blinked in startlement, and Professor Tawn winked at him. "Don't worry, I'm going to go mark them right after this anyway. Might as well allow your forehead to wrinkle less."

"Thanks Prof." Deke wasn't totally convinced that knowing his mark now would be a good thing, but often felt less confident about tests the longer it took for the grades to be posted, so was totally willing to get foreknowledge of the result.

"Well done. Oh that's close, the more correct answer would have been the assassination of John F. Kennedy, not his presidency," Tawn mumbled as he went through Deke's exam with lightning speed. The professor arrived at the last page and flipped back through them, tallying up a red-penned score he'd placed in the corner of each page. At the front page he wrote eighty-two and circled it. "Well done, Mr. Mills."

The grin on Deke's face couldn't be helped. That was the highest grade he'd ever received on a test. Professor Tawn returned his smile. "I've been very impressed with your turnaround, Mr. Mills. Tell Mr. Wett to keep rubbing off on you."

"Thanks Professor, I'll do that. It feels funny to know the mark of my last exam first." Deke had to hide the smile at the joke the professor clearly hadn't been meaning to make.

"Well, Merry Christmas?"

"Speaking of presents . . . I really appreciated you photocopying that Project Ultra book for me. I hate to ask, but do you think I could get a second copy... I seem to have misplaced the original."

"That's unfortunately one of the books I haven't managed to replace after the fire. It was extremely rare to begin with, I've been told. Insurance is giving me extra money to compensate me, but I'd rather have my book collection whole. If you know what I mean," Tawn said with sadness tinging his voice. Deke didn't know what he meant. He'd take an insurance payout any day of the week over some musty old books but he nodded along with Tawn, anyway.

Still, for that book to have been destroyed or to go missing on the same night as the photocopies, did give Lee's conspiracy theory some additional weight.

"Did the photocopies help you at all, at least?" Professor Tawn continued after a long sigh.

"Yeah they definitely did. I should probably get going, Lee was the first one finished and he was going to wait for me." Deke scratched his head. He didn't really want to get into explaining *how* the Project Ultra photocopies had helped him. While he wanted to ask if there was anything suspicious about its disappearance or the fire, that would be impossible to convincingly lie about. Or so it felt. Plus he didn't want to be associated with the strange occurrence...

Lee was waiting for Deke just outside of the classroom and he stood from his sitting position on a bench. "Gargantuan, that took you a longer time than I expected. Was it more difficult than I thought?"

"Anything is more difficult than you think it is, Brainiac. But also no. Professor Tawn graded my paper in front of me and I got an eighty-two."

"Really, do you think he would do the same for me?" Lee asked as he began walking to the door. Professor Tawn exited at almost the same time, carrying a white box that must have been filled with the tests.

"I'm afraid not, Mr. Wett." Professor Tawn interjected before Lee could officially ask. Deke wasn't sure if the professor had even heard the initial conversation or just been able to intuit what Lee wanted. Lee groaned, then turned to Deke before motioning toward the cafeteria.

"Lunch, then I get to go home for the break!" Lee exclaimed. Deke forced a smile onto his face on that topic. He was a bit far from home and there was no way his mother could afford a plane ticket. Not to mention want to spend that kind of money for the week he would have off. Lee must have seen his false smile because he snapped his fingers. "Why don't you come to my house for Xmas? I can't guarantee that we'll have a bed that fits your freakish frame, but it can't be worse than the dorms."

Deke actually smiled then. "That would be fantastic!"

They continued chatting about Christmas vacation on the way to the cafeteria. They hadn't even cleared the entryway when Valerie strode toward him. He grimaced. She hadn't really said more than two words out loud to him since the party, and all of her texts had also been one-word answers. He wasn't a Casanova with women but even he knew how to interpret those signals.

"I figured out how you can make it up to me," she said without even bothering to greet him, or Lee. "I need you to come to my place for the holidays. You're going to run interference between me and my parents." She placed a hand on her waist and cocked her hip out seductively. "Maybe if you do a good enough job, I'll reward you."

Deke looked over at Lee, who shrugged as helplessly as he currently felt. It wasn't like spending the holidays with Valerie would be *bad,* per se, but he had been really excited for Lee's. On the other hand, Valerie had been a bit cray-cray lately. Perhaps he should just end it now by choosing Lee?

Valerie took a deep breath in, and then released it slowly, visibly changing gears from cute and bubbly to apologetic. "Look, Deke. I'm sorry about the way I acted at the party. My dad had just told me he was coming home for Christmas and I... didn't handle it well. I shouldn't have drank so much and I definitely shouldn't have gotten in your friend's face." She actually said the last bit to Lee, and that actually made Deke smile.

"We can always go hang out with Lee at some point too, right?" Deke asked pointedly.

"Of course. We'll all get together for New Year's as well, right?" Valerie exclaimed, her voice growing excited when she didn't hear a denial from him. "After lunch we'll drive to my place. Thanks for understanding, Les."

"Deke has his last visit with the kids at the community center after this. And my name is Lee."

Valerie ignored the correction and turned to Deke. "You're not done with that yet? How long is your community service?!"

"I've got a few hours left," Deke lied. He wasn't about to tell her he was finished. She'd likely insist he skip it, and he wanted to see the kids.

"Like, that cop was a total douche, just call me when you're done. I'm so excited to show you my room." She winked at him and flounced back to her table of cheerleaders.

Deke looked at Lee. "Dude, I'm sorry about her and ... all this. I really wanted to—"

"Dude, don't worry. If some hot girl came over and invited me to her family's place for the holidays, I would have left you in the dorm and ghosted your keister. Let's get some food, man."

The kids were playing a third game of bump that Deke had chosen to sit out from. It was clearly a little unfair, since he had won the first two. Abbie got knocked out a few rounds later and she moved toward him.

"Those kids don't take any prisoners!" She lowered herself to the ground and pulled her knapsack-purse thing toward herself. "Honestly, they take after you," she said with a bit of a chuckle. Something about the chuckle sounded a little awkward and Deke took his eyes off the kids to look at her.

"What's up?" he asked when he saw that she was unwilling to meet his eyes. "I was just kidding with the trash talk the first two rounds."

"I know that, dummy." Abbie turned to look him full in the face while simultaneously blushing. Deke's breath caught. Their faces were just a foot apart and she was stunning, even while sweating. Maybe more so because of it. "Look, I got you something cause you never seem to understand Lee's and my humor."

Deke blinked and held up two hands, breaking the moment of

awkwardness. "Abbie, don't. I didn't get you anything. It wouldn't be fair."

"Shut up!" She cut off his rambling. "It's not expensive. Me and Lee hit the bargain bins all over the city. And before you go out and get something, I don't want a gift. I just think you might be into this sort of thing—seeing how well you and Lee get along."

Abbie pulled a very flat bag out from behind her laptop pouch in her book bag and handed it to him. The bag itself was white with a red circle on it. Inside the circle was "Comic Stop" in Comic Sans. He pointed to the font and made an "are you for real" face. Abbie punched him on the shoulder and Deke chuckled. "Fine, fine. So, what comic did you think was perfect for me? This better not be Cadet Moon or some other gag gift like that."

Pulling out the comic, he found that she had gotten him something called *Mutant X*. As soon as it was clear of the package and he was studying the rather hairy man on the front, she coughed. "This used to be my favorite as a kid. The character is pretty popular and heals fast. He's also Canadian, so I thought this was a good place for you to start your nerd journey."

Deke smiled. The comic wasn't shiny and new. In fact, it was quite clear that it had been through numerous hands. It made him smile all the same. He turned to Abbie and felt a lump in his throat. This might be the only present he got all Christmas, but was interrupted when a booming voice echoed over the cracked blacktop. "Deke, Abbie, I didn't know you had this many recruits hidden away!"

Turning to see who would know both of them and say something so amusing, Deke wasn't surprised to find Duke walking in through the rusted and bent chain-link fence. The big man actually had to duck to not hit his head. The kids abandoned the game of bump and rushed over to surround the giant of a center. Deke shook his head. Duke sure knew how to make an entrance.

"Sorry, I forgot I asked him to come surprise the kids," Abbie said as she got to her feet and dusted herself off. "I better keep the kids from dragging him to the floor. They haven't done it yet, but I've seen puppies with better manners."

Somehow Abbie leaving to go tend to Duke made Deke feel upset. The guy wasn't horrible anymore, but did he have to show up to the one place where Deke was getting admiration and steal the spotlight?

"Deke's been teaching us all about basketball," one of the kids responded to a question Deke hadn't heard.

"You couldn't ask for a better teacher!" Duke opened his arms wide and gestured toward Deke with one magnanimous hand. "That kid is going to be the next star of the Baguettes. If you're learning from him, I don't doubt that you'll all be stars too."

Deke stood up, his mood somehow feeling buoyed thanks to the infectious joy of the children, and he supposed Duke's compliments didn't hurt either.

"What were you all doing before I got here?" Duke changed the topic, clearly attempting to get the kids to make a bit of room so he wasn't at risk of crushing one of them with his size eighteen feet.

Within a few minutes the kids were back to playing bump, and Duke had goaded Deke into playing this round. "Let's see if you can take on someone your own size!" Duke said as he lined up right behind Deke.

Smiling, Deke drained the first three pointer and looked back at Duke with a cocky smile.

CHAPTER

THIRTY-ONE

FRIDAY, DECEMBER 23RD

"Daddy I'm bringing Deke home for Christmas"- Valerie

"Another one of your pity projects? If something goes missing it's coming out of your allowance."- Paternal Parental Unit

"Deke isn't like that."- Valerie

"Tell your mother, I'm going to extend my business trip a few days."- Paternal Parental Unit

Deke had been expecting Valerie's house to be big, but he just wasn't prepared for the sheer, nearly comical, size of it. The drive was twice as long as a basketball court, leading down a steep incline to an artificially flattened area on the cliffs overlooking the ocean. The house itself was a sprawling multi-story building with what he imagined the real-estate agent would have pitched as a "view to die for."

Two to three stories, with a half dozen different roofs that reminded him of "built on" houses from TV shows, although this one was clearly designed to emulate the look rather than having been added on by generations. The styles of each add-on were just too similar and while it gave off the generational house vibe, it was clearly recently constructed.

Behind the house was a pristine blue pool that looked nearly Olympic in length, if not in breadth. Large windows looked out over the shore amid palm trees and stunning yellow cliffs. Valerie parked her car in the middle of the driveway and an older man in a vest and slacks stepped out from a side entrance below a wide stairway which led to monstrous double doors.

"Good morning, Miss Valerie. Mister Mills," the older man said with a slight bow and a distinguished English accent. Valerie walked past him, pulling Deke with her and away from the gym bag he had packed his clothes in.

"Set Deke up in the room next to mine, Bernard. We're going to go soak," Valerie called out behind her as she walked up the steps. At the top she brushed past a woman in an apron, who opened one of the massive doors and stood just inside.

"Ahh, young miss, your mother has told me that your guest will be staying in the pool house." The woman said. Her accent was less pronounced, although Deke was pretty sure hers wasn't from England. Scottish maybe? Deke wasn't entirely sure. He had wanted to stop and greet the two staff members but Valerie had other ideas. With an exasperated huff of anger she threw the arm that wasn't holding Deke's into the air.

"Really? The guest house, Mother? If it's my chastity you're trying to protect you're too late. He's already sampled the goods." Valerie's voice was loud enough to reverberate through the entrance area. Deke looked up, mortified, at an older but still beautiful version of Valerie standing on the balcony above them in a lavender bathrobe.

"I'm right here, dear. And, quite the contrary, I figured you could be as loud as you wanted out there and not disturb your father," Valerie's mother said with a smile.

"Oh. Dad isn't coming home tonight after all. He said he had to extend his business trip," Valerie said, and Deke watched as the entire house almost sighed with relief. Val's mom's smile took on a more genuine tone and the woman behind him actually thanked God for this stroke of fortune.

"Oh, well... that's a shame," Val's mother said with a shrug that seemed false to Deke. "You two go get cleaned up. I've had Siobhan make that salad you like so much. Although... I think Deke will appreciate some red meat as well, so I'll have her put some steaks on. Come see me when you're done, dear." With that, Val's mom pushed away from the balustrade and back into the recess of the second floor.

"Come on!" Valerie said with a cheerful grin, already peeling off her shirt, revealing the bikini she had on underneath. She tossed it carelessly to the floor as she wiggled out of her shorts as well, throwing them to the side haphazardly and hitting a vase that wobbled slightly as she reached for Deke again and led him through the house.

For his part, Deke was just trying not to touch anything. Everything around him seemed to scream money. There were gilded mirrors and display boxes of random movie props littered around the house, like it was a museum. Even as beautiful as Valerie was, her near-naked behind wasn't enough to draw his eyes away from what was clearly a chunk of movie history. He followed her with a slow sense of awe; he saw coats, dresses and shoes, but what drew his attention the most was a framed shield. He recognized it from a famous movie about a Roman gladiator. Stationed right next to a pink blouse identified as being from the Brunch Bunch.

Deke shook his head—half the stuff in the hallway was from movies he had watched dozens of times growing up. His hand had escaped Valerie's when she had taken off her shorts and he realized he was left alone in the most expensive corridor of his life. Well, not exactly alone, the maid from the entrance was behind him.

"Best move along dear. The young mistress isn't prone to waiting for things." Deke looked and she was holding Val's shirt in her hands and bending over to pick up the shorts and straighten the vase.

"Yeah... I'm starting to realize that myself. Sorry for making you do that," Deke said, feeling awkward.

"Oh you're fine. The young mistress is just... feeling things, now that she knows her father isn't going to be coming home." The woman shooed him off and he wandered through a few large hallways until he came across a huge open living room, several large couches surrounding a massive entertainment system over travertine tiles, with a sliding wall that opened up onto the pool area where Valerie was applying lotion to her legs.

"Come get my back. I'm sure Meredith will have a suit down here for you in a bit," Valerie called out while pointing to the sunscreen bottle. Deke watched her body move for a bit and felt like pinching himself. This was the sort of life that he imagined he would have someday—when he was in the NBA—but he had never imagined living like this in college.

"This place is amazing," Deke said as he rubbed the cream into Valerie's back, while trying to avoid the leggy blonde's red bikini strap.

"Yeah, I promise it's going to be a great Christmas break." Valerie reached around her back to undo the strap of her bikini and help him out. Deke felt his breath catch, and he couldn't help but look around as she held the front of the bikini in place. He continued to apply the sunscreen, the act somehow more sexual now. Once she was done, she twisted around and gave him a kiss. "Mind tying it back up for me?" she said cheekily, her eyes twinkling.

It took a full thirty seconds for his numb hands to accomplish what his brain was instructing. Maybe his blood wasn't reaching those extremities at the moment. As soon as he finished, she pulled off his shirt and began spreading sunscreen on his back, returning the favor. Her slim fingers traced the lines of his muscles and goose-bumps rose on his skin, contrasting the sensation and adding some new ones too. Maybe this *was* going to be his best Christmas break ever...

Saturday, December 24th

Deke chewed his lip as he floated lazily in the early morning sun.

For the first time in months Deke was taking a break from the gym, basketball, and to a small degree even his remedial tasks. However, he had long since grown disappointed in those. In the weeks that followed the sports drink initiation, Deke had come to expect one evo point a week from those tasks but after five weeks, he never saw another. It was like he was a dog, and the system was just training good behaviour. Lee and he had discussed intentionally failing some of the tasks to see if it might kick-start rewards again, but Deke truly wasn't willing to go back to living the way he had before the system.

It was almost painful to look back at his foggy memories of those days. Had he really sniffed his underwear to find a tolerable pair? Still, feeling like a trained dog wasn't pleasant either. Not that he knew what evo points could do, other than heal injuries, but he really wanted a large backup of those. Just in case.

In fact, all around he had seen a pretty steady decline in the system of late. He was yet to get another skill like [Aim Assist], and despite pushing himself for personal bests in the gym on the daily, his stat gains were drying up. Lee claimed that it was something called dimming returns. No, that wasn't it. Dumbening? Diminishing? Yeah, that was it. Diminishing returns.

Essentially, his workout had gone from giving him as much as point zero four points, to two, then one. Not that it ever actually awarded him the total amount! It still seemed to be splitting those points somewhere unseen. And yet, even the half points weren't being awarded last week. There were still random tasks assigned and stats in other areas awarded, but he couldn't push the boundaries on those—meaning they weren't repeatable. Or as Lee called it, "farmable," whatever that meant. For example, him somehow getting the results of some of his exams had raised the power stat. Lee had joked that just meant he was a musclehead.

He sighed in minor disappointment, and lay back on his pool floatie in Val's infinity pool. She'd gone shopping with her mother and he had woken to a note letting him know to make himself at home. He hadn't left the pool house and pool area, terrified of getting lost in what he would term an industrial complex, more than a home. Not that he was complaining, but with the "invisible" staff, he just didn't feel right sticking his nose in anywhere.

Instead, he was taking this Christmas Break as just that, a break from most things. Unfortunately, the threat of a system purge meant that he couldn't just ignore his meals, and so he used that aforementioned staff to ensure he got healthy meals, the kind with no taste, for breakfast and lunch—that way dinner could almost be anything. Still, it felt so very wrong to not be swimming laps, working on passes, or slinging weights right now.

"What's the point, though, if I can't raise power!" Deke complained to the clouds. A nagging voice in his head, that sounded suspiciously like Lee, chastised him in familiar words. "Power isn't the only stat. It's okay to focus there but you don't want to be unbalanced." If Lee was actually here he would have argued with him, but the gentle lapping of the water over the edge of the infinity pool wasn't much of a fight.

He thought [Status], and went over his current stat sheet.

Status

Control - 6.005
Power - 6.405
Finesse - 5.575

Endurance - 5.485
Skills: Aim Assist
Physical Enhancements: [None]
Conditional Effects: [None]
Evo points total: 5
Operative rank designation: Trainee

Deke had gained some new lines to his page over the months since he'd first seen it, and a lot of those likely were due to Lee helping him really explore the thing. Still, he couldn't help but feel bummed that he wasn't becoming superhuman like that *Mutant X* guy. He'd read the comic and despite some rather corny moments, he liked it enough to have a few dreams of becoming the rather uncouth Canadian half-man-half-beast.

Lee and he had circled the Trainee designation the most lately in conversation. *Hypothesising...* Deke was fairly certain that wasn't the right word, just like it wasn't him making the guesses for what it meant. Lee believed that some of the diminishing returns could be because of that rank. Like, somehow Deke might need Evil Corps approval to unlock more things inside the sports drink.

He easily put all those thoughts out of his mind, thanks to Valerie practically skipping into the pool area with a fancy-looking shopping bag on her arm. "I can't wait to show you my new *swimsuit*. Wait right there!"

Despite wanting to respond, she was already in the pool house with the door wide open and falling out of her clothes. All thoughts fled his mind as his blood redirected itself to other areas. Valerie smiled evilly as she pulled on a single garment that would never be considered something to wear in public. To call it a swimsuit was a stretch. It truly covered the bare minimum of her body, and despite watching her totally naked body slip into the thing, Deke was aroused enough that he was out of the pool and by her side before she fully managed to tie the thing in place.

The following morning was amazing. The house staff were a polite, but almost invisible presence in the house. Making Christmas snacks, drinks and towels appear out of nowhere while dirty dishes or used clothing disappeared almost as invisibly, appearing a short while later, folded, pressed and clean. With Valerie by his side the huge mansion became much more homey and for the first time in his life, Deke got a taste of what real wealth actually felt like, which renewed his desire to earn this quality of life for himself.

The only thing that could have made this holiday better was to have Max share the experience. He couldn't help but think of the kid's face as he watched the waves from the custom hot tub next to the pool. Deke exhaled longingly, wishing for this level of care for his younger brother. Imagining not having to worry about him being hurt, by anyone. Not ever again.

The break continued to be idyllic until about three in the afternoon. He and Valerie were lounging on one of those massive couches, watching an old movie about a guy on a ranch in Australia. Suddenly Meredith, the head maid, stepped into the room. Her presence was unusual given her normally invisible existence. Valerie's body tensed as she saw her, as though preparing for grave news.

"Young miss, your father has come home," Meredith said and Valerie sat up and glanced around. "He has moved Christmas Eve dinner into the parlor and wishes for it to be a formal affair."

"Shit, he said he wasn't back 'til tomorrow! We'll get ready at once." Valerie swore, and the playful, relaxed attitude she had been using ever since she'd returned home was gone like a sun-scorched fog. She found the remote and turned off the movie; turning to Deke, she looked him up and down. "You brought your suit right?" When he nodded she continued, "It's a piece of junk, but it's still better than nothing. Damn, I would have had someone grab something better for you if he'd said he was coming home before Christmas dinner! Well, wear that, and shave." She touched his hair for a moment considering.

"See if you can't rein in your hair a bit. Father will like it better if you have a part." She jumped off and headed toward her room. "The white dress? No, the purple..." she muttered to herself as she left.

Deke looked around in confusion. He was suddenly alone, and he remembered that Valerie had asked him here to act as interference between her parents. They had spent some time with her mother and Deke actually liked the older woman. She had been trying to become an actor and had had a few jobs as an extra—a murder victim here, a distant relative there, but had quit acting when she got pregnant with Valerie and married. Valerie had never talked about her dad though, and judging by the eggshells the entire household walked on, and the way Valerie had changed as soon as the man had come home, he didn't think he was going to enjoy his Christmas dinner nearly as much as he had been expecting to.

Valerie had fussed over his suit and appearance for nearly fifteen minutes before she let him leave the pool house. She was wearing an elegant yellow dress; it was fluffy in a way that hid her body. As Deke considered the shift Valerie had undergone, he began to wonder if he was dealing with the same person. There was a stark contrast that extended across her personality, her clothing, and there was even a tension in the way she carried herself. They were seated at a table with room for six times as many people as were present and Deke immediately noticed that he had far too much silverware for a single meal.

Six forks? Who would need six forks? He wanted to make a joke, and the Valerie of this morning would have been fine with it, but he got the sense that this was not a table set for levity. He started to pull out Val's seat, but Valerie grabbed his arm, her eyes on her father. The man was standing at the head of the table, typing into his phone while Valerie's mom stood behind her chair across from them. Everyone was watching Valerie's dad as he fiddled with his device.

Deke assumed it was some sort of business email. There was nothing about the man that suggested he played Flappy Bird.

Putting his phone into his pocket and looking around, the man nodded firmly and took a seat. Deke pulled out Valerie's chair for her and she smiled at him appreciatively, even as a servant did the same for her mother. Deke then took his seat, which a servant pulled out for him. The whole dance was strange, and seemed to remove the necessity of the chivalry his mother had told him to display.

"Just the main course please. I'm not in the mood for a protracted event, and bring something..." The man paused, glancing around the table, and when his eyes landed on Deke there was a sense of judgement present in that steely gaze. "White and dry."

Immediately a third servant, one Deke hadn't seen yet, came out and placed a plate on the charger in front of the man, who pulled the domed lid off the plate and started in on the steak it held. Deke watched as Meredith took three of his forks away before setting a plate down in front of him as well. No one else at the table spoke. Deke waited until everyone was served to start into his steak. If this wasn't the most awkward dinner event ever, he would have called it the best steak he had ever eaten—the meat melted in his mouth.

"So, you're some sort of... athlete I assume? You're tall, so basketball?" Valerie's father said after draining his wine and holding the glass out for more.

"Yes sir, I'm a basketball player," Deke answered. He hadn't felt this nervous meeting Coach Skip for the first time.

"Any good?" The man asked as he took another bite from his steak.

"Daddy, Deke averages eleven points a game," Valerie responded on his behalf. "He's only a freshman but already gets a lot of minutes. He'll be the starting shooting guard next year." Deke supposed that scoring eleven points in the one game he had played did indeed give him an eleven point average. He was more surprised by the fact that Valerie knew the number.

"Hrmpf." The man expressed his opinion on Deke's skills with his mouth full. After a few seconds of chewing, he added, "Couldn't you have at least gone after a football player? I don't like basketball."

"Dear, you know UCSP doesn't have a football program," Valerie's mother said, her voice much quieter than Deke had ever heard it.

"Right, I knew there was a reason I hated that garbage school," Valerie's father muttered, as he drained his glass again. Valerie's mother's cell phone went off and the man glared at her until she silenced it.

"Sorry, it's my mother. She didn't know you were here. I'll silence it," Valerie's mother explained as she rejected the call.

"Your phone should have been on silent already. We're having a *family* dinner." The man shook his knife at her, his voice pitched with authority.

"I'm sorry," Valerie's mother pleaded even as she looked down at her food, and the table descended into silence as Val's father finished off his third glass of wine in as many minutes. Deke had been poured a glass but hadn't touched it, afraid of what having to purge after alcohol would mean with this man in the house. Deke slowly chewed his steak, which was no longer anywhere near as good as it had been.

Another ringtone broke the silence and Val's father picked up his phone and answered it immediately.

"Go for Howard." The man stood up and walked away from the table a few steps. "I'm going to take this in the study. You two continue without me." Deke had a feeling he wasn't included in the "two" the man had remembered were present at the table. He wandered off into a side room, the sound of shouting following his stormy exit. Val and her mother visibly relaxed a little as Howard left the room; it felt like a dark cloud had suddenly lifted.

"Vallie, why don't you take Deke out to a movie. You know how your father gets after his business calls," Valerie's mother said as she gulped down her own glass of wine.

"You sure?" Valerie asked her mother, and Deke had never heard this type of concern in her voice before.

"It's fine. I'll tell him."

Valerie didn't seem reassured, but her mother insisted.

"Thank you for the meal," Deke said to her mother as they left, and he wasn't sure if the noise she made as they left was a small chuckle of affirmation or a sob.

They quickly changed into less formal attire, Valerie moving at a frantic pace to get out of her dress. She borrowed some of his clothing, which was comically large on her thin frame, but somehow it felt right in that moment. She took off her face with practiced ease and then pulled him out one of the side doors and along the edge of the house. Her reluctance to get within sight range of her father was obvious.

Shouting from the house caused her to pause for a moment. Then there was a thump and the sound of glass breaking. Val bit her lip and waited, and Deke could feel her entire body tensing up as she counted seconds under her breath. On the count of three the shouting resumed, a woman's shrill voice part of the echo and with the renewed fighting Valerie darted off again, running like her life depended on it for her car. Deke followed along with a more measured pace, frowning. His longer stride allowed him to keep up with her easily.

Valerie jumped into the car and barely waited for him to get in before she took off. She was always a less than responsible driver, but she was careful not to squeal the car tires as she left the drive. Deke looked over once and saw tears in her eyes. He had never felt so helpless.

THIRTY-TWO

SATURDAY, DECEMBER 31ST
NEW YEAR'S EVE

"I expect you home without that gutter rat."-
Paternal Parental Unit - 7 days ago

"If you aren't home after your FOUR-DAY
MOVIE MARATHON, without your
distraction, then I'm cutting you off."-
Paternal Parental Unit - 3 days ago

"Valerie, I think your father is serious. He is
calling his lawyers to change his will. Please
come home."- Baddest Bitch Ever - Today

"Ill come home tomorrow morning, but only
for the day. Ive got New Years plans with
Deke."- Valerie

Deke clicked the mouse and held his breath. The feeling of nervousness while signing into Blackboard, his school's online portal for classes, was entirely new to him. In the past, he had never put in enough effort toward his grades to care. Now he really wanted to have improved his marks, and not just to validate all the extra effort his friends had made to help him. No, he wanted to have improved for himself.

The screen went white before changing to a list of his four classes. He clicked on grades at the top, which would summarize all of them on a single page. The screen went white again and he saw his first grade—Calculus, listed a C. It was a bit of a disappointment but he had never been overly hopeful for that one. He scrolled down with the fancy gaming mouse of Lee's home computer. American History B+, English B+ and Microeconomics a C+. His overall grade was a B-, and his heart thumped excitedly in his chest. He would have to brag to his brother Max about this later. These sorts of grades were still below his siblings' but they were closing in.

"I can hear you breathing heavily and I'm not sure if that's good or bad. Can I come into my own room now?" Lee asked from just outside the doorway. Deke looked around Lee's actual bedroom, and wondered, not for the first time, why the kid chose dorm life over this.

The room was almost the size of Rhonda's entire main floor back in London, and while the wealth displayed might be minor when compared to Val's place, it was by no means small. The fact that he had another massive computer here told Deke that Lee's choice to come to the dorms was likely more to avoid the conversations with his parents that might out his *actual* major. He smirked at the door after his scan of the bedroom.

"Yeah, sorry I don't want you judging me though," Deke responded, and debated closing the window. Lee's grades were bound to be far higher than his own, but he *proudly* chose to leave it open.

"B minus! Dude, congrats. Did you get any quest completion for that?" Lee strode into the room and immediately picked up the largest letter on screen. Deke scratched his head and called up his [Status].

"No, actually. That seems off doesn't it?"

Lee held up two hands, instantly fending off past arguments. Lee was well aware that Deke was growing frustrated with the system and wanting more answers, but thanks to Deke's constant questions, he also knew that Lee didn't have them—only theories. Lee pumped his hands once as he lowered them to his waist.

"Dude, don't worry. Just keep 'grinding', as you call it, and I bet we discover more. The lack of points could be because the grades aren't official yet, *or something*. Don't stress. By the way, Valerie just pulled into the driveway a few minutes ago. She hasn't left her car yet. Should you maybe go see if she is okay?"

Deke stood up and nodded. The two of them had chosen to stay hidden at the dorms and Lee's house over the last few days, but Valerie's dad had made some sort of threat that finally forced her home today. He had offered to go but was told that this time, it would only make things worse. Instead, she dropped him off here, and Lee and him had gotten the mix and snacks for a pre-drink that Valerie had insisted she would need after coming back from home.

Still, the last week of having the dorm and dorm room to themselves had been blissful. Maybe the first taste of what living together would be like?

As Deke walked toward the front door of the house, Lee asked a follow-up question. "Do you think you will still make it to the community center? I know Abbie was hoping we could show up."

"Honestly, I doubt it. I don't want to get into it but, if you had met *Demon* Howard you would understand. I think Valerie will need me to just hang out. You can go though, if you want. We could all probably meet at the dorms to hang out after."

"Remember the last time Valerie and Abbie met?" Lee reminded him, and Deke winced. Probably not best to have the two of them meet, at least not in Deke's dorm.

"True. Well let's just hang out. Text Abbie and tell her we'll meet her at the club or have her stop by here. I'm sure if it's at your house it won't be as bad." Deke opened the door and moved outside toward the small red Miata.

Valerie was just sitting in the driver seat staring straight ahead. His approach didn't seem to register on her face at all. Deke watched her for a long moment, his chest hurting. He had his own issues at home, so he felt a bit of turmoil on her behalf. Was there anything he could do?

Nodding to himself, Deke opened her door with more confidence than he felt. Valerie jumped, and an emotion he couldn't quite place flickered across her face before she seemed to come back to herself. Was that fear? Insecurity? It didn't matter, Deke supposed. Valerie's mouth trembled before she smiled. It never reached her eyes.

"Are you ready to get some dri—" she began to crow in mock-enthusiasm, as Deke took her hand and drew her from the vehicle.

"Shut up," Deke said simply, drawing her into his arms. He lifted her up and buried his face in the crook of her neck and shoulder, the warm scent of vanilla and spice forming a halo that seemed to reach for him in desperation. "Just shut up, Val." Valerie stiffened in surprise, her whole bearing drawn taut as piano wire. She began to push back against him as if to distance herself from the emotion of the moment.

"No, Deke... I—can't... I just can't... Not right now... It's all just too..." Her voice cracked with emotion as she tried ineffectually to push him away.

"Yes, you can," Deke murmured soothingly, his own voice thick with emotion, even as he wrapped her more firmly into his embrace. In that moment, he wasn't sure if he was talking more to himself, or to her. Images and memories of his mother's struggles and the heart-wrenching trials of his little brother played across his mind in vivid color. "You're not the only one who needs this, Val."

All at once, something seemed to break within the young woman, as her bones liquified and he suddenly found himself holding a mostly limp body. She didn't wrap her legs around him, as she might have when excited, but her arms, the only taut part of her, grabbed him more firmly than her small frame seemed to allow. The tears came in thick—choking sobs that wracked her fragile body, as the stifled wails of a little girl who just wanted a father, and not some authoritarian *demon* dictator, met the cool morning air.

"I'm here, Val. I'm here," he cooed. A tension he hadn't known was in him had loosened in his own chest as they held each other, taking what comfort they could in their shared misery. They were two people, with different lives but one problem in common. Family. They'd found each other. Time passed neither slowly nor fast, as they drew what comfort and strength they could from the moment. Eventually, Val drew back, dabbing at the mascara around her eyes.

"See, this is what I was talking about." He had put her down and stooped over her, wrapping his entire body around her protectively at some point. Now, she stomped her foot in mock outrage, that was far too cute to be taken as anything other than an attempt to break the tension. "Look what you did. Now I have to fix all of this."

"I don't see anything wrong at all." Deke smiled, taking in her disheveled appearance. "You've got this hot kind of damsel-in-distress thing going on right now that's pressing all my buttons."

Huffing out a breathy chuckle, Val rolled her eyes at him. "Hot mess, maybe." She took a slow, deep breath, her hands pantomiming the breath coming into and then leaving her lungs. "Okay. I'll admit that I really needed that. But *now*, what I really need is to get piss drunk and find someone to take advantage of me shamelessly." Eyeing him with a sultry smile, she gave him a once-over. "Anyone you know who might be interested in that?"

"I volunteer as tribute," Deke deadpanned a hand-raise. She reached out and put down his thumb and pinky, correcting his pose with a chuckle.

"Good, I thought you might—since you'll be the one driving. I hope you learned a thing or two from last time." As she spoke she slapped the keys into his chest and skipped past him like a twirling butterfly. The sunrise of her smile loosened the rest of the tension in Deke's chest as he smirked after her retreating figure.

"I'll manage." Deke clicked the door locks on the key fob as he followed Valerie into Lee's parents' house.

"I'll hop out here," Lee said as he slid over on the back seat toward the door. Deke was driving Lee's family's car, and he moved to the side of the boulevard to let Lee out. The Miata simply didn't have enough room, and admittedly if he never had to drive that death trap again, it wouldn't be a loss. "Abbie said she would meet me near that ice cream stand. We'll see you both inside?"

Lee had a bit of slur to his voice, having already drank one too many, trying to keep up with Valerie. Deke smiled at his friend and nodded. "Catch you in the VIP booth man. The team supposedly has the whole upper deck donated by a sponsor."

"You know what that means?" Valerie said, turning to look at Lee out her window. "Free drinks all night, bitch!" Somehow Lee had become something like a girlfriend or a gay friend to Valerie, now that they had shared pre-drinks. "Don't let me get too far ahead!"

Lee gave Deke a helpless look that said "save me" and Deke just smiled and winked at the kid. He would try to keep Valerie away from him at the party, and most likely it wouldn't be too difficult once they got inside and her cheerleader sorority girlfriends filled that void.

Deke parked the car in the first spot he found after dropping Lee off, and he moved around to open Valerie's door. He was too late and she had already shot from the passenger seat. He closed her door for her and locked up the car before moving to her side. She pulled him in for a quick kiss and he slid his hands down her back; she winced and pulled away slightly as he reached her ass.

"Sorry, I fell, and have some bruises there," Valerie said, slipping around and grabbing his elbow. Deke had noticed those bruises before, mostly on her upper thigh and back, almost always after she visited home. He had tried to bring it up with her before, but she always brushed it off.

Despite the bruises and alcohol, he was pretty sure she could walk straight at this point, but he did worry that she might be a bit unsteady with the size of her heels, and he didn't want to keep everyone waiting too long, so he let the matter drop. Val would hopefully tell him the whole story when she was ready.

They approached the back of the line and Deke truthfully wanted to wait in it, mostly to give Valerie some time to process the booze, but she tugged on his arm. "They've got us on the guest-list silly. All the Baguettes and staff get in VIP tonight!"

"Can you promise me you won't be too drunk to find my lips later tonight if we go in right away?" Deke asked, holding his ground in the line for a few moments. Valerie actually ran a hand through her hair and tucked some behind her ear, seeming to give the question more thought than it needed.

"All right, since you were so good all week, my first two drinks will be water inside. But if that bitch Lee asks, it's vodka-waters, deal?"

Deke laughed and allowed her to pull him to the front of the line.

"Deke Mills and *Veronica!*" She exclaimed when the bouncer held up his hand to stop them. "We're Baguettes." Deke managed to control his face at Val's usage of her false name.

The guard seamlessly lowered his hand, stepped forward and undid the security rope to let them pass. "Check your 'names' with the entry girl."

The bouncer had clearly been instructed to expect fake IDs by the way he enunciated the word. Deke smiled and pulled out his actual ID. It wasn't like he was going to be drinking and risk purging in a nightclub. Besides, he was the designated driver and he took that seriously.

As soon as they entered the first set of doors, the sound of the bass that was mildly audible from the outside ramped up, and the words to DMX's "Up in here" became much clearer. There was still a door separating them from the main part of the club and Deke led Valerie to the check-in desk, where he was admitted with his plus one, "Veronica Verdent." He was given a glow-in-the-dark stamp which indicated to bartenders not to serve him liquor and the two of them continued into the main club.

They entered through the second set of doors and Deke paused to allow his eyes to adjust to the red laser-lights that cut through the blackness near the ceiling. They weren't the only source of light, as blue lights shone down onto the dance floor and bar areas, creating a wave-like pattern. Clearly the theme was based on the name of the club, Wavemasters, and Deke was glad Valerie had instructed him to wear his best surfer apparel.

Valerie took off her thin zippered sweater to reveal her bikini and a lei underneath. Thankfully, the bikini she had chosen wasn't the one she'd shown off in the pool house. Still, this one gave a roundness to her breasts that made Deke stare for a moment. She caught him looking and grabbed his chin before giving him a kiss.

"I've brought another one in my purse for later. This is just a teaser!" she shouted into the din of the club music and close pressed bodies. "The VIP booth is that way!" She pointed to the other side of the dance floor and continued, "You lead the way."

Deke peeled his eyes away from her tiny purse. How in the world did that thing hold a piece of clothing? He swallowed as he realized what sort of treat he would be in for later. Taking her outstretched hand, he began doing as instructed and the dancers parted around his wide frame. He could make out some teammates dancing in a circle toward the back and changed direction toward them. It was easy to distinguish the basketball players, as their heads and some of their shoulders were above crowd level. Duke was by far the easiest to find and Deke was startled by the big man's ability to stay on point with the rhythm. As they approached, Deke watched enviously as the man popped and locked smoothly.

As soon as Duke saw them approaching he raised his hands and started a cheer, which was picked up by the other teammates, except for Mac. The shooting guard, who had been smiling a moment ago, narrowed his eyes and turned away to leave the dance floor. Deke thought the senior was looking washed out and pale, but considered that it might just be the lighting in the place. Together, Val and Deke closed the final distance and found the cheerleaders mixing in among the athletes. They were just regular size and hidden by the crowd from far away. Valerie popped out from behind his back at that point and was greeted by her sorority sisters giving a much more high-pitched and audible cheer.

"You made it, and with some fine arm candy!" Duke called, his deep voice trumping the music.

"Right!" Deke exclaimed, looking at Valerie as she began to sway in her bikini. Every so often the bikini bottom that was barely covering her ass would reveal itself. Duke got close beside him and pointed an arm toward Valerie's dancing partner. Deke realized it was Eva and took a moment to appreciate her extremely sexy scuba outfit. "Damnnn!"

"It shouldn't be legal." Duke put an arm around Deke's shoulder conspiratorially. "There ain't no way either of them should be allowed out in public. I swear the whole team is just bodyguards for the ladies at this point..." They both laughed and followed as their girlfriends motioned to the VIP section.

The section had two entrances. One toward the bar and one toward the dance floor. They entered through the latter and Deke looked around at the players and staff sitting on cushioned sofas that created a wall of sorts from the people outside. It wasn't until he looked back that he noticed the security guard who had let them enter. He assumed Duke approaching made it quite obvious they were part of the team.

The tables were filled with buckets of ice, and the ice was pincushioned with bottles of mix and alcohol. Too late, Deke saw the approach of Fisher and wondered how he could have missed the rotund man. "Boys, I insist you come have a drink with me!"

Deke held up the glow in the dark stamp on the back of his hand, thankful for the save, but Duke just nodded to Fisher and towed Deke along anyway.

"He's a part owner of this place and donated the booth for us. So let's at least go over. His table has top-shelf stuff anyway... Don't worry, I will pour you some water!" Duke said as Deke tried to protest. The big man leaned in and whispered conspiratorially. "More importantly, I'm not getting stuck with the guy alone, so you're coming with me."

They stayed around Fisher's table for a while and Deke noticed Mac sitting beside the man, sipping something that looked like an expensive cognac. With the music, Deke only caught snippets of their conversation, but it was clear that Mac was telling Fisher that he would be starting still, despite Deke's last game. Deke just smiled to himself and enjoyed his time with Valerie who had rejoined him. She was chugging her second glass of water whereas he was sipping his like a fine vintage.

"Okay, that's two cups of water and Lee and Abbie just got here. Can I have a real drink now?" Valerie asked as she tugged on his Hawaiian shirt seductively. He bent down to kiss her thoroughly, as she grabbed his hair and held the kiss for a long moment.

"Transaction complete," he gasped robotically when she let him have some air. She winked at him and took an expensive bottle of gin from Fisher's table before sashaying away to one of the other buckets of ice and mix. Deke looked at Fisher, who watched her go appreciatively and he gave a helpless shrug before following. She'd taken a bottle of Tanqueray Ten and when Deke got to the other station she used it to mix with tonic and ice. He wondered how much more expensive that bottle was compared to the Bombay Sapphire he saw in the lower sections.

Abbie and Lee came over to join them and Valerie began pouring a second glass. At first Deke thought it was for Lee, but she offered it to Abbie. "Hey look, I know it's not technically buying you a drink, but I wanted to apologize for the last time we met. I won't even try to excuse myself. I was wrong and I'm terribly sorry."

"Don't worry about it!" Abbie shouted over the music as she accepted the drink. Val looked at Deke after she said it and raised an eyebrow, as if to say "See? I can be nice." He just smiled in response. Valerie seemed to be less crazy lately, and he had to admit he was enjoying the tentative peace that she seemed to be forming with his friends.

"Good, now let's go dance, you *bitches!*" Valerie crowed at Lee and by association, Abbie.

The four of them made their way out to the dance floor and he swayed to the music, all hips and shoulders for the remainder of the night. Deke made it his goal to not get cornered by the ever drunker Fisher, and he miraculously managed it. One time, just as Fisher was coming toward him, two well-dressed men in black tuxedos inter-posed themselves and the three of them made their way into a door behind the bar. Deke shivered as the apparel and mannerism of the two reminded him of the Vaper.

Still, without having to dodge the man anymore, Deke's night became even better and pretty soon the end-of-year countdown began.

He found Valerie and they stood close together, ready to ring in the new year with a kiss. Deke looked around and found that all of his teammates had managed to pair up with someone. He frowned though, when he saw Abbie paired up with Lee. His gut churned, seeing her getting ready to kiss Lee, and he thought back to the moment at the community center, when she had given him the comic book. He shook the thoughts from his head and turned back to Valerie, who was looking up at him with excitement in her eyes.

She rose up in her heels and he leaned down as the ten second mark hit. She brought her lips close to his ear and ran her hand up his inner thigh below the shorts. "Do you think there is enough room in the back of Lee's SUV for some fun?"

Deke had just enough time to feel his heart start to race before she kissed him. He took one moment to register Abbie kissing Lee's cheek before he closed his eyes and rang in the New Year with Valerie.

CHAPTER THIRTY-TWO

Sunday, January 1st
New Year's Day

Systems check authorized. Evaluating performance goals and objectives.

Evaluation status: Trainee.

Skill(s) Gained: Aim Assist.

Yearly progress: 56/365 daily tasks accomplished.

Awarding 56 Evo Points.

You have 61 evo points.

Evaluation results: Adequate

*Learning grade average finalized. 2.7 GPA
Results deemed below average. 0.04 Power awarded.*

THIRTY-THREE

SATURDAY, JANUARY 7TH

"Mr. Wellington needs further persuasion."- Ed Rooney-Athletic Director

"The subject is being uncooperative, even with outside pressures."- John Smoke

"Surely there is more you can do."- Ed Rooney-Athletic Director

"We will up the ante but if this fails, we're pulling out."- John Smoke

Deke was crying.

The buzzing near his ears didn't stop, despite his play-acting. He was, of course, extra careful not to move too much during his façade. But he wanted to sell the scene, to play it for all it was worth. He was lying on his back on a bench with the Baguettes logo plastered on it, his head hanging way back so they could reach it, while above him two all-too-skinny kids shaved his hair off, laughing. The sterile banks of the pediatric ward lights provided a stark contrast behind them.

Around him, other kids were doing the same to Duke and the rest of the Baguettes basketball team. The entire scene was for charity. Grant Fisher had paid close to a thousand dollars to give these two kids the opportunity to shave Deke bald. He, like all the other athletes, knew where the money was going and his hair was a couple of inches long anyway, so it wasn't some huge loss.

"I can't take it anymore!" Deke yelled and he pulled the clippers from the kid's hand, careful not to injure the skinny kid's frail arms as he did so. Sitting up, he ran a hand across his scalp; he could feel an off-center mohawk and he glared at the two kids. "My precious hair!"

Trying to add even more humor to the situation, he reached down to grab some of the hair from the floor. He didn't care whose he collected as he pretended to try to stick it back onto his head. The kids giggled, and the other children in attendance turned to watch the spectacle, smiles bright on their wan faces.

"What do you think? Do I look fabulous?" Deke said, sculpting the purloined floor-hair up into a point and striking a pose. A little girl laughed while shouting her disagreement. "No? Well, maybe it's time for me to shave YOUR head!" Deke took a single step forward and gave mock chase to the child and she shrieked, turning around and running behind the massive frame of Duke who had already taken his turn, and thus was protected from the mock threat.

"Don't worry! I won't let our crazy man get you!" The big center said, picking the girl up and then throwing her over his shoulder before running off to the side to deposit her among her friends, to more giggles. Deke couldn't help but smile, despite his assumed role as the big bad guy, and he looked around. Off to the side was a thin child in a wheelchair. The boy's head swiveled in every direction, unable to participate but trying to watch everything at the same time. Deke headed toward the young boy, a genuine smile on his face. He couldn't help thinking about his brother Max, when he saw the child.

"What's your name?" Deke began, trying to familiarize the kid with him.

"David," he squeaked with a voice that screamed physical weakness.

"David, it sure looks like you have the strongest arms in here. Do you think you could finish the job for me?" Deke said, holding out the clippers.

The smile on David's face was warm enough to melt the arctic, and Deke felt his own heart swell. He wished Max was nearby, and reminded himself to call home later to check up on him. Grinning at David, Deke knelt down to let the kid finish shaving off the last of his hair with a great deal of good-natured banter.

Afterward, Deke spent thirty minutes wheeling David around the room so that he could talk to all the players. The nurses finally came in to grab the kids so that the team could rest. Deke was likely supposed to feel tired after all the interactions but the day had actually energized him. He smiled even as his teammates sat down to regroup.

Instead of joining them, Deke picked up a broom to help clean up. To his shock, Duke slapped his shoulder, holding up a dustbin and bending down, which for the big man was a long, long way, so that Deke could fill it up.

"You know, I'm surprised by how good you are with kids. Most of the guys have trouble finding what to say, especially with the really sick ones," the big center said, crouching low to pick up all the hair. It took Deke a moment to figure out how he wanted to answer that. While the interaction with all the kids made him happy, he wasn't ready to share his actual reasons. They were too personal.

"But it's so simple when they are great kids like those, don't you think?" Deke said, turning it into a question so he could hopefully steer the conversation away. Duke smiled as Deke swept his pile into the dustbin.

The large center gave a simple nod, seeming to sense his desire, and the big man changed the subject for Deke. "So, we never really talked about your performance last game. Let me ask; how do you think you did? What do you think you need to work on?"

"Oh." Deke switched gears as he tried to remember the last game. "Well man, I would say I did all right..."

"Just all right?" Duke asked as he stood to his full height.

"I mean I did pretty well, right up until they started taking me seriously." Duke nodded in such a way that encouraged Deke to continue. "Well, it might sound like an excuse but I think it's been too long since I shot with interference, you know?"

Duke dumped the dustbin and didn't respond, so Deke continued into the silence. "It felt like I needed to work on lining up my shots faster with a defense."

He somewhat skirted the actual issue, which was that Deke had gotten too used to relying on [Aim Assist] while shooting around at the community center. So, while it was true that he needed to practice with a defense, what he *really* needed to work on was actively moving while using the skill. Practicing with a wide open shot had made him lose the "feel" of his shot while under pressure, and he needed to get that back.

"I had the same problem as a freshman. Coach showed me this drill that helped me with those pressure shots—I'll talk to him and we'll run you through your paces." Duke headed off to find more hair to throw away and Deke watched him as he moved among the rest of the team, easily striking up a conversation with all of them.

Somehow that gorilla managed to include everyone, even the hospital staff who were working alongside the players. How do you reconcile that sort of open friendliness with the power and... the borderline cheating that came with using the sports drink? Deke wasn't sure, but he was determined to figure it out for himself.

Monday, January 9th

Duke had been true to his word, and Deke was now standing behind the three point line outside of the elbow. Boogie, one of the assistant coaches, stood near the top of the key, while Duke middled the distance between Coach and Deke. He was maybe five feet away, and thanks to his massive size it felt like the center was looming over him. Boogie dribbled once, then passed the ball over to Deke.

As soon as the pass left the coach's hands, Duke was released like a cage fighter and began closing the distance. Snagging the pass, Deke took a step forward, jumping up to take a full powered shot at the hoop. The [Aim Assist] glowed green as he pulled his hands back and he'd just begun his release when the line went red. Duke's massive hand interposed itself in front of the line, blocking the trajectory Deke wanted.

Since he was already in the air, he extended his reach up a little more, trying to go up and over the center's massive mitt. Unfortunately their height differential made it so that Deke couldn't get a clean shot off, though he tried anyway with a last minute high lob. Duke still swatted the ball easily out the side of the court.

Deke landed and Boogie's whistle sounded what felt like Deke's hundredth defeat, Coach's words granting him some reprieve. "All right, we've been doing this for a while, everyone take five and hydrate."

Deke allowed himself to collapse back on the floor in exhaustion, breathing heavily. They'd been doing this drill for almost an hour straight and all four of his appendages were burning from effort.

New task assigned.

Quick Shot: Created by Trainee's continued practice under pressure. Learn to make decisions and fire faster.

Rewards: Stats, ~~Quick Shot~~

Deke blinked and focused on the stricken-out reward.

~~*Quick Shot Skill*~~

Unable to display information at this time. Trainee's Radanium integration is insufficient to support additional active skills at this time.

"Catch," Duke said half a second before a water bottle landed on his stomach. Deke grunted in the middle of an inhalation, but managed to catch the projectile before it rolled out of his reach. He blinked away his current thoughts about the system and his own body, but made a mental note to ask Lee what the hell was going on. Twisting the top, he sat up and drained half the bottle in one long gulp. He was already thirsty before the radar bullshit system reminded him of his possible poisoning. He gave it one final thought. Could his body be slowly breaking down? That would explain why he hadn't gotten any new tasks or stats in almost two weeks. Now he had a task but was denied a reward...

"I think your problem is that you're catching the ball too low," Duke stated.

"Huh?" Deke asked, confused about what Duke was talking about.

"That's why I'm blocking your shots," Duke continued with a raised brow as he sat down on the court next to Deke. "I always have a harder time when the shooter is already most of the way to the shooting position when he gets the ball."

Deke shook off the system problems and brought himself back to the moment. He considered Duke's solution for a moment, before he nodded his head. He had to admit that it wasn't just [Aim Assist] that was giving him problems.

The weird double images he had been seeing off and on had started appearing more regularly, not every time, but at least two out of three. He was pretty sure it wasn't exhaustion or poison causing that issue, as when he caught a glimpse of the secondary image, it always preceded what the real Duke was going to do. Still, Deke was having a huge problem processing all the extra information.

"Okay, I'll try that," Deke huffed, as he pictured himself catching the ball already on his right palm. It wasn't hard to imagine, but likely would be infinitely harder to accomplish.

Then he kept thinking of this double image prediction-like ability. Unlike [Aim Assist], which mostly just told him where the thing in his hands was going to land, this new ability was proving much more difficult to use. In theory, it should be easy and Deke knew that. Take in the information and adjust to his opponent. However, in practice, he only got a split second of information before his opponent was there.

Duke and Deke sat in companionable silence as they finished their waters. Boogie whistled and they got back into position.

This time Deke's hands were near his chest when he caught the pass. The double image of Duke appeared as usual–the translucent image leading Duke's actual steps by a fraction of a second. With a thought he pushed down hard on his left foot, breaking his forward momentum and sending him backward half a step.

Unfortunately, he had been responding to the position of the image, and not Duke himself. The center pivoted, following him through the movement and slapping the ball out of his hands even as he raised up to shoot.

"That was actually better, despite the result," Boogie said.

"Yeah, let's run that one again. I think I've got it," Deke said, and Duke tilted his head before he bounced the ball to the assistant coach. Duke raised an eyebrow while everyone reset their positions, and Deke gave him a cheeky wink. He figured the worst that would happen would be Duke blocking his shot again.

Boogie slapped one hand against the ball before passing it to Deke. Deke's smile widened as he caught the ball on a forward step. He watched Duke's movement, as his actions were predicted and then, right as Duke committed his weight to a drive, Deke pushed off hard, backing up from the three point line by a full two feet.

Then, to Duke's wide-eyed surprise, he leaned back further and faded away with his hands back above his head. He lined up the tracking line until the shot went green. Duke tried to shift his arms to block. But it was too late, the line of [Aim Assist] flashed through the hoop and Deke released. The ball bounced off the back rim before dropping through the hoop.

"Well, that worked," Duke said, but gave him a look. "That wasn't exactly what I had in mind, but you still did release faster..." To blunt any sting in the comment, Duke clapped Deke on his shoulder and then reset his position. "Now let's just do it a few hundred more times."

Deke smiled in response to Duke's encouragement, but the sports drink had also finally come through for him. He took a quick break by grabbing another bottle of water, as he mentally called up the new message.

Successfully used motion prediction in combat.

Trainee Radanium integration is insufficient to support additional active skills. Partial unlock of [Motion Prediction] within integration limits. Acquire additional Radanium to unlock full functionality.

Deke sputtered; the idea that another skill was available to him but not going to unlock was infuriating. Was there a way to get more Radanium? Also the fact that [Motion Prediction] had been unlocked because he used it in "combat" unsettled him. Controlling the coughing fit that overtook him as he accidentally swallowed saliva, he felt Duke pound his back.

"I'm fine, just got excited and the water went down the wrong pipe," Deke managed to get out between the slaps and coughs. The distinctive shrill of Coach Skip's whistle echoed through the practice.

"All right, that's enough for the day. Good work everyone, keep up the energy level and I have no doubt we'll add another W to our season this weekend." Deke tuned out the head coach as he launched into his normal end-of-practice scripture. Deke spent the entire time reflecting on his shit luck. How could the system do him like that?

Deke was thankfully exempt from his after practice clean-up duties, but only because he had to go get checked out by Doctor Dan. Neither Skip, nor the doctor himself seemed to trust Deke's abnormal recovery, so he had to endure an extra bit of poking and prodding. He thought he had come to grips with that necessity, but his current mood made him upset to have to go through it *again*.

Duke followed him below along with Mac and Manny, the team's power forward.

"Hey Duke, you ever hear back from that recruiter guy who was chasing you a while back?" Manny's voice had a lightness that belied his muscular frame. "You know, the creepy one in the black suit that was always vaping?" Duke paused and Deke felt himself pull in a sharp breath, his problems with the system forgotten. He held that breath, not wanting to interrupt whatever the center was about to say.

"Nah, something just felt off about the guy. So I told him to take a hike." Duke picked up his pace. Deke narrowed his eyes and squinted at Duke. Lately the center had been growing on him, but here was another reminder of Duke's involvement in this whole thing. Still, no one else in the group even caught on to Duke's slight hesitation in his response.

Knowing what he personally knew about the vaping man, Deke thought "something off" was stating it mildly. Ronnie still hadn't shown back up, and Deke hoped that he had managed to escape whatever wrath the vaping man had intended for him.

Duke stopped, turning around to look the three other players in the eyes.

"Listen, that guy is a thug. I don't care what promises he makes. Don't take any deals from him. With the insane amount of effort he was putting into me, I imagine he'll probably be coming after someone else on the team. Spread the word. He's bad news, boys."

Duke caught Deke looking at him with narrowed eyes and canted his head. Something jostled Deke's shoulder, which broke the two players' eye contact.

"Why're you telling the rook this?" Mac said, pushing past Deke and Duke.

"Because with the way he's playing, he's likely to be taking your spot, dick," Duke answered even as he leveled a steely gaze at the point guard. Mac looked at him for a moment, then glanced over at Deke and scoffed.

"I'm not gonna lose my spot to some lightweight druggie who can't keep his clothes on," Mac said, continuing down the stairs.

"Don't listen to him, man. We all know it was Mac that gave you the extra doses, we just didn't have a leg to stand on without you on the team. He's our best bad choice." Manny looked after Mac's retreating back. "We all see how hard you're working to get back. You're obviously too serious about this to jeopardize your career over some painkillers." Manny slapped his shoulder and Deke just nodded his head.

Using his anger at Mac, Deke hid his guilt. While he hadn't chosen to take the sports drink, he had certainly been taking advantage of the benefits it gave him. Then again, the system seemed to be sputtering out or *something*. Manny walked a step ahead of him as they descended the stairs in silence.

About halfway down, Deke realized that he was indeed still taking advantage of the sports drink, and despite the thing's lackluster performance lately, he wouldn't even be healed without it. Still, this was his karmic reward for trying to save Ronnie from a beating. Was he in the wrong for any of this?

By the bottom of the stairs, Deke decided that he wasn't . . . *probably.*

CHAPTER

THIRTY-FOUR

MONDAY, JANUARY 9TH

"Duke! This rook is taking all my minutes!"-
Mac Attack

"We're winning. Wouldn't you rather make
Mercenary March?"- The Duke

"I'd prefer to still be starting at Mercenary
March. You seen Ronald around anywhere?
I know he quit but I need to see him…"-
Mac Attack

"I heard he left town." - The Duke

"I don't know!" Lee shouted, finally having had enough of Deke's pestering. "There is no game I can draw on that perfectly mimics what's going on inside of your goram body, Deke!"

Deke banged his head against the dorm wall behind his bed. He was sitting there, and until just now had leaned forward every time a new way to ask the same question entered his head. Essentially, *What does the rolandian integration shit mean?*

"This might be the first time anyone ever said this, and it's

304

certainly the first time I've said it, but we need a damn owner's manual or something," Lee grumbled as he flipped through one of multiple notebooks he was keeping. "We just have too many questions that we can't answer, you know?"

Deke bumped the back of his head into the wall again, trying to knock brain cells together in there. Surely there was something they could do. He thought back on everything he knew.

"So, from the beginning," Deke began and heard Lee groan. Before Lee could stop him Deke stated, "Just hear me out!

"Someone jumped Ronnie, presumably for the sports drink I took, but admittedly it could have been for the other drugs he was carrying. Still, those two thugs are one possible knowledge source—"

"That we'll never find," Lee interjected.

Deke ignored Lee and continued. ". . . then there are the papers that were in the bag—"

"That is likely in the city dump!" Lee interjected again.

This time Deke sat forward in a burst of speed and stared at Lee. Slowly Deke raised an eyebrow and watched as his friend's face fell. "We have no chance of finding the goram thing!" Lee argued. Deke just smiled. "Gorramit, you ruttin' reaver!"

Monday, January 16th

Deke picked up a tangle of charging cable and held it between two fingers in Lee's direction. Breathing through his mouth and a thin bandana, Deke admitted, "We aren't going to find the bag in all this garbage!"

"*Pi gu*, we just got here Deke," Lee responded without even turning around. "The guy at the front said each pile is from a specific week, and this is the right one. So we have a better chance than I originally thought!"

"You mean the guy we slipped a hundo to? The guy that took

money to let us in to search through garbage? That one?" Deke grumbled, mostly to himself. "And just because I haven't watched all of Firebug doesn't mean I don't know you just called me an ass, or idiot or something."

Deke's optimism at the garbage dump had dried up even faster than it had appeared. This place smelled horrible, and while Lee seemed to have flipped his skepticism in the opposite direction, actually believing, Deke could tell it was false optimism.

"Well then, *yeh lu jwo duo luh jwohn whei jian guay*," Lee quoted, and Deke raised an eyebrow. Lee glanced back and caught his expression. "Don't worry man, that one is more about our longshot odds of finding the bag. Basically, all we need to do is be here long enough or often enough."

"You've got garbage in your hair," Deke lied, and got the pleasure of watching Lee jump back and bring his hands near his head before realizing the gloves he wore were covered in goo. "I'm just kidding man, but honestly you were right. Happy, I said it? There's no goram way we're going to find a fake doctor's bag in this massive pile!"

Deke motioned to the pile that easily was three times the size of a house. Lee sneered at him for his "joke" and then looked back to the mound of garbage as well. The problem was that the bag could be completely buried under this thing, or the guy at the gate could be steering them wrong. They would never know, and while Deke wanted to find the contracts or user manual, he wasn't willing to dig through a literal pile of garbage for it.

"You're probably right, let's take one more lap around and over this thing. If we don't see the bag, then let's try to think of something else," Lee concluded. "What color did you say it was again?"

"Blue," Deke said as he walked up beside Lee. "You take that side this time, and I'll take this one," he added as he began carefully picking his steps around the edge of the pile. He looked up the pile and sighed. Another, larger issue was that they couldn't really climb the thing. The guy had made it very clear that pockets of air might exist inside of the massive mound, and if they climbed too high, they could get buried under it all.

"I took this side last time," Lee complained as he pointed to a rusty barbeque. "I swear I saw this thing eight times now."

"No you saw this thing, four of them," Deke pointed to another barbeque that was possibly bent even more out of shape.

"There is no way that many people threw out grills on the same day right? Which means the guard probably lied to us and this is pointless," Lee said as he glanced between the two identical barbecues.

"Okay, let's get out of here. I'll buy lunch since you bribed the guard."

As they climbed back out of the bottom of the pile, Deke froze. Eight men in wife beaters, all heavily tattooed, were walking toward them.

"Whatcha looking for?" the lead guy asked in a shout. Deke scratched his head, looked up the pile and then back to the guy. Just as his eyes returned, the guy revealed a gun in his waistband. The thing was silver and shining in the noonday sun. Deke blinked and put his hand in the air, showing he wasn't holding anything. Lee did the same.

Threat Level Orange.

Ruger Security-9. Ammunition size: 9mm. Loaded.

"Uhh—I threw out my friend's rare game, and after I couldn't replace it, he forced me down here to look for it," Deke lied. "The guard said this pile was from the week I tossed it."

"It worth anything?" the skinniest of the group of guys said from near the back. Deke looked at Lee, hoping for some help.

"I mean, I guess. I hadn't planned to sell it, but it's a vintage Play-Station disc for Breath of Fire. We can't find a replacement so I'd guess it's worth a couple hundred easy."

"How 'bout you pay us to keep looking for you?" the big leader said again. His tattoos of what appeared to be birds of prey rippled as he flexed intimidatingly. Deke was about to respond in the negative to the offer when Lee's wide-eyed look at him brought him up short. Once Lee saw he had Deke's attention, he pulled out his wallet and fished out the remainder of his cash.

"Thanks man, we really appreciate that." Lee held the money out, and the leader snatched it before looking at Deke expectantly.

"Oh!" Deke muttered, and fished out his own wallet. He only had two twenties but he pulled them out and reached them toward the leader as well. They were subsequently snatched.

"This it?" the leader asked, and only after they emptied their pockets and showed them the empty wallets were they allowed to leave. Luckily neither of them were wearing any jewelry or expensive clothing—thanks in large part to where they had been going.

As they left Lee whispered, "I think that was Los Condorés. They're a gang in the area. Somewhat tame as long as you don't antagonize them."

"You think they were looking for the bag too?" Deke asked, not sure why he jumped to that conclusion but feeling something familiar about two of the members.

"Nah, the guard probably told them we had money," Lee responded, and Deke looked back to find the group already leaving. Why were they so familiar?

Tuesday January 17th

Professor Pratt held up a hand in the universal "wait" sign, when Deke placed his English paper on the pile on his way out. Pratt pulled Deke's paper out and left it in front of him as Deke stepped out of the line of students exiting the auditorium.

Deke couldn't help but worry over what he had done wrong. Lee and Abbie had helped him somewhat with the paper, showing him the rubric and explaining what each line meant in detail, but other than that... he couldn't think of a reason to be singled out.

As the last student left the room, Deke swallowed and in an unsteady voice asked, "What's up P. Pratt?"

The very nondescript professor that was P. Pratt smiled at the use of the nickname students had given him—somehow failing to realize it was actually a bit derogatory, as far as Deke knew. P. Pratt was really a polite way to call the man peepee, but he guessed that the small bespectacled man just liked having a nickname.

"Nothing at all, Mr. Mills! I just figured you could do with getting your grades early, so you didn't have to worry about them before the games this week!" Pratt's voice was comically high-pitched, like he had never hit puberty.

"That would be excellent, Mr. Pratt," Deke responded, and even used a more respectable name for the teacher. His wide smile from the offer faltered and then fell as Pratt took the paper and flipped pages far quicker than what Deke thought was needed for a proper read-through.

The professor even seemed to make random red marks on each page, that Deke hastily read over, before he could flip to the next page. "Improper margins?" That couldn't be right; Lee had literally helped him navigate Office Suites to ensure his formatting was what the teacher wanted.

"Run-on sentence?" Really? He had used Abbie's Grammarly account to help him ensure the paper was as close to clean as a machine could make it. More and more marks on the pages were made until Pratt flipped back to the front and circled a C+. He handed the ten pages back to Deke and said, "Go Baguettes!" while tapping his nose.

Deke numbly took the stack, and tried to smile but only managed a small sickly grin. He was probably supposed to say something to the professor but all he could manage was a whispered "Go Baguettes" as he turned to walk away. He examined the lump in his stomach, after stopping just outside the door. He let his back crash onto the wall, which caused a mild pain while forcing the air out of his lungs in a rush.

Why was he upset? Last semester a C+ was a great grade, and honestly before Pratt's obvious display of favoritism, he probably would have celebrated that very grade if he got it back next week. "Okay, so you're upset at what then? That he just gave you the grade you wanted? *Pie gao.*"

Removing his backpack from the wall just outside of the classroom, Deke began walking toward the cafeteria even as he slammed the paper into the backpack he held by the top strap. He had lunch with Abbie and Lee before practice, and he needed the calories.

A hand waving from his usual table caught his attention. As he stood in the entryway, he looked over to find Lee. The kid motioned to a full plate of food, and Deke's mood turned around. Lee was definitely a godsend in all this. Who else would head to a garbage dump during his gaming time, and keep him honest to his nutrition plan?

"Figured you would be running late. What did Peepee say to your question about the rubric?" Lee asked, and Deke's smile fell for the second time. He had completely forgotten to ask.

"Ahh, I forgot to point out the descrep—umm the—"

"Discrepancy," Abbie helpfully said around a mouthful of food.

"Yeah, I forgot to point that out. Still, it doesn't matter 'cause he gave me a C+," Deke said.

Lee blinked and studied Deke's face. "You don't seem happy about that?"

"I'm real happy with a C+. I told you two yesterday that's a good grade in English Composition for me, but—well, look." Deke pulled the paper from his bag and flattened the now bent pages out in front of Lee and Abbie. He hadn't realized he'd bent them when shoving the thing into his bag, but figured his ability to carefully place it between two books from earlier that morning just wasn't there anymore.

The two began flipping through the paper.

"This is all nonsense! Did he even read it?" Abbie asked.

Deke shrugged. "I mean, maybe? I definitely couldn't read as fast as he was flipping pages. I barely read some of the mark-ups."

"That frog humper," Lee stated loudly, and a few people from other tables looked over. *"Qing wa cao de liu mang!"* he said a bit louder and Abbie smiled, which told Deke it was another saying from their favorite Firebug show.

The looks from people at other tables morphed into scrutiny, but midway through the clearly foreign language quote, most people turned back to meals. Lee pointed to the paper. "Deke, I didn't want to say anything till you got it back, but this isn't a C+ paper. If I handed something like this in, I would be aiming for an A, and be happy with a B."

Deke's mouth fell open, and he looked at the paper again. While he could get somewhat good grades in other classes, English wasn't even close to a strong subject for him. He might have dismissed Lee's words but Abbie was nodding along. "Really, you both think so?"

"Finish your lunch, and maybe go to Peepee's office hours. I think you should have him regrade this. Don't be rude or anything. But maybe say you worked really hard on it, or something."

Abbie swallowed a bite of her food, and said, "I think so too Deke. Even if your grade is lowered, it's better to do it right. *Like physio exercises!*"

She said the last playfully, and so Deke quipped back. "You mean the hand-holding stuff you wanted me to do, so I could play *next year?*"

The group broke into banter as they ate after that, which mostly consisted of Abbie quipping about Deke's abnormal recovery, while Lee and he shared knowing looks. They might not know what the problem with the system was, but they knew it was the reason for his *miracle...*

THIRTY-FIVE

SUNDAY JANUARY 29TH

> "CCES is showing up for annual drug testing tomorrow. Just got word from my contact."- Coach Skip

> "Do you need me to call my contact at CCES, to avoid testing certain players?"- Director Rooney

> "No, we ran some tests earlier this season on suspected individuals and they all came back clean. I think we're good."- Coach Skip

Deke climbed up the stairs to the practice floor and frowned. Usually a few minutes before practice everyone was warming up already. You'd have people doing stretches or shooting a few hoops. Instead, everyone was gathered in a clump near Coach Skip. Walking over to the group, he tapped on Manny's shoulder.

"Hey man, what's going on?" Deke asked the team's power forward.

"They haven't said, but I saw a CCES van outside. So probably a random drug test," Manny said after glancing over his shoulder to see who had approached him.

"Oh," was all Deke could say. Was he worried about drug testing? Sort of. The sports drink hadn't shown up on the tests Doctor Dan had given him, but those were just the cheap tests looking for normal drugs. The purge function made sure those weren't a problem. Even being around Val when she smoked sometimes made him sick. And because of that, she had even cut down on her use when she was with him.

The raderiminium stuff though? That was a whole different issue. Would the real tests find some trace of it? They must have had a way to get Duke off the hook for that right? Of course, knowing Evil Corp, they could just own CCES and have the results faked. Still, if Evil Corp owned CCES—that brought a whole different shitstorm down on Deke. There were just too many unknowns.

"All right men, I'm sure you have guessed but the nice men and women at CCES have come here to test our compliance with the drug use regulations. If I read out your name I want you to follow Doctor Dan down to the rehab area. Duke, Arthur, Mac, NJ, Big Tim, Mills, Wash, Chino and Larry."

Of course Deke was included...

"Man, why does the second string always get called up?" Big Tim complained before Deke got a chance to. His stomach bubbling with unease, Deke followed the other eight players as they shifted through the crowd over to Dr. Dan.

"All right, you know the drill. Line up, Abbie is going to give you your specimen jar, we have water if you need it," Dan said, gesturing for them to head over to a desk where Abbie was seated with another, unfamiliar man that Deke assumed was the CCES rep.

"This is such bullshit. I got tested last time. Deke is the only one you need to test anyway," Mac said, looking more surly than normal, which Deke thought was pretty impressive really. Still, his words soured Deke's stomach further.

"Just pee in the bottle, man," Big Tim said, pushing Mac toward

Abbie, who pulled out a styrofoam box with tape holding down a lid. Deke felt a moment of relief when he saw the familiar box—maybe it was the same tests? Abbie wrote on a sticker before handing it to the CCES guy, who put the sticker on the outside of the box before handing it to Mac.

In an overly loud voice, the CCES guy called out over the chatter. "Make sure the box is sealed and hasn't been tampered with. There should be two glass bottles inside and a plastic collection cup. The lids on those bottles tighten down and lock, so don't tighten them, but check the bottles to make sure they are clean. We're going to do groups of four"—he pointed to Mac and lowered his volume—"so stand to the side there and wait for the next three to join, please."

Deke hung to the back of the group, allowing the older students the chance to test first, so they could get back to practice

"Hey Deke." Abbie smiled at him as she wrote his name on the sticker and put it on the box herself. The CCES guy had left with the first four to head inside the washroom and oversee the actual depositing. Abbie continued, "I've got a bone to pick with you."

"What did I do this time?" Deke asked even as he swallowed hard, to try to wet his suddenly dry mouth.

"Lee just texted me that he's canceling our Wednesday pizza night because you wanted to do something else tonight." Abbie pointed at him, and Deke felt a tingle run over his shoulders as he exhaled in relief.

He managed a smile, thinking about finally paying his roommate back a bit for everything he'd been doing. "Oh, yeah. I was gonna take him to Beef and Baguettes, take advantage of the free meal they give the starters before a game."

Abbie wrinkled her nose. "I will never understand the appeal of that place, it always smells like provolone. You should take him to the Mignon Bistro instead, I know Lee has been meaning to go there and they still honor the starter's free meal, they just don't advertise it."

"He has?" Deke frowned, "He hasn't said anything to me about it... wouldn't that be a little weird though? That's like... a date spot, right?"

Abbie laughed. "Oh, the big strong man feeling a little insecure taking his friend to a fancy restaurant?"

"Why don't you come? I didn't realize I was forcing him to break some of your plans."

"Sure, that's the reason, totally not so it doesn't look like you're on a date with Lee." Abbie grinned at him and pretended to toss her hair, "Well, I suppose I could deign to accompany two such strapping gentlemen." She paused and then looked around. "You sure that's all right?"

Deke grimaced slightly. While he and Val were on better terms, Abbie was still a sore spot for his girlfriend.

"I'm sure it'll be fine," Deke said, even as Duke stepped up and handed his kit to Abbie. She needed to take a few seconds to explain the procedure to Duke, which essentially came down to taking responsibility for the sample. Duke tightened down the two lids of his piss and placed them back into the styrofoam as directed.

Deke's nerves started to come back as Abbie took a few more seconds to apply another sticker across the top of the box and over the sides, which sealed it closed.

"You're going to Mignon's?" Duke asked Deke as they waited. Deke blinked and turned to look up at the larger man.

"Yeah, uhh, just taking advantage of the free meal," Deke responded.

"You mind if Eva and I join? That's the sort of stuff that wins me big boyfriend points."

"Oh, uh, sure? I don't see why not."

"Sweet, I'll call and make a reservation." Duke waved at Abbie as he headed back up.

"For five, 'kay?" Deke said, wanting to make sure that Lee was included. Or Abbie was included? Why had his mind thought that they would leave Lee off, if the reservation was shortened?

"You're up," the CCES guy told Deke and he nodded to a busy Abbie, who returned a smile as he followed the man into the washroom.

"**S**top fidgeting," Abbie said, slapping Deke's hand away from the tie at his neck. It was pretty unfair given that she was wearing a blue summer dress that would have been out of place this time of year anywhere but Southern California.

"It's too tight," Deke said, fending her hand away while he loosened the offending noose-like accessory. He reached up and unbuttoned the top button and then pulled the tie tighter to cover the fact that it was loose.

"How are you an adult?" Lee said, shaking his head. His roommate was wearing a button-down shirt, tie and a sports jacket that were a near exact copy of Deke's. But somehow he managed not to feel any of the unease the attire inspired in Deke.

Deke offered a smile toward his friend. His nerves from the earlier testing were still there, but Lee seemed pretty confident that the sports drink was too unique for standard drug testing. Perhaps, Deke's feeling that the tie was a noose around his neck wasn't entirely due to his unfamiliarity with such an accessory. Instead, it felt like a metaphor for standing at the gallows of the potential end of his career as he waited for the test results.

He looked around again for Duke after Lee returned his smile. The three of them were waiting to be seated at Mignon Bistro. Duke and Eva hadn't shown up yet, so Deke turned away, pretending to look for them. He actually took the opportunity to make himself even more comfortable by further loosening his outfit. Abbie and Lee had forced him into this damned suit before they allowed him out of the dorm and he couldn't help but think about Beef and Baguettes fondly. Scanning the crowd, he caught sight of a familiar silhouette.

"Shit, it's Coach," Deke whispered. He quickly turned back, trying to pretend he hadn't seen the older man.

"Deke?" Coach Skip said and Deke turned around, plastering a fake smile on his face.

"Hello Coach," Deke said, giving a polite nod to the man that had been walking with Skip. Deke thought it might have been a Booster, but it could easily have been someone in the administration as well.

"Well, don't you all look refined," Skip said, giving Abbie and Lee a polite smile. "Look, Deke, I just wanted to take a moment to tell you that I've noticed the effort you've been making in the last few months.

"Your grades have improved, you've been doing all the work Dr. Dan has had for you and you've been excelling on the court. This is the sort of behavior I appreciate from my players. I know we had a bit of a rocky start to the year, but you've put in a lot of work and it has not gone unnoticed.

"I'm kind of regretting that I pushed you to delay coming back to the court until you were healed, but at this point it's clear that you are, and I couldn't be happier with the direction you're taking your life. You keep this momentum and you're bound for great things." Deke swallowed a sudden lump in his throat as he felt his cheeks flush.

Deke couldn't think of a response but luckily Skip turned to Lee and Abbie. He continued, "I hear I have you two to thank for Deke's turnaround, at least in some small part, and I'm glad that he's made such a good friend. And that he has a wonderful role model as his girlfriend—"

"Oh, we're not dating," Abbie interjected as she blushed. Skip shook his head for a moment and apologized un-sincerely for the mix-up. Clearly assuming that they were a thing still, but it just wasn't talked about. Deke felt a bit hot under the collar too, but he at least knew it was because of this damned tie.

Skip reached out to shake Deke's hand and he stopped fiddling with the thing to return the gesture. "You're doing great things, son, and I'm proud of you. Enjoy your dinner." Skip strode out of the building, saving him from having to respond.

"He really *is* lucky to have such good friends like us." Lee grinned mischievously, turning to Abbie. Abbie smiled at Lee, catching his direction.

"Indeed, we will tame his irascible tendencies yet. To you and me, my dear Lee, the saviors of Mr. Mills and his devilish paths." Abbie's voice was pitched in a clearly faux snobbish tone.

"Oh, come on!" Deke complained. "I should get some credit!"

"Pip pip, old chap." Abbie tipped an imaginary top-hat in Lee's direction, before they both dissolved into mirthful laughter.

From long experience, Deke knew the two of them would only get worse if he continued to protest, so he just rolled his eyes and turned away. Which is when he saw Duke and Eva walking in. Enjoying the excuse, Deke turned to the hostess and told them that they were all present. They were led to their table and sat down.

"Wow, this is great," Eva said with her overly enthusiastic smile. "Shouldn't we have waited for Valerie?"

"Oh, uh, she couldn't make it," Deke lied. He hadn't wanted to try to explain to her that Abbie was just a friend, again, so he hadn't asked her to join them. Eva glanced over at Abbie, who was talking over the menu with Lee, and nodded her head.

"Well, probably for the best then, I know she gets a bit jealous, but they make a great couple." She motioned at Abbie and Lee with her own menu.

Deke frowned, glancing over at Abbie and Lee. As far as he knew the two of them were just good friends. But he was interrupted as one of the Boosters came up to Duke and him, wanting to talk over the upcoming game with the two players. It was only after the second Booster showed up that he realized they had been seated in a position where all the current diners would see them and even have to walk past them to get to their tables.

Thankfully most of the patrons were very polite, only stopping by long enough to wish them luck or recommend a dish. There was no sign of Grant Fisher, which Deke thought was a blessing. The overly sweaty man had cornered him more than once since he started playing again and it was never a great experience.

"So, what are you getting?" Abbie said, a hand on Deke's elbow to bring him back to the conversation at hand.

"Oh, uh... I'm not sure. I was thinking... Porcini-rubbed Ribeye with Balsamic?" Deke paused, looking at the menu, "What's porcini?"

"It's a type of mushroom," Abbie said with a grin. "I was thinking of the kona crusted steak. But the ribeye looked good, you interested in splitting it?"

"Oh, I want in on that action. Let's add the Au Gratin Potatoes and the Tom's Mashed Potatoes too. I was thinking about getting the lobster," Lee piped in from the other side of Abbie. They bickered back and forth about what they were each getting and Deke was only a little upset that he was going to be forced to share his food. There was a deep-seated part of him that felt like Joey on *Friends*—he wanted his food and he didn't want to share. But if it was Lee and Abbie, that wasn't too bad.

"All right, so you're going to be the Blue Team this week right?" Lee said, switching from the food talk back to the game.

"Yeah, we're wearing the blue jerseys this week." Duke nodded his head in agreement.

"So does that make you Cyclops? Deke is probably Gambit right?" Lee asked, and Deke frowned.

"What? Gambit is from the south, that's like... the wrong direction," Deke protested.

"Yes, but you both speak French," Abbie said.

"I *had* to learn it!" Deke protested.

"Does that mean Mac is Jubilee?" Eva asked and Duke laughed.

"No, I think he's more like Psylocke. There is something mental there. And I accept being called Cyclops bee tee dubs. One of the best superheroes ever," Duke mirthfully responded as he put the menu down.

Deke groaned even as Abbie and Lee's grins grew bigger. They were going to be talking about which superheroes were best for the rest of the night at this point. He never would have imagined that Duke was such a closet nerd.

THIRTY-SIX

THURSDAY, FEBRUARY 9TH

"We missed you last night, hope you're feeling better. Mignon's was a blast!"- Big Sis Eva

"What? I never got an invite..."- Valerie

"Well Deke was kind of riding solo anyway."- Big Sis Eva

"Kind of riding solo? You better not say that bimbo was there?" - Valerie

Deke attempted to relax his leg as Abbie manipulated his knee in strange ways. It didn't hurt, but there were times that it protested certain movements, but those times seemed to be when Abbie was placing pressure on the joint in ways it wasn't meant to bend.

"It's insane. You've actually recovered your full range of motion and added some," Abbie commented as she lowered his leg back to the physio bed. When she let go, Deke's leg instantly felt a bit colder, because she had been using a great deal of her body to not only lift the limb but support it as she moved it around.

"Honestly, I kind of want to see what happens if I break one of your fingers." Abbie pretended to reach toward Deke's hand, and he pulled it back. She cackled with delight and shrugged. "I guess I shouldn't use the star shooting guard as a lab rat…"

"Stop it! Mac got more playing time in both games than I did," Deke protested half-heartedly, hoping she would state the obvious. The system was still seeming to slowly run out of new benefits, and while Deke was slightly disappointed in his own play, he was acutely aware that others weren't. So, he was hoping—

"Yeah, but you outscored him by ten to eight." Abbie paused and then scrunched her forehead while regarding him. "You know you're blushing, right?"

"Am not!" Deke countered lamely. Abbie lightly punched his shoulder, and then picked up her clipboard to make some notes. "So, you and Lee—" Deke cut off as Dr. Dan slammed his office door open. That seemed like a strange gesture from the usually placid man.

"I'm on my way up now, Skip." He turned and began striding through the clinic, but Deke caught his next response to the coach. "That's not how it works. They test the whole group as a batch, and if it's positive, then they move onto individual testing, so…" he faded off as the door to the stairs closed behind him.

Abbie looked at Deke, and he stared back, his eyes wide. Someone on the team had tested positive? Abbie tilted her head before she asked, "Look Deke, we're friends and I trust—"

"It isn't me!" Deke protested, even though his stomach was currently doing flips. Had Lee been wrong? Did the CCES tests pick up the sports drink, after all? Or worse, had Evil Corp?

"Has anyone seen Mac?" Big Tim asked, and all the players in the locker room looked around helplessly. Deke knew that the starting shooting guard wasn't in here, because he was acutely aware from the moment Mac was late, that he would be getting the start for the first time in his college career.

Would his stingy sports drink hold up? Should he call Lee?

They were playing the Lions, the current worst team in their division, which was something that, during the strategy meeting last night, had given Deke confidence. Now? Deke remembered that the Baguettes had lost to them in a tournament game, when he was back home for surgery. He bounced his arm on his pistoning knee brace, which he was required to wear to help prevent 're-injury', and watched the other guys slowly stop looking for Mac.

As if he was in some sort of eerie horror film, each time one of the others stopped looking for Mac, their eyes found him. He tried to nod to each as they paused, eyes focusing on him, but he was pretty sure that his nervous jimmy leg gave away his current conflicted feelings. If not the visual, the occasional whines of the knee brace from the movement couldn't have gone unnoticed.

Part of him was excited to get the start, but a far larger part of himself kept asking what would happen if he played terribly. Mac's absolute absence made that feeling even worse. There was no backup plan—no safety net. At least if Mac had just been late, Deke could have started and been replaced if his game was off.

Now, Deke looked over to Geoff 'The Brick' Jones. He remembered him coming off the bench when Mac got that bloody nose, and he couldn't recall what was uglier—Mac's face or Geoff's shot.

"All right gentlemen, we're in the thick of it now. We're playing tonight down one, after a grueling start to the season. So, let's try to get up on them early," Coach Skip began and Deke felt his stomach truly fall. So, Mac was sick or something. Coach Skip continued, which at least distracted Deke from the shot of jitters that came over his body. "Everyone take a knee.

"Give us the strength to not be weary. Even these young men grow tired, and can stumble or fall; but those of us who hope in the Lord will renew their strength. They will soar on the wings like eagles; they will run and not grow weary; they will walk and not be faint. Let us believe in the game plan He helped us make, and stride forth with confidence."

Everyone chanted ah-men and then stood up, many of the players jumping up and down in front of their lockers, warming up tense muscles. Coach smiled at them all, locked eyes with Deke and then nodded.

Duke shouted, "Let's go!" as he pushed through all the other players and out into the tunnel.

The warm-up before the game became a blur to Deke. He knew he performed his layups, and shots, and distantly even recalled making a lot of them, but he was definitely preoccupied with thoughts of this moment, right now. He stood shoulder to shoulder with the Lion's shooting guard, waiting on the ref to toss the ball up for the tip-off.

Duke squared off there against the opposing center and Deke felt himself vibrating with nervous energy. Just before the ref tossed the ball up, Deke saw Duke tense his legs, and then saw an image of the center driving his powerful legs into the ground as he leaped up, tipping the ball off right into the hands of the opponent's point guard. His almost-acquired [Motion Prediction] seemed to work this way, intermittently giving him tiny glimpses of what came next.

Hoping this wasn't one of those times it was wrong, Deke kicked off hard and sprinted to the image of the ball in the ghostly hands of the point guard. His shoes squeaked, and so did his brace, as he pushed harder with each subsequent step. He heard Duke grunt, and turned to see the ball on the path he was already on.

He reached out and snagged it just before the point guard brought it in. Deke immediately started his dribble and crossed the ball from his left to right hand. His defender was already trailing because of his quick change in direction, and the point guard had been caught flat-footed.

Deke had no one between him and the basket. He probably should have taken the easy two with a layup or dunk, but he pulled up for the three. He jumped and lined up the [Aim Assist], then released. The ball didn't even touch the mesh as it passed through the basket.

He held up his pinky, ring and middle finger to the home crowd, and twenty thousand voices roared their approval. It was game time and he was going to crush it.

System initiating power saver mode. Acquire additional Radanium to return full functionality.

The toes of his Air Jordan shoes caught the polished floor and he tripped as he ran back down the court to get on defence. His stupid knee brace prevented him from catching himself before he fell, and it banged loudly against the floor as he fell. He sprang back to his feet quickly, and any sign of the smile he'd held moments before was gone. He looked to the sideline to find Lee and help, but his eyes met Valerie's as the cheerleaders vibrated in excitement.

She gave him a worried look for just a moment but looked away far too quickly. He shook his head, because he didn't have time to deal with whatever *mood* she was in right now. His scanning didn't reveal Lee, and he was forced to turn away in the next instant to help his team defend the basket. That message wasn't good. The system was seriously going to abandon him?

The Lions missed a shot from near the top of the key, but unfortunately got their own rebound. Duke battled with the center on the opposing team but once the Lions came up with the ball, they converted it to two points from three feet. Deke stayed back to help Arthur bring the rock up the floor, but since it was early in the game the opposing team wasn't pressuring, and Deke's support wasn't needed.

When they reached the far end, they ran a play, which ended with Little Tim laying in an easy basket. Deke didn't touch the ball, but followed the game plan to help his teammate get an open lane. He chewed his lip as he attempted to catch up to his man, number eighty-eight. The opposing player had taken off from his own end even before Tim had put up the two points. To Deke's surprise, he closed the gap to Eighty-eight and even arrived before the inbounder's football pass attempt. He intercepted the intended 'touchdown' and blinked. Eighty-eight blinked.

Clearly, his hard work in the gym and the system awarded power increases were still functioning...

"There's our miracle kid, Deke Mills, clutching up and forcing a turnover! I think we're in for a wild ride tonight folks!" the game announcer crowed as Deke turned and dribbled the ball back up the floor. He had just crossed half and was fretting about the system message, and his loss of [Aim Assist] and the broken [Motion Prediction], when the former skill activated.

Admittedly it showed him a pathetic arc of a shot that landed on his defender's head. Considering his defender was on his own three point line, that wasn't good, but the fact that the line showed up at all meant Deke had misinterpreted whatever this "power saver" mode was. If this was like his brick laptop for example, he would likely be sprawled out on the floor unconscious, but clearly the reduction in functionality in this case didn't apply to his stats or skills.

"Let's give it a shot," he exclaimed and lined up a shot from well behind the three point line. The line went green and just a few moments later the ball sank through the net.

"Mills!" Skip shouted from the sideline as he waved his hands over his head. Deke backpedalled down the floor but turned to see what the coach wanted. "High-probability shots son, high-probability!" Deke nodded and grimaced. Right, that shot was definitely not part of the game plan, nor was his fast break three, he supposed.

But shit, didn't the coach also say something like, "Work smart, not hard?"

Still, they had a game plan for a reason...

"Boys, this game isn't over yet," Skip said with as straight a face as he could manage. Deke smirked in response. Sure, it was halftime and anything was possible, but he doubted the Lions were going to come back from down fifteen. Not with the way the Baguettes were playing. "When we get back out there, let's remind them why they are down, right away. Keep the pressure on, and stick to the game plan. High probability shots!" He said the last looking at Deke, who pulled a face, but nodded his head.

He hadn't taken any more of them after those first two, and had been mostly facilitating plays, but so far he hadn't missed a shot either. His stat line was already giving him fourteen points for the half and eight assists, plus a few steals. Basically, he was having a game—and despite Skip's "scolding," he knew it.

The team quickly returned to the floor and in the first possession, thanks to a steal by Arthur, Deke widened the gap to eighteen points with a dagger of a three pointer. Eighty-eight shook his head and ran up court, but Deke heard him mutter, "Fuck man, does this guy not miss?"

Deke gave the guy his biggest smile. He definitely wasn't going to miss with this low-rent-*Jason-Kidd* guarding him. It was like Eighty-eight was daring him to shoot. That's when it struck Deke, like a bird finding an "invisible" window. They hadn't game-planned against Deke...

They'd planned against Mac, the shooting guard they saw in preseason. The Baguettes' usual starter. They might have been aware of Deke, but they weren't prepared for him. He whistled to himself. "Well damn, maybe I can break thirty points and the Baguettes' record for rookies!"

As if his words were a jinx, Deke finished the game with twenty-eight points, twelve assists and five steals. Managing a double-double but not breaking the record for UCSP, which had never seen a freshman score above thirty.

Saturday, February 10th

"Valerie, it isn't like that," Deke complained as Valerie stood in his doorway with her hands on hips. "Lee and I were going to go to BnB's for the meal like I said, but Lee canceled his plans with Abbie and so I invited her too!"

"Yeah, right, and then you just happened to go to Mignon Bistro on a double date with Duke and Eva!" Valerie shouted, her volume increasing throughout the sentence till she practically shrieked her friend's name.

Deke was still in his boxers and had only been woken up a moment ago when Valerie started slamming her fist on his door. He was still in a bit of a daze, thanks to a massive lack of sleep. After a quick appearance at the victory party last night, where Val ignored him, and then the subsequent theorizing session with Lee, he had been hoping to sleep in...

Blinking at the furious Val, he wondered how she'd even managed to get into the dorm. As calmly as he could he pointed toward the exit, and said, "Hey, let's go downstairs so we don't wake anyone up."

"What. you're worried that people might overhear, and find out you're a cheater?!" Valerie shouted, and even turned her head to project the scream down the hallway.

Lee groaned from his bed and called, "Valerie, we came here right after the dinner. Just me and—"

"Shut the fuck up, mini-Deke!" Valerie shouted and Deke took the opportunity to walk by her and through the doorway to the stairs. He heard her harumph behind him but then heard her designer flip-flops start slapping as she followed.

Deke was still in a pair of old basketball shorts and shirtless, but he didn't feel like he could have returned to his closet and grabbed something else, without Valerie possibly getting more upset.

He walked right through the lobby and out into the morning chill. It probably wouldn't have been so bad if he wasn't currently shirtless. As it was, he instantly felt his nipples protest his choice.

"As I was saying up above, and *Lee* confirmed—we just went for dinner and then Lee and I came back here, Val. Duke even dropped us off with Eva in the front seat!" Deke stated his case even as he turned back to the entry doors.

Valerie pouted at him and seemed to shrink in on herself. "Okay, like I believe you didn't sleep with the skank, but why wouldn't you invite me?"

Deke sucked in air. That question was a valid one, but also brought to the forefront a larger issue in their relationship. "Honestly?" he asked, and she blinked at him before nodding slowly. "I figured you would respond exactly like this. I didn't want to start a fight and so just avoided it all together."

Valerie started to cry, and Deke immediately reached out and wrapped her in a hug. The warmth of her forehead on his chest was super welcome, and he squeezed her slightly even as he said, "I'm sorry, I know I shouldn't have assumed..."

"I get it, Deke. I did slap the girl. I'm just upset that I can't go back and change that. But I can't do anything about what Drunk Valerie did!" Deke chuckled at her joke. She liked to speak about herself in the third person when talking about her drunken antics, and Deke had to admit it fit. Sometimes it was like the woman in front of him, and the other one, were two different people.

"It's okay, babe, I get that you're jealous but I can tell you right now that I wouldn't ever cheat, not ever. Okay? Can you trust me on that?"

He felt her warm hand run down his stomach and shivered slightly as she pushed past the band of his old sports shorts. "I trust you. Now is this still morning wood? Or are you just happy that I came over for your victory celebration?"

Valerie joined him on his walk to the gym, and they held hands the whole way. They chatted aimlessly about the week when they hadn't seen each other. Mostly because Valerie hadn't responded to messages after her discovery of the Mignon Bistro night. Still, as if by mutual agreement, they avoided mentioning *that*, both trying to put it behind them and move on. Deke glanced at her and fondly recalled their "interaction" from the dorm showers. He smiled as he pictured it again.

"So, you sure you have community service that you have to attend today? I think Lee found a friend's room, after we kicked him out," Valerie teased as she leaned into him. Right, and the dorm room! Deke's cat-like smile widened.

"I'm sure, babe, the kids would miss me if I wasn't there. Still, how about a repeat performance tonight?" Deke asked and when he caught her looking up at him through her eyelashes seductively, he added, "You still owe me two," and winked.

Valerie licked her lips and jokingly reached for the drawstring of his new pair of shorts, which were beneath a pair of sweats. He fended her off playfully and turned the corner toward the front of the gym, but they both stopped dead as the familiar voice of Mac carried to them from a nearby open window.

". . . they're mine, yes, but I wouldn't take drugs knowingly. I'm telling you that I took those on Ronald's orders. He told me they were supplements!" Mac argued.

"Mr. McLeary, I can see right here that this bottle was assigned to you by our old team trainer. However, you brought this in and could have substituted the contents out at any time. Not to mention, you and only you signed the CCES agreement that said you're solely responsible for what enters your body. I'll look into your claims, but you're a senior and are supposed to be a role model for our younger players. I can't just let this go."

"You're telling me that I'm the only one on the team who tested positive? That fucker—"

"Language, Mr. McLeary," Coach interrupted.

"Wait, that Ronald guy probably did the same thing he did to me to like half the guys, even Duke! I know I've definitely seen him take stuff from the asshat!"

"Language, Chris McLeary!" Coach Skip shouted, and Deke cringed from the tone, even knowing it had nothing to do with him.

Deke looked at Valerie, who was blinking rapidly as she digested this new information. He was going to motion for them to move on and give Mac privacy when the kid added, "Whatever Skip! I'm the victim here. This all started with that stupid recruit Deke Mills. How the fuck are you going to replace me in my senior year! That's the reason I started training so hard over the summer. That's when that shitstain Ronnie gave me these bottles!"

"Language! *I will not warn you again, Chris!*" Skip's voice carried the warning of what Deke would call a threat of the belt from a parent, and Deke's ass clenched involuntarily. Skip continued, his voice still carrying a hint of menace, "Speaking of Mr. Mills and your catalyst to work hard—why did some of your teammates blame you for his missteps earlier this year?"

"Somehow I'm at fault that he can't manage his medication? Whatever, I think you're missing the point—there's no way his recovery is natural. He tore his ACL, Skip. That's like six months of recovery minimum, and he did it in two? Ronald was probably handing him drugs too!"

"So you admit that you knew that these were performance-enhancing drugs?" Skip asked patiently.

"No, that's not what I am saying, Coach," Mac quickly corrected. "I'm saying that if this happened to me, wouldn't the whole team *accidentally* be using? I know I've seen Ronnie supplying others with the same bottles!"

"Your teammates all tested negative, Chris." Skip's tone was firm, and clearly way past upset. "Look, based on your account, I will see if I can get you in front of a board of directors to overturn your expulsion from the school, but no matter what, your days of playing basketball are over!" Coach stated the last words like a gunshot in the quiet morning air.

When Mac started crying audibly, Deke shrank in on himself. That could have been him. Mere months ago, it almost had been. He recalled the folders laid out on Skip's desk that day with a shudder. Hurriedly, he motioned for Valerie to keep moving. She did so but her smile seemed to be all kinds of wrong. Deke groaned. "Don't go sharing this around just yet, please?"

She shook herself and nodded. "Of course not."

They arrived at the front of the gym and Deke pointed to Abbie's car. She had come to pick him up today. Valerie's smile morphed from playful, to sinister, to angry when she realized Deke was getting in the car with Abbie. He sighed and said, "I thought you said you trusted me, she's just driving me to the community center."

"Bullshit! I know your hours are over. You're just going to try to get some alone time with bimbo big-boobs in there!" Valerie shouted. Deke's eyebrows rose, and he looked between Valerie and Abbie's small car. Valerie continued though. "Forget about all of this!" She made a motion at her own body and cocked a hip. "Fuck you, Deke!"

She stormed back the way they had come and Deke was left shaking his head after her. He guessed he should have told her about Abbie before they arrived, maybe? He heard a car door slam behind him and turned to find Abbie looking after Valerie's retreating back.

"You've got some ground to make up with her," she commented and shook her head. "Lee texted me, why didn't you just invite her to Mignon's?"

Deke pointed at the corner she just disappeared around, meaningfully. "That's why! Anytime you come up, it's like she grows claws..."

"Well, with Valentine's Day coming up maybe you can show her how much you care?"

"I don't think she wants to hear from me ever again," Deke countered.

"Trust me, Deke, a girl doesn't get that jealous over a guy she doesn't want to see again. Just plan something nice, like a picnic on the beach or something."

"Yeah sure, and what? Just pick up already prepared food from somewhere?" Deke asked. His cooking skills extended to Craft Dinner and ramen noodles.

"Just ask Lee to help, he's actually a really good cook," Abbie offered.

"Awww... so you two are cooking for each other now?" Deke asked playfully, even as he felt his stomach twist. He chalked up the traitorous organ's actions to his morning of hot and cold with Valerie. He looked back to the corner even as Abbie punched him in the arm.

"Ow!" he said half-heartedly, but didn't even look back at her. The fist really wasn't more than a tap, and as Abbie shook out the offending hand, he couldn't help but flex a bit. His muscles had definitely grown a fair bit since the summer. Lee thought that might slow down, though, thanks to the "power saver" mode.

Deke really needed to find a plug.

CHAPTER

THIRTY-SEVEN

TUESDAY, FEBRUARY 14TH

"Higher authority has deemed Mr. Wellington as a waste of resources."- John Smoke

"What does that mean?"- Ed Rooney-Athletic Director

"We're pulling out, as discussed." - John Smoke

"No! You can't, we've already done the budget!"- Ed Rooney-Athletic Director

"Wait! What if I get you someone better?"- Ed Rooney-Athletic Director

"Are you certain you want to take on additional responsibility, Director?"- John Smoke

Deke collapsed onto his bed. It had been a busy day. He'd moved his evening workout up and smashed it right before practice, and had even buckled down and gotten his homework done between classes. There was a paper for history, but that wasn't due until Friday, and he was happy to say he was already halfway done.

Despite all of his hard work this week, he hadn't seen a single task, evo point or even a system message, and he distractedly wondered if it was still worth being this "good." He stretched his hands over his head and caught a whiff of evergreen mist or whatever the detergent was. *Okay, I guess it has some perks,* he thought to himself.

Part of him knew he should get off the bed, because he probably needed to take a shower, since he hadn't felt up to one after the intense practice earlier. Yet he just wanted to relax here for a moment, because without the sport's drink's increased recovery, his muscles were already protesting his day's remaining activities.

Hopefully, the quick hour's rest would re-energize him. A quick glance at the clock told him that he wasn't going to get that hour though. Lee's class was going to be over in thirty minutes and then the two of them were joining Abbie for an anti-Valentine's Day party at Shawn & Guster's, and then they were going over to Lee's parents' house. Val also hadn't responded to any of his messages about plans for Valentine's Day. At this point, he was half-assuming they were broken up. So, in protest of anything related to love, they were going to use the Wetts' movie room to watch what Lee had assured him was the "pizza da resonance" of zombie movies. Whatever that meant.

With a groan, he sat back up and peeled off his shirt. Leaning down, he pulled his laundry basket out enough to dump the shirt in the bin; he then spent a quick moment removing his clothing and transferring his practice gear from his gym bag to the basket. Only when finished did he grab his towel off the hook. He noted the almost overflowing dirty laundry and sighed—this whole being good thing sure was a lot of work. He used to just upgrade garments from casual wear to practice gear. Admittedly, he had reached a point somewhere along the way where he lost track of that system and just stopped caring.

Wrapping the towel around his waist, he shook his head at his "younger" self as he moved to the door. He took a glance at the time on his phone to see how much of a rush he should be in and frowned. His phone wasn't going to last the night if he didn't charge it now, so he returned to his side of the room and plugged it in. Once the little icon lit up, he walked down the hallway to the shared bathroom.

The tallest shower head still only came to his chin but at least that stall was empty. The other ones barely hit his shoulders and it was an exercise in futility trying to get the sweat out of his hair. The hot water felt good on his sore back and he sat under the heat long enough that someone might later complain about the lack of hot water. Only when his muscles felt loosened did he grab the soap and actually lather up.

Wrapped in his towel and feeling worlds better, he headed back to the room. A wolf whistle chased him down the hallway and he turned around to see Abbie grinning at him from the staircase.

"You're not dressed yet? Come on, we have places to be," she said, shooing him off to his room before claiming one of the couches in the lounge. She put her sneakers up on the coffee table and crossed her ankles as she offhandedly added, "Tell Lee he owes me five bucks."

"Why?" Deke asked with a frown, but she just waved him off. Grumbling, he headed back to the room. Lee was inside and already pulling a shirt over his head. "Hey bud. Abbie's in the lounge, says you owe her five bucks."

"*Bantha poodoo*! She's here already? How does she do that? I thought girls needed time to get ready!" Lee almost tripped over his own backpack, which was in the middle of the floor where he had apparently discarded it in his haste to get ready. "Your phone's been buzzing by the way," he said, grabbing his shoes and stuffing his feet into them. Deke closed the door, hung up his towel and pulled on some boxers before checking his phone and the missed call log.

"Shit." Lee looked over at Deke's exclamation. "Val," Deke said, holding the phone up so Lee could see the notifications. His room-mate groaned and leaned back in his chair.

"What's she want?" Lee asked, the urgency in his earlier movements gone.

"Let me check," Deke said. There wasn't a voicemail, but she had sent him a text message.

> "Hey, are we still on for Valentine's day?"
> Saturday- Dekester
>
> "Babe, you okay?" Sunday- Dekester
>
> "Val, please call me back." Monday-
> Dekester
>
> "All right. I guess we aren't doing
> Valentines?" Monday- Dekester

"Call me back loser."- :heart: Val :heart:

Hitting the button, he held the phone up to his ear as it rang. Val picked it up almost immediately.

"Hey hot stuff, so what's the V-day plan?"

"Uh..." Deke's mind blanked, glancing at Lee before turning away. "Lee and I planned to go to Shawn & Guster's and then grab a late movie at his parents'..."

"Just you and Tiny?" Val asked, and Deke winced at the nickname that Lee had asked him not to keep using a while back.

"Uhm, no? Look, you weren't responding to anything... I would have made other plans, but Abbie is coming with us."

"Are you fucking kidding me? Have fun with your little devil's three-way. I don't even know why I try," Valerie said before the line went dead.

Deke looked down at the phone and then turned back to Lee with a grimace on his face.

"That bad?" Lee asked.

"I think it's worse?"

"I'll go tell Abbie that it's just the two of us tonight. Call her back."

"Do you really think I should?"

"Deke, you know you're going to regret it if you don't. I'd love a wingman but honestly, I think I can do this on my own!" Despite his words to the contrary, his face paled a bit and Deke wasn't sure he would be okay. After a moment of hesitation Deke smiled and placed a hand on Lee's shoulder in support. Then he offered his friend a nod of encouragement, on what might have been his first date—ever.

"Thanks, man?" Deke turned the words into a final question while holding up the phone. Lee nodded shallowly again, and Deke dialed Valerie back. It might have been his imagination but he thought he saw Lee swallow a little too aggressively as he listened to the ring tone.

"I'll go tell Abbie," Lee said, slipping out of the room.

"What is it?" Valerie's voice was angry.

"I got out of the thing with Lee. Would you like to grab dinner somewhere?"

"Depends. What did you get me?" Valerie was back to a more normal-sounding tone.

"Well, I got you a present, I'm not sure you'll like it..." Deke had spent enough time at Valerie's house to know that there wasn't any way he'd be able to afford the kind of jewelry she was accustomed to. Abbie had helped him pick out a necklace all the same though.

"All right, suit up. I'll pick you up in an hour. I've got a place that'll let us in," Valerie said, before cutting off the call. Deke sighed, looking down at his phone. He pulled on pants and a shirt and then walked out to the lounge. Abbie and Lee were sitting on a couch waiting for him.

"I take it by the long face that you're ditching us?" Abbie asked.

"Yeah, sorry guys. Val told me to 'suit up' and she's gonna pick me up in an hour." Deke didn't want to make eye contact with his two friends; he had actually been looking forward to spending the night with them.

"Sounds like we've got an hour to make you look presentable for the cheerleader. It's a tall order but I think my good man Lee and I are up to the task," Abbie said, standing up and pulling Lee up with her. "Come on, can't let you screw this one up *too* badly." Abbie marched off to their dorm and Deke shared a look with Lee.

"We'll watch some romcom or something instead of the zombie movie. I really want you to see it," Lee offered with a smile. "Besides, this way I can call Abbie my Valentine's date," he whispered.

"I heard that! And if I'm going to be your Valentine then I demand chocolate!" Abbie shouted without looking back. Lee blushed bright red but also wore the biggest grin Deke had ever seen.

"I wouldn't suggest smiling like that on the date, you look like a serial killer," Deke quipped.

Lee punched him in the arm, and then shook his hand out.

Abbie and Lee were in her car, waiting to make sure Valerie actually showed up. Deke was standing in front of the dorm in a white polo, a blue sports jacket and paired the whole thing with tan slacks. He felt like he should be going to a yacht club or something. The small jewelry case in his hand felt heavier than it should have been—it had cost him more than he really should have spent and some part of him was still sure Val would call it cheap trash.

The Miata pulled up and Val looked him up and down with a big grin on her face. She was wearing a little blue minidress covered in sequins that left most of her long legs free.

"How much for the night?" She ogled, making him feel like she was trying to buy him off a street corner.

"Uh..." Deke stuttered; he hadn't been expecting her to say that. She laughed, seeming happy that she'd managed to stump him and unlocked the door.

"Come on, get in." Deke opened the door, folding himself into the front seat. "That for me?" Val asked, even as she pulled the box out of his hands and flipped it open.

"Oh." She paused, bringing her hand first to her chest in what was remarkably genuine surprise, before slowly reaching down and pulling the silver necklace out. It was heart-shaped, with a pompom and a basketball on either side of the silver ornament. Deke had worried it was cheesy but Val's small smile seemed to suggest she really liked it. She leaned in and kissed him. Her breath smelled faintly of peppermint schnapps.

"I love it." She twisted, pulling her old necklace off and motioning for Deke to put the new one on. He sighed contentedly and felt his shoulders relax. She liked it!

"All right we're off!" Val shouted as she put a fist up in the air and pressed the gas, scaring two students who were walking near her car as the car squealed out of the waiting area and made for the exit.

"Where are we going?" Deke asked, as he turned to wave at the two students to let them know he was sorry. He saw Lee and Abbie waving at him as well and he gave them a smile.

"Daddy's yacht, he's out of town and I told the chef to make us something," Val shouted over the wind.

"I've never been on a boat," Deke whispered, a bit embarrassed by the admission.

"Oh don't you worry. The boat adds a little something to the horizontal tango we'll be performing later. I want to get what I paid for!"

His excitement was suddenly piqued and Deke felt his heart drum appreciatively as he quickly forgot Shawn & Guster's. While he would have liked this to have been a group night, he admitted that his friends might get in the way of that particular dance on Val's boat. It was a partner-dance he would very much like to study all night. It wasn't one he knew the steps to, *yet*.

Plus, the setting made his—well Abbie's—choice of clothes far more appropriate.

THIRTY-EIGHT

MONDAY, FEBRUARY 20TH

"I think the sharks are starting to circle the Rook"- The Duke

"Do you think he will take it?"- Best Girlfriend Eva

"He is single mindedly driven toward the NBA. I'm worried he will…"- The Duke

"Well we got you out, so can we help him too?" - Best Girlfriend Eva

"You got me out." - The Duke

"Love you too." - Best Girlfriend Eva

"Mr. Mills!" Director Rooney exclaimed. Deke stood up from the waiting chair in the Department of Athletics. Rooney crowded him, extending his hand to shake Deke's. Deke smirked as they shook. This reminded him a lot of his recruitment trip. Even the tone of Rooney's voice was overly joyful, with massive salesman vibes.

"I'm so glad you came by today. The whole campus is buzzing. You might be the first freshman to score twenty-eight points in the history of UCSP!" Rooney fired the statements at him in quick succession.

"Thanks D. Roons! Nah, my roommate looked it up earlier this year, some guy got thirty. Plus, mine was against the Lions," Deke joked self-deprecatingly, even as the director placed a hand on his back to guide him toward his private office. His hand felt hot and clammy even through Deke's UCSP cotton practice tee. Rooney was also sweating quite a bit near his receding hairline.

"Don't be bashful, young man. I wish I'd gotten on Coach Skip's case sooner. I can't believe the man was keeping you on the redshirt list, even though you were healthy. And a star!" Rooney motioned to a chair once they crossed the threshold of his office door. Deke stepped forward quickly, glad to have the warm-damp hand off his lower back.

He heard the director close the door, and then a subsequent click as the deadbolt slid into place. Deke paused halfway down to the chair, but Director Rooney just smiled broadly as he turned to make his way to his desk. Surely he wasn't in any kind of trouble. Still, it was hot in this little office. Deke noticed that the blinds were down on both the windows, too. The one to outside likely should be open for a fresh breeze, and the one to the office being closed felt off, somehow.

Still, maybe this was pretty typical. Or maybe that horrible rumor about Mac was all it took for the school to realize that these meetings needed to be private. Deke still hoped Valerie didn't have anything to do with that but suspected otherwise, since the rumors were so unerringly accurate to what they'd heard. Deke shook off the thought as he lowered himself the rest of the way into the leather cushion.

Rooney sat down on the other side of the desk, moved a few papers around, opened a drawer and then closed it again—without taking anything from it or putting anything in. Deke raised an eyebrow. Was the director nervous about meeting with him? Maybe Lee had been right and this was a meeting to extend his scholarship?

"Mr. Mills, as you can no doubt feel on the campus and in practice: Things around here changed when you got that first start! When you pulled up and drained that three, instead of going for the layup," Director Rooney stated jovially. "That's the sort of high-risk, high-reward attitude this place needs!"

"I don't think Coach Skip would agree with you." Deke laughed, his tone and even the words meant as a joke. Coach Skip *definitely* wouldn't agree with Rooney. He had "politely" told Deke after the game, "If you *ever* pulled a stunt like that again, you'll be running laps until *your family* gets tired."

"Bahh, what does he know! He doesn't even realize that his best players aren't even his doing!" The disgusted tone Rooney described Skip with had obvious undertones, even if it took Deke a moment to make the illogical leap. He was upset with the coach? Or maybe he just felt like Coach Skip was getting too much credit for the team's success?

Rooney saw him frowning and smiled broadly. "He's a great coach, Mr. Mills, but who do you think gets him his recruits? Players alone don't win championships!"

Deke returned a nervous smile. Even though he strongly disagreed with that sentiment, he wasn't going to openly disagree with the director. Instead, he politely chuckled before bluntly changing the subject. "So, whatcha call me down here for, D. Roons?"

As most salesmen can do, Rooney flipped on a dime, returning to an overly large smile. "Of course, Mr. Mills. Part of it is obviously scholarship discussions for next season!" Deke leaned forward in his chair, surprised Lee had been right. From all of his internet research before he accepted his first scholarship, these usually didn't happen until after the season ended. Rooney's smile grew when he saw Deke's interest.

"We'd be stupid not to start these discussions, or at least give you some more direction." He gave a slightly awkward chuckle that stood out to Deke, but he wrote the oddity off as some sort of conversation change—especially as Rooney continued more seriously. "If you keep performing like you are, that is."

"So, like am I going to get a signing bonus added or something then?" Deke asked, confused as to why this meeting was happening. If Rooney was trying to give him some additional incentive . . .

"We have to work within regulations of course, but I'm sure we can bump your meal plan up a few notches and get you in some of our education programs that would allow you access to the technology and tools to let you focus your time here at UCSP on basketball." Rooney began, and then leaned forward to rest his sweaty arms on the desk. "Mills, as you know—I like you. I pulled you off a redshirt year, and that's given you this opportunity. I want to help more..."

He left the last statement hanging in the air, and Deke couldn't help his eyes widening. When Rooney made no move to continue, Deke prompted, "Help me more?"

"Certainly, Mr. Mills! With only you and 'The Brick' Jones available, I can't help but worry about this season's goals going up in smoke with a single *bad landing*." Deke's mouth twisted. Clearly that had been intended to remind him of his injury. Rooney saw his misstep and corrected course. "I just mean there are things we can do to ensure that injuries like yours don't happen again. Things that will ensure you keep improving. So you're ready to *take on the world!*"

That sounded a bit too sinister to Deke, at least in the way it was worded. Why hadn't the man just said "make it to the NBA" Olympics or something similar? He licked his lips to wet them and then swallowed hard because his mouth felt dry. "What do you mean, D. Roons?"

The drawer the director had opened when he first sat down opened again, and Rooney pulled out a leather case, which rested on top of a black leather Duotang-esque booklet. Deke tilted his head at the director, but returned his attention to the dark leather pair, as they were slid across the desk to him. They were plain, and clearly brand new. Deke could even smell the rich scent of the oils that must have been used to polish the new leather.

"This is a package we don't offer just anyone," Director Rooney said as he slid the leather over the wood the last few inches. "In fact, we know with a great deal of certainty that this offer turns players into *stars*."

Deke raised an eyebrow, and then looked at the case more intensely. Surely, this wasn't what they had given the Duke? The sports drink he currently had inside his body? He reached forward and paused, looking to Rooney to see if he was allowed to open the case. Rooney smiled at him as a bead of sweat trickled down from above his temple.

The case on top of the folder opened easily, as if the hinges had been freshly oiled for just this moment. As soon as the overhead lights of the office reached inside, Deke saw a fluorescent blue shimmer play over the case's interior. His mouth fell open as the vivuve man gleamed back at him from the somewhat familiar metal-enclosed vial.

This sports drink vial differed in one pivotal way from the one he'd taken outside of that fateful Halloween party. This one was about the size of his pinky, instead of the palm-filling one of that night. The second container was clearly the needle that he'd inadvertently used. The stupid liquid that had triggered this whole thing. The protective plastic covering the injector was still firmly in place this time.

The small window into the metal syringe showed a gray, mercurial liquid and the stopper was partially retracted—after only an eighth of an inch of fill. Deke couldn't be sure, but he thought perhaps this dose had been scaled as well. "As you can see, Mr. Mills, I'm quite serious in my offer to help. This could be a partnership that will help us all."

Rooney's voice allowed Deke to pull his eyes away from the two familiar vials. He stared at the director with eyes wide, mouth going dry from hanging open. Rooney froze at the look, and then held up both hands as if to placate Deke. "I assure you, Mr. Mills, that this is an opportunity of a lifetime, but after this taster if you want to say no... no one will force you."

From the tone, Deke could tell that the director took his current expression to mean he was shocked enough to go tell someone about this offer. He snapped his mouth closed and attempted to work some saliva back into it. Coughing, he said, "Sorry, I've just never seen anything like this before. What exactly is it a taster of?"

"It's the future Mr. Mills!" Rooney said excitedly, returning to his salesman smile. Deke scrambled furiously in his mind, debating how he could respond to the director without giving away that he had knowledge of what this box contained. Was it okay to assume it was drugs? Surely, that was logical...

"Is it some sort of drug? Didn't Mac just get caught for drugs?" Deke asked. He watched Rooney closely and thought he saw a few additional beads of sweat form on his forehead.

"No, no, Mr. Mills. This isn't a drug, at least not in the way you know drugs. This is an enhancer, but it won't ever show up on any drug tests, so you wouldn't have to worry about that. This is state-of-the-art... the tip of the trident. . . the cutting edge." The director's use of terms seemed off to Deke, like he was repeating what someone else had told him. Deke felt even more nervous because each of the terms felt Hollywood-esque, militaristic, or a combination of both.

"This product can guarantee you the type of success that most people only dream of," Rooney continued. "All you have to do is inject the liquid into a meaty part of your body, like your butt or thigh, and then swallow the blue stuff. After that, the world will open to you and only you!"

"What if I get caught?" Deke asked, attempting to sound nervous. He wanted—maybe even needed—more information.

"As I said, Mr. Mills, there is no chance of that. I can assure you, since that's what I was originally brought on to ensure. Even the contents of these vials have been specially formulated for you, from some of your samples Doctor Dan collected. If you don't use them they break down—disappear. If you do, they become a part of you, undetectable, untraceable."

Deke reached for the needle, and Rooney snapped the lid closed before his hand could make it inside the leather case. Rooney pulled the case back and flipped open the folder. "Here's a contract you can sign and this taster instead becomes a lifetime supply. It's mostly a common NDA to not talk about it, but it also contains some long-term offers for your future."

That sounded strange, and so Deke asked, "Like, you mean scholarships for the upcoming years?"

"Not really, but I'll certainly prepare them for your next visit, if you umm... want." Rooney slid the folder closer to Deke and even went as far as to put a pen on top of the paper. Deke's skin started to crawl, and he realized that his heart was pounding in his chest. Surely, he didn't have to sign right now.

"I was taught never to sign something without reading it over multiple times, and being sure," Deke stated, his voice a bit breathy due to the situation.

"Absolutely, absolutely!" Director Rooney visibly swallowed despite his tone of agreement. "We could go over it together?"

"Can't you give me some time? To read it over on my own first," Deke countered.

Rooney's forehead scrunched and his tongue played over an incisor. He clicked his cheek, closed the folder and nodded his head. "Sure, but the effects don't last forever. So, if you want more after this taster, you're going to need to sign. Also, do you remember what I said about these compounds breaking down?" He tapped the case. "You've got three days. After that this stuff goes inert and I can't get you another sample. Okay?"

Director Rooney's voice was stern, verging on hostile, and Deke nodded shallowly, then added a few more in quick succession. "Yeah, I understand. I'll read it over."

Deke stood up hurriedly and started to make his way to the door.

He could feel the air cooling his body as he walked, and it blew over his sweat covered skin. He reached for the handle and Rooney called, "You forgot the contract and the sample, Mr. Mills."

Standing at the door with his fingers almost on the deadbolt, he paused. Should he just fling open the door and run? He turned around with a plastered smile. "Duhh! I'm going to need those..."

He strode back, collected the case and folder, before reversing directions.

"Can't wait to see what this does for you!" Rooney said, his voice truly excited.

Deke gave a nervous grin over a shoulder, unlocked the door and then strode hurriedly out of the Athletic Department.

"Lee!" Deke shouted as he flung open the dorm room's door. "You're never going—" he cut off as he found Lee curled up on his bed, and not gaming on his computer. "What are you still doing in bed?"

"I'm sick," Lee said piteously from somewhere in a pile of blankets.

Deke scoffed and pulled on the edge of the blanket, flinging it off of his friend. "You're not going to die of heartbreak, Lee!"

"It's a legitimate ailment, you barbarian!" Lee shouted as he tried but failed to catch a corner of his blanket before the whole thing flew off.

"Look man, we've got class soon and I think I've got just the thing to cheer you up," Deke responded while shaking his head and brandishing the leather case stacked on the folder.

"I don't care! I can't ever show my face out there again—everyone's already making fun of my humiliating crash and burn," Lee responded as he curled into the fetal position.

Deke dropped the blanket on the floor. "Maybe you shouldn't have told everyone you had a date with Abbie, *Romeo*."

"Oh shut up," Lee retorted and threw his pillow at Deke, who easily caught it and dropped it atop the blanket.

"I've got *the contract*," Deke countered, in his best impression of speaking to a dog. He even moved the folder back and forth with his one-hand grip on the corner. Lee shot to a sitting position and eyed Deke, then the leather, more seriously.

"What contract?" Lee questioned incredulously.

"What kind do you think? I think a wedding contract for you and Abbie is a little far off, don't you?" Deke quipped.

"Shut up you ruttin' jerk!" Lee couldn't stop the small chuckle at the joke, though. Then he must have realized the contracts would have fit in the folder alone. "What's in the case?" he asked with a point.

"Nothing much, just more sports drink."

"Goram, way to hide the lead!" Lee shot up and grabbed both the objects. "Do you think I can take this one?" Lee opened the case, and immediately took out the blue vial to look at. Clearly, his excitement over the possibility of getting a system had trumped his memory that Deke also could use the vial. Not to mention the poisoning...

"I don't think so. Director Rooney said something about it being made for me with my samples?" Deke responded.

Lee gave him a shocked look. "This came from Rooney?!" He held up the vial, and Deke nodded. "Wait—he confirmed that the sports drink needs to be calibrated for the person?"

"Not in so many words..."

Lee put the vial back in the case, exchanging it for the syringe. He didn't respond, and Deke could tell he was thinking. He held the syringe up to the light with a frown.

"How come Duke's worked for you then?" Lee asked. Deke flinched back. In the office, with Rooney right near him, he hadn't considered that. He knew that the Cotton Candy bastard also assumed anyone who took the stuff would get poisoned—but Deke hadn't... So were they both lying then?

"That's a really great question. You-know-what might have answers." Deke pointed to the folder.

There wasn't a brick of a book inside the folder, so they went through the contract and the instructions multiple times each in under a half an hour. When Deke finished reading his second time through, Lee held up the contract. "I've read this about five times, and it feels like they are trying to draft you into the army—kind of. It feels more like a contractor, but I don't see an end date on this thing. Not even a real company name. It only says you have to show up for training a week after you graduate."

Deke tilted his head. He had read that part too, but honestly had not realized how sinister that sounded. He remembered the militaristic terms Rooney told him and repeated them for Lee. Lee made a noise of disbelief and then brandished the papers again. "That makes me more certain. The only thing Rooney didn't say was 'military grade' in his sales pitch."

"So, you think it's shady?" Deke asked.

"*Shen sheng de gao wan*, yes!" Lee responded. Deke gave him a questioning look at the new term. "Umm... holy testicles, yes..." Lee flushed red.

Deke smiled, but held up the instruction manual. "Did you see the part in here where it's coded to me, and giving it to someone else will poison them?"

"I did. I just don't know if I believe it. Like, why aren't you in a hospital then?" Deke didn't respond; the implications hadn't hit him when he talked to Rooney. "So, are you going to take it?" Lee asked for a follow-up when Deke didn't answer.

Rushing back after talking to Rooney, he hadn't taken the time to consider just how badly his heroics trying to save Ronnie could have gone. He shook off his spiraling thoughts about why he hadn't died and met Lee's eyes. The kid seemed excited, but also reticent.

Blinking, Deke considered that further. Last time he hadn't chosen to take the drug. He had gotten the injection and been forced to take the radar namy stuff. That or have something terrible happen... His brain tried to run down that path, thanks to the recent talk about poison, but he held the reins firmly on point. Now, if he took the taster in front of him, he would knowingly be consuming a drug.

"Last time I had to take it. I understand that it isn't improving anymore and I can't unlock skills or tasks without more, but taking it feels wrong," Deke mumbled, still not a hundred percent sure of his decision.

"That's true," Lee began and Deke realized at that moment that he had been hoping for the opposite response. Lee seemed to pick up on his wavering mind and continued in a bit of a rush, "You scored twenty-eight points while you were out of Radanium. Plus, you were going to go to the NBA without it anyway, right?"

Deke didn't correct Lee, but he desperately wanted to. It had been his decision not to take the taster, so those were all reasons he shouldn't. Still, he knew that he had only scored twenty-eight against one of the worst teams in the division, and he *maybe* would make the NBA without it but that definitely wasn't a guarantee. Plus, how many people in the NBA were taking it? In the end all he said was, "Yeah, exactly," before finally allowing his brain to return to the rabbit hole the instruction manual showed him.

He'd been worried early on that he was poisoned but since nothing had happened, he'd put it out of his mind. Still, this instruction manual stated in no uncertain terms that he should be poisoned. So was that still a possibility?

THIRTY-NINE

TUESDAY, FEBRUARY 21ST.

"Operation Fishing Creek stage one complete."- Agent Smoke

"Affirmative. Reception?" - UPLIFT Einherjar

"Skeptical. Will continue to monitor."- Agent Smoke

In the end Deke—with Lee's help—chose to try to make the NBA the right way as much as he could after the accidental injection. He still had a lengthy discussion with Lee about the possibility of him being poisoned, as well. Lee had divided it up into four different main parts, organized by what he'd called the "order of prescience."

First, this juice was tailor made for Deke specifically, and the stuff meant for Duke was also in his system. This led to four big problems that Lee had written up on the white board, usually reserved for the kid's gaming schedules, in the order of likelihood.

A. They lied.
B. Bad things are coming.
C. Deke was different.
D. Mixing doses could poison Deke.

They had discussed it at length and the simplest solution was that Evil Corp had just lied about it being tailor-made for him. The issue with this explanation was there was no way to safely test it. Basically, any test would mean risking exposure to a possible poisoning. So, on the off chance Rooney and his backers weren't lying, someone might die—and that just wasn't acceptable.

That left the other options as potential problems they could investigate. Perhaps there was, as Lee put it, a Sword of *Demon Clay* hanging over Deke's head at this moment, and things were going to hit the fan at any moment. That issue, however, was one that they would have to deal with if—and when—it came. Another thing they took into consideration was that even if he couldn't use the injector and the drink, perhaps they'd need both as evidence if they needed to go to the authorities. They also couldn't completely set aside the long-shot possibility that Deke had some unique quality that allowed him to integrate with the sports drink in a way that any other person would be poisoned by.

The simplest solution that they had to dismiss, however, was that this was a new policy that was implemented in response to the loss of Duke's original kit. It would explain so much if Evil Corp got spooked and added the targeted formulation as a defensive protocol, but that didn't explain Cotton Candy's assumption that whoever took the drug would be poisoned and in the hospital early on. So, Lee set that option aside reluctantly.

Finally, the last problem. On top of not knowing enough to conclude anything on the first three, they couldn't be sure what would happen if Deke took a second dose of the stuff. While this batch was made for him, the original juice was made for Duke and it was still in his system. So, he could possibly trigger a poison just by mixing them...

Most infuriatingly, there wasn't anything to be done right now. Other than admitting to Rooney he already had the sports drink in his system, which they had dismissed. Lee concluded that would likely end up with Deke in a lab, being dissected. So for now, they decided when and if Deke started to have problems with poisoning, they would handle it then.

Lee had still argued that they should get extra medical help until Deke pointed out that he was getting weekly check-ups already from Dr. Dan and the team's medical staff.

Second was something Deke hadn't noticed right away. Lee noticed the problem when Deke had recapped the conversation. According to Rooney, the sports drink was expected to run out, just like it had. Thus why it was called a taster. So, it might be possible that side effects happened after it did.

The director didn't seem to think there was going to be a problem with him going off the drug, and given the differentials in sizes of the blue liquids... it was likely that Duke had taken the sample and then turned down future supplements after his shipment on Halloween *arrived* in Deke's body. So, Duke was definitely in "power save" mode already, and he wasn't dying, right? That meant as long as there wasn't already a problem with Deke having taken Duke's sample, there shouldn't be a problem after the randy rim stuff ran out. Well, aside from losing access to some of the system's functionality.

Third. The contract and being forced into some sort of military training after he graduated.

It was all too much. Deke stood up from Lee's chair and grabbed the eraser out of his roommate's hand. With five swift strokes he erased the entire whiteboard.

"Why'd you do that?" Lee asked with a frown.

"Because it wasn't helping. We're just rehashing things over and over and going nowhere. It's clear that we aren't going to figure it out; the only way to know more is if I take the vial. There aren't really any other moves that take us forward. It's like you said—if I have a reaction after taking it, then the backers will likely help me. Other than that possibility, we can't get any more information than we had when we started. So, since I've already decided not to take the dose, we're fucked!

"I'm done. We've been stuck in here for hours—we've skipped classes, which is going to be noticed. I need to get out of this room and get some air, and maybe moving, getting my blood pumping will help. I'm gonna head down and see if I can't get a pickup game at Mr. Roger's Community Center." Deke picked up his gym bag and headed toward the door.

"Deke, you can't, it's only like... four hours until the game," Lee said, even as Deke angrily tossed the bag onto his bed, annoyed with himself for forgetting that he had a game tonight.

"You're right, I need to start getting ready. All right, maybe food will make me feel better." It was about time for him to grab his pregame meal anyway; any later and he'd be running late on the rest of his pregame ritual. "Come on, I need to get out of here. We'll get stuff from the student center."

Leaning down, Deke grabbed his other gym bag, the one that he only used before games, pulling it open to look inside to make sure it had everything he needed. Setting that on the table, Deke pulled off his shirt, annoyed that the coach made them wear a tie into the stadium. Even when he wanted to leave the room there was more to do...

Four Hours Later

Deke watched as number twenty-one on the other side dribbled past him. His incomplete [Motion Prediction] gave him a ghostly image of where the player was possibly heading. He saw the quick shift of the player's weight as he tried to feint to the left while continuing right. Hoping the image was right this time, Deke stuck his hand out and felt the ball connect with his palm. He felt the leather pull at his skin as he flexed his fingers around it, to attempt to maintain control. Once in possession it was easy to push past Twenty-one and charge back down the court. Blinking red lights in the corner of his eye told him that the system had a message for him. That took him off guard—they weren't normally red.

Still he drove forward. He could hear Twenty-one behind him, trying to make up the distance before he could score on an unde-fended hoop. But the kid was racing someone who had been ampli-fied by the system, albeit for a short time, and Deke's muscles were stronger and more ready than ever to respond to his commands.

Deke drove past the three point line. He considered pulling up for three, but Twenty-one behind him wouldn't likely give him the unobstructed shot that [Aim Assist] needed, plus Coach Skip had told him to always take the easy basket. So, he went for a layup. The ball slid smoothly down through the net and he turned around. He gave Twenty-one his best smile, even as he heard the announcer overhead.

"And the Smiling Assassin takes another two points for an early Baguettes lead." He winked at the opponent before heading to his defensive spot, giving Duke a high-five along the way.

While he waited for the other team to make their way back down the court, he called up the red letters, since they were more annoying than usual.

Power save mode deactivated.

Additional milestone reached: 1000 predictions studied.

Attempting to acquire full [Motion Prediction] at reduced cost. Trainee's Radanium insufficient.

Re-entering power save mode.

There it was again. Deke's stomach fell out from under him. Another reminder that the system was on the fritz. Not to mention this ongoing power save mode! Wasn't that when your computer shut down? What did that even mean when it was *inside* him? Could it be the poison shutting *him* down?

Movement out of the corner of his eye caught his attention and he shifted as he realized that Twenty-one was making another drive down the center. At least this time he was more cautious. Deke watched, but the telltale flicker of a predication didn't appear. He stuck to Twenty-one even as the man pivoted around him. Deke's fingers brushing the ball for half a second before Twenty-one passed it to their team's forward, who rolled off of a teammate's screen on Little Tim, to make an easy layup for two points.

Distantly, he could hear the announcer give the point to the other team but he was looking at his hands. If he had the full [Motion Prediction] would it trigger every time, instead of rarely? When it did trigger, it was almost like a superpower that *Mutant X* might display.

Yet here he was, with a power saving system, while the skill remained tantalizingly out of reach. He glanced up to the score and found exactly what he remembered. The Baguettes were down two with only thirty seconds left in the half. Why had he not taken the taster again? They needed to win this game. If they won, the Baguettes would be one step closer to winning their entire division and all he needed was that slight edge to *crush* the opposition.

The ball bounced off his chest, and he realized that the inbounder had passed it to him so that he could take the ball up the court and start the next play. He held his hands up in a T to call a timeout.

"Mills, you all right?" Duke asked, as he got to him first.

"No, I'm..." Deke shook his head, "I think..." What could he say? That he had been reminded that he ran out of go juice for the secret system that was powering his body and enabling him to predict the arc of his shots or the motions of the opposing players? That he even had a booster of neon blue juice in his sports bag and if he took it they would surely win the game? His teammates would think he was crazy.

Well, everyone except Duke, who would probably know what he had done. Would Duke be able to piece together the fact that he stole the drug that was intended for him? What would he tell Coach? What would Rooney say?

"I think he hit his head or something, Coach," Duke said, his arm around Deke and guiding him toward the benches.

"All right, Chucker, you're in. Mills, sit down. Abbie, get Doctor Dan to come look at him," Skip ordered, and the team had a quick meeting before returning to the floor. Part of Deke knew that letting Chucker take his place was even worse than him being out there, while out of power for the system, but Skip wasn't an idiot. Out of the corner of his eye, Deke saw his team dribbling the ball near the half, waiting for the timer to run down, so they could take the last shot of the half.

The timing of this reminder notification was suspicious, right? Was it trying to bait the trap with more honey? Did Evil Corp know that he had taken Duke's serum? There was no way they could know... right? Besides, if they did know, why would they lie and tell him the serum was tailored for him specifically? It just didn't make sense.

"Deke?" Abbie was kneeling next to him and he realized she had said his name several times. "Deke? Can you follow my finger?" Deke nodded numbly, his eyes following the finger that Abby put in front of his face as she waved it around.

"Okay good, your eyes are tracking properly. Did you hit your head?" Deke shook his head. "Does anything hurt? How many fingers am I holding up?"

"Three," Deke said with a sigh.

Dan appeared next to him and distantly, he could hear Abbie and Doctor Dan talking, he even heard his name a few times, but his focus was on his water bottle. Should he just dump the vial into there and drink the thing at half time? The pass intended for Duke hit his hand after he got bumped by an opposing player and bounced out of bounds, giving the opposition possession with only two seconds left in the half. They called a timeout to come up with a play, and take the inbound pass nearer to half-court.

Deke tangled his fingers in his hair and gave a tug. Was his resolve this weak? He had decided not to take the taster, and to make it to the NBA without it. Yet, if the game continued like this Deke's gut told him it would be close, but they would lose. Lose the shot at Mercenary March. Deke shook his head, trying to focus in on the things that mattered. He was still faster and stronger than he had ever been before, the power saving mode hadn't robbed him of that. It wasn't like he couldn't just get better at defence with practice. Did he really need [Quick Shot] or [Motion Prediction]? He still had a fully functioning [Aim Assist]—he raised his water bottle and saw the familiar dotted line appear just as the teams retook the floor.

Abbie and Dan were looking at him strangely so he changed his "shot" motion to take a drink from the bottle.

"Deke, what's going on there buddy?" Doctor Dan asked, a kindly smile on his face. "What happened?"

"I... just got dizzy for a moment there, must not have been drinking enough water," Deke said, taking another gulp from the water bottle. Dan reached out and grabbed his other hand, pinching the skin there, and then watching the response.

"Well, you've got good skin turgor. Abbie, check his temperature?" Dan put his hand on Deke's wrist and felt for his pulse. Abbie scrambled to grab the forehead scanner and rolled it across his forehead.

"Normal," Abbie said, showing the temperature to Dan, who nodded.

"You've got an elevated pulse, but nothing too high considering you were just playing. Take the halftime break easy and rest. Abbie, get him one of the candy bars. Rest up and we'll see how you feel in the second half warm-up," Dan said, patting Deke on his shoulder.

Deke took the drink he had been commanded, draining half the bottle easily. Dan went off to talk to Skip and Abbie handed him a chocolate-covered granola bar, which he ate mechanically. He was watching the last seconds of the game. As if Twenty-one had [Aim Assist] he caught the inbound pass, dribbled twice and let fly a shot that Deke knew was going in as soon as it left his hands.

The halftime buzzer sounded.

"Oh, I'll be *better* after the half," Deke growled to himself. Seeing Dan out of the corner of his eye, he followed the dejected-looking Baguettes back to the locker room for a break.

Abbie followed close behind him, likely watching him for any sign of dizziness. He chuckled when he thought about her attempting to catch him. He would pancake her. As soon as he got to his locker, which was now on the starting bench where Mac's used to be, he waffled again on the sports drink. Abbie still watched him, even as Skip and Dan approached.

"So, what happened out there?" Skip asked with a frown on his lips.

"Just got dizzy Coach, not enough water I think," Deke answered and Skip narrowed his eyes.

"Deke, go with Doctor Dan for a bit. Pee in the cup, we'll have it tested, if you're on something..." Skip left the threat unspoken and Deke opened his mouth to protest, but Abbie jabbed her finger into his back and he closed it again.

"That's fine, I'm not on anything. I promise, Coach." Deke felt more confident in that answer after the talk to Rooney. There was no way Rooney would let him pop positive on a test. Deke wondered what Rooney thought was happening, and how was he interpreting this dizzy spell?

In five minutes Deke had peed in a cup, and Dan had run the quick tests to clear Deke of the suspicions. The rest of the sample would still be shipped off to be tested more thoroughly but he could tell that Doctor Dan didn't believe he was on anything. Unfortunately, or maybe fortunately, Deke thought, five minutes was enough time to miss the rest of the team in the locker room. They were all likely warming up for the second half already.

Dan told Deke to go join them, but he made a stop at his locker. With no one around, he found the taster vial wrapped in socks, and hidden in the inside deodorant pocket of his sports bag. Not even taking the metal canister from the socks fully, he opened the lid and downed the contents in one gulp. He'd consider taking the injection later.

Infusion of Radanium detected. Specially formulated for Trainee, no assimilation required. Power of infusion increased by 25%.

Power save mode deactivated.

[Motion Prediction] skill unlocked.

Deke had begun to smile when the messages started, and the feeling of euphoria only grew but unfortunately the messages weren't done.

[Quick Shot] skill partially unlocked.

Insufficient Radanium to fully unlock.

Entering power save mode.

He had begun to run toward the tunnel and hit the door extra hard, slamming it wide open to bang off the brick wall it was set into. This was a pretty common act of the Baguettes' and the door and the wall were battered by years' worth of players running high on adrenaline. Yet, Deke's current actions couldn't be classified as adrenaline, but instead anger-fueled.

The door swung back toward him and he gave it another shoulder for good measure. Was that all the taster had? So, wait, did Duke only have a single skill? Or perhaps he didn't have any...

Somehow the thought of the big center not being quite as hopped up on the serum as Deke originally thought, made him feel better about what he had deemed a lackluster result from the taster. He reconsidered and even nodded to himself. Surely, a new skill and one partial skill was enough to change the outcome of this game!

And if they won this game, they only had to close out the rest of the season games to finish top in the division. Then it was a much easier path to Mercenary March! Deke felt his anger and nerves at taking the taster evaporate.

Only a few seconds later, Deke exited the tunnel. The home crowd roared with approval as they saw him jog onto the court to join the last few minutes of the team's warmup for the second half.

They had five points to make up and Deke had a new system skill to help.

Fifteen Minutes Later

Deke juked around Fifty-seven, who had replaced Twenty-one earlier in the game. Not that Fifty-seven had made a difference, but Deke guessed that after four steals from him the other team had to do something. Fifty-seven fell for the misdirect and Deke stepped back over the three point line, wide open with a decent shooting angle. [Aim Assist] went green and he swished a ball home to extend the Baguettes' lead to five.

The fact that the game was still so close only reinforced Deke's choice to take the taster at halftime.

"Come on guys, only three more baskets," an opposing player from the Badgers shouted.

"Yeah, we got this. Still plenty of time on the clock," another player responded, which made Deke glance up at the clock—9:37. Midway through the second half.

The buzzer sounded and Deke looked to the sideline, finding the starters for the opposition all subbing back onto the floor. They had taken a break to recharge and now the real push to the close of this game was about to start. Deke eyed Twenty-one as Twenty-one did the same to Deke.

The blood in Deke's veins already felt alive, full of electricity as he fought against what the entire country deemed a "superior" team. Plus, the Baguettes were winning. If they closed out this win and kept winning they'd seal first place, which gave them even better odds to make Mercenary March.

"Worried?" Duke asked as they waited for the opposing players to reach them and play to resume.

"Nah, nah, we're fine," Deke said, still eyeing Twenty-one, who was taking an inbound pass. Deke moved forward to meet him at the centerline, forcing him to pass it outside. Deke's fingers touched the ball, but he wasn't quite able to get the steal. With a quick pivot he moved back to his position at the top of the key.

Arthur came up behind him, his man trying to screen both Deke and the point guard. But Deke slipped around him. The ball returned to Twenty-one, who had gained a sliver of space thanks to the screen. He was lining up a shot and Deke watched an apparition hold the ball instead of shooting it right away. It was a fake. Deke closed to the man but didn't jump to block the shot, and instead stayed firmly planted on the ground. Twenty-one's eyes widened ever so slightly and he attempted to turn the fake into a real shot.

[Motion Prediction] gave Deke plenty of warning and this time, he did leap and slap the ball out of the shooting guard's hands.

"Add a block for the Smiling Assassin," the announcer called even as Deke gave chase to the ball which was bouncing up the floor. He caught up after four steps and scooped it up. When he looked up, he found Manny out ahead of him and made the easy pass to the wide-open power forward. Twenty-one, who had been close behind Deke, cursed openly as Manny dunked the rock.

Deke returned to defence and was forced to watch as the Badgers cut the lead back to five on their possession. Perhaps, sensing trouble this time, the Badgers avoided running anything through Twenty-one. While shadowing a decoy player was frustrating for Deke, he had one more "half-skill" up his sleeve.

Arthur took the ball up the court and called a play. Deke smiled. The play, while meant to free up Little Tim for a shot from one of the wings, was run through a pass to Deke first. Arthur passed him the ball just outside the three point line and Deke, who was praying for the semi-unlocked skill of [Quick Shot] to activate, felt his body react.

As if he was preparing to shoot without the ball in his hands, his arms began to rise from near his waist on a track that met the ball near Deke's chest and continued the motion up to Deke's shooting position. [Aim Assist] triggered almost before the ball arrived, and in one smooth motion, Deke caught the pass, and rose up for a jumper, from behind the arc. The ball just barely clipped the rim and bounced through the hoop.

"Fuck," Twenty-one swore. Deke was looking at the kid's back. Mostly because the opposing shooting guard only had time to spin and watch the shot sail over his head. While Deke had tried to activate [Quick Shot] earlier and failed, this time it had worked, and the *quick* in the name wasn't for nothing. Even his teammates seemed a bit confused by what just happened.

"That was unreal!" Duke shouted as he pounded a massive mitt on Deke's back. "You turning into Curry, now?"

Deke smiled and rushed back down the floor to get on defence. A comparison to the best three point shooter, ever, was something he could deal with...

Two hours later

Deke had opted not to go to the afterparty; he wanted to celebrate the victory but in the time it took to leave the court and meet the Boosters, somehow the win began to feel hollow. It was a strange feeling, at least when he looked back on the game. Was the team capable of coming back from five down without Deke taking the serum? He was starting to think the answer was "certainly." Deke had made the decision to win or lose with what he already had. So, why had he changed his mind at the first sign of pressure?

"So, what if taking the taster puts you on Evil Corp's radar?" Lee asked from his side of the room.

"Yeah. I'm an idiot. I just felt like I needed that slight edge, you know?" Deke attempted to explain. Lee nodded but his lips were firmly pressed together, which made Deke feel like he did understand but he wouldn't have made the same choice.

After a short pause Lee answered, "If I had the system, I would like to believe that I would be looking for any and all ways to power up. To become superhuman, but somehow knowing that you had been forced to take the serum the first time was an easy way to justify everything. Now that you chose to take it? Something has changed."

"Yeah, but with this win we could be first in the division by the end of the year. If we had lost we might have been out of Mercenary March, just like that." Deke snapped his fingers. It was hard for Deke to meet Lee's eyes.

"Sure, but you weren't guaranteed to lose if you didn't take it," Lee began, which caused Deke to finally meet his roommate's eyes. As if something in that look hurt Lee, he stuttered to a stop before continuing in a rush. "Look, I'm no expert on basketball, but do you feel like you are becoming too dependent on the sports drink?"

"No!" Deke answered immediately, then after swallowing a lump of saliva to clear his throat, he followed it with a quieter, "I don't know."

"I think we should tell Abbie," Lee said. "She's got more medical knowledge than both of us combined... she'll know if taking that taster was safe."

"No," Deke said as he stood up. That suggestion had caused him to sweat, which admittedly made him worry about poison but he was pretty sure it was for a different reason. "You didn't see her face when I first met her. I've already promised her I didn't take drugs. She would never talk to me again—or she would blame me for not being able to play volleyball anymore. She'd say I took the easy way out." By the end Deke felt like he might be a bit manic as he threw out reasons to not tell Abbie. A part of him wondered why he cared so much, but he retorted to himself that he just didn't want to lose a friend.

"Well, first of all, Abbie isn't the kind of girl that blames other people for her issues... But more importantly, is that what you think you're doing?" Lee asked with a wince, clearly thinking that same thought. "Taking the easy way out?"

"No..." Deke responded slowly as he felt a surge of confidence rise within him. "I think I was taking the only way out."

The air in the room felt heavy, and eventually Deke sat back down onto his bed, feeling that strange surge of confidence evaporate like water in the Sahara.

"I'm not so sure," Lee whispered to himself, repeating a thought Deke was having as well.

FORTY

THURSDAY, FEBRUARY 23RD

"How is he doing? You seemed worried about him…"- Abster

"You know how he is. Do you know of a reason I should be worried?"- Leeroy Jenkins

"Nope, all the drug tests were negative and he's been 'crushing' it in practice from what I hear. Should we take him out for a meal?"- Abster

"Valerie is here, best you stay away."- Leeroy Jenkins

"Oem gee! Like, I could totally be the next Kardashian. Teaching all them basketball skanks about fashion!" Valerie gushed. She was sitting next to Deke on a bench outside the math building, where his next calculus class was to be held. She leaned into his arm and squeezed. The heat from her hands and face was pretty intense, so Deke looked at her. She was flushing with pure excitement.

He felt his stomach twist even as he smiled. He was happy that Valerie was excited but there was something disturbing about the timing of this visit from an "NBA agent." Deke tried to find the right tone of voice and appropriate words to stop her from getting her hopes up. "Just because an agent says he wants to sign me doesn't mean I'm getting drafted, babe."

"Deke, I know agents. My mom has had several—this guy wasn't a joke. He looked like a serious badass. I bet he could crack some skulls of the GM's if he needed to. His cologne I could do without, though," Valerie rattled off and then held her nose.

"Cologne?" Deke asked, not understanding how a fragrance could change Valerie's mood that much.

"Yeah it was sickly sweet. But like, who cares what he smells like, right?" Valerie's jubilant mood returned and she squeezed his arm tighter. "Just insist on phone calls in the future! He swears he will get you to the US NBA after next year's season!"

"Just NBA, babe. No US in front..." Deke said absentmindedly. He felt like his veins were burning in his arms. He knew that it was his imagination, but taking that "taster" of the serum might have been a really bad idea, and not because of the chance of poisoning. Lee and he had already hidden the injection, deciding not to take it just in case.

"Deke, baby, just think of how much money you would be making! You could buy a house nicer than my dad's!" Valerie urged. Deke couldn't help but picture that. A nice big house that had plenty of rooms. One for Rhonda and another for Max! Still, there was something strange about Valerie wanting more money. She could turn around and more money than Deke had ever seen in his life would fall from her purse, and she wouldn't even notice the loss.

Could this really be about her father? Deke had seen those "unexplained" bruises. His stomach sank further. After a moment he shook his head. "Did the agent say anything else to you?"

"Just that you should sign the contract you have, and the world would open up to you, to us!" Valerie responded while staring into his eyes. A smile froze on his lips as he ran a nervous hand through his hair. He only had one contract in his possession and it was given to him by Rooney. Not some "badass" NBA agent.

"I'll think about it, babe. I've got to get to class, though."

"What? Why are you going to class instead of signing the million-dollar deal you have! Fuck class, what's math going to do for an NBA superstar?" Valerie countered, her voice starting to change tones.

Deke leaned in and when she didn't respond in kind, he kissed her forehead. She glared at him even as he stood. She was forced to let go of his arm after the first few inches, and she plopped back to the bench looking somewhat hurt by his decision. "I've already told you, babe. This guy is just promises—there's no guarantee he'll make it happen."

"Well if I see Mr. Bubbalicious cologne again, what should I say?" Valerie asked over her overly acted pout. Deke's heart screamed as it froze in his chest. Bubbalicious? It took his mind a moment to connect the dots. Sickly-sweet smelling... cotton candy! It was the Vaping Man!

"Just tell him I'm thinking about it," he responded and fled. He was sure that Valerie would be upset by his sudden departure but at the moment he wanted to get inside and out of the courtyard, where he was clearly visible from nearly every direction. It almost felt like he had a gun pointed at his back—like he could picture the crosshairs between his shoulder blades, lining up a kill shot.

"You swore to me that you didn't take anything!" Abbie hissed at him after she closed the door to the much smaller rehab room. Deke flinched while narrowing his eyes at her. She had claimed that she had a new rehab workout for him, but her red face and tone conveyed something entirely different. Had Lee told her?

The smell of stale sweat on rubber hung heavy in the air, and

Deke wet his lips, his mouth suddenly dry. This was the second such instance of him being ambushed by women today. First Val, and now Abbie?

"What are you talking about?" Deke asked, truly confused by her attitude. If Lee had told her, he was sure he would have explained enough for her to realize that it hadn't been a choice. Right? Well, at least the first time.

"Some suited-up douchebag came in and told me he could fix my knee—make it like I had never been injured in the first place. Told me that he was offering me a miracle, and all I had to do was get you to sign some contract to go to the NBA!" Abbie strode across the small room as she spat her angry sentences at him. By the end, she was poking him in the sternum. "It isn't hard to put together your miracle recovery with all this!"

"Abbs, I can swear to you that I only got the contract he's speaking of a few days ago!" Deke responded, skirting the actual issue. Abbie stopped jabbing him in the chest with her finger and blinked up at him.

"So, what? This company is actually offering me some sort of experimental treatment, just to sign a freshman college player to a multi-million dollar contract? And don't tell me it's not. These kinds of guys don't go after players like this for peanuts," she said, her voice confused. Deke took a deep breath and looked around the room. After a moment he moved to a weight bench and collapsed onto it.

"You're not the first one they've approached, either," he began. "Valerie drooled all over me between classes, gushing about how *we* were going to the NBA."

The bench shook as Abbie sat down next to him. He looked at her, and found her staring at her braced leg. "Do you think that they could really fix my leg?"

"I mean, I'm sure they could get you in for the surgery you need, and with your discipline, you'd be playing again in no time, but a miracle? I don't think those are so easy," Deke quietly said, and he meant it. His "miracle" sure wasn't feeling like one right now. He felt guilty about the lies, but it was for her own good. He didn't want Abbie of all people getting tangled up with the Vaping Man and Evil Corp.

Abbie looked up and met his eyes. Something in them must have convinced her that he was being sincere. She reached over and put an arm over his back, then leaned into him, almost like Valerie had. Still, the difference was night and day. Where Valerie clung to him, Abbie was supportive. Where Valerie demanded and didn't listen, Abbie had just pulled a one-eighty simply because of his mood...

His shoulders relaxed a bit and he leaned into Abbie, putting his arm on the back of her head. "What is it you always say to me? Hard work is the only thing that is proven effective?"

She chuckled. "Speaking of, maybe you should stop distracting me from the workout, huh?"

"Right, because I brought you into a private room to yell at you..."

She leaned away and punched him in the arm. He chuckled in response, even as he stood up to start.

"You still good to get a bite?" Duke asked, as he approached Deke at his locker. He was just getting changed after a shower, and he suddenly recalled the big center asking him, mid-practice, to eat together at Beef and Baguettes.

Deke shrugged. "Sure man. Do you want me to invite Val?"

"Actually, I'd prefer you didn't."

Deke finished tying a shoe and looked up to meet Duke's eyes. His current flat-lipped, serious expression looked ominous. "Everything okay?"

"I think so. I just want to talk, man. Not too much to worry about..." Duke's tone and his words didn't quite match, which caused Deke to frown. Still, this was Duke—the team's captain. He had a feeling he knew what the talk was going to be about, and maybe it was past time to have it.

Deke stood, grabbed his T-shirt from the hanger in his locker, and pulled it on. "Okay, let's go."

The walk to the restaurant was quiet. Deke kept his thoughts to himself, and Duke did the same. Deke could tell the center was wrestling with something, and he didn't want to be the one to break the silence either, because he had his own worries. Had they promised Duke something as well, if Deke signed?

That seemed unlikely, considering that Duke had been given the very same offer. Or close enough to the same that it didn't matter. So then, what did he want to talk about? They entered the restaurant and Deke stopped his walk. Eva was sitting at a table, watching them walk in. Why was she here, if he wasn't bringing a date?

A deep inhale brought the scents of fresh-baked breads, pickle juice and pastrami to his nose, which made his stomach rumble suggestively. Plastering on a smile, he moved to the table, even as Duke greeted Eva with a kiss and sat down.

"Hey Deke," Eva said sheepishly. "Look, this isn't an ambush," she continued and made a motion with a hand at the place where he'd frozen. His smile became a bit more genuine. Eva saw his smile and her body relaxed a bit. "Well, I guess it *is* an ambush, but a friendly one. We just want to talk to you about everything *we know* is going on."

Deke scratched the nape of his neck.

"With Rooney, and all the 'agents'." Deke formed air quotes around the final statement. Eva and Duke looked at each other, clearly surprised. Then they met his eyes and nodded.

Leaning forward, Deke met their eyes seriously. "That's good, because I could really use some perspective on all this."

Duke coughed as he averted his gaze, and Eva looked at him. Since Duke was clearly trying to get the attention of a waiter, she sighed and met Deke's eyes. "Rooney is involved?" She began slowly before shaking off that question. "Never mind, that part doesn't matter. It's more Duke's story to tell than mine, but I think I can say that before you, all this was happening to him. When we pulled out, they were bound to find someone else. We're not stupid enough not to realize that it started after your 'miraculous' recovery. We know you took the sample, Deke. That's how you healed up so fast."

Duke returned his gaze to Deke for just a moment. In that glimpse, Deke could see a swirl of emotions. Jealousy, desire, fear, and so much more, that he felt a shiver run down his spine. Clearly, Duke getting out hadn't been an easy decision.

"So, the case—" Deke started, but Duke slammed his hand down on the table.

"Could we get some service please!" he said over-loudly. Still, he wasn't looking around the restaurant, his eyes were wide, and fixed firmly on Deke. Duke shook his head ever so slightly. "If we're going to talk about the *offer* you received, that's fine, but let's order first, okay?"

Deke got the message. Don't bring up the case, or what was inside. Still, Duke had practically called out the entire restaurant, and a server rushed over to remedy the situation. They each ordered a meal with the flustered-looking guy.

As the server rushed away, Duke looked chagrined. "That made me feel like a real asshole, but yeah, we just want to discuss the offer you currently have in front of you. We know a little bit about it, and *strongly* suggest you don't sign anything!"

Deke floundered. If he couldn't talk about the drug, that likely meant he couldn't or shouldn't mention the interface. So, what? They just wanted to talk about the contract itself. That felt superficial. Deke eyed Duke, and again the center widened his eyes and shook his head slightly. Clearly, he didn't want to talk about the "taster," and so Deke asked the only thing that was left. "Why shouldn't I sign? The guy has a compelling offer—he's even approached people around me with promises."

"And you don't find that strange?" Eva cut in, before Duke could respond. "If the offer was so good, why would they need to go around and use the pressure of your friends?" Eva seemed to notice that she had Deke's full attention, now. "It was the same with Duke. He'd actually have been in the draft next year, according to Sleazy McSleazebag. At first I was really excited about it all, but I told him we should at least run the contract by a lawyer."

She paused for a moment and looked down at her hands, Duke, and then back to Deke before continuing. "We left that office *absolutely* convinced to not sign the contract. The lawyer practically laughed at some of the clauses. He called the original writer 'predatory', and suggested numerous more reputable sports agents for Duke. I was so glad we brought it to him."

Something in her tone and the words didn't match. It made Deke's skin crawl, so he waited for her to drop the other shoe. She didn't disappoint. "Then a day later he called us back, told us he was wrong. Said we would be idiots if Duke didn't sign. Basically, tried to strong-arm us into a meeting right then. This was *my dad*'s lawyer, he'd worked with him for years—told me he was the smartest and most trustworthy man he knew, but I could tell he was lying. I could feel the difference in his tone of voice from the man we'd met the day before. It was almost like someone else was speaking with his voice.

"Still, even if I thought it was a lie, Duke didn't. The guy insisted that they were amending the contract to address all the problems he found. Duke promised to meet with the lawyer and then sign on Halloween, before the party—"

"If the lawyer was wrong, and they were amending the contract like he said, why wouldn't I say yes to the NBA—to all that money? To my life basically being set," Duke chimed in, cutting Eva off. He was whispering and not meeting anyone's eyes, which looked seven shades of wrong on a monstrous man like him.

"Then, I missed the meeting that night because Eva refused to drive me to the office." Eva was smiling fondly, which told Deke this wasn't a sore spot in the story. At least not anymore. "She drove out of the city instead. We went out into the Mojave and just talked. I convinced her that I should sign just after midnight."

"That was when we drove back, and when we re-entered cell service..." Eva added, clearly prompting the next part of the story.

"My phone had gone crazy. Just, bat-shit insane, Deke. All those people around me who had been offered something *miraculous* were messaging me. Telling me I had fucked them over. Told me that because I didn't sign their lives were ruined."

Deke felt his blood go cold in his veins. That was certainly something he hadn't considered. If these people could giveth—certainly they could taketh away. Duke saw his expression change and he nodded sagely. "That wasn't even the worst part."

"People started claiming I stole . . . *something*." Duke changed what he had been about to say at the last minute but Deke felt his stomach fall further. He knew what Duke had been accused of stealing. It was running through his veins, right now.

"They threatened to 'take it back', told me that they wouldn't stop until they had it. My room was broken into four times in the next three days..."

"Mine too," Eva added in a whisper.

"If it makes you feel any better, someone broke into my room, too," Deke offered, trying to lighten the mood.

"It doesn't." Duke started, but paused. "Actually, yeah. That does make me feel better... Why is that? Anyway, for some reason, after those three days, they changed tunes and wanted me to sign again, but it was too late. I'd already seen their true colors, Deke. They may offer rainbows, but it's just colorful hellfire. I got lucky—truly lucky— we went to the Mojave that night." He reached over and squeezed Eva's hand.

Deke took in a shuddering breath. He opened his mouth before closing it. There wasn't anything to be said. He knew they were right. After thinking it through, he realized there was one thing he did need to know. "All those people that they ruined the lives of...?"

Duke didn't answer right away, and Deke realized that it was because he had spotted the server coming with three plates balanced on his arms. After the guy put down the sandwiches, Duke and Eva both turned to him. "They're living their lives normally again, but not many of them will forgive me for taking away what 'could have been'."

Deke's fingers went white on the table, as he clenched it hard. Would he lose Lee, Abbie, or Valerie if he didn't sign? A hand on his shoulder made him look up. Duke was looking at him with true heartfelt sympathy in his eyes. "I know it sucks, Deke, but if you do lose some friends over it, just know they weren't really there to begin with. They were your champagne friends. Only there for you in good times." His grip became almost painfully intense as Duke locked eyes with him.

"I ain't a champagne friend, bro."

FORTY-ONE

THURSDAY, FEBRUARY 23RD

SPIDERSLAYER LEE: "HAVE YOU GUYS EVER
HEARD OF UPLIFT ENTERTAINMENT?"
CLERICTIGHTPANTS:" THAT SOME SORT OF
CHRISTIAN ROCK BAND?"
SPIDERSLAYER LEE:" NO, THEY MADE THIS
WEIRD GAME, HERE I'LL LINK IT."
LEEROYJERKOFF: "LOOKS TOO HETERO
FOR ME."

Deke opened the door to his dorm room and was assaulted by a wave of pepperoni pizza scent that wafted out from inside. It made him smile. Lee would likely be "raidering" with his friends tonight then. Yet when Deke stepped over the threshold and adjusted to the lower light, he found Lee's monitor on, illuminating his friend's face in blue, but there wasn't the expected accompaniment of furious keyboard clicking or Lee's trademarked lightning-quick mouse movements.

"I thought pizza night was *rage* night?" Deke asked, allowing the confusion in his voice to come through.

"Ha. Ha. I got upset one time, Deke, *one time*—and admittedly that kid ruined a two-hour attempt at the World Boss, so I had every right to rage. Plus I didn't even say anything! You just were awake and saw my teeth grinding and heard my mouse protest my hand clenching." Lee was still clearly somewhat embarrassed about the outburst, as evidenced by his immediate defense of his actions.

"I mean if I cared as much about my computer as you do about yours, I wouldn't be abusing the mouse that way..." Deke added with a chuckle and closed the door to their room.

"You mean that brick paperweight that you keep under your bed? Please don't call that thing a computer, man. At this point it's an artifact of ancient society."

Deke smiled as he moved behind Lee and gestured at the screen. "My original question still stands. What's... UPLIFT Entertainment?" Deke scratched his chin. That name was familiar for some reason.

"It's the company that developed the game we've been using as a baseline for your sport drink's effects." Deke blinked as it came together. His reaction made Lee continue. "I've been over their website numerous times for that reason but this time's a bit different." He scrolled to the top of the page and Deke read the page's headline to himself. "Join our Team."

"You thinking of applying?"

"I mean, that wouldn't be a terrible idea if we were absolutely out of other things to explore, but I wouldn't even have to apply. They sent me a job offer directly that seems too good to be true." Lee manipulated the keyboard and mouse in a way that seemed to toggle open windows, which pulled up an email. Deke bit his tongue and made a note to ask Lee about how he did that. It seemed like it might be helpful for writing papers.

"Why is this job offer too good to be true?" Deke asked, looking at the salary and terms that seemed high to him. Still, his mothers salary wasn't a good baseline. Plus hers was in Canadian dollars...

"First, I only have a JackedIn profile, and its resume is out of date. I think I updated it to being a student but I couldn't even say I was a computer science student—in case my parents saw, Deke!" Lee exclaimed as if that explained everything.

"So, you're saying they shouldn't have any idea you want to be a game developer?" Deke asked, trying to clarify the problem. Lee's voice had been nervous, and a bit manic even.

"Maybe?" Lee began, actually turning to regard Deke instead of looking at the computer. "I mean, in theory my teachers and fellow students all know my aspirations, so it isn't impossible for someone to have tipped off a recruiter. I think what's bothering me is that it's UPLIFT Entertainment, out of the blue and starting at ninety thousand a year. Tack on the fact that their game mechanics function is eerily similar to your sports drink, and we have a prime recipe for a conspiracy."

Lee's voice this time was definitely manic, so Deke sat on his friend's bed to give him his full attention. Admittedly, Deke still didn't see the problem, so he said, "Okay, I want to help but I'm lost, man. Walk me through like a total boob."

Blinking, Lee seemed to recognize his own anxiety. His face morphed before his head drooped with a chuckle. His head still down he mumbled, "First, we call them *noobz*. Second, earlier when you called it rage night—it's raiding or raid night. Okay?"

When Lee's eyes came back up and met Deke's, he seemed a bit more like his usual self. He even wore a cheeky grin. Deke smiled at him and shrugged, trying to convey that he was likely going to forget the terms again as soon as the conversation moved back to the problem. Lee sighed. "Okay, ninety thousand a year may not seem like a lot. But my TA was just bragging about getting hired on for fifty-five *after* he graduates... Like sure, maybe if I had proven myself to be a top recruit already, but a first year... the industry is too brutal for this. This isn't poaching a talented asset early. Deke, it feels like a payoff. Like, Uplift knows I've been looking into them."

"Oh, yeah, I know!" Deke responded, taking a deep breath. Clearly he also needed to explain his statement more, because Lee's eyes went a bit manic again. He held up a hand to inform Lee that an explanation was coming. "Everyone I met with today got an unexpected offer. Go back to that email—is there anything about *me* in there?"

Lee's mouth flattened as he turned back to the monitor. He rolled the mouse wheel and scrolled through the contents of the email again. It was at such a speed that Deke couldn't have read it, even if he was facing the monitor directly, which he wasn't. The scrolling stopped and Lee said, "*Gorramit*, how did I miss that..."

Deke stood and moved to read the paragraph in the dead center of the screen. It alluded quite heavily to how great of an opportunity this was for Lee but also, his friend. While it didn't explicitly say Deke needed to sign the contract for Lee to get the job, it did say "We look forward to working with your friend, and you."

"That's more subtle than what happened with Abbie and Valerie," Deke stated. "No wonder you missed it. They were told directly that I should sign the contract and they could benefit..."

"Wait, start at the beginning. Abbie was approached with an offer, too?" Deke smiled at Lee's dismissal of Valerie's involvement to focus on Abbie. He was clearly still a bit smitten, even after the "rejection."

Deke explained the conversations he'd had today, ending with Duke and Eva's retelling of their experiences. "Wow. This group sure knows how to bring the pressure, huh?"

For the first time in the conversation, Deke felt like he couldn't meet Lee's eyes. He stood up and began to pace off some of the energy that seemed to jolt through him. So, now that Lee knew, would he pressure Deke to sign like Valerie had?

"Do you think they were so subtle with me because they knew I would say no if they spelled it out?" Lee asked, and Deke felt a wave of relieved euphoria wash through him, loosening the muscles in his back and shoulders—making his next exhale feel longer.

"Dude, I think they are thinking that my relationships with Valerie or Abbie might be a bit more *personal* than with you."

"Oh!"

"Yeah," Deke said, and laughed at Lee's deep red face.

"Well, at least they don't know everything, I guess." Lee met Deke's eyes and in them he saw an unspoken question about Abbie. He gave the answer with a minor shake of his head—no, he hadn't slept with Abbie... As if to break the tension, his stomach chose that moment to rumble loudly, and he realized that the smell of the pizza must be getting to him. He sat down on his own bed to access the low-hanging "fresher" air.

"The way I see it, you're going to have a tough time explaining why you're saying no to people that don't know the whole story—maybe it's time we tell Abbie?" Lee said, bringing the conversation back on track.

"No, man. If she finds out that I took drugs at this point, she'll never talk to either of us again!"

Lee's face fell and he scratched his head. "She would be mad we kept it from her, I think, but it isn't like you had a choice..." Lee faded off, and Deke cheeks heated up. At first that was true, but he had made the choice with the taster.

His pocket vibrated, and Deke felt a moment of relief as he began fumbling in the pocket to pull it out. "Someone calling, one sec. And still no telling Abbie!"

He read the caller ID and saw that it was his mom. He smiled as he picked it up. "Mom! How are—"

"It's Johnny, sport," Johnny responded, interrupting Deke. Deke considered just hanging up the phone but realized that something could be wrong at home. He gritted his teeth, stood up and began pacing again

"Everything okay?" Deke asked. Lee gave him a raised eyebrow look and he mouthed the word "Johnny" by way of explanation.

"Everything's better than okay, kiddo! I heard you've got a real shot at going to the NBA, down there!" Johnny responded, slurring some of his words, which made Deke think he might be drunk or on something.

"Johnny, I don't know what's going on but can I talk to my mom or Max?" Deke asked, feeling his stomach flip a few times.

Deke heard a door open, and then close again. Wind blew into the receiver now and Deke assumed that Johnny had gone outside. "Both fast asleep after all the celebrations, I'm afraid. We got the news, and I told them about how I'm going to take them to a brand new house, with a yard. Rhonda won't have to work again. I didn't even know you had this kind of pull kid, congrats."

"What are you talking about?" Deke asked, already suspecting the answer.

"My company just got lifetime contract offers for eight buildings with the city of London. I hadn't even put in a bid for five of them. They stipulate I'd have to change the name of my company to include Mills in the title—you know, pull on some of that hometown hero magic, and that you'd have to take the offer on your end, but like who wouldn't go to the NBA? That's like your dream, right?"

Deke flipped the phone to speaker on his end, placed it on a table and then ran both of his hands violently through his hair in exasperation. His slightly longer curls fought back and trapped the digits, giving him a satisfying tug to his scalp, which fit the situation. He couldn't think of much to say, and so mumbled, "It's not that simple, Johnny."

Lee looked at Deke with concern but held his tongue. Likely realizing that a bit of context was forthcoming. Johnny sucked in a breath on the other end, and Deke inferred that he must be shocked or upset for his breathing to be audible through the phone.

"Don't be an idiot, Deke. Opportunities like this don't come along every day! It's the NBA, too—you'll be making bank. Why wouldn't . . . I mean what possible complication . . . just say yes!" Johnny sputtered to an ending of his argument.

Lee wrote something hurriedly on his computer screen and Deke strode over to read it. Deke sighed in relief at reading Lee's plan. "I can't just say yes to the first agent that makes an offer, Johnny!"

"So what, you think that a better offer is coming down the pipeline?" Johnny asked breathily. Deke was willing to bet that the drunk man was getting more excited by the minute.

"No clue, but I just got the offer recently, and this guy is already pulling out all the stops, so I'd be an idiot to just jump on board, right?"

"Okay. Okay, so you're holding out for a bigger fish. Kid, I always told Rhonda you were smart!" Johnny slurred excitedly. Deke knew for a fact that Johnny had never called him anything other than a failure, meathead or similar derogatory slurs.

"Sure. I'm just waiting for all the offers to come in."

"But this one isn't going to just go away, then? Cause if you sign now Rhonda and Max are taken care of. There's a clause in the city contracts that says she has to become my VP. Not only that, but they've already set up an appointment time with that doctor you've been trying to get Max in with..."

"Fuck," Deke mouthed to Lee as he felt his legs go numb under him. He crashed onto Lee's bed. Something rose in his throat and he swallowed hard, fighting against the vomit or tears or whatever was threatening to emerge right now.

"Dekester? You still there?" Johnny asked. Deke couldn't attempt a response, his throat felt constricted, and his eyes were burning. Should he sign the damn contract? Wasn't Max his whole reason for working so hard in the first place?

The doctor in question wasn't a guaranteed fix, but an appointment with her would mean a consultation and a possible plan for the future. A possibility of improvement, even though Deke had given up on that route a while back. That was why he needed the NBA and money. Max didn't need more consultations. He needed to get bumped up the priority list and start getting multiple surgeries. Only the rich could go the private route and totally avoid long waits in the Canadian healthcare system.

The realization snapped Deke out of his stupor and he realized Johnny had still been talking. Without a response from Deke, Johnny was likely checking his connection, because Deke's phone was making small noises that indicated Johnny fiddling and pushing buttons on his end.

Lee had stood up and moved to collect the phone off the table. Deke met his friend's eyes and Lee motioned at the end call icon. Deke nodded, and Lee hung up on Johnny.

"Well, this is getting scarier by the second," Lee said as he collapsed back into his computer chair. "These *ruttin' reavers* are attacking on all fronts..."

As if mocking Lee's words, Deke's phone started buzzing again, displaying Rhonda's name. Deke didn't answer. He needed to think— he needed to breathe. He stood up and walked out of the room, the air cool on his wet cheeks. Lee stood up and followed, grabbing a dorm key, which Deke had forgotten in his haste.

FORTY-TWO

FRIDAY, FEBRUARY 24TH

"Starting the game plan for Bailor! I can't
believe that our team could finish first."-
Assistant Coach Boogie

> "Getting that easier first round draw sure
> would help, but it's a tight division Boogz. A
> single loss could change the layout
> significantly, so let's not start celebrating
> too early. We've got three more games to
> win. We need to keep the boys on task."-
> Coach Skip

"Totally! After tomorrow we've got some
tough teams to close out the year."-
Assistant Coach Boogie

> "The Hornets aren't that bad of a team,
> Boogz. Don't underestimate them, they
> beat us in preseason. - Coach Skip

"It's time to dance!" Leslie shouted from halfway down the immense harvest table that Deke currently sat at. A good number of the cheerleaders, basketball players, and invited friends of the latter stood up, taking the energetic statement of the small cheerleader as a call to action.

Deke smiled and checked his phone. It was already approaching ten at night and his cut-off for the evening, so he stayed in his seat. For the briefest of moments Val remained in her seat as well, but a glance showed Deke why. She tossed back the remainder of her gin and tonic in one motion before shooting up. Once standing she looked at Deke, and even reached down to grab his bicep and attempt to pull him to his feet.

The smile he wore grew, even as he shook his head. "Sorry babe, it's a game's night and I need to be in bed by ten. If we leave now, we can still—"

"Oh come on! Your whole team is here," Valerie shouted over the distant music from the dance floor in the background. "Let loose and come dance, then we can both cum later." She finished the statement with a knowing wink.

A surprised laugh broke past his lips at her innuendo, and he did stand up, but only to give her a long kiss. He figured he did a good job because she collapsed into his chest breathless after the affair. "I'm sorry babe, but it's a fifteen-minute walk back to the dorms, and I still need to shower—"

"Fuck your stupid routine tonight, Deke. Come on! Everyone else is letting loose, even though you have a game tomorrow. Why can't you?"

"Babe, the starters need to get some rest. Every game is important right now. Skip said—"

"There's Arthur, Manny, Tim and Geoff right there! I know for a fact that two of them are trying to pick up Leslie tonight—" Deke was already shaking his head, and Valerie surprised Deke by cutting off her argument with a smile. Then his look of confusion morphed into some mix of desire, amusement and disappointment as she spun around and began walking to the dance floor. "I bet you can't say no to this."

Tonight Valerie was in a blue A-line skirt, and a glorious red open-back bodysuit. One of those skin-tight, almost lingerie-like deals that buttoned up in the crotch area and doubled as underwear. How did Deke know that? Well as Val walked toward the dance floor, she pulled up the back of her blue skirt to give him a glorious view of her tight butt. Deke almost ran after her, but despite most of his blood flow diverting to a new region of his body, he sighed. Coach Skip had made it clear during game prep that tomorrow's game was important, despite it being against the Hornets.

When he didn't follow, Valerie pouted, but reluctantly came back to join him.

"I can't believe you don't want to undo this outfit with your teeth," she teased, but the words had an edge to them, and Deke felt the hair on his arms raise.

"Let's get out of here, and I'll do a lot more than that!" Deke attempted to tease back and defuse the situation he thought was coming. He already knew she was mildly upset with him for not spending more time out with her, like this, which was why he had allowed her to drag him here tonight. Of course, he had made it clear then that he had a bedtime.

"Deke!" Valerie whined. "It's okay to break curfew now that you're back on the team. No one is going to kick you off anymore. Especially with Mac gone. Has a coach even knocked on your door recently?"

Deke frowned. He had somewhat forgotten about the curfew set by the coach after his injury. Valerie was right that no one seemed to be enforcing it anymore, but he would put money on the fact that it was because of his new, better habits. The trust he had cultivated with the coaching staff and players. Regardless, he wasn't going home early because he *had* to. No, he was going home because keeping the routines the system had drilled into him made him better. Right?

Valerie must have seen that infinitesimal moment of hesitation, and she attempted to pounce. "Manny, come help me! Deke wants to bail!"

"Come on Val, I was just getting my courage up to go join Leslie!" Manny complained. Deke frowned, glancing between the two. When did they become close? Instead of answering, Valerie moved to Manny's side and whispered something in his ear. After she was done, she flounced away to the dance floor.

"Fuck, man," Manny said as he closed the small gap between himself and Deke. "I sure hope she comes through and puts in a good word for me. Dude, let's go dance, be my wingman tonight, I could use the help."

Deke blinked in surprise before huffing a breath out through his nose. So, this was Val's plan. "Man, we've got a game tomorrow. I don't know if this is the right night to be wheelin' Manuel."

"Dude, don't use the dreaded full name now. You make me feel like Skip is sighing in disappointment. It's just the Hornets tomorrow —plus, it's a late game so we can sleep in!"

"Man, I'm heading back to my bed. Unlike the rest of you, I'm actually still on a curfew," Deke said, which was probably true?

"Shit, right!" Manny responded while scratching his head. Deke was happy to use the curfew as an excuse when it was against peer pressure. "Don't worry about it, then, you can be my wingman tomorrow night. We're having another backyard bash after the game. It's going to be lit!"

"Yeah okay, I've got you," Deke answered, and offered his fist to Manny. Manny bumped it and smiled. Deke turned his fist into a point, "Now can you go tell my girlfriend I'm heading outside and will wait five minutes. Plus, that should give you an excuse to get close to Leslie on the dance floor. Be smooth with it!"

"Thanks for looking out, Deke!" Manny answered and spun to follow the path Valerie had made a few moments before.

Deke moved in the opposite direction and ended up on the sidewalk outside of the nightclub. He waited for ten minutes longer than he said he would before he realized that Val wasn't going to join him. Turning, he headed back toward campus. If he ran he might be able to get back on time...

Saturday, February 25th

Deke sat on the edge of his over-cushioned seat on the bench, practically twitching as he waited for his short break to end. Even as he picked at the edge of his knee brace angrily, Abbie swatted his hand away, her glare reminding him that he 'had' to wear the thing to keep coach happy. He nodded at her and at least stopped playing with the brace, but sighed and allowed his knee to bounce nervously. He knew that this rest was just part of Skip's game plan to give the starters rest, but in close games, it only gave him anxiety.

"Is no one going to tell Chucker that those shots are why we don't call him Charles?" Deke growled to no one in particular, as the aforementioned team member sent a desperate shot at the vicinity of the basket. Somehow the ball found the rim, which honestly was better than Deke thought would happen. Truly, a shot like that had no business going in, even if Deke was using his [Aim Assist] he'd be beyond lucky to sink that type of shot.

The Hornets managed to rebound when the ball bounced out on the opposite side of the hoop from where Duke was furiously guarding the Hornet's center. Deke sighed and joined the bench in the chant for a defensive stop. Unfortunately, they only got about three stanzas into "De-fense. De-fense," because the Hornets ran a fast break that saw their small forward lay the ball in, stretching their lead to eight.

Turning his attention from the scoreboard, Deke looked over at

Skip, hoping for the indication he was getting subbed back in. As if the coach felt his scrutiny, he sighed. Looking at the game clock and then saying something to Doctor Dan, Skip nodded gravely at the Doc's words before pacing the sideline and placing a hand on Deke's shoulder on his way by. Only when Skip's hand landed did Deke realize the man was twitching more than his own legs were.

"You need another ten minutes of total downtime, son. Go stretch if you can't sit still!" Skip said. Deke was sure his voice was meant to sound confident, but he heard the same anxiety in it that he himself felt. The Hornets were not a team they should lose to! His earlier assumptions counted this as an easy win to clinch first in the division. A loss here could drastically alter that finish, moving them down as far as fifth even, maybe worse. A change like that would match them up with a stronger team come playoffs...

Deke jumped to his feet and moved to the team's warmup box at the end of the bench. The box was an area where players like him could ride the bike, stretch or stand. Right now, he didn't have the patience to stretch, and instead just bounced from foot to foot.

Duke managed to grab a rebound after Manny's floater trickled out of the basket, and the big man immediately two-hand jammed the ball back down with authority. Deke's lips twitched up in a small smile as he prayed for a momentum shift.

The point guard on the Hornets inbounded the ball and Manny pressured him as he dribbled to half-court. Once he crossed the centerline, he picked up the ball to pass, but some good defense by an agile Little Tim made him hold the ball. Chucker bounced out to double- team Little Tim's man. Deke's eyes widened as he watched Chucker's abandoned defender, the opposing shooting guard, step out wide past the arc.

"Watch the three!" Deke shouted, and pointed uselessly. The opposing point guard had already bounced the ball right past Chucker and into the hands of the wide open number two. Number two shot the ball and held his finishing pose as if he was some type of superstar. Deke cursed under his breath as he watched the flight path of the ball and the waiting basket. It sank home, and Deke felt the air leave the stadium, his own heavy sigh matching the crowd's. The Hornets were now up by nine.

Five minutes later, number two had sunk home four additional threes. Despite some baskets from the Baguettes, the lead extended to fifteen. Skip called a full timeout, using a whole minute, which made Deke smile. Maybe Coach was starting to realize that they needed him out there.

"Gentlemen, it's time to regroup. We are letting one hot-handed player beat us, on a team that is dead last in the league." Skip looked around the circle and met eyes with each player. "I'd ask you where your pride is, but I can see some vacant looks. Is there a party or something after this game that you all can't wait to attend?"

Deke blinked as he saw a few of his teammates grimace. Skip caught them too. "Okay, why don't we try this then. Since no one wants to party with losers..." Skip let his words hang in the air and Deke looked at Duke, the only other team member who Deke was reasonably sure wasn't out last night. "If we lose tonight, we'll run sprints every fifteen minutes until midnight. I wouldn't want to ruin someone's festivities by allowing losers to attend, after all."

A few too many teammates' eyes widened at that, and Deke felt his stomach twist. Luckily, the meeting from that point became one of strategies to contain number two, and Chucker was replaced by "the Brick" Geoff. So, perhaps the squad would turn it around.

The next four minutes showed Deke the opposite. Instead of playing with confidence, the team seemed nervous about the punishment. Like they had already lost. The only person out there keeping pace was Duke and somehow—through heroic rebounding, and some very powerful spin moves—he kept the score gap from getting outrageous. Deke didn't even wait for Skip to call him as the ten-minute mark approached; instead he chucked his long-sleeved warmup to the floor and jogged toward the center table.

He did, of course, glance at the coach to get an affirmative nod, but he didn't think that ruined his swagger. He'd ask Lee later, to see if the kid noticed. His eyes found Valerie on the sideline as he knelt and waited for a stoppage in play. Somehow the thirty seconds felt longer than the ten minutes had, and perhaps even more unfortunate, was that the stoppage came just as Geoff fouled number two, which awarded him two free throws.

"You've got number two," Geoff growled to Deke as they walked by each other, trading places on the court, Deke's knee brace squeaking annoyingly.

"Like I didn't know," Deke growled. He didn't bother joining the rebounders until after the first shot sank home, extending the lead to nineteen. The second shot drained too, and the lead became twenty. Deke glared at the time clock. With eight minutes left, and a score of seventy-five to fifty-five, he wasn't sure if Skip had waited too long.

Trusty Arthur got the inbound pass and quickly moved it up the floor, with Deke's help and a few passes between them. The final pass landed with Deke. Quickly, he held up a three over his head to call for an isolation play for Arthur. His intention wasn't to get Arthur a shot, but to have his two wing teammates to screen down, bringing their defenders with them. Arthur and Little Tim began to move down to screen out Duke and Manny, and Deke dribbled to his right, making it seem like he was going to pass to Duke as he sprang free. The brace hindered his movement slightly, but he was getting used to it.

Two stepped back to play off of him and possibly jump the pass route to Duke. Deke smiled and lined up his shot with [Aim Assist]. The ball was in the air even as Two blinked his eyes. Deke watched the kid turn to watch the ball sail over his head and into the basket. Instead of watching the shot, Deke turned and began jogging back.

The announcer let Deke know the ball had sunk home, even as he turned back around just shy of the half-court.

"You know Skip isn't going to like that!" Duke said, as he sprinted by following his own man toward the key.

"The team needs the pick-me-up. We have to change the momentum, and a little show-boating does that, Mr. Shaq-attack." Deke mimed the big man's earlier dunk, complete with warrior-face and shaking the imaginary hoop like he was trying to shatter the glass backboard. Duke rolled his eyes in response.

While he did know that Skip wasn't going to like that "risk" because he had essentially pulled the rebounders out of the key right before the shot, at this point in the game, they needed fast baskets more than they needed smart gameplay. Deke didn't deny the element of ego involved in his actions—but as impulsive as it seemed, it was a carefully planned ego and to him, that made all the difference.

Arthur let the opposing point guard cross half relatively unmolested, and Deke kept a good position with his player, number two, to prevent an easy pass. As soon as the ball crossed, a moment of déjà vu seemed to occur. The point guard attempted a pass and Manny jumped the route. Deke smiled, and took a step toward the now "stuck" point guard, making it seem like he was going to trap him in a double-team.

He heard the squeak of Two's sneakers as he moved wide, and suddenly [Motion Prediction] created a faint outline of a ball near Deke's foot. The point guard was going to try to bounce-pass right beside him. Deke took an extra hard push forward off of his back leg and snagged the pass about two feet before it would have hit the ground. With only the point guard in front of him, Deke continued his forward motion, adding a dribble to his movement, and was past the only remaining defender before he even registered the steal.

Deke pulled up at the three point line, and could almost hear Skip cursing him out over at the bench. He drained his shot and held his finish, looking back at Two in mockery. The game wasn't over yet! All Deke needed to do was get back fourteen points!

"And there's another miss! Sprint," Skip crowed, seeming to delight in the torment of the players, who were all breathing heavily. While Deke was sick of running sprints after losing the game, he also admitted that they were, somehow, improving his mood.

Directly after the loss, Deke felt like his world was ending. How could he make the decision to take the taster to win a big game, then lose to the Hornets? That loss completely negated Deke's arguments with himself. Taking that taster had become one more stupid decision that made him want to bash his head into a wall.

The team hadn't even left the gym after the game, and perhaps that was a good thing. Instead they began the punishment, and instead of finding out which was harder between a wall and his head, Deke was running suicide sprints. Somehow, though, the punishment was bringing context to the loss in a way Deke hadn't expected.

While losing this game was going to have unfortunate ramifications for the end of the Baguettes' season, from the reaction of the coaching staff and the other players around Deke, it wasn't the end. This wasn't a do or die playoff game or a sudden death tournament like Mercenary March...

Deke was one of the first to finish his current sprint, thanks in large part to the aforementioned serum and the stats it had helped him increase. That gave him the opportunity to watch each player labor back to the starting point of the suicides. Maybe it shouldn't have been amusing, but the third string and redshirt players wore expressions on their faces that told a story of absolute disgust.

Thor, Wash, and Mr. Glass hadn't even been dressed for the game but were now running lines as a punishment for a loss that Deke knew they had no part in. So, the looks on their faces were justified and somehow amusing. Chino, who also was a third string player but did get to dress, wore the look of a try-hard. His brows were pulled down in concentration and each sprint for him seemed like the finals of a hundred meter dash. Unfortunately, Chino was a first year with no true shot of playing due to his lack of skill and athleticism, which was saying something when Chucker and Brick were off-the-bench players.

Speaking of players that mostly sat on the bench but came in to rest the starters, those were the next most upset group. Deke scanned over the faces of Big Tim, Larry, NJ, Brick and Geoff. This group, while upset, also seemed to carry a burden of shame or embarrassment as they stood around heaving for air.

As if in contrast to the two other groups were the starters, whose eyes seemed to blaze with an emotion Deke hadn't been able to place at first, but thought he was starting to feel himself. Retribution. They'd lost the game tonight, and while the loss was entirely on the Baguettes, they were going to try to make every opponent they faced from now on pay for it. These were the looks that gave Deke the feeling that this loss wasn't the end. He almost felt bad for their opponents in upcoming games.

Thor, who was known to be a terrible free throw shooter, missed his next shot, and despite the team's love of the large Viking of a man, a groan went through the gym.

"Sprint," Skip called.

The new fire in Deke made him change his approach. He had learned something from the system when he had it. It had never awarded Deke points for completing a task with minimal effort. Just like now, these sprints weren't about winning or losing—Skip was trying to teach them a different lesson, he thought. They had taken a game for granted, and not studied the game plan. Most of the players had indeed already been celebrating the win, by planning a party after. Even Deke had plans to attend with Val. All of them had approached this game *wrong,* and Skip was trying to teach them about doing it *right.*

Deke changed his approach to the suicide sprints, no longer standing tall when he turned. Instead, as instructed, he began touching each line with his hand. This changed the dynamic of where each player usually finished the punishment. Deke was now in the middle of the pack during the drill. Still, he managed to make up some ground on the final full-court sprint and turned around in second place behind Arthur. He tried desperately but didn't manage to catch up by the starting point, and doubled over panting, even as Skip threw the ball his way. Deke reluctantly took his hands off of his knees and caught it, attempting to catch his breath as he made his way to the foul shot line.

Each time a player missed, they were forced to run, which admittedly was getting more frequent by now. Sometimes they also had to run if they sank the free throw too. Deke took a couple extra seconds to line up his shaking [Aim Assist], and managed to hit the throw. He turned to the coach expecting what came next.

"Did you do everything you could in that loss?"

"Yes, sir."

"Do you have a prior engagement tonight?"

"Yes, sir." Deke responded with the truth.

"Did you read the game plan or were you on a hot date?"

Deke wanted to swear under his breath. This was his third time hitting his shot but the first time Skip asked this final question. The previous two times the team was forced to run after Deke admitted he had plans tonight. Hoping the new question didn't stem from his "trouble" in the sorority, he debated for a moment and chose his response somewhat carefully. Others on the team had answered a question like this untruthfully with a simple "no sir," but still caused the team to run.

In the end he settled on a response that might make them run. Grimacing, he asked, "Just a date with my pillow, Coach?"

"Don't listen to him, Coach. We all know he's got a date with Rosie Palm and her five sisters later tonight." Lacking the ability to even see straight, some joker still had the energy to bust his balls, even now. It sounded like Chino, and Deke made a mental note to get him back.

Skip canted his head, a lip twitching up before he controlled himself back to a glare. "You're lucky you scored double digits, Mills."

Skip snatched a ball off the rack and threw it to Chucker Charles. The whole team groaned. Skip broke into a full smile.

"What? You don't trust your teammate?" Skip asked. Deke shuffled back to the baseline even as Charles moved out to take up his prior position.

The groans weren't because Charles couldn't hit a shot. No, they were because out of everyone present, Chucker had been given double, if not triple, the chances. The ball clanged off the rim before bouncing out. Deke let his head fall even as he got ready for what came next. Skip's whistle rang through the large gym and he started another sprint.

Skip had left practice about an hour ago. Still, Boogie and the other assistant coaches kept the team running.

"That's it, maggots. As my Staff Sergeant used to say, 'the more you sweat, the less you bleed'. And boy did we ever bleed out on that court today. We have a list of weaknesses identified from this game, and we will be shoring them up over the next days and weeks. Also, you'll be happy to hear that Coach Skip has a final message for all of you. If he gets a single report of *anyone* on the team going out tonight, they will be off the team. No exceptions," Boogie said by way of parting, and simply left.

Pulling himself out of a puddle of sweat on the polished court, Deke limped out of the gym and went through changing and walking back to the dorms on autopilot. He took the old and horribly slow elevator up to his floor, not trusting his numb legs on the stairs. When the doors dinged open he slowly made his way to his room.

Lee was wrapped up and completely concealed by his blankets when Deke came in. Deke mechanically leaned down to grab his towel from the hook near his bed. His mind was a dull burned-out coal, but the habits he'd built completing his "daily quests," as Lee had called them, had finally entered a place that went beyond thought. However, as he leaned over, his body betrayed him—giving out after the long, grueling hours and pitching him to the floor in a tangled heap. A small, distant part of himself attempted one last act of coherent thought, but was washed away in a tidal wave of sleep.

CHAPTER

FORTY-THREE

FRIDAY, MARCH 3RD

"Your totally lame lately"- Valerie

"WOW way to leave me on read"- Valerie

"Babe these two weeks have been nothing but practice and school. Plus I've seen you every day at lunch..."- Dekester

"If I was important youd make time!"-Valerie

Thanks to the loss against the Hornets, Skip ran extra practices, keeping Deke and the entire Baguettes roster effectively confined to class, the gym, and bed. Deke was currently groaning as he sat up from the latter.

"You would think Skip would give you all a rest since you *crushed* the final two games of the season," Lee complained on Deke's behalf.

"Coach Skip," Deke corrected, a habit that had been formed in the last two weeks from hell. "Sorry, didn't mean to correct you, but yeah, we were all hoping the same thing. However, that loss to the Hornets meant even with those wins we have to play the number three, UC Alameda, tonight, and Coach Skip knew it would cost us."

399

"Still, not everyone has the sports drink you do. So, if you're feeling and looking like this . . ." Lee let that foreboding statement hang in the air. Deke smiled though, which seemed to surprise Lee.

"Man, I wish I still had the system giving me abnormal recovery. Truthfully, I don't think I'm even that far above where I could be without the stuff. I know you think the stats are still helping but I miss the good ol' days, when they were climbing daily," Deke mock-whined.

"I mean, sure, but if you had a working system, wouldn't you just be in more pain right now? It was compacting DOMS!" Lee pointed out, and Deke recalled just how painful some of those next mornings were with the full serum.

"Good point! I mean it still gave me a small amount of physical points the other day, so maybe it's—" Deke began but was cut off.

"You know as well as I do that if you work out you get stronger. I think that 0.01 to physical stats was just natural growth. Just like if you studied, you'd get smarter," Lee retorted. Deke winced a bit at Lee's final friendly ribbing. It hit a bit too close to home. It was true that he could do with some more studying, but honestly it was playoffs, and if Lee didn't understand that, Deke wasn't sure how to make him see.

"You sound like Valerie," Deke complained, partially as a joke, but entirely to change the conversation.

"I notice she hasn't been having lunch with us anymore?" Lee asked, sympathetically.

"She claims that I'm not making enough time for her," Deke explained.

"Well, have you been?" Lee asked, and Deke flinched as if shot. Seeing the reaction, Lee explained, "I'm not saying you aren't. I'm just wondering how you feel about it. Abbie and I are your friends and we only see you because one of us works on the team you play for and I'm your roommate. Valerie is somewhat peripheral to all that..."

"Okay, so what exactly should I stop doing to make more time for her? Remember, you just called me out for not studying as much as I could," Deke said incredulously.

Lee shrugged helplessly as he swung his chair out from his desk to face Deke. "I'm not saying you should. I'm more pointing out that she doesn't understand all of that. She doesn't see you leave the dorm at seven, and stumble back at ten with only breaks for food in between. As far as she knows you're just lying in bed and avoiding her."

"I've told her. You've even told her, Lee," Deke growled.

"*Liú kǒushuǐ de biǎozǐ hé hóuzǐ de bèn érzǐ.*" Lee practically growled the words, giving Deke the impression that he was being insulted in "Firebug."

"What the heck does that mean?" Deke asked.

Lee didn't bother explaining what was said and instead offered, "You're being an idiot. Just because you're busy doesn't mean that others have to understand. I doubt Val is even that angry with you. She just wants to see you. What I wouldn't give to have Abbie complaining about—" Deke coughed, which seemed to bring Lee back to the present.

Lee's cheeks grew red, and Deke finally understood where this was all coming from. "Little heart-sick, buddy?"

"A little?" Lee asked sarcastically. Deke felt for his friend. He wanted Lee to be happy, but Abbie had made it quite clear that they were just friends. Deke felt his stomach twist as he considered what to say. Part of him wanted to try to make Lee see reason when it came to Abbie, but another part wanted to encourage his friend. Unfortunately, both were losing options, so he kept his mouth shut.

"I better get to breakfast, or I'll be late to the game tape session," Deke said, changing the subject yet again. Lee nodded and stood up, taking his words as the invitation to join that it was.

"We've already lost to this team twice in the season, which means we have nothing to lose." Coach Skip spoke to the team in the locker room right before the game. Deke listened with half an ear as he continued. Instead, his primary focus was on himself. Both losses to UC Alameda had been before Deke was allowed to play. While the game plan hadn't mentioned that fact specifically, small comments from teammates and even the coaching staff hinted at that point. Almost like everyone was counting on him.

"—we aren't the same team we were last time they saw us, either. The end of our season has been nearly perfect, if we ignore one minor hiccup," Skip continued, using the exact same wording that seemed to place the weight firmly on Deke's shoulders. He took a sip of water and considered—was he up for that kind of pressure without the working system?

A small smile crept onto his face. The end of the season had truly firmed his resolve. Even without the system, this, what he was doing right now, had always just been a pathway to the NBA, and if he wanted to play in the pros, what was UC Alameda? His twisting stomach changed from protests of worry to the thrum of challenge. That feeling of retribution from the loss to the Hornets returned and his smile became much toothier. He'd show UC Alameda!

Fire seemed to course through him as sweat and goosebumps broke out across his skin. Tonight, he planned to rise above even the team's high expectations.

"That's a double-double for Mills!" the announcer called out as Arthur's baseline floater sank through the net. Smiling, Deke nodded to himself. It was only the start of the second half, and he was having a game! Deke only had nineteen points, but that bucket had given him ten assists, and he was on the cusp of a triple-double or maybe even a quad.

Double-doubles were something relatively common in college basketball, where a player managed to get double digits in two of the five major stat lines. Triple doubles, while less common than a double, were still pretty achievable by the top players of each team. However, a quad? Deke didn't even know if more than a handful of them were recorded for NBA players.

Deke stayed just outside of the opponents' key, picking up the opposing shooting guard full court. Arthur did the same, marking the point guard as soon as he caught the inbound pass. Deke checked the score, confirming they were still up by fourteen. Fifty-five to forty-one.

He glanced back down just in time to have his [Motion Prediction] notify him of a possible pass coming to his man. Deke caught a faint holographic trace of both the ball and a ghostly outline of number forty-five, his covered shooting guard, intercepting its path. Could he move fast enough to cut it off? A quick assessment told him that he had given Forty-five too much of a cushion. So he closed the distance instead of trying to steal the pass. Almost as soon as the Alameda's Forty-five got the ball Deke was already on him, denying him the first bounce of the dribble.

Forty-five spun in a flash, his elbows held at head height. Something collided with the side of Deke's head, just missing his temple. The next thing he knew he was lying on the ground, shaking his head as his vision blurred. A whistle sounded, and the Baguettes who were on the court were suddenly all surrounding Deke.

Power save mode deactivated.

Threat detected: Threat level: White

Injury detected. Injury classification: Mild gash. Evo

points not required, trainee's current level of recovery will suffice.

Re-entering power save mode.

Deke shook his head to clear both his spinning head and the message, which he was already surprised to get thanks to the mostly inactive system, but as he considered the wording he started feeling vaguely insulted. Really? *A white threat?* The lowest he'd seen before was green. Was white even lower than green? Had the system just called him a bitch for getting hit with an elbow?

"Number forty-five, flagrant," someone announced, as Deke's focus started to return. The first person he found in his vision was Abbie, as she slid over the court to his side. She had a towel in hand, and Dr. Dan was about half a court behind her, but clearly rushing as fast as his old age allowed.

"Hold still, you're bleeding," Abbie firmly said as she pressed the towel to the side of Deke's head. He winced as the pressure from the towel sent a spike of pain through his head. He could tell Abbie wasn't even pressing hard, and instead, only attempting to stop the bleeding. This couldn't be happening.

"Mr. Mills, do you know where you are?" Dr. Dan said as he slowly got to his knees beside Abbie.

"Of course, it's only the biggest game of the year, Danno," Deke said, and saw Abbie grimace at his choice of address for Doctor Dan.

"*Doctor* Dan if you please, Mr. Mills. Look into the light," Dr. Dan ordered as he began to flash a small flashlight in and out of Deke's eye. "Pupil response satisfactory. Remember these three words, Deke: chair, orange, bicycle." Coach Skip suddenly loomed over the kneeling duo of Dan and Abbie, and the doctor turned to him. "He seems to be okay, but his pupil response is slightly erratic, and he'll need to pass Concussion Protocols. Plus we'll have to stop the bleeding."

Skip profaned and Deke's eyes widened. Was it that bad? Abbie removed the towel for a moment and Deke saw the red contrasting its starched white fabric. It definitely seemed to be a good cut. Abbie leaned in, her breath hot on Deke's ear as she tried to get a view of the cut through Deke's hair.

"It might need stitches, doctor," she reported. The profaning from Skip continued.

"It doesn't feel that bad," Deke suggested.

Dr. Dan ignored him, and looked at the nearby Baguettes who were clearly ready to fight, while still looking nervously at the group around Deke. "Can I get two volunteers to get him to the therapy room?"

Duke and Little Tim grabbed Deke under his armpits, heaving him up to his feet even as he looked at both of them. "Guys, it's not that bad. Come on—I've got to keep playing," he pleaded, becoming more frantic as they ignored the first bit and started walking him somewhat forcefully off the court. "Guys! Abbie!" Deke looked back over his shoulder at Abbie, who was following with the towel still pressed to his head.

"Dr. Dan is a wizard with the needle, Deke," Abbie explained. "He'll have you back out here in no time." Her final words got his sneakers to stop squealing as he began walking with Tim and Duke, instead of being dragged.

Duke and Tim dropped him off with a, "Answer Danno's questions and you'll be back out there in no time." Then to "Danno" they shot a pleading look.

"I'll do my best, gentlemen."

"Mr. Mills, repeat the words I told you earlier."

"Bicycle, orange and chair," Deke rattled off the doctor's earlier list.

"Good. Let's see the pupils' response again." Dr. Dan went back through the flashlight routine and nodded to himself. "It's getting better. Okay, let's take a look at this cut."

Abbie pulled the towel off, and Dr. Dan pulled a nearby lamp over. He then used his latex gloves to part Deke's hair around the gash. The movement so near the injury hurt, but strangely not as bad as Abbie's towel had at first. "Ms. McDugal, this doesn't look like it's as serious as you thought. Bring me the glue."

"Really?" Abbie asked, her voice sounding surprised. She still obeyed the doctor's orders and got something out of a nearby locked cupboard. When she brought it out, she paused as she looked at the cut Dr. Dan had made more obvious with his parting of Deke's hair. "That's odd. I swear it was closer to an inch and a half long, when I last saw it."

"Sometimes the court lighting casts strange shadows," Dr. Dan responded as he took the glue. "Let's be happy that it's less serious. Ms. McDugal, can you begin concussion protocols as I glue this shut?"

Abbie gave Deke a squinting appraisal before reaching for a nearby clipboard which was affixed to the wall with a screw.

"What do you remember just prior to the elbow?" she began.

Deke closed in on number forty-five, giving the player no room again. It was the final minutes of play and the Baguettes were up by five. He didn't need to pressure this hard, especially with under a minute to go in regulation, but he wanted some revenge. Petty? Certainly, but he wasn't going to let the kid elbow him and do nothing.

Plus he was one steal or three rebounds away from a triple double. All told, Deke had only missed about ten minutes of this second half, and while the team looked like it was going to still manage to pull out a win, he couldn't help but be a bit upset. He was so close to a quad, and this asshole stole ten minutes from him.

Forty-five didn't even dribble, and instead passed directly to his waiting point guard.

"Scared?" Deke asked, hoping to goad the kid into dribbling the next time. Instead, Deke saw the shadow of a fist coming for his face.

"What the?" he spat as he ducked under the image. Instead of trying to back away, he wrapped his arms around the opponent's waist. Something scraped his shoulder and he realized he had been a hair too slow to fully dodge any contact his [Motion Prediction] showed. It had been Forty-five's elbow brushing by him as he extended. The kid then leaned back and attempted a true elbow, but since Deke was hanging on to him it wasn't anything more than another weak bump to Deke's back near the right shoulder.

"Mills!" Skip shouted from the sideline, and Deke released his hug, opting out of the suplex he wanted to pull. Instead, Deke jumped back out of reach of Forty-five. The wild-eyed kid managed a single step before his own teammates restrained him. Deke was also grabbed from behind, and he turned to find Duke.

"It's okay, I realized I can't retaliate or the league will likely suspend me," Deke assured Duke. It had been a close thing. If Skip hadn't shouted at that moment, he likely would have thrown Forty-five to the ground and started swinging. No saying who would have won, but the Baguettes definitely would have lost either way.

Duke let him go, and the referees came to announce that Forty-five was out of the game. Deke wondered if the kid was a senior. Perhaps the taunting had solidified to him that their season was coming to an end. That his career would be over, and his dreams were going up in smoke. He read the last name on the back of the jersey even as "Harding" ripped it off and balled it up.

The crowd booed but they seemed conflicted. Some jeered at Deke since it was UC Alameda's home court, and some directed their displeasure to Harding. The Baguettes were awarded two free throws. Skip gave Deke a thumbs up from the sideline and motioned for him to move to the free throw line.

In technical foul situations like this, two free throws were taken and the opposition wasn't allowed to stand in the key. Instead, both teams lined up at half-court and the Baguettes would also get the ball on the sideline after Deke's attempts. He made them both count thanks to [Aim Assist] and extended the lead to seven.

Duke inbounded the ball to Arthur and they began spending the seconds on the shot clock with some passes, well outside of scoring range. As the shot clock hit ten seconds Arthur held up two fingers. Get the ball to Duke inside after a ball reverse.

Arthur passed to Little Tim, who dribbled to the top of the key before dishing it with a no-look pass to Arthur as he cut inside. This play was meant to culminate with Duke's possession but the Yellow Bears knew that and had double-teamed him. Still, when someone was double-teamed, that meant someone else was open, and Little Tim must have seen that. Arthur laid it in, extending the lead to nine.

The Yellow Bears hurried to inbound and Deke began pressuring the new sub, number fourteen. Fourteen did dribble and despite [Motion Prediction], Deke didn't manage a steal. Still, he dutifully wasted time forcing Fourteen to cut back and forth.

As soon as the ball crossed the half Fourteen threw to a wing, another option that left Deke no chance of stealing it. The next few passes happened fast, culminating with a two-handed dunk from Duke's opponent. Duke grabbed the ball and passed it to the ref even as the other team postured. Deke smiled—there was no way Duke would have let that go normally. Right now, though, just like Deke, they couldn't afford to respond.

Their lead was seven again. Deke needed a three to break thirty, or a steal for a triple double. He decided that one of those would be his goal. Either he would tie, maybe even break the freshman scoring record, or he would get that elusive triple double. The inbound pass from Duke came to Deke, and he was immediately hugged tightly. This was a tactic for an intentional soft foul. He blinked before looking up at the clock. There was just over a minute left. So, they were going to start fouling and hope the Baguettes missed free throws.

[Aim Assist] made sure that didn't happen, extending the lead back to nine. Unfortunately, the other team managed to cut that to six with a timely three on their possession and the inbound from Duke was forced to go to Little Tim, since the Yellow Bears double-teamed

Deke and stuck close to Arthur—the Baguettes' best free throw shooters.

"If Tim misses, we need this rebound!" Duke ordered, the clock reading forty-five seconds after the opponent's last possession. Deke nodded, taking up Tim's usual spot on the key for free throws.

Tim hit the first, and blew on his hands before rubbing them together. The ref returned the ball to him and Tim lined up the shot. Deke watched [Motion Prediction], and saw that the ball was going to lip out to a place behind him. Instead of moving forward and attempting a box out, Deke stepped back, and as if choreographed the ball landed atop him.

Deke dribbled away, forcing a game of chase to waste time. He only managed to reduce the game clock by six seconds before the Yellow Bears point guard "hugged" him, forcing the foul call. Deke smiled wide as he got his opportunity to break thirty points for the first time in his college career.

The green line showed the ball's path and point thirty sank home. He had just tied the record Lee had looked up all those months ago, and he'd done it in the playoffs to boot. Now he was left with a decision. Deke could sink his next shot, putting his team up by nine. However, nine wasn't an insurmountable deficit in thirty seconds. So, while sinking his second free throw would earn him that record for UCSP freshman, the Baguettes would be better off sealing the win by running down the clock.

If this had been a few weeks ago, Deke knew he would sink the shot and celebrate that milestone, but a glance at Coach Skip sealed his current decision. He would do this right.

The second shot Deke chose to miss. He lined up a miss with a rebound landing far outside the key. He shot the ball and started moving to the spot. He easily snagged his own rebound as it lipped out. This time as he ran away, he watched for the point guard, and passed to Arthur just before he was fouled. Arthur took off, and the Baguettes managed to wind the clock down to eighteen seconds with some smart passing before the Yellow Bears fouled Duke.

Duke didn't miss his shots and the lead became ten.

Once the lead became ten, Alameda gave up, and held the ball after the inbound pass. They too realized that ten points in fifteen seconds was impossible to overcome.

The game was sealed.

FORTY-FOUR

MONDAY, MARCH 6TH

"Like if I get Deke to sign, you all will get me a movie role?"- Valerie

"I will be your agent, Ms. Star. Meaning I will start getting you roles. It might start as commercials or TV. But let me assure you that as your name suggests we will do everything to make you a star."- Agent to Celebrities

"We spent yesterday at my house and he totally was digging the life."- Valerie

"I'll wait to hear from you. Thank you Ms. Star."- Agent to Celebrities

"When you didn't rise to that number forty-five's punch, I totally knew the game was over!" Grant Fisher pumped Deke's hand as he practically shouted his words in overexcitement. Fisher let go of his hand a moment later, and Deke hurriedly stuffed it into his suit jacket. Partly to dry off the sweat, and mostly to avoid any more over-enthusiastic handshakes from the round man.

They were at an extremely large Booster Party, being hosted at UCSP's reception hall this time. The reason for the change in venue? The two big wins over the weekend and the upcoming finals.

"The semis yesterday were a foregone conclusion after you took out the trash against Alameda, my boy," Fisher continued and looked down to try to find Deke's hand. Smiling, Deke raised his eyebrows and nodded along. Fisher gave up on finding a hand to slather with his sweat, and continued, "Even the number two couldn't keep up with the Baguettes! Now, the finals against the cross-town rivals too! With you on the court, Mills, we simply can't lose! Baguettes in Mercenary March—I don't think I've seen it in decades. Go Baguettes!"

Everyone who heard Fisher's shout returned the cheer, and when the large man turned around to engage someone nearby, Deke made his move, backing up into the crowd and ducking his head. "Mills!" he heard Fisher call, but he turned and threaded his way out of the crowd as fast as he could. He saw Valerie sitting at a table with some of the cheerleaders and made a turn to rush in her direction.

"Save me!" Deke said by way of introduction. Valerie looked up and smiled. Deke's breath caught. They'd spent all night yesterday after the semis at her house, and while it was only about six hours total, it seemed to have worked. Deke made a note to thank Lee for his advice.

"Just the boyfriend I was looking for!" Valerie crowed. The volume was a bit off, and Deke wondered how many drinks in she was. Still, she definitely wasn't sloshed, which kept Deke from running away.

"So, you've got multiple boyfriends now?" Deke asked playfully.

Valerie came over and stood on her tiptoes to give Deke a long, meaningful kiss. When she disengaged from the tongue war, she said, "Don't worry, you're my favorite!"

Laughing, Deke nodded to the other cheerleaders who were

watching the show. "Ladies," he said, before turning to look at Valerie. "If you see Fisher coming this way, warn me—or kiss me like that again."

She promptly grabbed his hair and kissed him even more passionately. Deke needed a deep breath after the impromptu kiss. When he had his breath again, he said, "Thanks, I really think he might throw my shoulder out if he gets a hold of me again."

"Oh, he wasn't coming. I just wanted to practice." Valerie winked at him and then motioned to a table that had no one occupying it. "Let's go hide over here," she said.

Valerie led him to the standing table and immediately pulled out a flask. "Want some?" Despite the system being in power save mode, Deke wasn't willing to test if purges were still possible. So he shook his head at her offer and she took a short swig before returning the container to somewhere inside her skirt. Where that space was, Deke couldn't begin to guess.

"So, like that agent guy has totally sweetened the deal! He says if you sign the contract and go to the NBA with him, he'll like, totally get me a commercial, movie or TV role right away. I don't know which one I prefer yet, but figure you could help me decide, right?"

Deke frowned. He'd talked to Valerie yesterday about all of this. When had the agent "upped the ante?" It would have to have been after midnight. Deke immediately felt sick to his stomach. "Val, baby, I can't sign with the first agent that makes an offer. We've been over this!"

"Holding out for something better is all good, Deke, but I don't see a line of agents looking to represent freshmen. Do you?" Valerie tried to make it a statement of logical fact but her sneer took away from that.

"No, but that's what's worrying. I've never heard of freshmen signing with agents. Not even MJ. And. I'm. Definitely. Not. Him." Deke enunciated each word, making his point as best he could.

"Deke, you're averaging twenty-six points in the playoffs, you're tied for the UCSP freshman scoring record and you almost pulled off two triple doubles. Come on, have some fucking confidence!" Valerie answered, but instead of the confidence booster those words could have been, she used them as a weapon. Deke rolled his eyes. "Don't fucking roll your eyes! What does it matter if you sign, and then don't make it? They can't hold you to making the NBA. And, to go you'll need an agent, regardless. So why are you being so fucking stubborn?"

She was hissing the words, and while they had some privacy at their table they were also drawing looks thanks to Val's language. "Val, I've already explained my reasoning. Just because—"

"Your stupid reasoning!" Valerie countered. "Why can't you just sign it already? Do it for me?"

Deke shook his head and despite knowing it was going to cause problems later, chose to walk away. Sure, he could stay here and argue with her, but he only saw her getting angrier with him repeating the same reasons. He couldn't tell her the actual reason either, and maybe that's what she was feeling...

The sound of a hissing kettle followed him as he turned his back, and he tuned out the barrage of words that she shouted after him. They weren't pleasant, and he could only hope it was because she was intoxicated. Thanks to her volume, a great number of faces turned his way, and he made out Lee and Abbie giving him wide-eyed stares from across the room. Hunching his shoulders, Deke zigzagged in their direction.

"Seems like you messed up, kid," Abbie said, punching him in the arm. He felt a blush that almost matched the one Val's kiss had given him, and he grabbed a carrot off Abbie's plate to hide it.

"I'm only like eight months younger than you, Abbs," Deke retorted with a crunch as he bit into the carrot.

"Which makes you a kid. Right, Lee?"

Lee looked like he too wanted to protest, but Deke could see the war that was waging between his two brains.

"You are the youngest, Deke," Lee answered after a long pause. Deke snorted. That wasn't his best option. Lee was only a few months older than Deke, and by admitting Deke was a kid, he'd basically agreed he was one as well. Not that Abbie had used age as a reason with Lee.

Shaking his head, Deke smiled at the two of them. "She just wants me to sign with that agent."

Lee gave him a wide-eyed look, even as Abbie clenched her jaw. A moment later she explained her response. "The same one that offered to fix my knee if you signed, and Lee got that job offer?"

"The same," Deke mumbled.

"Something is really suspicious about that. I asked Doctor Dan about it, and he said no athlete should sign until they know their worth. For what it's worth, I think you're making the right choice." Abbie looked at Lee, who nodded along eagerly agreeing with her point, despite the fact that he knew the whole truth.

"Thanks Abbs. I've told her all that, but I can also understand how a movie role or a TV show gig would make it hard to say no."

"Wait—what?" Lee said, and Deke explained what they clearly were missing. Once he finished, Lee looked across the room to where Valerie was openly drinking from her flask. "Yeah, that would put a different kind of pressure on her—especially with her mom being an actor."

"What are you talking about?" Abbie asked, giving Lee a stare that seemed to question his sanity. "You can't just roll over and accept anything she wants." This next line was directed at Deke, who raised his hands from her tone. "Okay, okay," she said and dialed back her volume while making a "lower your hands" gesture with her own. She wore a small smile, and Deke couldn't help but wonder if his and Lee's apparent fear of her made her happy. "I'm just saying, if she really cared about you...." She trailed off, leaving her opinion about Val's obvious selfishness unspoken.

Lee clearly wanted to disagree, but instead closed his mouth and looked at the ground. Deke ran his tongue over his teeth. Lee had it bad, and clearly thought that Abbie wouldn't think the same of him if he disagreed with her stance. Deke's churning stomach told him that was likely a mistake on his friend's part, but there was no helping it, without being glaringly obvious.

"How's school and your clinic hours progressing, Abbie?" Deke asked, instead of continuing the earlier conversation.

"Good?" Abbie responded, giving Deke a strange look, as if asking him if what she had said was wrong. Deke just shrugged, so Abbie started to give a bit of a more detailed answer. "For a second year, Doctor Dan says I'm doing really well. I'm way ahead of my clinical hours, and so am about to take some time off to focus on studying for exams. How are you managing right now with how much time basketball is consuming?"

"Lee has been helping me, since we have a few classes together. Plus he's smart enough to help me in the classes he isn't even taking." Deke tried to bolster his friend's attempts at pursuit, but only earned Lee a look from Abbie. The look cut Deke like a dagger on Lee's behalf. She paired it with a shoulder squeeze that told Deke just how doomed the relationship was. She might as well have just petted the head of a puppy that had done a cute trick.

"You're lucky that he's willing to take time away from gaming to help you," Abbie responded, and despite the good-natured tone, Lee shrank in on himself.

Deke had been planning to try to say something to change the way Abbie saw Lee, but Lee's current hangdog look made him swallow it. Normally, he might have made some sort of offhand comment about Lee meeting with a bunch of girls, or something, but it would have been a tough sell already. Now? Now, it was impossible.

"I'm going to go find Duke, anyone want to come see if we can snag an hordeeves plate?" Deke suggested, glad that his two friends didn't capitalize on his inability to say the French word.

"Won't that just bring Grant Fisher right to you?" Abbie joked, and Deke snorted. The snort and the well timed joke allowed the three of them to relax and get back to some joking banter.

"Mesa thinks youza right!" Deke responded, trying his best to imitate a Star Wars character he knew.

Both Lee and Abbie punched him in the arm. Lee explained, "Don't ever try to quote that character around me. Ughhh," he finished with a disgusted noise and a shiver. Abbie nodded along in total agreement.

"Come on, I didn't think I could pull off the Mr. Hut guy!" Deke complained.

"Of course you can't! He speaks Huttese," Lee responded, sounding even more incredulous.

"Huttese? Never mind, I don't want to know." Deke chuckled. "But you obviously see my problem, right?"

That got a laugh from Abbie, and Lee followed a moment later. "The *hors d'oeuvres* come out from that door back there," Lee explained with a point. "My guess is all of your teammates are over there too."

"I wouldn't take that bet. I can see the heads of most of the starting line!" Abbie answered and they began threading through the crowd. Deke was in the lead, easily able to clear a path that Lee and Abbie could follow in. He was also the first to exit the crowd, to find each of his teammates with an entire plate of hors d'oeuvres on a table.

"They're like piranhas," Lee whispered, as each and every one moved from table to table snatching even crumbs from the ill-gotten silver trays.

"I guess I wasn't the only one with this idea." Deke scratched his head as he scanned the area. "Dang, I don't see Duke. You two okay if I leave you here?"

Abbie strode forward confidently, aiming herself directly at a table with four silver platters. "Oh, I've got this!" she said. Deke chuckled and looked toward Lee.

Lee didn't immediately follow Abbie, and instead looked at Deke. "I think she's wrong, by the way," Lee said, clearly intending to return to the earlier conversation. "To Valerie it probably looks like you're saying no to something that is clearly good for you, and her. Since you're not able to tell her the whole truth, she probably is sensing something is off. You know?"

Deke winced, and glanced back across the room to where he last saw Val. "You're probably right, but it isn't like I can just tell her all about the sports drink." Lee gave a nod that spoke volumes. More of a head tilting bob of his head. Deke clenched his teeth before admitting, "Okay, I *could* tell her, but I don't trust her..."

"And therein lies the issue," Lee said. "That's likely what she's sensing. I think your problem might be bigger than this contract, Deke." It was Deke's turn to nod along.

"All right, maybe if she talks to me again, I'll consider telling her," Deke said. Lee raised an eyebrow. "Oh eff off man. Aren't you going to go get some food with Abbie?" Lee's face fell, and Deke grimaced. "Sorry, man."

"That obvious?" Lee asked. Deke could only nod. "Maybe I'll come with you to see Duke then?"

"I mean it might be good to have you there to ask him questions," Deke said, thinking Lee might be able to come up with some circumspect ways to learn more from the big man.

"Deke, I've been meaning to bring this up, but it's probably better if you find someone else to be your Eva," Lee joked, comparing himself to Duke's girlfriend.

Despite the joke, Deke twitched. Lee's offhand comment really brought up just how well bringing Eva into the fold had gone for Duke. Deke couldn't help but make comparisons between Val and her "big sis" and knew that Val came up wanting. He shook his head sadly in response to his own internal question. Val wasn't Eva.

FORTY-FIVE

FRIDAY, MARCH 10TH

"Was the sample taken by the recruit?"-
UPLIFT Einherjar

> "Sample has been delivered, and possibly taken. Some signs of possible improvements to physicality. Contract unsigned."- Agent Smoke

"Applying pressure through usual avenues?"- UPLIFT Einherjar

> "Affirmative."- Agent Smoke

"Deke!" Lee shouted, which startled the recipient out of his vacant state.

"What?" Deke asked, blinking away the daydream of winning tonight's game.

"I was just asking if you gave any further thought to signing the contract?" Lee repeated. Deke groaned—it was such an easy question to ask, but impossible to answer. Lee knew that, as Deke had clearly avoided this question in the past. He had told Lee that he wouldn't take the taster, and didn't want to lie to his friend again.

While the option to take the contract wasn't entirely off the table, right now, he wasn't going to even think about taking the offered deal. Still, maybe if the pressure got high enough or the right offer got made, he would change his mind. Instead of answering, he gave his friend a look he hoped conveyed his disdain for the buzzkill.

"I'm going to focus on winning tonight's game," Deke mumbled and then even more quietly added, "Let's start there," to himself.

"Okay, but like, can we be sure that Evil Corp doesn't have a way to track that you took the taster, or worse, take it back?" Lee asked, his tone clearly stressed. Deke gave him a meaningful look, again trying to convey that this type of conversation might be more appropriate for tomorrow. Or never...

"Lee, I've got no clue, but I think we can assume that Duke took the sample, and they haven't come reaping yet! He's even said they've mostly backed off," Deke answered, some heat entering his tone. He hadn't meant to raise his volume but the last thing he needed today was to think about a possible bloody future. He couldn't help the foreboding scene of his family used as leverage, or his friends. He shook off that thought. Clearly, he had been watching too many thriller movies with Lee lately.

Despite Duke being safe and giving Deke a feeling of ease, he had to admit that the possibility of strong-arm negotiations existed. That daymare could become a reality. Still, his conversation with Duke after the Baguettes' win in the semis had been what helped. Lee of course had a better recollection of the conversation with Duke from the Booster party. "He never said that, Deke! He specifically said he's worried about what will happen after school!"

"He meant he's worried about what he's going to do for a living Lee, not that some shady nefarious group is going to kill him to take back the sports drink!"

"I don't think so. Remember, he told you how much trouble he was having finding an agent to represent him?" Lee countered.

"So?"

"So! So, that could be the influence of Evil Corp, or them just applying pressure in a more subtle way!" Lee answered, clearly exasperated by Deke's lack of foresight on the issue.

"Lee, that's quite the conspiracy theory. Why would they want him to go to the NBA so badly? Like what does an NBA player have for a skill set that they would want?" Deke pointed to a poster on his side of the room. The poster was of MJ, and the next one was of Lebron. "Those two made a ton of money, and have or had influence, but creating the next MJ or Lebron isn't going to get Evil Corp much..."

"You brought this up last time and I still agree, but I've been thinking. What if Aim Assist, Motion Prediction, and other skills this system is giving you aren't really intended for basketball? The threat response alone gives me goosebumps. So, what if like, that knife . . ." Lee motioned to his poster with the hole in its alien head. Deke grimaced in apology. "What if the assist in throwing knives or other weapons is the actual use of the sports drink?"

"Then why would they let these super killers go to the NBA?" Deke asked, his brain pumping static into his ears at Lee's point. Deke's stomach growled, reminding him that he'd already skipped breakfast due to nerves. "Can we talk about this all after the season?" Deke asked, pointing at his stomach while simultaneously wiping sweat from his brow. "Today, I've got enough on my plate."

Lee nodded once, and then followed it with several other quick head bobs. "Sure, let's go get lunch, but we really need to talk more about this. I've got a theory, and it might be worth checking out."

Deke made all the right noises, but truly hoped that Lee would forget about this particular subject by the end of the season, which hopefully wasn't tonight. Together they walked down to the cafeteria and Deke found himself moving the food around on his plate but not taking a bite. Lee must have noticed and he apologized for his earlier line of conversation. Deke attempted a smile to reassure his friend but ended up just showing Lee his teeth.

"Maybe I'll take this to go. Then go shoot the ball a bit to get rid of these nerves. See you at the game?" Deke said as an excuse. It wasn't Lee's fault for bringing up an issue that likely had at least some merit. Still, Deke needed to sweat out the negative thoughts, or at least be around other athletes right now. Every athlete knows that you don't bring up outside issues on game days...

"Hey Dekester!" someone called in an overly friendly kind of way. Deke turned and found a very disheveled Mac jogging his way. Deke was about a meter from the doors to enter the Athletic Center, and truly considered sprinting inside. What in the hell was Mac doing here anyway?

"Dude, it's not contagious," Mac said, as he slowed to a stop in front of Deke. "You can't catch what I've got. I just wanted to talk to you." Mac's tone changed to something more akin to what Deke was used to. More of a haughty sneer. Deke rolled his eyes and was about to turn for the door, when Mac held up both hands. "You're going to want to hear me out, I think," Mac stated, a clear threat in his tone.

"What are you on about now Mac?" Deke asked.

"Well, I've been looking for Ronnie, and it suddenly struck me. How did a rookie who just underwent surgery recover so fast?" Mac clearly was now threatening Deke.

Just struck him, huh? Deke clearly recalled overhearing him making that assertion in Skip's office. Deke schooled his features and rolled his eyes again. As derisively as he could, Deke explained, "I got tested at the same time you did, moron!"

"Right, right. I considered that, but then I recalled who I saw buying a scream mask at Value Village on Halloween. Ronnie sure was adamant about finding that guy. I didn't think anything of it at first, cause you were a cripple, so how could you be the thief. But now..." Ronnie left the conclusion hanging and Deke narrowed his eyes while looking at Mac.

"But now—what? I bought a scream mask, so did hundreds of other people. It was Halloween? What are you trying to imply, Mac?" Despite his tone and questions, Deke's mind was whirring. Did Mac know? Surely, the idiot just thought that Deke was taking drugs. Right? Mac laughed in a way that made Deke's already upset stomach knot tighter.

"You're not bad. Maybe you should be the aspiring actor instead of Val. But you see, you can't fool me, I started piecing it all together. The end of last year, Duke had a few meetings with some NBA agents—the same NBA agents that are sniffing around *you*." Mac pointed at Deke's heart. "And then he started meeting with Ronnie far more regularly than in the past. Then all I had to do was pair that with his sudden spike in play! Look, I just want to know where Ronnie is. He needs to help me get back on the team. I don't care about all the other shit. It gives the Baguettes a better chance at winning anyway. But don't fuck with me, okay? I know that there is some sort of designer drug Duke was getting from that slimeball, and I know you stole it."

Deke shook his head and turned away. He took a few steps to the door before turning over his shoulder to address Mac. "Mac, are you hearing yourself? When was the last time you slept?" Mac looked down at his own clothes as if realizing for the first time his appearance was beyond bad. "I don't know where this is all coming from, but I didn't take any drugs. I definitely didn't *steal* any drugs, either. Plus, I have no idea where Ronnie is."

Deke's final words seemed to anger Mac again.

"Well, I can tell you with one hundred percent certainty that piece of shit didn't go back home. His family hasn't seen or heard from him in months!" Mac hissed. Deke rushed inside the Athletic Center instead of answering, his already upset stomach now truly heaving. He managed to make it to the entryway's bathroom before he dry-heaved a bit of bile into the toilet bowl. Had that Cotton Candy Vaping thug really killed Ronnie?

"These aren't the Baguettes that I've seen all year," Skip said from the front of the team room. "You look like you're scared you might actually win or something." Skip slowly scanned over the players and Deke did the same from his locker. The only one meeting the coach's eyes was Duke. To say that the Baguettes were playing poorly was quite possibly the understatement of the year. Maybe Deke should have seen this coming when he'd heard four other players vomiting due to nerves in stalls beside him.

Would [Quick Shot] turn this around? Maybe. And with that thought, Deke was forced to admit that if he had another taster on him, he'd take it, hands down. Luckily, the coach continued and stopped him from going down a rabbit hole he really would like to avoid.

"They might be up by eighteen after the half, but I believe that there is always a path forward. All we need to do is seize it. Proverbs three-six says, in all your ways submit to him, and he will make your path straight. All we need to do is trust in the path. We worked every day to get to this point, and now, we just need to let that practice, play. Let those hours in the gym shine through, because they are God's preparation!" Skip preached at them from the front of the room. Deke nodded along. He had made his choice, and signing the contract for more serum, while tempting, wasn't needed. He could do this without it! Looking around the room, he found a few teammates raising heads to finally meet Skip's eyes.

"CIT might be undefeated this year, but do you all know what that means?" No one answered and that bit of a silence started to stretch, sucking the new energy Coaches' speech infused into the room. Skip didn't allow it to go on too long and answered his own question. "It means that we have nothing to lose, and they have everything! All we have to do is show them a glimmer of a chance that they could lose, and we will get to see their true hearts. Do you boys want to slay Goliath or do you want to be known as the Baguettes who *almost* made Mercenary March?"

This got a few cheers before Duke stood up and roared. That seemed to give others permission to let loose as well, and the cheers turned from a polite, subdued affair to something primal and barbaric. Deke joined in and thought he could feel something like shackles, that had been gripping his stomach, release. He turned to his locker and snatched a protein bar, ripping it open and devouring it since his stomach seemed to have forgotten its earlier distress. They still had the second half!

The team exited the team room like bullets from a gun. The metal door that led to the hallway, which traversed the back of the building to the gym, banged against the concrete bricks as each player gave it a hard shove. Unlike the Baguettes' home gym this brick wall didn't show signs of constant abuse, but maybe that was because they were in the away change room.

Deke followed the group somewhere toward the middle and watched as the players seemed to bounce their way back to the court. The crowd booed them as they roared through the baseline to begin the second half's shortened warm-up. However, the boos only seemed to energize the Baguettes more. Deke could feel something in the air, and hoped it was a comeback.

Skip reiterated some points from the game plan in the huddle, and made a few changes as well. The CalTech Beavers were relying heavily on two players. Number sixty-two—a large center who was already at twelve rebounds and eighteen points, and number fourteen, who was their point guard. He was very effective at initiating the plays, and had a killer mid-range shot that he'd sunk home far more often than normal. Luckily, as this was the finals, Skip didn't plan to "rest" any players in the second half. Each of the starters was given a look and told, "If you need a break, you tell me! Otherwise, we survive or hang on your shoulders, you understand?"

Arthur, Tim, Duke, and Manny nodded seriously. Skip's eyes

lingered on Deke and he realized he hadn't responded yet. He nodded eagerly. He didn't want to be subbed out, either. He wanted to win!

They broke the huddle, and moved into a defensive call based on who they were marking. The possession arrow was to the Beavers and that meant they would inbound the first ball. Some of Deke's earlier nerves returned now that the game was about to restart, but he mentally attempted to squash them. All they needed was a good run of points. The other team had a good first half, and now it was the Baguettes' turn. A satisfied smirk came onto his face as he marked Fourteen.

"You've got no idea what's coming your way," Deke said, hoping to rattle the opponent a bit.

"I'm guessing more brick shots?" Fourteen quipped back. Deke's smile only grew. Fourteen jerked forward, crossing back into his half as he attempted to get open and take the inbound pass. Deke reacted a split second earlier thanks to [Motion Prediction], and the pass which was meant for Fourteen ended up seeming like a perfect inbound to him.

He took the ball to the basket and laid it in, turning even as the ball sank home to smile at Fourteen. Still smirking, Deke responded, "Hard to brick a shot if there's no defense in front of me."

Deke forced the inbounder to find the shooting guard of the Beavers instead of Fourteen, which made the point guard curse. Fourteen tried a few pivots and fakes to shake Deke, who was guarding him like he was a receiver in football. "All the plays run through you," Deke growled as he pushed himself to keep in front of multiple possible passes. "So, I've just got to stop you from getting the ball."

"Sure, but what happens when you tire yourself out?" Fourteen asked as the shooting guard gave up on getting him the ball and instead reversed the play to the small forward.

"Now you're making an ass of you and me," Deke responded as Duke fronted the opposing center and cut off that pass.

"What the hell does that even mean?" Fourteen said, clearly not understanding the comment about "assuming."

The shooting guard ended up with the ball again at the top of the key, and the shot clock of forty-five seconds only had about five seconds left. He checked Fourteen again but seeing Deke smothering the player, he forced up a shot. To Deke's horror it swished home. Fourteen gave him a shove as he sprinted back up the floor to get into their zone defense. As he left he called, "Looks like my teammates don't need me as bad as you think."

Deke just smiled as he muttered, "We'll see about that..."

The next ten minutes were some of the hardest Deke had played. He and Fourteen were panting up and down the court in both directions, but Deke refused to sub out first. The lead was down to ten thanks to this tactic, and the Baguettes had a real shot of closing it further in the last ten minutes of play. The Beavers were already in foul trouble and two of their starters were sitting at four each, which put them one away from fouling out of the game.

Despite the Beavers' lead, they were in desperate straits. Arthur managed to thread a pass through traffic to Duke, who attempted a layup but got fouled by number sixty-two, the Beavers' center. That put him at three fouls as well, and sent Duke to the line for two. Fourteen was subbed out and went to the bench, leaving Deke with a decision. He was currently huffing in air, attempting to catch his breath. While he was in fantastic shape and even had some help from the sleeping system, marking Fourteen was taking its toll on his endurance. Right now he could pull himself out for a rest, and return to marking Fourteen when he inevitably came back in, or he could try to use this opportunity to close the gap even more.

Duke's first shot sank home and the lead was cut to nine, then eight in quick succession. Deke chose to stay out on the floor. The Baguettes' biggest disadvantage all year had been their lack of depth, and if Deke went to the bench it would bring Chucker Charles or Brick Jones out to replace him. They couldn't afford to lose Deke right now, or at least, that's what he decided.

The lead of eight became six, and then four over the next five minutes, and Deke was forced to admit that the Beavers weren't going to go away easily. A buzzer that signalled subs rang through the gym and the crowd, which had been growing silent, roared back to life. Fourteen was coming back on for the last five minutes of play.

Deke could feel a kind of numbness in his legs, but called out his intention to return to marking the Beavers' best player. Thanks to [Motion Prediction] he had the edge, so he assumed he could do it. That was when Deke's [Motion Prediction] warned him that Fourteen was going to cut to the inbounder. Deke got the jump on the player but Fourteen's speed seemed to have increased.

For the first time in the half, Fourteen got the ball and Deke had another decision. Pressure him up the court or let him get to half? He chose the latter. They only had a four point lead and wasting the game time would only help the Beavers, not the Baguettes. He slowly backed off and watched a grin come onto Fourteen's face. Even as he took his first dribble he taunted, "You got any energy left?"

Deke flashed his biggest smile back. He honestly wasn't sure, but he wasn't going to let Fourteen know that. After Deke crossed a few feet into his own half, he waited as Fourteen took the full ten seconds to cross over. This was a classic delaying tactic for the team with the lead, and Deke now knew that the Beavers would be aiming to shoot the ball as close to the forty-five second shot clock violation as they could. Deke was willing to gamble. With five minutes, and a lead of four, the Beavers would need to hit more shots down the stretch than the Baguettes did. With his [Aim Assist] and Duke playing the way he was, Deke was confident in that gamble.

After ten seconds of dribbling in place, Fourteen called a play. Deke got into a deeper defensive position and got ready to stop the Beavers' offense. Fourteen didn't even dribble in, and instead passed to the right of Deke, hitting the shooting guard, who immediately relayed the ball inside to Sixty-two. Duke was caught a step behind and Sixty-two jammed it home. Deke shrugged as Duke inbounded the ball to Arthur. If the Baguettes scored on this possession, nothing would have changed.

Arthur called a give and go play for Manny, and Deke screened down to free up Duke, who was meant to facilitate the next pass. Duke seemed to be moving in slow motion though, and Arthur was forced to hold on to the ball, instead of passing it to the closely covered big man. He reversed the ball to Tim, who tried to thread a long pass through traffic to Manny. The ball bounced off of the defender's heel and into Deke's scrambling path. Luckily, his [Motion Prediction] had warned him.

He spun and lined up [Aim Assist] but blinked as the line that normally was at least near the basket was about three feet short. He adjusted in midair and released, but the shot rattled off the front rim, then the backboard, before bouncing out and into Duke's hands. Duke landed and jumped back up, attempting to slam the ball down, but Sixty-two fouled him, which prevented the basket. Despite Duke not scoring, Deke smiled. That was four for Sixty-two now as well!

Duke missed his first shot, and Deke winced. Deke looked at Duke and found the center looking back at him. His eyes were slightly unfocused. Deke blinked. The big center looked half dead on his feet. Deke signaled to the ref for a time out, and the whistle blew. Skip saw what Deke did and made it a full sixty-second time out.

Deke grabbed Duke under the arm and practically dragged the big man back to the bench. The players handed him Gatorade and Abbie quickly unwrapped a protein bar for Duke. Skip asked, "Everything okay, Deke?"

Deke nodded toward Duke. "I think we needed a quick break. That's all."

Skip nodded as he looked over the clearly exhausted starters, currently sitting on the cushioned chairs trying to recuperate. Skip glanced at the clock. "Gentlemen, we're down by six. That's nothing when compared to the eighteen we started down this half. However, I'll ask you all now, is that all we could do?"

Arthur was the first to shake his head, and then all of the

starters began to shake their heads too. "Good!" Skip shouted. "Win or lose, this is where you're meant to be. Fight with everything you have left boys, and show the world what the Baguettes are capable of!"

Skip ended his speech and then looked around. "We've got forty-five seconds left. So, use it to catch your breath. Deke, we still have one more thirty-second timeout. Use it when you think it's appropriate."

The starters looked down the chairs at Deke, who nodded at Skip's words, confirming that he would use the final timeout when he thought it was the right time. After forty-five seconds, they cheered and moved back to the opposing end for Duke's second free-throw. It rattled around before sinking home, returning the lead to only five. After the break, Deke managed to stop Fourteen from getting the inbound pass, and he heard a few choice curse words from the point guard, thanks to his effort.

On the far end the Beavers missed a floater by their power forward, and the ball ended up in Tim's hands on the rebound. After a short fight over the rock, Tim passed it to Arthur to take it up the floor. Deke stayed nearby as an outlet pass but the Beavers didn't pressure. Deke hoped that was because they were also tired.

Arthur called for a three, which was a play designed for Deke, and a three pointer. He took a deep breath and began his route through the key to lose Fourteen. He popped out on the far side just as Manny reversed the play back to Duke at the top of the key. Deke came to the big center and received almost a handoff pass, before stepping back behind him. This put Duke between Deke and number fourteen, which gave Deke the gap to release his shot.

Deke lined up [Aim Assist] and felt [Quick Shot] activate as well. He wanted to curse. [Quick Shot] wasn't exactly a boon right now, but he managed to add in enough power just in time to get the ball to go through the basket. He heard a grunt as he released, and found Duke's back closing in on him. Fourteen had run right into Duke, pushing the center back. Deke felt the big man's back clip his braced leg and for just a moment he recalled his injury from the preseason tournament.

His eyes widened as he tried and failed, just like the last time, to land properly. Instead of getting his feet under him, Deke landed in nearly the same bad positioning he had during the ACL injury. The brace that he was so used to by now screamed, but held his knee in a solid, uncompromised position. He felt the pain before his brain registered where it was coming from. Unfortunately, that's when his brain caught up to the situation. His ankle had buckled.

A small pop sounded as he played back the moment.

Power save mode deactivated.

Injury detected. Injury classification: Mild ankle sprain. Evo points not required, trainee's current level of recovery will suffice.

Re-entering power save mode.

The sports drink informed him of the issue, even as he screamed his pain to the gymnasium. Duke looked down at him with wide eyes before turning back to shove Fourteen, hard. Fourteen ended up on his butt some ten to fifteen feet away, and two fouls were assessed. One personal foul for Fourteen and one technical foul for Duke. Deke tried to keep track but he saw Abbie and Dan rushing onto the court with that stupid stretcher. He tried to wave them away and stand but his ankle protested, causing him to fall back to the floor.

While a part of his brain registered that his damn squeaky brace had done its job and prevented a worse injury, the other part of his brain was attempting to scream at the stupid system to use evo points. What were they good for if not for right now!

Nothing happened, and after a few seconds Deke fell fully onto his back and brought both hands to his head. He stared at the score clock—two minutes left and a lead of two. They had been so close!

Fourteen walked through his swimming vision and smirked. He didn't say anything, but he didn't have to. Fourteen had just removed Deke from the game, and he'd been awarded two free throws on top of it, because of Duke's retaliation.

This was total bullshit! Or as Lee would say, *fus roh da*. Or something like that.

FORTY-SIX

SATURDAY, MARCH 11TH

"Now that basketball's over, I think I'm going to like dating a player even more :wink:"- Valerie

"Just don't bring him to the sorority house. He can't get anymore strikes, Val."- Big Sis Eva

"Well he has to get workouts in somewhere :kiss: :peach:. You fun sponge :nerd-face:"- Valerie

"Better than a cum sponge :sweat-droplets:" - Big Sis Eva

eke snoozed his alarm for the fifth time, and rolled over on his stupid, small dorm bed.

"Dude, you've got to get up eventually. Stop hitting snooze!" Lee said, and accompanied his words with a tossed pillow. The pillow hit the wall and fell on top of Deke softly.

"Why do I have to do anything?" Deke asked, his voice gravelly thanks to his general dehydration and the early hours.

"Well, can you at least turn off your alarm? I was sexiled again last night and would like some uninterrupted sleep!" Lee complained. "Now give me my pillow back."

"Fuck. Fine," Deke retorted, and threw the offending pillow back with a great deal of extra force. Lee caught the thing out of the air, and Deke blinked. Maybe the practices on passing had helped the kid more than he thought.

Clicking his tongue, he made the decision to get out of bed; he had to get up anyway because he had an appointment with Doctor Pinsonneault. Deke clicked off the alarm on his phone and then rolled to sit on the edge of the too-small bed. His still braced foot landed on his "exploded" suitcase that he had torn through last night looking for a toothbrush before giving up and crashing into his bed.

The team had flown back after the game last night in complete silence. Not even Coach Skip had words of encouragement for the group. Deke kicked all the clothes under his bed in frustration with his heels as he recalled the dour mood, but more importantly the loss that caused it. His ankle twinged a bit, reminding him it was injured. Not that an injury mattered when the season was over.

Standing up, he kicked the laptop and the duffle bag under the bed as well for good measure. He would try to remember to buy another toothbrush on his way back. Or just go without. It wasn't like he hadn't done that for weeks, earlier in the year.

Deke pulled a shirt and shorts from a shelf a bit too aggressively, which caused the clothes under them to crash onto the floor. He yeeted them under his bed with a grunt before throwing on the selected clothes and leaving the room. The bright California sun burned down through the wisps of fog left over from the night before as he walked across campus, his mood souring further.

The low hanging fog looked like the last vestiges of his hopes as the sun burned it away. That same sun singed his skin, adding an uncomfortable heat to his face, shoulders and neck. The buildings blocked the wind too, making his shirt stick to his back as he worked up a sweat. Deke glared at the four kids who were singing an obnoxiously cheerful acapella song as he trudged through the main square. The walk felt longer than normal thanks to the ankle brace, but he finally arrived at the doors to the Administrative Building. He yanked them open and ran right into Director Rooney coming the other way.

"Ahh. Mr. Mills, just who I was looking for," Director Rooney said, his voice filled with an excitement that made Deke lower his eyebrows in suspicion.

"I've got the scholarship papers for next year all put together. I think with some *work* in the off season we'll be heading to Mercenary March next year. Especially with you and Duke returning." Director Rooney gave a smile that Deke remembered thinking was a winning one, back during recruitment. Right now it just felt sleazy, perhaps even gloating. "Follow me to my office and we'll *sign everything*."

Deke felt his jaw clench. This man wanted to pressure him the day after the loss? After all the pressure from his friends and family, and *the loss*, it made Deke feel like he was going to either be sick or breathe fire. "Sorry director, I've got a mandatory appointment with the school shrink right now."

Not waiting for a response, Deke brushed past the director and began climbing the stairs with ample use of the railing thanks to his foot. He did glance back, once, only to find Rooney on his phone texting someone. A part of him felt great about walking away from the man, but another part of him silently prayed he hadn't just ruined his scholarship for the upcoming season. The churning anger in his gut squashed that thought. Who cared if he didn't come back to UCSP? Surely another school would grab him, right?

Better responses, or perhaps, just angrier responses echoed in his head as he found his way to the office of Doctor Pinsonneault. As he walked in, he was surprised to find her standing at the reception desk with her attendant. She looked up and took a deep breath before her face morphed into a small, sympathetic smile. "I'm glad you made it, Deke. I've cleared my schedule for the next hour for you. I hope that's okay?"

Sympathy was an odd emotion, and honestly if anyone else wore that look right now, Deke might have torn a door from its frame, but somehow Doctor Pinsonneault made it feel like soothing water on the fire in his gut. He met her eyes, and her sympathetic look, for too long before taking a deep breath and letting his anger out. She came over and placed a hand on his back, guiding him to the room and the chair inside.

She didn't even sit down before she asked, "This is about more than the game, isn't it?"

Deke tried to answer but found that in place of a word, his body convulsed and a sobbing sound escaped. He swallowed a lump in his throat as he brought his hands up to find lines of tears on his cheeks. The doctor was beside his chair with a box of tissues and Deke grabbed a handful, not trusting his body for fine motor control as sobs wracked it.

It took several crumpled tissues before Deke felt capable of trying again. Deke stuttered, "I just—I wanted to see them—no, I wanted to see him."

"Your brother?" Doctor Pinsonneault asked, as she put the tissue box on a side table and returned to her chair and notebook. Deke, after hearing his own voice, didn't trust a response, so nodded instead. "They were going to make the trip to Syracuse to see you. I remember your excitement over that. What's stopping you from going to see them instead?"

A surge of embarrassment washed over Deke. He didn't have the money for something like that. He probably couldn't even go home for the summer, if the team didn't purchase his tickets. Thinking back on his response and imaginary responses to Rooney, he felt new sobs rack his body.

Power save mode deactivated.

Re-balancing surge of neuroinhibitors, amino acids, and hormones complete.

Re-entering power save mode.

A wave of cathartic comfort overcame Deke, as his convulsing body stuttered and then slowed to a few shakes before abating. The sudden nothingness of his emotions allowed him to get his first full breath since he arrived in the office. He looked up to meet Doctor Pinsonneault's caring eyes. "I don't have the money for that. They don't have any money either. They were going to drive down to Syracuse."

She nodded knowingly before asking, "Is that why you push yourself so hard?"

Deke gave that question more thought than a simple yes or no question merited. In his exploration, he discovered the spark of his anger was still smoldering in his chest. It didn't threaten to consume him like before, but it still existed, and with Doctor Pinsonneault's question he could even see some more of the reason for it.

"That's why I needed to go to Mercenary March. That's where the scouts and agents are. That's where I can test myself against the best and show them I belong in the NBA."

"When you say NBA, you don't just mean playing basketball against the best in the world, do you?"

"No. That's just the fun part of it. I want—no, I need the money. My fam—" Deke blinked and took a deep breath, cutting himself off. "Max needs the money!"

"I was told you already have an offer from an agent. Why can't you take it?" Doctor Pinsonneault asked. Deke felt his eyebrows rise and then fall back into a familiar scowl just as quickly. He scrutinized Doctor Pinsonneault and found her inquiring look to be genuine. She canted her head, studying him in turn.

He licked his lips before giving her the standard response he gave everyone, it seemed. "I was told that I shouldn't take the first offer that comes along..."

The room that had felt safe just a moment before suddenly didn't anymore. Deke looked around, trying to discover recording devices or signs that Doctor Pinsonneault might be working for Evil Corp. He didn't find any of course, but he stood up all the same. Deke hurriedly said, "I'm sorry. I really need to go. I should call my family..."

Doctor Pinsonneault frowned before she closed her book. She stood up slowly and gave Deke another smile. This one, a bit sad and commiserating. "I understand, Deke. I know it might not feel like it right now, but we made a great deal of progress today. Can we make an appointment for this week to continue?"

Deke wanted to agree but his stomach twisted, turning his nod into a shrug. He made a few sounds that were neither agreement nor denial as he rushed out of the office. Once outside, he ran the entire way back to his dorm room, feeling like eyes were on him.

Flinging open the door, Deke expected to find Lee still sleeping but instead his roommate was up and at his computer. Deke was glad he was up because he would have woken him anyway as he hissed, "I think Doctor Pinsonneault might work for Evil Corp!"

"What?!" Lee said as he turned to the sweating Deke, who was closing the door. Deke raised his eyebrows and hands as if to say "you heard me." Lee snorted air through his nose before shooting down Deke's theory. "Don't be an idiot. Did she do more than ask questions about things that have happened in your life?"

Deke frowned, and then shook his head.

"That's kind of her job, man. She has to ask questions, preferably ones that make you think. Now, if she told you to sign the contract that would indicate she might be in cahoots. Please tell me you didn't shout at her or something?"

Sighing, Deke leaned against the wall and slowly lowered himself to the ground. By the time his butt touched down he realized Lee was right. "No, I didn't shout at her, but I did run away. Did you really just use the word 'cahoots'? This isn't some no-air detective film."

"*Hakka.* Are you not the one who just ran in here and whisper-yelled about a conspiracy?" Lee pointed out, and from previous conversation, Deke knew the first word used meant idiot or something similar. Lee continued after a moment, though. "Well this might cheer you up, do you want to hear the good news Abbie told me?"

Deke blinked at Lee before leaning forward. "Okay, but it better not be something stupid."

"She says that UCSP could still make Mercenary March. The league still has to bid on at-large berths. Come here, I've been looking it up," Lee exclaimed.

Deke shot to his feet. Did UCSP have a legitimate chance for what he would term a wildcard entry for Mercenary March?

FORTY-SEVEN

SUNDAY, MARCH 12TH

"I really don't know if we should have told him…"- Browncoat Lee

"Didn't you say it helped?"- Abbie

"I don't know. Honestly, I feel like if they don't get it, things will be twice as bad."- Browncoat Lee

"Shoot. Well let's not count out the possibility. Doctor Dan seems excited about their chances.."- Abbie

"This is where we had our end of season meeting last year too," Duke grumbled. They were currently in an auditorium meant to seat five or six hundred. It looked comically empty with only the twenty or so people inside, spread out in small clusters. Deke could see Abbie and Doctor Dan leaning against a wall to the side, whispering.

Deke's mouth turned down into a sickly frown as his stomach protested Duke's words. It seemed no one had much hope left. It was rare that two teams from their conference were sent to Mercenary

March, but from everything Lee had made him read, it wasn't impossible.

"I'm sure Coach Skip has good news," Arthur chipped in from the side. "Maybe they reviewed that blatant foul by Ivanov, and..." Little Tim punched Arthur on the shoulder and motioned to Deke as if that explained the action. Deke shook his head while rolling his eyes. His ankle was already eighty percent healed, according to the system, and even Doctor Dan was claiming it wasn't as bad as he originally thought. So, he could play as long as the season wasn't over...

Of course, Abbie, who had run some of the original tests on the ankle, seemed skeptical about another "miracle healing" but luckily, Doctor Dan's acceptance of his misdiagnosis due to swelling helped her get over any suspicions, or so Deke hoped.

"If we played the first half of that game like we did—" Manny began and Little Tim slugged him even harder in the arm. "Ouch. Hey! I'm just saying, man!"

"You're all a bunch of idiots. Look around the room and just think how much stronger we'll be next year. Only Mac was going to graduate this season—" A raised hand from Arthur cut Tim's attempt at a motivational speech off.

"I'm probably all done too," Arthur said, and hurriedly continued when he found multiple open mouthed stares turned his way. "What? I've been taking summers too, I'm here to get my degree and start working. I'm not good enough for the pros, I'm just glad I got to play as much as I did."

Tim opened and closed his mouth, seeming to consider trying to keep going with his earlier attempt at encouragement, but failing to find the words. Deke chose to speak up instead. "Guys, it's not hopeless! There's still the at-large bids..."

He faded off because Duke was giving him a look that promised pain if he kept going. Arthur leaned in close to Deke. In a whisper he explained, "We don't talk about the—that. It's bad luck."

Deke wanted to scream, but recognized that it was more or less akin to what he had been doing with Lee. He didn't want to get his hopes up too high, and put the sentiment out there into the ether, so he had been unwilling to talk about it. However, now all of the conferences across America had finished their finals, the results were in, and their at-large bid was either given or it wasn't. Nothing they said in this room could change that, right?

Despite knowing all of that, he shut his mouth and leaned back in his cushioned seat. Maybe they had a point. Who knew what a spiteful Basketball God might do if he jinxed it.

The air current in the room shifted as the snick of the heavy metal doors resounded throughout. The room went deathly silent as Coach Skip, Boogie and the rest of the coaching staff walked in. Director Rooney was at the back and moved to join Doctor Dan and Abbie. The sound of the doors closing sounded like a gunshot in the silence.

"Gentlemen, the coaching staff are going to come around and collect your cell phones." Skip's words were like an electric current through the team. Deke felt himself leaning forward, his legs banging against the seat in front of him, as far forward as physically possible.

Skip made it to the podium and fiddled around with some electronics, which initiated a whine as the large projector screens on both sides of the podium descended. The assistant coaches collected all the cell phones. Duke groaned beside him, handing their phones to Boogie. Deke's eyes widened as his gaze flew over each face in the room. Rooney was sweating, Boogie didn't wear his customary smile, and Skip—Skip looked like he was chewing rocks.

"What is going on?" Deke whispered. He felt a hand land on his shoulder and squeeze. He turned to find Duke's mitt there. He looked at the center and found his eyes filled with just as much confusion as Deke felt. Goddammit!

Both white screens turned blue, with white lettering claiming no connection, before flickering on to the computer screen that must be mirroring the one at the podium. Skip held out his hand to Boogie, who handed him a memory stick. Everyone watched as the external memory was recognized, and then opened. Inside was a list of videos. The first one was titled Season Highlights.

Skip double clicked it and a paused video popped up. He maximized the screen and hit the play button. Deke felt his stomach sink. They were going to watch their season's highlights? Now? He felt like throwing up. The first highlight seemed to be a point guard taking a shot from just past the half-court line. Deke looked at Arthur, who was likely the teammate who took that shot. Arthur was squinting at the screen and his head slowly canted to the side. He looked confused.

Deke turned back to the screen and found a big man jamming a ball through the hoop. This time he squinted. They didn't have a big man with long hair on their team and the jerseys were the wrong colors? The images kept coming and the more he watched the more confused he grew. Had Skip clicked the wrong file?

Skip paused the video and glared out over the auditorium. "I don't see anyone taking notes! How are we going to beat the third-ranked team in bracket A of Mercenary March if you all won't take this seriously?"

Boogie's face finally cracked into his normal smile, before growing even larger. Deke blinked and looked down at his empty desk. Wait, notes?

Deke's eyes found Skip, as he scanned back up to the podium. Skip wore a large smile that seemed self congratulatory, like he was a cat who got into the cream. "All teachers have been informed that you won't be attending classes today or possibly for the rest of March. We leave tomorrow for Syracuse, and only have so much time today to prepare for the Syracuse Wildcats. Once we arrive, we will have a few days of practice as well, before our first game."

"See how statistically this player pulls up from well outside the three point line?" Lee showed Deke a printed spreadsheet of numbers that made absolutely zero sense to him.

"No, Lee, I don't see that!" Deke stated flatly. Abbie laughed from Lee's computer chair, where she was playing MoonCraft or something like that. Deke didn't recall the name of the game, but he recalled it had three races that seemed to be in perpetual war with each other. Oh, and among themselves too.

It was early in the morning on the day of departure for Syracuse and Abbie had come by with her bags to wait in the dorms for the bus to the airport. Somehow, seeing her so early in the morning, almost as soon as he woke up, made him feel a certain way. He couldn't put a finger on what that feeling was, but it consisted of brain fog, clenched gut, and tingling fingers.

"Okay, maybe the visuals will be better." Lee flipped to a different printout which showed the key, the arching three point line and then a collection of dots. Deke's eyes widened. How long had Lee worked on this? Lee saw his look and shook his head. "Don't worry, I had the computer analyze it for me. Since you're guarding number eleven on the Wildcats, I just had it focus on him."

Deke blinked and then snatched the page. This was actually better than what the team had given him yesterday. Lee seemed to misinterpret something because he mumbled, "I just thought it might help."

Looking up, Deke found Lee looking at the floor. Hurriedly Deke exclaimed, "Dude! This is more than helpful!" Lee smiled as he looked back up and began pointing out areas where the dots were more congregated. Lee paused in some of his explanation as Deke's phone buzzed. Deke glanced at it and put it back on his pillow.

"Wasn't that Val?" Lee asked.

"Yeah, but I told her earlier that I'm in basketball mode," Deke explained. Lee frowned, shrugged and then kept explaining.

"Eat that, Zorgling!" Abbie shouted occasionally as Lee brought out more and more printouts with explanations. Deke chuckled at the outburst, even as Abbie spun the chair with both hands raised. "Abbie wins again!"

Lee shook his head. "You know playing against the computer, on easy, isn't what most gamers would call winning."

"Pshh. Then clearly they haven't met DragonSlayerAbbie!" Abbie retorted, which caused Lee to blush furiously. Abbie stood up in her comfy-looking athletic wear before moving to the door. "I'm sorry to cut this coaching sesh short, boys, but the bus is arriving in ten. Deke and I need to be on that carrier!"

Lee chuckled and even said, "Carrier has arrived," in a deep, machine-like voice. Deke assumed he missed something there but wasn't in the mood to ask for an explanation. He had packed last night, and simply grabbed his duffle and backpack from beside his bed. Seeing him ready to go, Lee fiddled with his hands as he tried to find something to say. Deke clapped him on the upper back.

"Can I take those with me?" Deke asked, and Lee seemed to relax.

"Yeah for sure. I'll send you all the notes and homework for this upcoming week too. Umm. Good luck, *dude*," Lee said the last word as if it was his first time using it, and Deke couldn't help the large smile that came over his face. He pulled Lee into a hug, then scrambled out the door after Abbie before it got awkward.

"Your bromance is coming along nicely, I think," Abbie commented as he matched her stride. "Is that why you're ignoring Val?"

"Nah, she just got pissed that I wouldn't come over to her place last night. She said she could get her mom or servants to drive us to the airport, but despite me telling her I needed to study the opponent, she claimed I was ignoring her... I think she even broke up with me."

"Really? Over text?" Abbie asked, her voice incredulous. "Let me see?"

Deke hesitated for a moment, not wanting Abbie to read some of the more sexualized lines that Val had sent. Still, he needed a bit of validation that he hadn't done the wrong thing, and a girl's opinion might help. So, he handed her his unlocked phone.

He watched her face carefully as she scrolled through the messages. There were a few twitches of her eyebrows but otherwise her reaction was pretty subdued. Finally she handed the phone back. With a shrug she announced, "Well, she did and didn't break up with you."

"That's nice and ambiguous. Thanks Abbs." Deke sighed, feeling like he had just exposed a part of his soul only to have the recipient react like it was totally basic.

"Well, she gave you an ultimatum. She heavily implied that if you didn't go over there last night you two were done, but she never really said it. Add that to the messages wishing you luck and asking if she will see you at the airport, and I'd say she was probably just horny—"

"Abbie!" Deke hissed, and watched the girl shrug.

She seemed to consider for a moment before clarifying her statement. "What? It's perfectly natural."

"I thought you didn't like Valerie?" Deke asked, wondering why Abbie seemed to be taking her side.

"You're right, I can't stand that plastic witch, but that doesn't mean I can't understand another woman."

Deke canted his head as they exited the elevator. Was Abbie implying she understood being horny or was that just Deke's male brain connecting dots he wanted to see? He chose to ignore that part of his brain and move on.

"Well, I mean I guess I'll find out if you're right by how she treats me and my family in Syracuse."

"I'm so excited to meet your family!" Abbie responded, her voice carrying genuine happiness. "Especially Max. I want to see the person who stopped you from being completely unsalvageable as a human being!"

"What in the hell does that mean?" Deke asked, projecting as much hurt into his voice as he could.

"I've already explained how useless I thought you were at first. However, you're pretty good with kids, so..."

"Right, so you assume Max is my saving grace?"

"Absolutely!"

"He is pretty great," Deke said with a smile.

Valerie waved from behind the plexiglass divider that led into security. It turned out that they weren't broken up. Deke waved back, having enjoyed the affection she'd shown him. He'd wondered why she couldn't come through security with him, but found out the cheerleaders weren't flying until next Saturday, since they didn't need time to acclimatize and practice in a foreign gym. There went Deke's semi-plan to join the mile high club. It probably wasn't realistic anyway.

Valerie's smile suddenly became a sneer as Deke joined Abbie in repacking his carry-on bag with his electronics. Deke looked away, pretending he hadn't seen the look. If Valerie knew they'd spent the morning together, even as platonically as they had, she'd probably find a way through security just to stab Deke.

"Oh, shit! Look, Lee came to see you off too!" Abbie pointed. Deke followed the gesture and allowed a broad smile to come onto his lips. Lee rushed over to Valerie's side and quickly held up a sign.

"Eleven can't guard the Smiling Assassin?" Deke read, allowing the question into his voice. He looked past the sign to Lee. The kid smiled back and then wrote something on his phone. Deke's phone buzzed in his pocket almost on top of the moment Lee looked back up.

> Since Mercenary March is sudden death, I convinced my parents to let me go watch your first game. I fly out Friday!"- Lee the Rager

Sweat broke out on Deke's upper back, but he managed to school his drooping smile back into a happy look as he looked back to meet Lee's excited one. He probably should have responded to the text, but Lee's reminder that their first game could end the season made his brain fill with static. Instead, he gave a thumbs-up to his friend. Lee looked down at his phone and read something on screen.

"Don't worry, I responded for you," Abbie said. "He doesn't understand the superstitions of athletes. I'll talk to him later about it." Abbie patted Deke's back and gave Lee a second thumbs-up through the glass.

Deke looked at Valerie one last time, expecting her to celebrate with them all, but found her scowling at Abbie. He hurriedly looked back at Lee with a sigh. It would be great if his girlfriend chose to get along with his friends. It wasn't like Lee was cutting into her time with Deke. Well, actually, maybe he was?

A security agent came by to move Abbie and Deke along, and they waved one final time to Valerie and Lee before turning and checking their gate number. Deke sighed once he was out of sight.

"Stop grousing, it was an honest mistake," Abbie said from beside him.

"I just hate being reminded how important this game is," Deke mumbled.

"That's one way to look at it," Abbie coached, almost sounding like Doctor Pinsonneault for a moment. "Remember, this is where every college athlete wants to be. Sure you could lose, but what if you win?"

That was all it took to send Deke into a daydream of hoisting the finals trophy over his head. His smile returned, and he nodded to Abbie as his walk became something closer to his previous excited gait.

FORTY-EIGHT

FRIDAY, MARCH 17TH

"Have prepared a full dose for Operation Grindstone."- John Smoke

"Last time we spoke, Mills ran away, I don't believe he's interested."- Ed Rooney-Athletic Director

"Was this before or after the at-large bid was arranged?"- John Smoke

"Before."- Ed Rooney-Athletic Director

"Operation deemed salvageable. Wait for contact."- John Smoke

"All right gentlemen, you have the rest of the day to relax, but we'll be taking the bus to the Golden Corral around six," Boogie said to the gathered Baguettes. Deke mixed in among his teammates in the hotel lobby. They had just finished their daily practice and the bus had returned them to the hotel for the afternoon, it seemed. A glance at his phone told Deke that they only had about four hours before they left again. He was relatively sure the coach had "gifted" them this time for schoolwork, but doubted a single member of the Baguettes would use it as intended.

They were all wound too tight; yesterday Deke had heard Geoff tossing and turning most of the night. While he might have made a joke about Geoff's nerves, Deke had also been up most of the night feeling a mixture of excitement and fear. He doubted he could sit still and concentrate on anything other than his internal thoughts. He definitely missed Lee as a roommate, though.

A group of about eight members rode the elevator to the ninth floor before getting off. Geoff was likely with the second group and so Deke made his way to the room they shared by himself. He tried the card five times on the door before the light lit up green and finally admitted him. His first step into the room made a noise that was so distinct he knew he'd stepped on paper.

He glanced down to find a yellow note slid under the door. He stepped back and picked it up. "Message for Deke Mills, we're in room four hundred and four. Call us when you get in, Rhonda." he read out loud. He stood stunned for a moment, not understanding the message. They were already here? Max had said Rhonda couldn't get off work early enough and they weren't showing up until early tomorrow.

He rushed to the hotel phone and hurriedly punched in four-zero-four. The rings of the earpiece sounded loud, and Deke forced himself to breathe when he realized he was holding his breath. "Deke!" Max's voice shouted through the phone and Deke felt his heart make a single erratic thump. His brother was here! Max said something more but Deke missed whatever that was due to his brain refusing to piece together the noises.

"I'm coming down!" Deke shouted and hung up. He left the room and sprinted back to the elevator. He was forced to wait as Geoff, Duke, Arthur and five others unloaded, most of them giving him a questioning look. He was going to explain, but then stopped dancing from foot to foot instead.

"Did you forget your key?" Geoff asked as he pointed back

toward the room Deke just left. Deke shook his head and slipped into the elevator.

"Nope, Max is here!" he exclaimed as he hammered the number four repeatedly. The seven teammates smiled broadly on his behalf, seeming to all now understand why he was so excited. The doors slid closed and he impatiently waited as the elevator went up to pick up some people from higher floors. On the fourth floor, he rushed to the right of the elevators, following the metallic sign with arrows that distinguished which direction four hundred and four was.

Instead of knocking he tried the handle, which of course didn't work. So, his "knock" became a shoulder to the door first, before he pounded on the heavy wood. "Maxie!" he shouted three times, accompanying his knocks with shouts. The door swung open and Deke fell to his knees to greet his brother—only to find Johnny staring down at him.

Johnny wasn't a looker normally, but more so than ever before, he looked rough. Deke was sure he had dressed up, and had even taken a shower, but he still looked like he had just finished a hard day of manual labor in the sun. It was like the Johnny he had met back in July had shriveled away. Deke had nothing against manual labor jobs, but he did have something against the current way Johnny looked. He was super lean, almost skeletal, but was corded with rope-like muscles that stood out on his exposed arms. The look screamed habitual drug use to Deke, and not the legal kind.

His mother had claimed he had stopped drinking earlier in the year, but then Deke had gotten what he thought was a drunken phone call just a few weeks ago. Now, Deke could tell his assumption might have been wrong and that there was more to the story.

Normally, Deke would have immediately tried to send Johnny and his clear bad habit away from his family, but behind Johnny was who he wanted to see, and instead of focusing on the hateful man, Deke transferred his gaze to the smiling face of his brother Max. Deke held his arms out wide while his face attempted to break in half. Johnny followed Deke's eyes to Max, before he seemed to breathe out disdainfully through his nose. "Hold up, brat," Johnny said, and motioned for Max to back up so he could get out of the way.

Max reluctantly reached down and used his hands to maneuver his wheelchair backward. Deke's smile dried up and he glared hatefully at Johnny while the man squeezed himself out of the entryway, and let Max reverse directions again. Max's arms pumped furiously as the distance between the kneeling Deke and him closed. The two rubber protectors on the wheelchairs' foot stands collided with Deke's thighs but he didn't even feel it as he wrapped Maxie in a joyful hug.

Deke would have held his brother like that longer, but the twitching muscles of his brother told him that Max couldn't take much more. So, Deke released him and leaned back. Max did the same before seeming to explode into an animated story. "I saw your conference finals! That last shot!" Max lifted his arms and mimicked a fadeaway, even though he was confined to the wheelchair. "It was perfect. Like a silhouette on shoes!"

Smiling, Deke nodded along, even making a swish sound for Max shortly after the kid released his fictitious shot. "That guy who pushed Duke into you was a real jerk though!"

"Language!" a female voice said from inside the room, and drew Deke's attention from his brother to the two people standing behind the chair. One of the two was Johnny, who had his arm possessively around Deke's mother, Rhonda.

Rhonda wasn't looking great either. Again, Deke was sure she was dressed up, but her best dress seemed to not fit her properly, not the way it did in Deke's memory. Johnny and her almost seemed to look like siblings with some of the same DNA, because both of them were lean in a way that made Deke's teeth clench, even as he attempted to hold his smile for Max. Rhonda was nowhere near as skeletal as Johnny, and Deke hoped internally it was just the stress causing her to lose some weight.

Ruddy brown and normally straightened, her too-thin hair was hanging down to her shoulders in curls, and she smiled slightly blackened teeth at Deke. "Hey Deke," she said, not meeting his eyes straight on. Deke felt the threat of tears in his eyes, but fought them back. Looking at the floor she asked, "You got a hug for me too?"

"Mom," he managed to croak out, as he stood up. Tears streamed down his cheeks as he squeezed by and carefully embraced her. Thankfully, she felt sturdier than she looked, which caused a sigh of relief. While he wasn't happy to see her looking so stressed, he still loved Rhonda deeply.

Something in his stomach clenched itself into a solid mass, almost feeling like a chemical reaction. The lump might have started soft, but like carbon turning to graphite it hardened, and kept going. Seeing his mom and Max was all the reminder he needed for why he was pushing for the NBA. He tried not to glare at Johnny, but must have failed.

"Don't be looking at him like that," Rhonda said as she shrugged out of Deke's hug and pushed him away. "He's the one who brought us down here!"

Max had spun his chair around and was now behind Deke and halfway into the hall. Deke spun around and moved toward Max instead of answering Rhonda. To his brother Deke asked, "Do you want to go for a walk and meet the guys?"

"Hold up there, *sport*," Johnny said from behind Deke. "Max will have plenty of time to meet the team, but to make this whole trip a business expense, you and I need to talk. Rhonda, can you take Max down to the lobby for a few minutes? Deke will join you both in five to ten, cool?"

Deke ran his tongue along his front teeth, while his mouth was closed. He looked down at Max, who was still beaming up at him, not sensing that anything was wrong. Max even said, "It's really good news Deke. Johnny says that you two can go into business together and we'll all be set for life!"

Trying to not show his anger, Deke blinked but then held that closed eyed position as he breathed in and out. Finally, he managed to force out a smile. To Max, Deke said, "I'll see you downstairs soon, buddy!"

Rhonda slipped by but instead of immediately taking Max's wheelchair, she put a hand on Deke's shoulder. "Just hear him out, okay. He's shown me the contracts. This is a sure thing, and you don't even have to make it to the NBA for it to happen!"

Deke patted her hand and she sighed before wheeling Max away. As they left, Deke could hear Max excitedly telling her about the clothes he had that he wanted signed by all the players. He even wanted the bench players' signatures, which made Deke genuinely smile, right up until Johnny said, "Come on in and sit down."

"Look, man, I appreciate you bringing them down here and everything, but there's nothing you can say that is going to make me sign that contract..." Deke whispered, trying to make sure his voice didn't carry to his two family members waiting by the elevator. He started to turn to follow them both but Johnny reached up and placed a hand on his shoulder, preventing his departure.

"Just come inside and sit down, Deke," Johnny said, a threat in his voice that made Deke's hair stand on end. It was like he'd left an "or else" out of the statement. Deke brushed off the hand but did as requested, entering the room and sitting in the computer chair that was nearer the door. This left the cushioned chair in the back corner of the room for Johnny. It wasn't that Deke was trying to be nice or anything. He just wanted to have a quick escape available where he didn't have to rush by Johnny.

Johnny sat on the edge of the bed near the door, thwarting Deke's plan. Trying not to show any of the nerves he felt, Deke said, "All right Johnny, I'm here now. What do you want?"

"I already explained most of it over the phone, but since then the deal has gotten even sweeter!" Johnny excitedly said, gesticulating wildly with his hands. "Now, they are saying that Rhonda will get hired at the center they send Max to, and get a salary for twenty hours a week, on top of everything else. It's almost too good to be true!"

"Come on, you must know that something too good to be true usually is, right?" Deke countered, his voice dripping with disgust.

"This agent doesn't want what's best for me. He's just dangling stuff in front of all my relations to force me into a contract with him. Can't you see that?"

"Deke, do you think I'm stupid?! I brought the contract you have to sign to a lawyer and he said everything checks out, and that it's even a better deal than most draft-worthy athletes get!" Johnny spat, his excitement replaced with derision.

Deke leaned back blinking. What was Johnny on about? Even a cursory glance of the contract Deke had to sign would have raised a bunch of red flags with any decent lawyer. Even between Lee and him, they'd found one glaring one. "How did you even get a copy of the contract?"

"The lawyer for my own company—I've been using him for more than a decade, Deke," Johnny began but then cut himself off and added the last bit when he saw Deke's squint. "He called me up and told me he'd read it over. That you would have to be an idiot not to take the deal!"

"So, you never saw the contract and your lawyer just called you out of the blue?" Deke asked.

"Of course not, you moron. I had him looking over the city contracts that the agent said would belong to my company if you signed. He reached out to the agent with some inquiries. That agent sent over your contract right away. Said, you needed a lawyer to look over it anyway!"

Deke frowned. There was one of two possibilities here. Either the contract that was sent to Johnny's lawyer was a different version than the one Deke and Lee saw. Or, and Deke was leaning toward this possibility, the lawyer had been paid off. Deke tried to use the argument he made with Valerie. "Do you think the first agent that comes sniffing around is going to offer the best deal? If we wait, something even better will come along!"

"Maybe!" Johnny shouted, his agreement with Deke's point throwing him off. "Still, you can't accept any money while you're in the NCAA. So, while you might get a sweetheart deal in three to four years, what's going to happen to your family between now and then? Have you even thought about that? This deal ensures that they're taken care of now, and later..."

Johnny's face was red as he stood, and he was even sweating. Both of his fists were clenched, and he was shaking with emotion. He truly looked like he was walking on a razor's edge. Deke could tell that if he didn't need Deke to sign the contract and get what he wanted, Johnny would have already been swinging to enforce his opinion. Deke knew this man, and had fought his entire adult life to remove people like Johnny from Max's life, and by extension, Rhonda's.

"You can unclench those hands and sit your ass back down, *Johnny*, or you can get the same thing I gave you back in July," Deke spat, standing up to his full height.

Johnny shook for a few more moments before a sick smile crossed onto his face. "Oh yeah, so big and strong now," Johnny sneered under his breath. "Who the fuck cares how big and strong you are when you're halfway across the world chasing some pipedream. I'm the one in London. I'm the one looking after Rhonda and Max, and here you are with your first fucking chance to be more than a parasite, and you're holding out for something better?"

It was Deke's turn to clench his fists. Not because he wanted to punch Johnny. Well, he did want to do that, but deep down, his heart was telling him that Johnny had a point. That he truly did have an opportunity to help his family right now, and was he just running away from it? No, that wasn't the whole situation, and Johnny having a good point didn't make him some knight in shining armor. Johnny was an insect—the parasite he accused him of being actually, who only wanted Deke to sign for his own gains. He might even leave Rhonda and Max as soon as he got what he wanted!

"Johnny, if you touch even a hair on Max's head, I'm going to come back to London and make sure you're the one in a wheelchair. One that's for people paralyzed from the neck down. Do you under-stand?" Deke growled. He was relatively sure that Johnny had meant the implied threat in his earlier words and chose to nip that particular line of thinking off right now.

Johnny stood up to his full height, still a foot shorter than Deke, and jabbed a finger into the latter's chest. "You think being big and tall will stop me and my boys from pulling the tire irons from the trunks. You might have gotten the better of me alone in your house in July, but if you ever come back to London looking for trouble—I can guarantee you'll find it."

Johnny was spitting all over Deke's Baguettes warm up T-shirt, and Deke chose to leave. Sure Deke could have fought Johnny here, where again he wouldn't have a group of friends with weapons to back him up, but he didn't want to escalate this situation any further. He needed to figure out another way.

"Don't fucking walk away from me, you ungrateful little shit. You sign that contract or when we get back to London, Max is going to have a little accident. End up in the hospital again..." Deke had one hand on the door handle and had half-pulled it open but turned back, ready to pummel Johnny despite the consequences. Something wrapped around his chest and he even felt hair tickle his nose as it brushed by him. Whatever was clinging to him didn't stop him from stepping back into the room.

However, Abbie's next words did. "Don't Deke, it's not worth it. I'm a witness to the threat he just made. We can file a report! Don't ruin your life over this cokehead," she pleaded.

Deke looked down to see the top of the tall trainer's blond head. He played back what she'd said. She'd heard his threat? Johnny had finally messed up. There was someone around who heard it all. Deke managed a sinister smile toward the now paling Johnny. "You hear that, shitstain? I want you on a plane out of New York tonight. When you get back, you get your shit out of the house in London, and never come back. Abbie and I are going to go report what just happened to the police!"

The next few hours became a bit of a spectacle as Deke sat in the lobby with Abbie, explaining the situation to the police. The police didn't find Johnny in the hotel, and Deke somewhat hoped that they would catch him at customs crossing the border. His running made him seem even more guilty and if he was in jail here, he definitely couldn't harm his family. Max sat in his wheelchair next to Deke, their hands clasped together. His brother was looking a bit shell-shocked from the news that Johnny had threatened him and Deke.

Child Protective Services was also in the room and attempting to get Max alone to ask questions, but Deke wouldn't allow them to ask Max anything alone. Deke had an internal debate with himself about whether CPS would be better for Max, especially when Rhonda spoke out against the charges against Johnny, but surely Max was better with their mother, right?

Surprising Deke, Abbie held his other hand through almost everything, giving him worried looks but not moving. She only left once to speak with Doctor Dan and Coach Skip when the team was leaving for Golden Corral, but then she was back beside him, giving his hand a light squeeze. He gave her a tight-lipped smile, and kept unwaveringly telling the police the events that occurred in room four hundred and four. It must have already been the eighth time he repeated it all.

FORTY-NINE

SATURDAY, MARCH 18TH

"Mamma i just talked to deke's mom."-
Valerie

"And?" - Baddest Bitch Ever

"She was getting beaten by her ex. Deke
stopped it."- Valerie

":heart:" - Baddest Bitch Ever

"At the beginning of the year, I thought I was going to end my NCAA career without ever even smelling the chance at Mercenary March." Arthur spoke eloquently from his standing position in front of his locker. "But then we won the game against the Badgers, and I started to hope. Suddenly, the rest of the year had meaning."

Arthur continued to give his speech and admittedly, it was a good one, but Deke couldn't help but look at the small conversation happening between the coaches and Doctor Dan. He knew they were talking about him. What happened last night still felt surreal to Deke, like it had happened to someone else, but the looks of his teammates when they thought he couldn't see told him just how worried everyone was.

Deke shook off his distraction and turned back to focus on Arthur. ". . . win or lose, I can now say I made Mercenary March. In my first year I would have been happy with that. Hell, earlier this year I would have been happy with that, but now that I'm here—I want to go out on a win. I know that's a long shot but that's what I want. That's what I think this team is capable of. Let's win this whole fucking thing!"

The people nearest Arthur patted his back as he sat back down and Duke started up a cheer that seemed to be a bit too unenthusiastic for just how good Arthur's improvised speech was. Skip motioned for Deke to come join Boogie, Dan and himself in the therapy room, and when Deke stood to comply the room went deathly silent.

Every eye followed Deke's path, and even after the door closed behind him, Deke didn't hear conversation pick back up.

"Come sit down, son." Skip motioned to the only chair in the room. Deke looked around at the other three and then shook off the offer. He'd stand with them. "Okay, look, we've been on the phone with local authorities on and off all day," Skip continued, "and I'm sorry to say that Johnny hasn't been found."

Deke closed his eyes for a moment before opening them again. It was frustrating for Johnny to still be on the loose, and likely already back in Canada, but the events of yesterday still were a good thing overall. "That's okay, Coach. The events of last night are still a good thing, I think. This has been going on for a long time and at least now I don't have to worry about my family, cause they're right here."

"Speaking of," Doctor Dan interjected from his seat beside Boogie. "We've managed to get your mother and brother seats right behind our bench. Abbie and I will keep an eye on them throughout the game."

"Thank you," Deke whispered. His voice still sounded tremulous despite the low volume.

"Until that horrible man is caught, it's the least we can do," Dan answered. "Still, what Skip isn't saying is that if this was any other game, we'd bench you and make sure you spoke to a psychiatrist before you came back. None of us were aware of just how much you were going through, son. I don't think anyone knows how to handle the events from yesterday."

Deke felt like someone had dumped a bucket of feces over him, and despite his earlier choice to stand, he slowly lowered himself to the floor, with his back against the wall. They were thinking of benching him? Wait, Dan had said *any other* game...

Deke looked back up, hope sending small jolts of electricity through his body. He pierced Skip with a look. "You can't, Coach. That's why I'm here! This sport has always been how I've coped. *Please* don't take it away from me."

Skip studied Deke with eyes that matched Deke's ferocity with kindness. It was an odd experience to not only have your emotional state assessed, but to know that someone had the power to sit you on the bench because he felt you weren't "right in the head." After a chin scratch, Skip gave him a tremulous smile. "I understand, Deke, I really do, plus the team needs you. So, I'd rather have you out there. Yet, if for even a moment it feels like it's too much..."

Skip let that hang in the air and Deke's held breath came out like air from a bellows. He jumped to his feet and nodded emphatically at Skip, Boogie and Dan, not trusting his currently constricted throat to form words. While he knew that was a sign of his possible crying, he also knew that this was from joy, and not concern. Johnny wasn't beside his family anymore. He'd taken care of the asshole again, and this time might be permanent.

Each individual in the room gave him a pat on the shoulder, and Deke managed a nod to each. After a few deep breaths, Deke felt more in control of his emotions again and pointed a thumb back to the locker room. "Can I go use a foam roller?"

Coach Skip nodded his assent and he was allowed to leave, but the silence of his departure seemed to be like a coiled spring, waiting for the door to shut before it was filled with speculations. However, for Deke, the silence truly followed him, just like when he walked into the therapy room. As soon as he exited the room, he felt the eyes of his teammates on him, and could sense that just a moment ago the air had been vibrating with chatter.

Deke chose to nip this in the bud. "Guys, I'm okay. The cops weren't there because I did anything wrong, but because of some guy threatening me and my family. So, let's get ready to crush this team!"

"That wasn't a disciplinary meeting then?" Wash, the team's third string power forward, asked. Deke shook his head, and added a middle finger in the guy's direction. A few members of the Baguettes broke into startled chuckles, which allowed the floodgates to open.

"You can't blame us for thinking—" Arthur started.

"With the way your season started—" Timmy said.

"All right, I get it," Deke stated, giving Duke a glare. He assumed Duke was the only one who knew about his run-in at the Winchester Hall, and didn't want him to say anything about it. Duke's eyes widened, and he even tapped the side of his nose, like some old-timey detective. Deke could only shake his head and go to his sports bag to get changed.

It was another twenty minutes before the coaching staff joined them in the cramped team room. Doctor Dan and Abbie were still working in the small therapy room, attempting to tape and provide other pregame treatments to any athlete in need. With the arrival of the coaching staff, Deke reluctantly strapped into his knee brace. It squeaked at him as he got it in place, and he scowled back at it.

Skip took the next fifteen minutes to go over the game plan for the eighth time, and Boogie circulated to the starters ensuring that they knew their man-to-man coverage. Deke was forced to stand throughout the entire process because his body didn't want to sit still. He could feel an almost electric buzz moving through every cell of his body.

It took a few jumps and a bit of pacing before he managed to sit down. Unfortunately, he had missed a great deal of what the coaching staff had said in those moments but now that he was listening again, he did catch some minutiae of the game plans. The team moved onto the floor to warm up and the opposing team wasn't out yet.

Deke didn't miss a shot. His body felt light, and each action paired almost flawlessly with the [Aim Assist] and [Motion Prediction] skills. [Quick Shot] even triggered what felt like an abnormal number of times. After each made shot, he took a look over to Max to find his kid brother with his hands in the air. This was the first time in almost a year that Maxie got to see him play in person.

Deke felt better than great at the sight. He felt amazing, which was why the pit that formed in his stomach in the next second seemed to come out of nowhere. Since the system was "sleeping," the letters that scrolled across his vision as he watched Max react to a two-handed jam from Duke were definitely not expected.

Power save mode deactivated.

Competing agent has been detected.

Head-to-head mode activated.

All System actions will now require drastically increased Radanium.

Analyzing trainee condition…

New Task: Win your First Live Combat Engagement. Defeat the opposing agent in combat. Reward: 2 evo points.

Error: Task unable to assign.

Error: Insufficient Radanium.

To prevent system cannibalization, all skills will be unavailable to trainee during combat.

Re-entering power save mode.

The world crashed to a halt as Deke read the message.

Deke watched Duke spin around under the hoop to glare at the other team, as they exited their tunnel and took the floor to the extreme cheers of the crowd. A detached part of Deke wondered if Duke got the same message as him, even as he studied the last four players to enter the court lines. Was the system that literal, that it only sent the message when an opposing player with the 'sports drink' entered the court?

None of the players who just entered looked their way, and Deke tried to narrow down who the other agent could be based on who was a star player of those four. That eliminated two of the four but left the opposing forward, number fifty-two, and the point guard, number double-zero. While Deke didn't want to body shame anyone, he knew how the system worked, and number fifty-two was about forty pounds overweight, whereas number double-zero was yoked. Deke wasn't sure he had an ounce of fat visible.

"Not to mention the jersey number, double-zero," Deke mumbled. "Agent double-zero, huh?" While Deke still couldn't be sure, his suspicions fell firmly on that player. That man was Arthur's man-to-man coverage assignment and Deke glanced at the Baguettes' point guard. While Arthur was a great player, he had always been a relatively weak defender. Or at least Deke thought so.

Should he go to the coaches and ask for a swap? Wait, was Deke a better defender than Arthur without any of his skills? Not to mention, Deke couldn't even be sure that Double-zero was the one with the system. He thought back to the scouting report and shook his head. Double-zero was more of the play facilitator than he was a scoring threat, wasn't he? Deke missed his first shot in warmups on his next attempt, thanks to the total absence of [Aim Assist].

"Dude, you okay?" Duke asked, and Deke realized he was staring at the other team again. The line in front of him for rebounders had moved and his teammates had filled in, in front of him, leaving him to glare at Double-zero.

"Yeah, just trying to size them up," Deke said, and went to move back into the line.

Duke grabbed his shoulder. "There's always bigger fish out there. Still, a team can catch a whale. Got me?"

Deke managed a weak smile and a nod. He hoped that was true. He made his next three shots and then heard the buzzer sound to end the warmup. Before moving to the bench, Deke took one more look over to the Syracuse Wildcats side. It was hard for Deke to remember a time without the system. Especially, after the last six months of it almost always being at the forefront of his mind. Still, sinking those last three shots gave him hope—maybe he didn't need [Aim Assist], [Motion Prediction] or [Quick Shot]. He had been good enough without the system to begin with. That's why he was on scholarship at UCSP. He kissed the back of his thumb and looked up to the sky, past the ceiling and the bright lights. Maybe this was like Skip said, a test from some higher power.

Maxie made the same motion of kissing the back of his thumb and looking up as Deke made his way to the bench. Max, however, added a bowed head with clasped hands after, which told Deke he was praying for the Baguettes to win. Every gesture made his heart melt, and his drive to win without the system that much stronger. For his little brother! Assistant Coach Boogie broke Deke's distraction when he started his speech.

"We traveled nearly across the entire country to be here, gentlemen, and while our opposition has home court advantage, I don't think they've played a team like us," Boogie said. "We match up with them well defensively and I think with our three-ball threat, we can really spread them out when we're on offense."

Boogie finished and looked at Skip, who nodded once before stepping forward. The entire team knelt down. "Just remember. In a game like this all the players—both on your team and against you—are here to fight, but only one gets the prize. Today, play in such a way as to get that prize. Everyone who competes in these types of games has gone through strict training. Most do it to get a crown that will not last, but we? We do it to get a crown that will last forever. A crown that says we are better men because of our hardships. That we have learned and fought through things that would break others."

Goosebumps rose powerfully on Deke's skin, causing him to shiver, as Skip looked right at Deke. He nodded, affirming the point Coach made. The words were so similar to a thought he'd just had. With all of the challenges he'd overcome in his life, he didn't need the system!

Johnny couldn't break him, not ever again. Deke peeked at his family and found Rhonda biting her nails nervously, but Max— Maxie was looking right back at Deke with a huge smile. Abbie was knelt down beside Max, clearly saying something, but they were too far away to hear.

As if time sped up, Deke blinked and he was standing on the court, surrounding the tip-off where Duke and number fifty-two lined up. The ref got into position and Deke didn't see the fuzzy image of a ball going up, nor its system-estimated trajectory, and that somehow comforted him. He smiled as the powerful Duke touched the ball and pushed it back toward Arthur.

First possession and a chance for first blood; Deke couldn't help but widen his smile. He pushed forward, trying to get a jump on his defender, who wore a number eleven. However, to his shock, the opposing team all started moving toward the Baguettes' basket. Deke turned to look back, confused, and found Double-zero with the ball and Arthur guarding him. At that moment, Deke was sure that Double-zero was the enemy trainee. Had he just used [Motion Prediction]? Was this how it felt to be on the receiving side of the system's abilities?

Wait—how the hell did this guy have Radanium to spend? Deke had hoped that they'd both be without skills in this contest, but reality was a cruel mistress.

Unfortunately, Deke was way out of position and number eleven was left wide open. Double-zero didn't miss that sort of opportunity, and found Eleven after making a sharp cut to draw defenders even farther away from him. Eleven shot and banked in a two from just outside the key. Deke heard coach Skip shouting his name, asking what he was doing, and he clenched his jaw. He'd thought for sure Arthur was getting that ball, but hadn't seen Double-zero making a move. So much for first blood.

Arthur took the inbound pass from Timmy and they got a chance to counter attack. Double-zero didn't bother pressing until Arthur got over the half, which meant Deke could release and get into position with the rest of the Baguettes. Arthur called a one, which today meant two things. This play was designed to leave either Duke unguarded inside, or Deke alone on the wing. Deke sprinted through the key, attempting to pull Duke's defender off of the big man as he cut to the open corner.

Smiling, Deke watched Fifty-two take a few steps off of Duke to guard a back door inside pass to Deke. That was all Arthur needed as he passed the ball to the now-open Duke. However, Double-zero snatched the pass out of the air like it was an inflatable beach ball. Two of the Syracuse Wildcats broke off of Timmy and Manny, sprinting past the stunned Arthur. Double-zero fed a long pass to one of them and they laid in a basket.

Deke swore even as Skip's yelling from the bench transferred to Arthur. What in the hell was going on? Even if Deke's currently sleeping [Motion Prediction] had seen that pass coming, he never would have been able to get in position to intercept like Double-zero had.

During the next three possessions, Deke slowly discovered that the opposing team planned to double-team him whenever he made a move to get open. He started thinking about how he could use that but continued to keep a sharp eye on Double-zero. Something was going on there for him to steal that pass from Arthur.

During one of those next three possessions, Deke noticed the trick that Double-zero was using. Whoever moved to double-team Deke, Double-zero moved to cover a passing angle to that defender's man. While this worked one additional time, on the next possession Deke managed to get open on a wing once and sink a shot without [Aim Assist].

With that single shot to boost his confidence, Deke managed to pull defenders in strange directions on the next possession, and Duke crushed a slam dunk thanks to his efforts. Still, the score was already ten to four, and Deke wanted to regroup. He made a T with his hands to call a timeout.

Coach Skip looked at him curiously and he explained what he had noticed. "Shoot. Good eyes, Deke. Did everyone hear that?" Skip addressed the team. "If your man moves off of you to double Deke, you need to look at Double-zero and get open in relation to him. Send passes away from his lanes, as he has unreasonably fast hands. Now that we know the strategy, let's use it against them."

Skip followed that up with a cheer and the Baguettes returned to the floor. Over the next seventeen minutes of the half, Deke learned what it meant to face an opponent using the system while he couldn't. It felt like a never-ending stream of tough, out of position shots without [Aim Assist] for Deke, and he didn't like it at all.

Now that the Baguettes knew not to pass to the open man, the ball usually found its way to Deke after the double-teaming defender returned to his original man. Unfortunately, that was when the next point in the Wildcats strategy seemed to take over. Double-zero charged over, and kept himself firmly between Deke and Arthur, denying a pass.

Worst of all was when Deke faked a shot, and discovered that Double-zero wouldn't leave his feet, likely thanks to what Deke assumed was a working version of [Motion Prediction]. Unfortunately, Deke had already picked up his dribble to make the fake and despite knowing the danger, was forced to pass to Arthur. As if Double-zero was superhuman, Deke found him directly in front of the pass . . . just another reminder of what it was like to be on the receiving end of the system's incredible support and guidance. He cursed nonsensically under his breath as Double-zero got another steal on his stat line.

From that point on, Deke was forced to start shooting, but with a double-team, he was only able to force up shots from his back foot, or deep fadeaways. He still hit eight buckets of the fifteen he shot, which was exceptional, and confidence boosting for Deke, but the lead kept extending in the Wildcats' direction.

The halftime buzzer sounded and Deke looked up to the jumbotron to find the score at 42–28. They were down by fourteen, and from the team's body language, everyone was just as confused as he was. Max waved from the sideline vigorously, which got Deke's attention.

"When you win this game, people will say you fell behind for a more dramatic victory, right bro?" Max said as he walked by. Deke laughed. That was a line he had fed his brother once in high school, when he had almost lost a game. It was total bravado but it effectively reminded Deke that they had nothing to lose now. Only things to gain. A weight seemed to vanish from his shoulders at that moment.

He gave Max a wide smile and a thumbs-up to show him that he heard his message. He couldn't let Maxie down.

"I can't believe you made us all fly down here for this. You boys going to start playing basketball, or do you want us to take over?" Valerie said to Duke as he walked by. Duke blinked at Val before looking at Eva. Eva interposed herself and pulled Valerie back from the court, but Deke was already glaring at her. What in the world was her problem? Did she think they weren't trying or something? Right, her father used negativity to entice results...

Even knowing that this was her attempt to pump them up, Deke's blood boiled from her comment to Duke, and she caught his look. Her face seemed to switch eight times in the next nanosecond before she shouted, "I was just trying to pump you boys up," confirming Deke's thought.

Not trusting himself to respond, Deke managed a shallow nod in her direction. He wondered if his sudden anger with her was for the way she'd acted with his brother. She hadn't even been able to say more than two words to Maxie, and even seemed to be suddenly taken with the idea of social distancing, but only when it came to Maxie.

Deke hated when people treated his brother like he was going to break or was something already beyond repair. And while he would always give people a chance to get to know Max first, he had hoped for better from Valerie. Max was his family, after all, and didn't she love him and everything about him?

A thought struck him. Thinking back over their relationship and time together, he couldn't ever recall a single time that they had told each other they loved the other. That couldn't be right... could it? He cast a long, thoughtful glance over at the blond cheerleader.

FIFTY

SATURDAY, MARCH 18TH

"As we anticipated, this may be the best opportunity to make another offer."- Agent Smoke

"I can't just go into their team room again. Skip is still upset about the last time..."- Director Rooney

"Either you go, or we find a suitable replacement for future dealings."- Agent Smoke

"What does that mean?"- Director Rooney

"Hello?"- Director Rooney

"Deke, we noticed the changes you made, but you have to stop forcing up shots. Double-zero might be good at intercepting passes but if you're double-teamed, that leaves someone open!" Coach Skip said and Deke frowned, distracted for a moment.

Power save mode deactivated.

Competing agent no longer detected.

Head-to-head mode deactivated.

All System actions will no longer require drastically increased Radanium.

Re-entering power save mode.

Immediately upon entering the locker room Duke had pulled Deke aside, just before Skip and Boogie joined them. It seemed that they all felt the same way, which likely meant the entire team felt that he was causing problems by forcing shots. Deke felt his temperature rise. He thought he had been playing well, especially without [Aim Assist]'s help. He looked at the three people who now seemed to be cornering him. "I'm trying my best already, but sometimes no one is open."

"Deke, this isn't an attack," Duke said. "You're one of the only reasons we're down by fourteen and not twenty-five, but we still believe we have a chance. If you truly can't find someone open then keep forcing shots up before the shot clock, but—" Duke looked at the coaches and then continued. "We all think that you can find that open man. We believe in you."

"It's a lot to put on a freshman," Boogie grumbled and got stared into silence from Skip and Duke.

"Some of us think you can't handle this, but I've seen your growth this season. Not just as an athlete, but as a man," Skip said as he turned back to Deke. The coach put a hand on his shoulder. "If nothing changes, I think we can all see where this game is going, and that's fine. Losing is just another lesson, son. However, your teammates and most of us coaches think you can change the game!"

Deke felt the hair on his arms rise, causing goosebumps all over his body. His body felt like it was at odds with itself. He was beyond gratified to have heard Skip and Duke say what they'd said, but wasn't it all because of the system? Would he have eaten healthy, worked out daily, gone to classes and changed like this without it? Now it was gone, and even worse, someone on the other side was using it against him. Despite his inner turmoil, he nodded, and the three allowed him to move to his seat in front of his locker.

As if his teammates had been part of the small gathering, each player he passed met his eyes and gave a nod. Deke nodded back, even though he felt like each nod was a nail under his fingernails. If they knew, would they trust in him? Surely, he could do something more to help his team with his natural talent as a player and the sports drink's stats, though, right? Just as his butt touched the seat, the door slammed open and Rooney shouted, "Mills! I need to speak with you."

Deke stood up as if he had sat on a pin, and stared at the director in confusion. Skip, who had likely been about to start a speech, glared daggers at the man. Rooney ignored him, his face flushed red from his obvious rush down to the locker room. He reached up and dabbed sweat from his forehead before frantically looking around the room. Rooney pointed to Doctor Dan and Abbie, who were in the therapy room treating Arthur and Manny. Director Rooney ordered, "I need the room. Continue outside!"

Deke looked at Skip, Boogie and the Duke in turn. Skip moved to the therapy room and Boogie was only a step behind, but Director Rooney blocked the door with his bulk. Finally meeting Skip's eyes, Rooney growled, "This is a private discussion about motivation. Don't you have a sermon to give, or something?"

Skip's eyes widened to a size Deke had never seen before, and he stopped his approach to the room. There was no way he was going in there with Rooney if it was going to piss Skip off. The room had gone absolutely silent as everyone held their breath. Skip jabbed a finger into Director Rooney's chest. "I'll be bringing this up with the board, so if you're crossing any NCAA guidelines you'll be gone."

"Go for it," Rooney said instantly before turning to Deke. "Now if *you*"—Rooney pointed at Deke—"want to play the second half, get in here. We need to talk."

Skip turned back around and met Deke's eyes. Seeing the confusion on Deke's face, he moved to his side. Leaning down, Skip whispered, "You can tell me what this is about later. For now just go with him. While I don't truly believe he would pull rank to bench you, he's already jeopardizing his position by coming in here again."

Rooney was already pulling the blinds inside the room, as if the team would somehow forget that Deke and the director were in there if the visual was obscured. Doctor Dan was standing beside Director Rooney when Deke entered the doorway.

"This is highly unusual Edzel, and I will also be bringing it to the board's attention," Dan said, before joining Abbie, Manny and Tim outside to continue treatment. Deke was forced to step into the room to get out of the doctor's path.

He replayed what he had just heard. What was this board and who was Edzel? Rooney followed Dan to the door and slammed it shut, as Deke realized that he had just learned Director Rooney's first name. Confusion fought with amusement at the name that definitely didn't fit the man, but Deke managed to control his features. Rooney spun and pointed at the therapy bench, "Sit down, young man. I have an amazing opportunity!"

Out of a jacket pocket Rooney pulled a leather pouch and a folded wad of papers. "The..." he paused, collecting himself, and then continuing at a much quieter volume. "The people have upped the offer. We have a full dose ready for you right now, as long as you sign the contract. With the cost of production this offer is a luxury, only to help the Baguettes win!"

Deke felt the heat return from earlier, but far stronger. It was enough for him to start sweating. Internally, he was fighting a war with himself. Skip, Duke, and Boogie had made it clear that the team was relying on him, and surely the serum would reactivate his system and skills for the second half. Rooney was flattening the contract down beside Deke, and reaching to his front pocket for a visible pen.

Deke's mind spun as he tried to make connections in light of what was going on. On one hand, it did seem like this Evil Corp group was taking a big risk having Rooney present this offer in this particular way. However, what were they risking, in truth? Rooney's position? Apparently they were confident enough that nothing would come of the complaints, or that their interests wouldn't be strongly impacted one way or another. But why now? Did they plant Double-zero to increase the pressure on Deke, knowing about the "head-to-head" mode of the system? Were they relying on the emotional impact of looming defeat to add another layer of pressure? One question loomed above them all: How badly did Deke want to win? If he took *another* full dose of the Radanium it would definitely help, right? Double-zero was using the system to its fullest.

The thought about Double-zero woke Deke up and clued him in to the controversy in Rooney's words. Surely only one company was offering the sports drink, and that meant they were the ones who had given it to someone else. Deke glared at Rooney as he placed the pen atop semi-flattened papers. [Motion Prediction], as if taunting Deke with its functionality, showed the pen rolling off and hitting the floor thanks to the cushioned tabletop, but Deke didn't bother catching it.

"Director, are you aware that the other team has a player with the same offer?" Deke asked, wanting to see Rooney's reaction to that news.

The pen clattered to the floor as Rooney visibly paled. Deke's eyes narrowed as *Edzel* met them. The director seemed to notice his mistake and attempted to put on a smile. "Of course I'm aware. This shot is a superior model, and will give you the opportunity to beat out others with the same 'gifts'." Deke could see Rooney's gears turning and even noticed when Rooney came up with a reason. "In fact, this is actually a test of this new product. So, let's sign and move on to the round of thirty-two, hmmm?"

It was a very tempting offer, even though Deke suspected that Rooney was lying about the "new" product. If Deke had more Radanium right now, then he truly could live up to his teammates' expectations. He could take on Double-zero on even terms. And based on the first half, that would surely change the game.

And yet, Deke was playing well without the system. If he hadn't been stuck with that needle on Halloween—no if he hadn't been injured back in July, he wouldn't even be aware of all of this. He'd be playing his best, just like he was now. Competing against the Wildcats with his talent alone. If he thought about it, in a certain light, his dose of the serum had only erased his injury.

His confidence in himself began to grow. He could turn this game around without it. He had made a decision earlier in the year to take the taster when the team needed a win—and it had felt hollow afterward. Maybe he was growing up, because it felt like he had learned from that lesson.

Deke's eyes narrowed as he thought of a way to decline without insulting Rooney, but more importantly, Evil Corp. "No, this is too convenient. If they really wanted to help the Baguettes, wouldn't they have given everyone on the team the serum? Or if they had wanted to test out a new product, wouldn't they have offered it to me before half time? I think I'm going to do this right, D. Roons. Thanks but no."

Rooney reached up and wiped sweat off his forehead again; his white pinstriped shirt was see-through in areas thanks to his copious sweat. However, he shrugged off Deke's suspicions. "I can't say why they do what they do. I can only plead with you to take this offer, as it may never come again."

Deke stood up, towering over Rooney. There was a moment where Deke thought Rooney would attempt to shove him back to the table or shout, but since Rooney had just pulled the needle and glowing vial out of the leather satchel, he instead used the moment to hurriedly shove them back inside. That gave Deke the opportunity to cross the tiny room and reach for the door handle when he heard Rooney let out a long sigh.

"He can walk again, you know."

Deke froze as every hair on his body stood on end at the director's quiet words. They hung there in the air like a lead weight—heavy with meaning.

"Like many great innovations, this little thing started in the medical field. Now, it's privately owned, and all I had to do was look the other way and they'd become our school's greatest donors. They even gave me a flier for the thing. A very neat and concise info-graph." Rooney chuckled wistfully. "It looked like they were advertising the next smartphone for Christ's sake, or any other professionally marketed gimmick. Except they were offering not gimmicks, but miracles, and the target audience were groups like the Department of Defense and a select few in the World Health Organization.

"They took the flier back, by the way, or else I'd show you it. Quite remarkable, I must admit. I think your brother could use a miracle, don't you think? They convinced me, that's for sure, and as you might assume, many others as well." Deke heard Rooney ease himself into the only chair in the therapy room. The salesman vibes, nervousness and even anxiety seemed to have evaporated as he spoke. Deke listened, his hand still on the door handle. They could use a miracle too, after all...

"You haven't left yet, so you must be considering. Capitalism sure has its upsides when you're a hot commodity. I'll be frank with you. You've got leverage here, Deke. You've seen their first offers but I'm saying you can write your own check. Your mom? She can have a meaningful career in whatever her heart burns for—receive care from the best mental health professionals to help her overcome her addictions. She wouldn't need anyone else around to make ends meet, wouldn't need some scumbag like that Johnny guy to help her." Rooney chuckled darkly as the chair he sat in creaked.

At that moment, Deke couldn't move his body an inch if someone were holding a gun to his head. His mind whirled with the possibilities as Rooney continued speaking in that relaxed voice, so at odds with the direction this conversation had been going.

"Johnny is a rabid animal, and you've backed him into a corner. I think we both know what wild animals do when trapped, Deke."

Rooney paused for a moment to allow his words to sink in. "He might be a threat to you, but have you ever seen Animal Control handle a rabid creature? They're so efficient and at ease that you can just tell, what would be terrifying for another person is just a Tuesday for them. Tuesday's coming up, Deke and your pest problem can be handled more simply than you would believe." The chair creaked again, likely because the director was leaning forward.

"But all of that, while important and valuable, isn't enough to get you to sit back down on this table, is it?" Director Rooney seemed to come to a thought, before speaking his next words. "You might not be aware from that simple taster you took, Deke, but I can assure you, this full package can heal almost anything. I want you to close your eyes. Close your eyes and imagine little Maxie—"

"Don't you fucking call him that." Deke spoke for the first time, his teeth gritted in barely restrained rage. Rooney was touching on the deepest desires of Deke's very soul. Everything he had set his mind and body to achieve—the NBA—was so that he could take care of his family and give them the life they should have had from the beginning. But to hear his nickname, the name he always called his little brother in the depths of his mind, coming out of Rooney's mouth at this particular moment, it set Deke's teeth on edge. No matter how old Maxwell Mills got, he'd always be little Maxie to Deke.

The sound of cloth sliding against itself reached Deke's ears and he imagined Rooney raising his hands in a placating gesture.

"You're right Deke. I've overstepped myself. I apologize and hope you'll forgive the slip, I didn't mean anything malicious by it. Please, just humor me for a moment, and close your eyes and take a deep breath and let your emotions go for a moment. This is a decision you want to make with your head and not just your heart, though the heart has its place as well. Imagine for a moment—checking a basketball to a strong, running, dribbling, shooting, *playing* Max.

"Imagine you as his coach in both life and the game—both of you in one of these mansions that pop up like weeds around California.

Both of you with a common goal, learning life lessons alongside each other—and you, being there every step of the way. That's what I'm offering here, Deke. You just have to reach out and take it." The sound of fabric sliding again made Deke think that Rooney was holding out the leather package with the serum and needle inside.

Deke ignored the sounds and closed his eyes tighter. Really, imagining it. His white-knuckled grip on the door handle relaxed as he let a laughing image of Max dunk on him. Deke stuffed three-point shots and was stuffed in return—flagrantly fouling his younger brother by picking him up and spinning him around and collapsing in a dizzy heap as they both couldn't control their mirth.

It was everything he'd ever wanted, and just as he began to turn away from the door and open his eyes to return to the table, a different image of his brother was suddenly there, still in his mind's eye. Deke froze.

Max had the most serious look he'd ever seen on his little brother's face. He sat in his wheelchair, young and vulnerable, and Deke's heart ached. Max held Deke's gaze firmly, as he locked out the wheels on the chair to keep it from rolling. With his eyes still trained on Deke, Max gripped the handles of the chair and began to stand. Deke made to rush forward to help his brother, when Max raised a restraining hand, telling Deke that he had this. As Max stood on the shaking and thin matchsticks of his legs, he began to change. Max's muscles filled out, his jawline firmed, and he began to grow into a mature reflection of Deke himself, but instead of a smile, Max's face was still deathly serious. There was no doubt that the young man standing in front of Deke was still his little brother Max—only as he could be, or would be, depending on the choice Deke would make.

Max took the only steps Deke had ever seen him take in his life, as he stepped forward. Maxie's strength fled and he suddenly tripped and despite his solid form, he didn't manage to catch himself. Deke caught the image of Max before he hit the ground. His brother's face was pale and his lips looked so blue they could be called black. Just as

Deke had resolved himself to do anything, sign any contract to have this moment, the image of his little brother whispered.

"What happens when my Radanium runs out?"

Deke was plunged into a cold lake of realization, and Max confirmed his fears with those words, even as he still held an image of his dying brother in his mind. Deke might not be the smartest tool in the shed, or whatever that saying was, but he understood what his brain and knotted stomach were trying to tell him. If he signed that contract with Max as the fulcrum, they would own him, down to his toenail clippings.

Max faded away like smoke, leaving a yearning emptiness inside Deke, who found himself still standing at the door, his hand wrapped around the handle. The only evidence of his struggle were the tears that tracked down his face. Doctors had told him that Maxie could have a normal life as long as he got multiple surgeries before he was eighteen. If Deke managed that, Max wouldn't need a drug. Just like Deke didn't need a super drug.

"Thanks for letting me know what's really at stake, D. Roons." Deke's voice was thick with emotion and conviction, and he truly meant every word. "I appreciate the offer, but I think I'll take it from here." And Deke opened the door and stepped back into the locker room, wiping the tears from his eyes even as he almost ran into Duke.

Beside Duke was Boogie, but a glance behind Deke told him Rooney was successful at hiding the leather satchel before getting caught. The papers were still very visible on the black cushion. Boogie frowned at Deke. Deke shook his head, telling Boogie that it wasn't the time to talk. Deke could tell he had interrupted Skip's speech as he returned and all of his teammates were looking at him. Duke mouthed, 'Hell yeah, man!" making Deke nearly one hundred percent sure the center had heard the conversation inside the room. Or at least connected the dots.

A smile crossed Deke's face and he held out a fist for Duke to pound. Duke bumped his own much larger fist into Deke's and smiled back. They had made the same decision. They would win without outside help. They would prove they were elite players who didn't need Evil Corp and its serum.

Deke met eyes with Coach Skip, before taking his seat in front of his locker. Unfortunately, his brain wasn't going to drop the decision he'd just made that easily.

Luckily Skip returned to his speech, which distracted Deke from replaying his decision repeatedly in his mind.

"As I was saying. Defeat is a state of mind gentlemen; we are not defeated until defeat has been accepted as a reality. To me, this first half's defeat is temporary, and should only spur us to exert greater effort to achieve our goal. We have an entire half remaining and the final score has yet to be written. Are we going to accept defeat? Or are the Baguettes going to show the world what we can do?"

"Hell yeah!" Manny shouted and a chorus of other enthusiastic agreements sounded out.

Skip nodded at each player who shouted and Deke joined his voice to the cacophony. Skip nodded at him and waited for the room to return to relative silence. He placed a hand on Duke's shoulder as he said, "Everyone kneel."

The prayer Skip gave was the same as always, but for some reason it spoke to Deke more. As if he had never heard the nuance in it. As if Skip knew the decision he'd just made, and approved. Despite feeling Director Rooney's eyes on him, Deke felt invigorated, and clearly the rest of the team did as well because as soon as Skip finished, the team room went crazy.

Both starters and bench players jumped and shouted, bouncing into each other in a show of comradery and a crazed release of pent-up energy. Deke smiled as he and Geoff bumped shoulders and came back to the rubber floor. Duke slammed the door open to the hallway and the Baguettes roared out from the locker room.

They had a ball game to win.

FIFTY-ONE

SATURDAY, MARCH 18TH

"The AssBagues got us all the way up north to play like this!"- Valerie

"Tone it down Val. Who do you think is more upset about them playing poorly? You or them?"- Big Sis Eva

"Well they should use that to fuel them to play better!"- Valerie

"Did you not hear that roar in the tunnel? I think they're going to try!"- Big Sis Eva

Power save mode deactivated.

Enemy agent has been detected.

Head-to-head mode activated.

All System actions will now require drastically increased Radanium.

Error: Insufficient Radanium.

To prevent System cannibalization, all skills will be unavailable to trainee during combat.

Re-entering power save mode.

The roar of the team was somewhat answered by the New York crowd. Of course, they tried to match the Baguettes' enthusiasm with pessimism but that only made Deke smile. This far north was likely a completely foreign environment for most Californians, but as a Canadian, he was closer to home than ever before. Even the air smelled crisp, with fragrances that reminded him of growing up in London.

Nothing sank that fact home more than Max sitting right behind the bench. Deke chuckled as he found his brother waving at him as they began the second half warmup. A weight seemed to free itself from his shoulders at finally having made a decision, and he refused to look back. He softly passed Max the ball, and held his hands up after indicating Max should send it back. Excitedly, his brother complied and Deke caught it and spun. He heard Max give a "two, one, buzz" commentary as he faded away and released. This was just like it had been in the driveway back home as they grew up.

Deke presented his fist to his brother even as he heard the basketball hit the rim and bounce out. The result wasn't important, he was going to fight and attempt to win this game the right way. Max bumped fists and Deke returned to his warmup, feeling even more confident in his decision. The second half shoot around was a very short affair and soon they were huddled around Skip as he reiterated the change to the game plan. It all hinged on Deke finding the open man. In the locker room that had bothered Deke a bit. But now, his teammates were beaming at him, and among them was Duke—maybe the only one who knew most of the story.

Deke didn't need [Aim Assist], [Motion Prediction] or his semi-activating [Quick Shot]. He would pit his best effort against Double-zero, who clearly was someone who'd signed the contract, and had Radanium in his system right now. It was time for war, and not just one against the Wildcats, but against Evil Corp too!

Duke inbounded to Arthur and the game got underway to the jeering of the Syracuse crowd. As soon as they crossed the half, Deke moved behind Arthur and took the wide open pass that positioning provided. This was step number one of the new strategy, and Deke watched as Double-zero followed Arthur as he replaced Deke on the wing. This switch of Deke handling the plays wasn't something entirely new to the Baguettes, but Skip hoped it would force the double-teams to make earlier commitments.

Deke's defender followed him and made a huge mistake. Instead of pressuring Deke like he had been for most of the game, he treated Deke like a playmaker, someone who was going to initiate the offense. Eleven played off of Deke, giving him a "cushion." With [Aim Assist] Deke would have sunk a three right now, but remembering Skip's lessons and not to force shots, he instead chose to use the cushion and only partially retreated from Double-zero's inevitable double-team as discussed.

Dribbling forward, Deke entered scoring range, and as in the first half, Double-zero initiated the clamps. Deke looked for a passing angle that would avoid the too-quick hands of the "agent" and found none. He then looked behind Eleven, and discovered everyone covered. Yet, Fifty-two was fronting Duke, which left a pocket behind the big man, nearer the basket. Deke lobbed a pass over Eleven and Fifty-two.

Duke caught the pass but found the Wildcats' power forward between him and the net, with Fifty-two behind him. This stopped Duke's traditional slam dunk approach and Deke, seeing that, charged the basket, passing Eleven but trailing an already sprinting Double-zero. Duke took the short shot, as everyone in the gym expected, and the fight for the possible rebound began between the big bodies that were nearer the hoop.

Deke however, watched Double-zero and shadowed him, following him to a spot outside the key. Deke had four inches on the kid and, he hoped, a better jumping ability. So, when he saw the ball rim out toward Double-zero, he cut inside and pushed off the floor hard. The ball touched his fingertips and Deke curled it into his palm as gravity returned him to the court. He landed and crouched down while bringing his elbows in close to his torso to protect the rock.

Something squishy collided with his elbow and he heard a surprised grunt.

Power save mode deactivated.

Combat between agents detected.

Error: Unexpected EOF, error out of bounds.

Recalibrating... Recalibrating... Recalibrating...

Infinite Recursion error present, halting System analysis.

Dump and Reboot initiated.

Trainee is advised to report to [Unassigned] for debrief.

A buzzing started in Deke's ears for a moment, as if the strange text after the error was attempting to read itself directly into his ear canals. The whistle sounded over a jumble of noises, and Deke immediately wanted to complain about what he assumed was a foul call on him. He glared at Double-zero, somehow blaming the ref's bad call on him. What he found was a look of wide-eyed fear on the kid's blood-covered face.

Not only was the kid clearly terrified of Deke, but he was bleeding from his nose profusely, which had been the actual reason for the stoppage in play. Again a shitty stoppage for the Baguettes, since Deke was a few feet from the basket and wide open, but blood covered Deke's arm from elbow to hand and was already pooling on the floor.

With the stop in play, Deke had a moment to consider the message he'd seen. What had that been about? It read like those "blue screen of death" messages in movies. Had Double-zero sabotaged his system in some way? Was this what the people behind all this did when someone refused to play ball? Do they just send in the clean-up crew, but without the obnoxious body count that could complicate matters? It did seem somehow elegant in its simplicity to Deke, whose emotions were conflicted at the moment. He'd already decided he didn't need or even really want the system. So why did the idea of it breaking fill him with complex emotions that he didn't know where to begin to untangle?

The trainers for the Wildcats rushed onto the floor. Duke wrapped an arm around Deke's shoulder to steer him away from the downed Double-zero and toward the gathering Baguettes near their own bench.

"It looks like they're taking him out till the bleeding stops," Skip said from the sideline a few feet away from the group. "Use this time to close the gap!"

As soon as Double-zero stepped over the sideline, Deke felt a sense of relief pass over him. It was a bittersweet moment. He had made his decision to do this without them. Refusing the dose Rooney offered was a brutally difficult decision, but now his system abilities would work again without signing the contract. Deke was conflicted on how he felt about the issue.

Should he refuse to use them? Deke decided that he'd be an idiot not to use them. He might not have asked for any of this, but he'd be a total moron not to use everything he had to win.

Using a combination of a wet towel and a dry one, Deke wiped the blood off his forearm. The ref blew his whistle and summoned the Baguettes back to the far end. They had the ball for an inbound pass.

System rebooted.

System operations nominal.

That was it? Deke thought to himself. No head-to-head? Just... rebooted? What did nominal even mean?

"Fucking cheap-shotting little bitch." Eleven swore at him as he got into position to try to stop Deke from getting the ball. Deke just shook his head. He hadn't elbowed Double-zero on purpose, plus with [Motion Prediction], Double-zero likely could have seen it coming. Deke didn't bother responding and instead got ready to move.

With a massive shove from his legs, he exploded from the standstill position and instantly gained a few feet of separation from Eleven. Tim saw the gap and [Motion Prediction] showed Deke the path the ball was likely to take. Deke caught it and instantly dribbled to the three point line. Eleven was five feet behind him at this point and [Aim Assist] went green as he fired a jumper, turning the unfortunate whistle into three points instead of the likely two the Baguettes would have gotten otherwise.

Duke and Little Tim boxed out down low but both released as soon as the ball passed through the hoop. Both gave a small fist pump as they did, celebrating the lead being cut to eleven. Only because Deke was already on the other half of the court did he see Eleven glare at him.

Still, it was Deke's peripherals that caught something strange behind the Wildcats bench. A man in a black suit and shaved head slid something to Double-zero. The bald man looked so much like the Cotton Candy vaper that Deke didn't need to think hard to put the pieces together. However, this man was tall and skinny with almost "caretaker-esque" vibes. Deke shivered even as Eleven crossed the half and he was forced to return his attention to the Wildcats' shooting guard.

Eleven clearly wanted some revenge, and he rushed forward, attempting to take Deke on in a one versus one scenario. The crowd roared its approval at the "heroic" intention for revenge, but [Motion Prediction] showed Deke only a single path. Even without the skill it was clear that Eleven wanted a three pointer to assuage his fragile ego. With the skill, Deke could even see where the shooting guard was going to pull up to shoot. Deke waited for Eleven to stop his dribble and then pounced, stripping the ball from him even as he attempted to move it up for the shot.

The guy hadn't even called a play to try to trick Deke. Clearly, Double-zero facilitated plays for a reason. Deke burned back across the half and turned the mistake into an [Aim Assist]ed three pointer, which reduced the Wildcats' lead back into the single digits. While it felt good to be closing the gap, the minor victory felt hollow. This was only because Double-zero was out and his teammates' subdued cheers told Deke they knew it too.

Thankfully, Double-zero was still holding a towel to his nose when Deke glanced at the Wildcats bench. Now however, Double-zero wasn't sitting on the bench any longer. He was in the warmup area behind the bench and Deke found two pairs of eyes trained on his position. His mouth went dry at the second set, staring out from a black suit and giving him a cold, calculating look. The owner of those eyes was tall, even when compared to basketball players, and Deke couldn't help but feel like a victim in a horror movie under the man's hawk-like appraisal.

The familiar sound of a bouncing ball on the floorboards broke Deke out of his unintentional stare-down. Still, as he looked away, the staff of the Wildcats took Double-zero back down the tunnel and into what Deke assumed was the therapy room, to speed up the stoppage of blood.

It was time to refocus—maybe the Baguettes could even the score before Double-zero returned.

The next four possessions resulted in only two scores for the Wildcats. Thanks to the loss of leadership and the return of Deke's skills, it resulted in a perfect four for the Baguettes, though. After five minutes without Double-zero the lead was now narrowed to 46-40.

The crowd jeered the comeback, adding their voices in an attempt to stop the UCSP's momentum. Fifty-two missed a short jumper, thanks in large part to Duke's defence. The ball ended up in Arthur's hands after the stop. Arthur made a beautiful pass down court to a fast breaking Manny, who laid in a two-point basket.

After each score from the Baguettes over the past few minutes, the crowd had booed and jeered. However, this time they started out silent before roaring to life. The noise of the crowd wasn't negative, though. Eleven took the inbound pass as Deke blinked with confusion. All the Baguettes froze for a moment, thanks to the unfamiliar noise after the basket.

The crowd was roaring, cheering and even chanting. "Moralis. Moralis. Moralis."

It didn't take Deke long to piece it together. The name Moralis had been in the scouting report and game meetings. Double-zero had returned to the gym, and the Syracuse crowd approved.

CHAPTER

FIFTY-TWO

SATURDAY, MARCH 18TH

The ball was already in bounds when Double-zero rushed to the scorer's table to wait for a play stoppage and a sub, which meant that the Baguettes could possibly close the gap to a one possession game before he made it onto the floor again, and cut off Deke's skills. Unfortunately, they needed a defensive stop for that. The Wildcats seemed to be surging with energy, imbued by the crowd—or Moralis's return.

Eleven, while animatedly taking the ball up the court, had wised up in the last five minutes of play, and didn't want to take Deke on

490

anymore. It was as if Deke could see the reins of the coach from the Wildcats pulling on an imaginary bit in the kid's mouth. Sure, Eleven wanted some payback, but was willing to wait for agent Double-zero to get it.

After crossing half, Eleven gave the ball to number twenty-four, the replacement point guard, who began running a play. Every play since Double-zero left had been an attempt to find Fifty-two inside, and Deke had no reason to believe this one would be something new.

Deke chose to try to capitalize on that with a tactic he had been watching since the beginning of the game. Instead of sticking close to Eleven, who had become a bit of a non-threat, Deke halved the distance between Eleven, the ball carrier, and Fifty-two, attempting to create a closable gap to cut off passes, just as Double-zero had done in the first half.

Eleven moved into the lane and set a pick in the path of Manny, who was guarding the opposing power forward. This move also brought Deke with him. Normally, Deke would cover Manny's man for a moment, but Deke somewhat wanted to keep his position between Twenty-four and Fifty-two. Twenty-four faked a pass to the power forward by looking at him, but Deke's [Motion Prediction], plus the general path of the kid's hands, telegraphed the ruse. Deke stepped the opposite way he was expected to, and caught the pass, feeling for just a moment like he was Double-zero.

Deke held the ball and moved it back and forth as a few passing Wildcats attempted half-hearted swipes at the rock. He could feel the glare from the scorer's table and he met eyes with Double-zero. Last they'd locked, Double-zero looked a bit scared, but now Deke swore he could see a blue glow in them. It probably was his imagination, but Deke could feel waves of power coming from the kid. Had he just taken another dose?

It didn't matter, Deke supposed. Either way, he was going back to a game without his skills after Double-zero subbed in. So he figured he should make the most of this situation right now. Deke started his dribble and moved down the floor. He made a play call, asking for the team to run a one, which admittedly was a bit selfish. Just like earlier, this play was meant to get Duke or Deke open. Still, if Deke hit a three and reduced the lead to a single point, the Wildcats, but most importantly Double-zero, would feel the pressure.

Deke passed the ball to Arthur and made his cut as Eleven jostled him. Together they crossed through the key, and Deke smiled as he saw Duke make an adjustment to the intended play. Instead of springing out to the wing to get open for a pass, he set a screen in the path of Eleven. Deke heard his knee brace squeal as he changed direction to force Eleven into the big man. Deke's shoulder brushed by Duke as he rushed by, and he heard a grunt from Eleven as he got marginally clipped by the screen.

That was all the spacing Deke needed, and Arthur, who had been following the play, found him as he sprang free. Unfortunately, there was still about ten feet between Deke and the three point line, which would give Eleven or another defender time to pick him up. So, instead, Deke listened to Skip's teachings and jumped up for the easy two pointer. It banked home and the score was now forty-six to forty-four.

The buzzer sounded and Deke, along with every other eye in the gym, moved to the scorer's table. Double-zero threw his warmup to the side as he stood up and strode onto the court.

Enemy agent has been detected.

Head-to-head mode activated.

All System actions will now require drastically increased Radanium.

Radanium detected. Unlocking Radanium pool.

Current Radanium 5 / 100

Skills:

- ***[Aim Assist] - Cost 1 Radanium***
- ***[Motion Prediction] - Cost 1 Radanium***
- ***[Quick Shot] - Locked***

What in the world? He had Radanium now? How in the hell had that happened? He glanced at the crowd to find Lee, but couldn't see the kid in the massive gym. He eventually looked to the Baguettes' bench, or more specifically Max, and that's where he found Lee. Sitting with his kid brother, and they were clearly both excited.

Lee saw the look and his head canted, even as he stood up in clear concern. Luckily, Deke didn't have to call a timeout, because Coach Skip chose to regroup. The whistle blew and the Baguettes made their way to the bench. Deke rushed to his water bottle, which was closer to Lee and Max. As soon as he picked it up he whispered, "Something fucky is going on."

"How so? It seems like you've given the team a real shot at a ropey-dope." Lee's misuse of a famous athletic quote hurt Deke's soul, but it wasn't time to correct him.

"For the first half I couldn't use *stuff* cause I was out of *sports drink* and the other team has a player with it. Now that player is back and I have more *sports drink...*" Deke prayed for the ever-intelligent Lee to piece together that rather terrible message.

Lee looked right to the Wildcats bench and then back to Deke. After a moment he mouthed, "Double zero?" Deke nodded. Lee blinked and then looked around before shrugging helplessly. Clearly the kid had no answer to the conundrum either.

"Mills!" Skip shouted, and Deke was forced to move onto the bench where all the starters were already seated.

Almost as soon as he sat down, Boogie handed him a different bottle filled with Gatorade. "Here, if you need more just ask. We need you at one hundred percent, Mills!"

"This changes nothing!" Skip shouted over Boogie and the

roaring crowd. Deke first saw and then felt popcorn hitting him and the other Baguettes. Boogie looked up at the crowd and shouted something while pointing into it, likely identifying the perpetrator. Thankfully security and the refs saw it too, because the Baguettes were awarded fifteen more seconds for their timeout.

"Double-zero is just one man, gentlemen. You've now shown the Wildcats that you aren't going to just roll over, and because of that they are going to be hesitant. They're going to be worried that they can lose. You fought hard and made that possibility a reality in their minds. Now, we just have to remind them. We just need to show them that even with Double-zero, that we aren't going away." Skip continued to shout over the crowd.

Deke was still confused about the system messages. Had it not re-entered power save mode after Double-zero got injured? He tried to think back on that moment. He didn't think it had. Had him "fighting" the other trainee somehow awarded him Radanium? No, that didn't make sense. There had been an error, and surely he could only get Radanium from more shots, right?

"Mills!" Skip shouted for the second time, and Deke shook off his thoughts to meet eyes with the coach. "You ready for this, or do you need a break?"

"No, I'm ready Coach! I was just going over the coverage. Sorry!" Deke shouted back.

"Don't worry about it, *eh!*" Duke shouted from beside him, elbowing him in the ribs lightly. The team often made fun of him for needlessly apologizing, because he was Canadian, but this time Deke could tell it was Duke's way of alleviating the ire of Coach Skip. Deke nodded to Duke before locking eyes with Skip. He would focus on the man from this point forward. What did it matter where the Radanium had come from?

"I was saying, I think we need to make a personnel switch. Take Arthur off Double-zero and put you on him, Mills, but maybe you aren't *focused* enough for that?" Skip shouted. Deke felt the rebuke in his words but began nodding vigorously. Deke didn't know how badly he needed to make that switch, but as soon as Skip spoke the words, he felt his heart begin pumping a challenge in his chest. A war drum!

"I'm gonna crush it, Coach!" Deke shouted, and he saw all the starters nod encouragingly at him. Skip called for a cheer and Deke spared a look at Maxie over his shoulder.

Max was holding out a hand as if he was in the huddle, and when Thor shouted, "What do bakers do?" Max joined Deke and the other Baguettes as they screamed, "Bake 'em!"

When Deke moved on to the court he walked right toward Double-zero instead of Eleven. The point guard smiled before saying, "And so it begins!"

Deke blinked, having expected one of a million insults, an angry exclamation about Deke's elbow, anything. But he hadn't expected this, which was his only excuse for his eloquent "Ummm..." as a response.

"It's a new game now," Moralis continued. "May the *best* agent win."

Deke couldn't find any words, and settled for a nod. *May the best agent win* said everything the two needed to say. It acknowledged the system, and the upcoming battle between them. Deke looked around the gym as Fifty-two took the ball out at midcourt.

While watching a basketball game, the energy of the players always fascinated Deke. He believed you could tell which side was going to win based on how hyped up a team was in comparison to their opponents. While playing, it was hard to tell sometimes, but looking around now, Deke thought that the Wildcats and the Baguettes looked pretty even.

Coach Skip had made it clear before even boarding the plane that conserving his starters wasn't going to happen in Mercenary March. There was likely no one more aware of the Baguettes' shortcomings, one of which was the lack of depth. Too much of the team's talent and skill were focused on the few starters. During Mercenary March, they would be doing their very best to minimize the use of the bench, but that was a double-edged sword.

Luckily, it seemed that the Syracuse Wildcats also suffered from a lack of depth because despite the Baguettes tiring, the opponents were as well.

Deke put the next game out of his mind. They might eventually run into a team that could take advantage of their biggest weakness, but the Wildcats weren't it. They could win.

The Baguettes marked their opponents and stuck very close to them. With under fourteen minutes left, each possession was becoming more critical and important. A single stop could create huge swings in the point differential, and Deke could tell the whole team understood it.

Double-zero cut back to his own half of the court, and Deke willed [Motion Prediction] not to activate. He might not be sure what had happened to award him Radanium, but he understood Lee's video games enough to know that he had a limited number of skill uses. He pressured Moralis as he moved up the court. It was odd to think that Moralis could likely see what Deke was going to do before he did it. Was there something he could do to prevent that, or better yet—to use it against the other player like he had on that rebound earlier?

He considered his own system and Lee's hypothesis on how it worked. It read intentions based on flexing muscles, body position and the like. Deke canted his head, and attempted to play in what Coach Skip called "neutral." Ready to react to what the opposing player did, and not attempting to anticipate it.

The game plan for Moralis was to force him right when you could, and baseline if he was already on your left. Deke repositioned, giving Double-zero the lane to his right. Moralis smiled and took off, and Deke shuffled desperately to try to keep up. It was too late, and Manny peeled off of his man to block the lane Moralis charged down. Double-zero found the man Manny left open and the Wildcats' lead became four again.

"Shit," Deke swore. He was more than upset with the result, but he still felt he was onto something. He'd seen his own [Motion Prediction] spit out multiple possibilities before. Admittedly, that was before he had the full skill, but surely he could create that same scenario now, against Moralis. Arthur took in the inbound and Deke blinked.

Eleven was on Arthur now. So, it seemed like the Wildcats made the switch as well. This was truly turning into a duel between Fifty-two and Duke and Double-zero and Deke. "Bring it on," Deke growled as he sprinted forward to clear their half. Eleven wouldn't be able to stop Arthur alone, and Deke would prefer Moralis was farther away from the rock.

Deke moved to a wing away from Arthur, and saw Double-zero attempting to play off of him, but still sticking close enough to contest. That gave Deke an idea and he looked at Manny, while raising an eyebrow. Manny understood and nodded, even as he moved to swap starting positions with Deke. Deke moved into the post, and Double-zero followed with a slightly reluctant step.

Arthur called a one, but Deke held up a fist with his thumb out, changing the call to a six. Deke had an idea that he thought would give the Baguettes a chance to score an easy bucket while simultaneously conserving his Radanium.

Call six saw Manny screen down, and Deke pop up to the far side of the court. Double-zero fronted him but Arthur passed the ball to Little Tim, who hurriedly relayed the ball inside to Manny, who broke his screen and also moved to the same side as all other Baguettes, except Deke. Double-zero's eyes widened as Manny passed the ball to Duke inside, as Fifty-two came out to double. Duke scored a two point basket and the game was a one possession lead again.

Double-zero didn't bother passing in the next possession, and shot a three over Deke almost as soon as he arrived across half. It sank home and Deke growled as the score not only increased, but increased by more than two. Deke took the next inbound pass and used [Aim Assist] to return the favor.

Deke picked up Moralis full court on the next possession, unwilling to let him have another easy basket. The crowd cheered Double-zero on, but the noise amped Deke up as well. He kept working on neutrality, as he turned Moralis back and forth. After crossing half, Double-zero raised his head and brought his feet together. Deke made a split second decision and stayed ready. He wouldn't jump until the ball rose to a shooting position. He knew that [Aim Assist] could be interrupted with just a tiny bit of pressure.

"You're learning," Moralis said, and continued to dribble up the court. Unfortunately, this possession still ended with two points from Eleven.

Double-zero picked up Deke full court, both of them no longer willing to let the other player take easy points. The clock crossed the ten minute mark as Deke managed to cross half. It had been a close call, though. Double-zero had pressured him hard, and while it clearly hadn't taken the entire ten seconds to cross half, it had stretched close. Based on the shot clock of thirty-six seconds, it had taken a full nine seconds to cross half.

Deke was still at a major disadvantage when compared to Moralis, who likely had a full pool of Radanium to draw on.

Deke called a four, which was a play to open a shot opportunity for three from Deke. However, with him starting the play, the new shooter would be Arthur. While it was a risk, Deke needed to trust his teammates. He clearly wasn't going to win this game on his own, and he only wished he had done more to help all of the Baguettes. Maybe they would even have a deeper bench.

Dribbling to the side, he passed to Manny and then cut to the net, drawing Double-zero away from the side the play would send Arthur to. His ears picked up the problem before his brain did. Even over the crowd Deke could hear Moralis chasing him, but suddenly the squeak of his shoes and heavy breathing were gone. Realizing what was going to happen, Deke shouted, "Off! Off! Reverse it!"

It was too late, and Manny attempted to hit Arthur just as Double-zero ended up cutting in front. A fast break to Fifty-two ended with a dunk, and the Wildcats lead extended to six. Deke swore, and Manny gave him an apologetic look, likely thinking Deke was swearing at him.

Deke gave Manny a look he hoped conveyed that he didn't blame him, but simultaneously began running back up court. Arthur moved as well, and since Fifty-two had just scored a one on none, Duke took the inbound pass. He sent it to Arthur who found himself double-teamed. Manny's man was on him and Arthur looked for Deke as an outlet. Deke crossed his arms but was too late. Arthur threw the ball directly to Moralis, who laid in another basket and extended the lead to eight.

Deke looked for the nearest ref and called a timeout. Just over seven minutes were left. The team needed to regroup, and he needed to explain that he would try to keep Double-zero away from the play. That he would be a decoy.

Movement out of the corner of his eyes made Deke look at Max. Lee was waving his hands above his head to get Deke's attention. He moved to his water bottle, which was close to Max and Lee, and Lee didn't waste any time. "Deke, you've got to stop holding back. I think I understand what's going on, but conserving mana in a boss fight can also lead to the enrage timer running out!"

"What?" Deke asked, totally lost on the lesson Lee was trying to impart.

"Just stop holding back," Lee answered, and pointed at the clock.

"Okay!" Deke managed to say between sips before he was forced to turn away to join the team. Skip was talking again, using this opportunity to encourage Manny. Everyone knew that the intercepted pass wasn't Manny's fault. Double-zero led the entire country in steals, and Deke now knew the exact reason why.

Deke glanced back at Max and Lee as Skip continued to speak. Max and Lee were huddled close and clearly discussing the game in whispers. Something about the scene made Deke feel light and bubbly. Abbie joined them a moment later and the feeling only grew. It had always been hard for Max to make friends—

"Mills, you need to sit out or are you with us?" Skip called.

Deke shook off the moment of euphoria and turned back to Skip. He nodded seriously and took the opportunity presented to explain his plan to his team. While he agreed with Lee that he needed to stop holding back, he also knew he needed to spread out his system usage to continue being a threat to Moralis. Deke had barely finished his explanation when the timeout ended. The buzzer seemed to sound too quickly.

Thanks to the timeout and Deke keeping Double-zero occupied, the Baguettes scored on the next possession. This time Deke used [Motion Prediction] on Moralis and immediately began to shadow him, attempting to prevent an inbound pass going to him.

Still, Moralis was way better with his system than Deke was, because four different versions of Double-zero sprang to life. Deke watched one cut to the sidelines, two sprint up court and one pretend to move up court before stopping and turning back to the passer.

Deke chose that last option, because that would be the decision he would make. The pass ended up in his hands and he moved to lay it up. Suddenly all the hair on his arms and neck stood on end as his instincts screamed a warning. Gripping the ball, he forced his nearly engaged muscles to stop the intended jump. The difficulty involved with truly committing to the shot enough to trigger his opponents' system calculation, and halting that same action, nearly pulled a muscle in his back. Double-zero sailed through the air by him, and Deke began to resume the layup even as a foot hit him on the shoulder.

Normally Deke would have chalked it up to poor body control, but not only did the foot hit him, but it also kicked out, pushing him off balance—and if he had been airborne as he had intended, possibly even chancing an injury.

The whistle blew and a foul was called. Deke went to the line under the glare of Double-zero and Fifty-two. Deke glared back, even as the ref passed him the first ball. He chose not to use [Aim Assist] on the free throws but drained both in the next few moments before he again marked Double-zero.

Double-zero allowed him to get right beside him before he leaned in, using his weight to stop Deke. In a growl he said, "That's as close as you're going to get!"

"That lead? We're gonna crush it," Deke responded. He wished he had a wittier comeback, but in the spur of the moment and with so much on his mind, Deke was just happy he responded at all. At least it was better than Double-zero's response, which was to give him a discreet shove after a hard pinch. Some people just had no originality!

Deke smiled at the point guard, feeling like he had gotten under his skin. Double-zero didn't bother going for the inbound pass and instead led Deke up the court. Deke smiled, thinking his steal was at least making Moralis have to think. The time was counting down and Deke attempted to closely shadow Double-zero, to not allow him the chance to handle the ball. Frowning, Deke followed Double-zero throughout his own end, but quickly discovered a problem.

Was he trying to prevent Deke from getting near the ball too? Double-zero didn't seem to go anywhere near the ball handler of his team, and instead was moving to the far side over and over again. In theory, Deke was doing a good job preventing him from getting the ball; however, the other four players of the Wildcats ran a play that culminated in Fifty-two's basket right near the end of the forty-five second buzzer. The lead returned to eight and it was Double-zero's turn to smirk at Deke's frown.

Moralis was using his own tactic against him.

CHAPTER

FIFTY-THREE

SATURDAY, MARCH 18TH

"If I keep you out of the play, your teammates aren't going to be able to stop the rest of us!" Double-zero crowed. Deke forced a smile onto his face. While Deke knew that the Baguettes' bench wasn't strong, he had complete faith in the starters. Not to mention Duke! If Deke lost this game betting on his teammates like this, he probably would be okay with it, right? His smile became genuine and even widened a bit.

Double-zero's confident look changed slightly—instead of glaring menacingly, Deke thought he saw a bit of worry. Deke continued to use the same strategy as his opponent on the next possession, and made sure he stayed as far from the ball as possible. Arthur saw his intention right away, and ran a play on the other side which saw Duke return the basket in Fifty-two's face. The best part was the Baguettes managed to only use ten seconds for the entire play.

The stalemate continued for the next three minutes, cutting the remaining time in the game in half, before something changed. The Wildcats missed a pass inside to Fifty-two and Manny managed to fall atop the loose ball. Manny normally would have called a timeout, but with Deke's earlier uses of them, he was forced to throw a low pass in Duke's direction. Duke barely got to it before a scrambling Double-zero.

Deke sprinted forward, seeing an opportunity with Double-zero off balance and out of position. Duke hit him on a fast break and Deke, seeing a trailing Eleven on his heels, chose to take the ball in for a layup. It was now a two possession game. The Wildcats only had a four point lead again, and looking around, Deke could tell that his teammates felt the momentum shift.

Double-zero felt it too, though, and called a timeout. Deke moved to the Baguettes' bench with a spring in his step. The game was definitely tilting away from the Wildcats. For the first time, Deke felt confident they might dethrone the third seed of Mercenary March, bracket A.

"Good work, gentlemen. They're feeling the pressure now!" Skip said, his voice excited and loud. He knelt down in front of the five starters right after they took their seats. He had his clipboard out and was clearly going to illustrate a defensive or offensive option. "With two and a half minutes left, we're going to move to a four man zone. Deke, you're going to shadow Double-zero. The rest of you are trying to prevent easy inside shots by Fifty-two. We know that those are the Wildcats' two main threats. If they pull up for any shots outside the key, let them take it. Right Boogz?"

Boogie caught the cue "That's right. The rest of the team is hitting twenty-five percent from outside of three feet. So, force them to take those shots and we'll close this gap!"

They cheered before returning to the court and instantly got into their new zone defense. It was quite clear that the Wildcats planned to get the ball inside to Fifty-two or take shots from close into the hoop, which theoretically was exactly what the Baguettes were trying to stop. So it was going to be a direct competition of strength. Yet, Double-zero wore a small grin...

Deke followed Double-zero relentlessly, like a dog and a beloved owner. It was particularly frustrating because Deke knew that Double-zero was essentially attempting to tire him out, as his teammates wasted time near half, but he couldn't allow him to handle the ball if they wanted to keep closing the score difference. At the two minute mark, the rest of the Wildcats began to move. Deke saw the play developing because he was quite literally a spectator of the two teams as he sprinted around the court after Double-zero.

Something told him that this play would end with a basket and Deke reluctantly used [Motion Prediction].

The opportunity came when the Wildcats reversed the ball back to the top of the key, and Deke moved to cut the path which [Motion Prediction] told him would be a bounce pass past Arthur to Fifty-two inside. To Deke's horror, Double-zero cut Deke's path to the ball and picked it up before it even bounced. Deke threw on his brakes, but he was off balance and not expecting the pick off of his attempted pick off—his brace whined and Deke could only watch as Double-zero drained a two pointer from the top of the key just as the shot clock was hitting five seconds remaining.

Duke slapped his ass on his way by. "Dude, it happens, let's get it back!"

Deke's fists shook as he clenched them by his side. He had wasted a use of Radanium. It felt like he was in a clinic of all the ways to use the sports drink system. Could he do what Double-zero just did? Certainly, but he hadn't even thought about it. With under two minutes left and two skill uses left, Deke was forced to act. It was now or never.

Arthur took the ball up court, not needing Deke's help to shake Eleven, who was giving him a wide cushion. A quick play ended with a pass to Duke inside, and Deke saw that his teammate would fumble the throw a bit thanks to [Motion Prediction]. This time, he managed to get a true jump on Double-zero and recover the ball and throw it back inside with a better pass. Duke closed the gap back to four even as the whistle blew. And one!

The lead of the Wildcats was cut to three and Deke smiled. One stop, and one [Aim Assist]ed shot would tie it up. Deke marked Moralis, but the player didn't even bother going for the inbound pass.

There was just over a minute and a half left, and the Wildcats had forty-five seconds. They needed to stop them right now. Deke's stomach was in turmoil as Arthur attempted to force a half-court violation, along with Manny.

They failed and retreated to get into their zone defense, daring Eleven to shoot from behind the arc. Eleven didn't take the bait, and just dribbled in place while watching the shot clock. Deke, of course, spent that time chasing Double-zero around like paparazzi on a celebrity.

At the fifteen second mark on the shot clock, they began to play, and Deke chose to fully rely on his team to make the stop. Just marking Double-zero. The Baguettes would live or die from this possession. Even as Deke thought that, Tim tipped a pass, which ended up finding its way into Duke's hands. Fifty-two latched on to the ball as well though, and a jump ball was called. The possession arrow was pointing in the Baguettes' favor and that meant it was still a turnover!

They had just over a minute left and a chance to tie the game, which of course prompted Skip to use their final thirty-second time-out. As soon as the starters were near the bench, Skip started talking, attempting to make full use of his limited time. "Okay, we need a three to tie, or to get a two point bucket within twenty seconds. So here is what we are going to do!"

Skip outlined the plan. If the Baguettes saw an opportunity to quickly score a high probability shot from near the basket, they were going to take it. However, if the shot clock hit thirty seconds, they were going to run a play that included Deke again, intended to free him up to shoot a three point shot and tie the game. Skip didn't have time to explain any more because the buzzer sounded.

They moved back out onto the floor and Deke frowned as Eleven ended up defending him. Deke looked at the bench and saw Skip standing with a tilted head. He shouted to get Arthur's attention and called an audible change to the plan by holding a five above his head. The goal now was to get Deke an open three-point shot in the first twenty seconds. Deke took the ball up the court instead of Arthur, because Double-zero was no longer on him.

Eleven was attempting to keep Deke contained right after he crossed half this time, not going to allow Deke to hit a thirty-five footer uncontested. Deke initiated the play as Arthur took Double-zero on a tour of his own end. Deke watched him closely though. Something felt off about the switch and Deke didn't blink as he tried to figure it out.

It was when Deke cut through the key, and moved to the corner that he discovered a clue. Deke had looked away for a split second, and when he turned, Arthur was entirely alone. Deke's eyes widened and he crossed his arms in front of him while shouting Little Tim off from passing him the ball. He still hadn't found Double-zero yet, but knew that Arthur being left wide open meant he was coming.

At a pointed gesture from Deke, Tim passed the ball to an open Arthur, and he hurriedly reversed the basketball to the senior—who took his opportunity to dribble forward into the key, and drain a two pointer. Deke found Double-zero then, and turned to smile at him, only to find the opponent smiling at him instead. Shit!

Deke's head spun to the inbounder, who was wound up and prepared for a baseball throw. Deke followed the pass as it sailed through the air and ended up in the hands of Fifty-two—wide open for an easy slam dunk. The entire sequence took twenty-two seconds and the Baguettes now had forty-eight seconds left to tie the game. Clearly, the Wildcats realized that if the Baguettes made a two they would move to a foul trouble strategy, attempting to exchange a single point possession for the Wildcats for a two pointer for them. Now, though, they could only shoot a three, which might make them predictable. They also didn't have any timeouts remaining.

It was the Baguettes' turn on this possession to waste time near the centerline. However, Deke wasn't going to be allowed to be involved, as both Double-zero and Eleven shadowed him. He could tell that the Wildcats were daring the Baguettes to run a play and take a shot quickly instead of waiting out the shot clock and attempting to send the game into overtime. Coach Skip shouted to take the opportunity, and the Wildcats allowed Duke an easy basket in the next fifteen seconds. While they still played defense, they were also clearly being cautious to avoid drawing a foul.

This time, the Wildcats managed an inbound pass to Double-zero and Tim fouled him. Unfortunately, the Baguettes were four fouls away from foul trouble, and so they each picked up man to man again as the Wildcats took the ball back out. This time, Deke fouled Double-zero. Next it was Arthur, but unfortunately another four seconds peeled off the game clock, dropping the remaining time to twenty-three seconds.

Deke stuck even closer this time to Double-zero, not wanting him to get an inbound pass and be the opponent going to the line. If he had [Aim Assist] that was like giving him, and by extension the Wild-cats, two points. It ended up being Eleven who got the pass and was fouled. He sank both baskets and returned the gap to three.

Deke was marked too closely by Double-zero and clearly wouldn't be allowed to shoot. So he used his final Radanium point on [Motion Prediction]. To his surprise, he didn't get a system message telling him he was out of the substance, and his heart sped up.

Arthur took an open three pointer, but [Motion Prediction] told

Deke it wouldn't go in. He moved to a spot where the ball would be at the peak of his jump and took off. This tactic prevented Moralis from contesting, even though he was right beside Deke. Before even landing, Deke relayed the ball to Manny, but Eleven moved to double-team, which forced Manny to settle for a two pointer from just outside the key.

Deke immediately found Double-zero and stuck so close to him he could smell Moralis' sweat. Unfortunately, he was watching the man too closely and crashed into the edge of a screen by Fifty-two. The inbound pass found Double-zero a moment after, and Deke fouled Moralis as he dribbled up the court, wasting more time off the game clock. Deke's stomach sank when he did it. He and his whole team deflated.

Moralis didn't miss, which gave them a three point lead. Deke had one desperate hope left. Duke took the ball out to inbound it this time, knowing that he wasn't going to be useful on the far end of the court. Arthur got the pass, and was instantly pressured by Eleven.

Deke remained absolutely neutral, attempting to make it look like he was going to move up court to get open for a three pointer. It must have worked because he managed to fake out Double-zero and double back to get the ball. Double-zero didn't go far though, and by the time Deke got the ball he was back on him.

Deke heard the crowd counting down from two, and glanced at the clock to see four seconds. Clever tactic, but he wouldn't fall for it. Unfortunately, he only managed to get about eight feet closer to the centerline in three seconds and was forced to launch himself sideways to open a shooting lane. Airborne, he watched his [Aim Assist] line go grey before shattering to pieces. The ball left his hand even as a sudden system message shook him to his core.

Error: Insufficient Radanium.

All skills will be unavailable to trainee during head-to-head mode.

Power save mode engaged.

It might be the worst feeling in the world to know your final hail Mary could have been a sure thing if only you'd made a different decision... The crowd, the team, and everyone else watched the ball fly. Admittedly, it looked like the line was good, but Deke knew it would rim out, not because of any System indication; he simply felt it down in his very soul.

Double-zero confirmed his fears as he said, "Too bad, that was a fun game.."

He sounded genuine but Deke couldn't even look at him. Instead, his eyes found his family, Abbie, and Lee. All of them except for Lee were watching the ball.

Deke heard the clang of the ball on the rim, and despite the noise of the building, it sounded like a gun shot in his ears. The closing game buzzer was a death knell to the Baguettes.

They had lost.

Lee pursed his lips but sent Deke a look of commiseration that spoke volumes. Deke thought back on Double-zero's words even as the buzzer rang out over the roaring crowd. He turned to look at his opponent, who was holding out a hand. Deke gripped it and shook. Deke managed a smile even as his eyes watered, "Great game man, next year we won't lose."

"With how fast you adapted? Yeah, I'll look forward to it!" Moralis patted his arm. "You were a frickin' pain in my ass this year. Name's Cam, what's yours?"

Deke introduced himself, but shortly after was separated as multiple other players mingled around the two of them, waiting for a chance to shake hands.

Only after Deke had shaken every opponent's hand was he finally able to collapse onto the bench, exhausted physically and mentally. That had been a great game.

EPILOGUE

SATURDAY, MARCH 18TH

"Don't worry, I'll totally take your mind off that loss later!" -:heart: Val :heart:

"Oh, yeah. What do you have in mind?"- Dekester

"I'm sharing a room with Leslie at the hotel. She already knows not to come back before midnight..."- :heart: Val :heart:

"Well, damn. Max's bedtime is eight. See you at 8:01!"- Dekester

D eke slouched in the cushioned bench chair and let a towel hang over his head to block out the scene of the Wildcats celebration. He heard the cushion seat beside him exhale as someone sat on the thing and sighed.

"I know what you're thinking," Duke stated, and Deke could hear the sadness he felt mirrored in those words. "What if?" Duke allowed the two words, which encapsulated so much more, to hang in the air. Deke pulled the towel off and met the big center's eyes. Those words usually held the power of contemplation for any athlete, but for the two of them, they seemed to have substance. Almost like they manifested concepts as great as time and space.

Deke studied Duke's face, and due to his scrutiny he noticed the small smile start from the corner of the big center's mouth. It spread quickly, crinkling his forehead and creating crow's feet on his eyes. Duke reached a hand out and placed it on Deke's shoulder.

"This is already a year ahead of schedule for me!" Duke said. Deke managed a small chuckle at the change in subject. He grabbed a water bottle and took some deep draws between heaving breaths. For the next few moments neither of the two men spoke.

Both of them stared up at the scoreboard as they caught their breath and attempted to replenish the water they had sweated out during the game. It was a good sentiment and Deke understood it. Duke continued while looking at the big jumbotron. "That score up there doesn't reflect the choice we both made. It may say we *lost* by three, but I'm feeling like we both won!"

Deke flinched and looked at Duke, who slowly turned to look Deke in the eyes again. His hand still rested on his shoulder. "I think we made the right decision. Even without taking that offer, we pushed a high seeded team to this point. A high seeded team with a guy like Double-zero. If we keep it a bit closer in the first half, we win. Period. So, let's work hard and get back here with a deeper bench. Then we can show that agent we'll be in the NBA without him."

A wave of heat ran over Deke's shoulder, raising goosebumps in its wake. He didn't bother responding, as a war waged inside of him. It was tough to let go of that heavy "what if" question. Yet sitting there and translating Duke's unspoken words let him put it down for just a moment, and Deke felt a hint of the pride Duke was conveying. If the Baguettes had a better bench—if Deke joined Duke in trying to push the others to be better, they could do this without the super serum; no they *would* do it... After a moment Deke nodded to Duke, not needing to say anything. He understood. Next year, with a great deal of work on the Baguettes' other players, they would have an even better chance in Mercenary March. This year had been an at-large bid, which put them against a powerhouse, and they had still come close.

Finally smiling, Deke stood up and returned the gesture by placing his hand on Duke's shoulder. "Thanks man. I'm going to console my brother now. He might be more heartbroken than I am."

Duke chuckled, and Deke let go of his shoulder without comment. It was only a few steps down the bench to arrive at Rhonda, Lee, Max, and to Deke's surprise—Abbie.

"Sorry we couldn't pull that one out," Deke said as a way to break the ice, and admittedly also as a way to get the response they all gave. Everyone took the time to console him and tell him how well he played.

"If a twenty-five, eleven, and nine night wasn't enough, you'll just have to get more next year, right bro?" Max said, and Deke's smile almost hurt his cheeks. Max still had lines on his face from the tears, and his kid brother was still consoling him. It made him happier than he could recall being in a long time.

"That's right, Maxie!" Deke exclaimed. That was when a man in a black suit stepped into their circle. Deke thought it was the vaping man for a moment, but thanks to the individual running a hand through brown hair, quickly realized he wasn't.

"Sorry to interrupt. I just wanted to take a moment to introduce myself. I'm Sean Strong, an agent that represents some well-known athletes. I don't want to take much of your time, but wanted to say, keep up the hard work and I'm sure we'll be sitting down around a table to discuss the draft in a year or two."

Deke blinked in shock. Abbie punched his shoulder. "Turns out holding out on that other agent was the right thing to do!"

"Other agents?" Sean asked, sounding confused. "I'm surprised I'm late to this party. Who approached a freshman before Mercenary March?"

"Actually, he works with that guy over there," Lee said, pointing across the court.

They all turned to see Moralis talking to the freakishly tall Evil Corp agent that Deke had seen giving Double-zero more of the sports drink during the game. Deke caught Sean twitching out of the corner of his eye, and looked at the man to see him play with a wedding ring on his hand. Sean caught his gaze, and explained, "I know the reputation of that particular agency, Mr. Mills. They've taken a lot of freshmen in, and while I haven't heard anything bad, I can't condone signing and promising young athletes so much. Everyone knows how difficult it is to make the show. All the best, though!"

Sean fled after that explanation, and left Deke and the others to watch after him.

"Well, that was certainly disconcerting," Deke said.

"Maybe you should take what the other agent is offering if no one else will make the deal now, though," Rhonda countered.

Lee and Abbie spoke up together. "It's too good to be true!"

Max frowned at the two before he nodded along. "They're right, Mom. Don't you always say that someone too helpful should be watched twice as close."

"That's to stop people taking advantage of you, Max. Deke's an adult," Rhonda said.

Deke smiled. "And because I'm an adult and heard that lesson preached to Max so much, I know better."

After that, the group silently looked on as Valerie leaned in close to a suited man with a portfolio under his arm, definitely flirting. Deke shook his head, and Abbie groaned from beside Deke. "Does she have no shame?"

Deke considered some of their more... athletic activities before answering with a helpless smile. "None at all."

Val turned and found Deke in the crowd. With a smile she gave him a "come hither" look and beckoned him closer. He exchanged a look with Lee.

"Want me to come with you?" Lee asked, and Abbie gave a look between them that made Deke shake his head in the negative.

"Don't worry about it, I'll be right back. Keep Max and my mom company, okay?" Deke answered. Deke felt a moment of dread as he walked over to join Val.

"Deke, Brodie was just saying how great of a game you had for a freshman!" Valerie said, her voice high and excitable. Almost overly enthusiastic. "He's said we should talk to him soon about getting some representation."

"I'm not really looking just yet..." Deke said, and Brodie nodded his head.

"Totally understandable. I was thinking sometime after next Mercenary March anyway."

"You might not wanna wait that long, my guy here already has some offers," Val quipped and Brodie looked surprised.

"You already have offers?"

Present Day

"Honey, I'm taking the kids to their sports. Do you need anything?" Deke's wife called from the bottom of the stairs, well outside the office. It effectively interrupted the story, and Deke's eyes came back to the moment for the first time in hours. The interviewer lifted his pen from his notepad also. This was the first break he'd taken as well, and now with the ability to finally digest all the information, he started to sweat. This was huge, a scoop—something that could make his career!

Deke called back in the negative in the next moment, before turning to look around the room. The afternoon sun had clearly begun to fall over the horizon, turning the light sources of the room firmly to the overhead fixtures. Deke rolled his shoulders and looked at the reporter before explaining his thoughts, "I'm sorry for the interruption, but that might have been a great place to stop for today.

"As requested, if you could stay here for the next few days, we can get an earlier start on the story tomorrow. As you can probably tell by now, this story is large, and quite dangerous. I would feel far safer if you not only stayed here in the meantime, but wrote the story and published it while under my roof. I can't protect you anywhere else."

"Protect me? Are you... capable? This seems like quite the dangerous organization we're talking about here," the reporter said, swallowing the lump that formed in his throat.

"I am quite capable. While my story today might have seemed tame, I can assure you that things devolve from this point forward. Plus I'm making my famous ribs. My wife loves them," Deke finished, his voice sounding excited to have a guest for dinner.

The reporter slowly nodded as he stared at two prominently displayed items that he now recognized from Deke's story. Trying to banish the chill from his blood, the reporter asked, "If you hated that thing so much why did you frame them both?"

"Well, that injury is a defining time in my life. I kind of think of it as fate now. Without each event happening as it did, or what I'm going to tell you moving forward, I don't think I would have made it here. To this point, where I can finally openly defy *them*."

"You sure put on a lot of muscle between the two injuries," the reporter said, pointing out the smaller of the two framed braces.

Deke chuckled and looked out the window as the sound of a car started from the driveway. "My legs were never that thin. Fate, my friend. *Fate...*"

AFTERWORD

We hope you enjoyed Freshman Drive! Since reviews are so very important to us Indie Authors, please take a moment to go leave a positive review of the book on Amazon. Follow this link!

ALSO BY XANDER BOYCE AND RYAN DEBRUYN

Xander Boyce

Advent: An Apocalyptic LitRPG Series

Red Mage

Temper

Fracture

Farming Livia: A Fantasy LitRPG Adventure

Tallrock

Ryan DeBruyn

Ether Collapse: A Post-Apocalyptic LitRPG

Equalize

Excise

Earthdom

Equatorial

Ether Flow: A Fantasy LitRPG Adventure

Tech Duinn and the Birth of a Void God

Edda Gaia and the Origins of Ragnarok

System Misinterpret: A Post Apocalyptic Cultivation Tower Climber LitRPG

Starred Tower

Endarkened Spire

GREAT COMMUNITIES

If you love LitRPG, GameLit, or cultivation (Western Cultivation and Cultivation Novels) join these awesome communities on Facebook!

Or if you just want to be part of the community, try LitRPG Legion.

Finally, there is LitRPG + Gamelit Readers.

LITRPG GROUP

To learn more about LitRPG, talk to authors and just have an awesome time, please join the LitRPG Group.

www.ingramcontent.com/pod-product-compliance
Lightning Source LLC
Chambersburg PA
CBHW051307190726
48290CB00001B/40